Praise for
The Tomb

"A vivid retelling of a Bible story we've all heard but perhaps never completely understood in all its facets until now. With a main character human enough for us all to identify with, *The Tomb* is a poignant tale of secrets too long guarded, the tenacity of love, and the freeing power of grace."

—Tosca Lee, *New York Times* bestselling author of *Iscariot*

"*The Tomb* by author Stephanie Landsem brings the story of Martha, the over-anxious sister of Mary and Lazarus, into a dramatic and unexpected light. Often when we read the biblical story, we don't stop to think about who these people were, what they thought, how they lived—especially when we are unfamiliar with the culture of the day. *The Tomb* gives us a rich glimpse into that culture and into the lives of these characters: their hopes, their joys, their fears. You will never see Martha quite the same way again. An intriguing, fascinating read."

—Jill Eileen Smith, bestselling author of
the Wives of King David series

"Stephanie Landsem delivers a fascinating perspective on Martha, Mary, and Lazarus. Gripping yet tender, *The Tomb* weaves these Bethany siblings into the lives of supporting Gospel characters, beckoning readers to that poignant moment when the Son of God wept. Satisfying. Inspiring. Beautiful."

—Mesu Andrews, award-winning author of
Love Amid the Ashes

"Stephanie Landsem has a gift for telling stories of eternal significance through the eyes of ordinary people. Powerful and tender, *The Tomb* carries us from the shadow of the valley of death to the glory of the resurrection, while keeping the hopes and dreams of its characters relevant to today's readers."

—Regina Jennings, author of *A Most Inconvenient Marriage*
and *Caught in the Middle*

"Once I picked up *The Tomb* I couldn't put it down. Landsem's novel about Martha is not only a riveting page-turner, it's a profound and uplifting story about people transformed by faith."

—Rebecca Kanner, author of *Sinners and the Sea*

"In Stephanie Landsem's latest novel, Martha, Mary, and Lazarus are real enough to invite you into their Bethany home, sit you before the fire, and fill your belly with barley stew and warm bread. *The Tomb* is an enthralling tale, impeccably researched, full of delightful characters. As women, we have always been told to emulate Mary, the sister who chose to worship at Jesus' feet. But Landsem's Martha has much to teach us about love, loyalty, honor, faith—and the true measure of a family."

—Carole Towriss, author of *In the Shadow of the Sinai*

"Once again, Stephanie Landsem weaves a masterful tale of danger, intrigue, and love as she draws from the familiar story of two sisters, Mary and Martha, and their brother, Lazarus. Landsem pulls the reader into unexpected corners of history as this humble family does their best to figure out who Jesus really is and what his radical message means for them. She pulls from scripture and traditions passed down through the centuries to explore the human experience behind these beloved characters, breathing new life into the story in clever and surprising ways."

—Laura Sobiech, author of *Fly a Little Higher*

"Landsem creates a beautiful tapestry of familiar New Testament stories, woven together with fresh insight into what it looked like to walk alongside Jesus, encountering both the mundane and the mysterious in the man who brought the kingdom even to small villages."

—Tracy Higley, author of *The Queen's Handmaid*

"Triumphant! Landsem's words resound with hope and healing, with freedom from the chains which bind us all."

—Siri Mitchell, author of *Like A Flower in Bloom*

ALSO BY STEPHANIE LANDSEM

The Living Water Series

The Well

The Thief

THE *Tomb*

A NOVEL OF MARTHA

STEPHANIE
LANDSEM

HOWARD BOOKS

A Division of Simon & Schuster, Inc

New York   Nashville   London   Toronto   New Delhi

Howard Books
A Division of Simon & Schuster, Inc.
1230 Avenue of the Americas
New York, NY 10020

Copyright © 2015 by Stephanie Landsem

All Scripture quotations are from the Revised New Testament of the New American Bible, St. Joseph's edition © 1986 CCD. All rights reserved. Catholic Book Publishing Co., New York, NY.

First Howard Books trade paperback edition March 2015

HOWARD and colophon are trademarks of Simon & Schuster, Inc.

For information about special discounts for bulk purchases, please contact Simon & Schuster Special Sales at 1-866-506-1949 or business@simonandschuster.com.

The Simon & Schuster Speakers Bureau can bring authors to your live event. For more information or to book an event contact the Simon & Schuster Speakers Bureau at 1-866-248-3049 or visit our website at www.simonspeakers.com.

Interior design by Davina Mock-Maniscalco

Manufactured in the United States of America

10 9 8 7 6 5 4 3 2

Library of Congress Cataloging-in-Publication Data

Landsem, Stephanie.
   The tomb : a novel of Martha / Stephanie Landsem.—First Howard Books trade paperback edition.
      pages ; cm— (The living water series)
   1. Martha, Saint—Fiction. 2. Lazarus, of Bethany, Saint—Fiction. 3. Jesus Christ—Fiction. 4. Bible. New Testament—History of Biblical events—Fiction. I. Title.
   PS3612.A5493T66 2015
   813'.6—dc23
                                                              2014022826

ISBN 978-1-4516-8912-9
ISBN 978-1-4516-8913-6 (ebook)

Fear not, I am with you;
be not dismayed; I am your God.
I will strengthen you, and help you, and uphold
you with my right hand of justice.

—ISAIAH 41:10

*To my sisters, Jennifer, Rebecca, and Rachel
and my brother, Steven,
because family is where every story begins*

Dear Readers,

The Martha of Bethany that you are about to meet may surprise you. I hope she does.

As always in The Living Water Series, my intention is not to rewrite the Bible but to reimagine it in ways that bring us closer to Jesus. My hope is to open all of our eyes to a new way of looking at familiar biblical stories to discover new meaning for our own lives.

The Tomb: A Novel of Martha is not an attempt to recount the historical events that took place in Bethany two thousand years ago. Instead, it is a re-imagining of how Martha, a woman who was "anxious and worried about many things," might have been transformed into the faith-filled woman of John 11:22, who said to Jesus—as her brother lay in his tomb—"Even now I know that whatever you ask of God, God will give you."

We'll never know Martha's true story. Instead, I hope to bring to you her message: no matter what sins and doubts haunt our pasts, we can lay our worries and anxieties at Jesus' feet, and he will, in return, give us "the better part."

In Christ,
Stephanie Landsem

Chapter One

Hear, O children, a father's instruction, be attentive,
that you may gain understanding!
—Proverbs 4:1

*M*ARTHA CLENCHED HER teeth so tight her jaw ached. She'd kept quiet for seven days. *Seven days*. Now she felt like a pot left too long over the fire. If another old woman gave her a pitying glance, if one more village girl whispered behind her hand . . . by the Most High, she'd boil over.

She filled a cup for Josiah, her sister's new husband. Who would have believed it? Sirach of Bethany's daughter—his younger daughter!—choosing her own husband. And what a husband he was. Josiah had many good qualities. He was kind and patient, and everyone knew how he loved Mary. But he was also poor and none too smart. Even his own mother admitted that he was about as useful as a three-legged donkey.

She took a deep breath and poured a cup of wine for her father, careful not to spill a drop on his fine linen tunic. When Abba agreed to the betrothal a full year ago, the women of Bethany had gossiped for weeks. Most had concluded that Sirach was eager to be rid of Mary, his grown daughter who spent more time playing with the village children than taking care of her father's household. But they were wrong. Abba loved Mary just as much as he loved Martha and Lazarus.

Now, at almost fifteen years, Mary was ready to start her own family with a man she adored. Martha was glad that Abba had allowed Mary her heart's desire. If only he would allow Martha hers.

If Mary can choose Josiah, why can't I have a say in my husband? But of course, she knew why.

Her eyes strayed to the center of the meadow that stretched between the Mount of Olives and her father's many fields and vineyards. The afternoon sun cast a patina of gold on a pair of musicians—an old man playing the flute and a young one strumming the *kinnor*. Lazarus sat at the kinnor player's feet, watching him with admiration.

Martha sighed. Even her little brother got to be closer to Isa than she did.

A group of village girls linked arms and began to dance, each eyeing Isa as if he were the last honey cake on the plate. Didn't they have anything else to do but stare and giggle about how handsome he was?

Isa didn't even look at them. He never did. He looked into the distance, where the Mount of Olives rose between Bethany and Jerusalem. The love song of Solomon was on his lips, but Martha knew his thoughts were on her. Small comfort, with all the work she had to do.

Mary's wedding feast had lasted the full seven days. Abba's excellent wine had flowed as generously as the music, and laughter had filled their courtyard and the meadow that surrounded it. It had been good to celebrate Mary's joy, but with all the rejoicing, Martha had found only a few moments to be alone with Isa. And tomorrow he would leave for the Decapolis. She had to find a way to talk to him today. Who knew when they'd see each other again?

Mary and her new husband rose from their seats. The men nearest Abba elbowed each other and smiled. Martha averted her eyes from the couple. The sun wasn't even behind the blossoming apricot trees, and they were already going to the marriage tent? Of course, they wanted children, and there was only one way to get them. But did they have to look so *eager?* People would talk.

"Leaving us so soon?" Simon, their neighbor and one of the most respected men in Bethany, was a handsome man—at least that's what the village girls said—but his large, wide-set eyes and full lips had always reminded Martha of a fish. He pursed his thick lips and raised his brows. "I've never known a man to need so much sleep."

A chorus of twitters sounded from maidens clustered in the shade of the olive grove. Older women, those with babies at their breasts and sleepy toddlers, exchanged knowing glances.

Martha watched as the bridal couple took their leave of her father. She had to admit, marriage agreed with her sister. Mary's softly rounded face glowed, and her eyes, the same deep brown as Martha's, shone with what must be the marital bliss Martha had heard of. The linen dress Martha had made for her—the best linen, dyed Mary's favorite shade of pink—fit her plump curves perfectly and suited her bronze skin and the deep blush on her cheeks.

As Mary moved beside her new husband, her arms jingled with a dozen brass bracelets, her betrothal gift from Josiah. They weren't silver or gold—in fact, they were practically worthless—but the best Josiah could afford. Mary hadn't re-moved them since the *ketubah* had been signed at their betrothal.

Josiah shrugged his thin shoulders as if to brush off the laughter. He looked down at his new bride, and a ridiculous smile stretched from his crinkly eyes to his wispy beard. Josiah wasn't much to look at, but when he smiled at Mary like that Martha could see why her sister had pleaded with Abba—even though Josiah owned little more than the cloak on his back and a tiny home in the village.

No more servants for Mary, no fine linen from Galilee, no meat in her cooking pot—not with Josiah as a husband. They'd probably live on barley bread and water. Mary didn't seem to care, and, at this moment, Martha could see why. What would it be like to be adored? To have a husband so in love that he couldn't keep his eyes, or his hands, off you?

Yes, Abba gave Mary to Josiah, but he would never let Martha marry Isa. It was unthinkable.

As Josiah took leave of his new father-in-law, Mary threw her arms around Martha. "It was beautiful. Everything was perfect. Thank you, my sister. I will remember my wedding feast forever."

Martha's throat tightened. Her only sister: beautiful, exuberant, not afraid to announce her love for all the world to hear, even the gossips of Bethany. Martha had worked for weeks to make Mary's marriage feast—what they'd dreamed of since they were children—perfect. And it had been. But now she felt as though she stood on the edge of the sea, watching Mary sail away while she stood onshore alone. She kissed her sister's hand and blinked back tears.

Mary's smile faded, and she glanced toward the musicians. "Have you talked to him?"

Martha shook her head.

Mary squeezed her hand. "Talk to Abba," she urged. "At least ask him . . . perhaps after another cup of wine?"

Martha tried to smile at Mary's outlandish suggestion—at her hope in a hopeless cause. There wasn't enough wine in all of Judea to make Abba let her marry Isa. Josiah at least lived in Bethany and worshipped at the Temple. But the elder daughter of Sirach, the most respected Pharisee in Bethany, marry someone like Isa? Never. "Go." She gave Mary a gentle push. "Josiah is waiting."

Teasing calls from the women followed Mary and Josiah to the marriage tent, tucked discreetly behind the olive trees, while Martha went back to serving the men. Simon leaned close to Abba, but his commanding voice carried far. "Let's hope your grandsons have more sense than their father."

Martha clenched her teeth. How dare Simon mock Josiah when he was barely out of earshot? *At least I kept my unkind thoughts to myself*. She tossed the dirty bowls on a growing pile of dishes and hefted the next delicacy for the guests, rounds of soft wheat cakes, drizzled with honey and sprinkled with pomegranate seeds.

The other men chuckled, but Abba frowned. "Josiah is a righteous man, despite his lack of wealth. He will be a good husband to Mary."

Abel, a tool merchant and one of Bethany's city judges, snorted and mumbled, "If he can keep food on the table."

But Simon nodded as if Abba were Moses himself. "You are a wise man and a loving father, Sirach." He tipped his cup to take the last of his wine, then clapped it on the table. "Where are your kinsman Jesus of Nazareth and his parents? They are not ones to miss a wedding."

Abba looked thoughtfully at the cakes. "Jesus sent a message that they could not attend. His father is not long in this world."

"May the God of Abraham and Isaac watch over him." Simon leaned toward Abba. "I remember talk of Jesus, many years ago. The priests in the Temple said he was a great scholar, although he was little more than a boy. Some even whispered that he was the Messiah." Simon smiled as he said it, as if he were remembering a joke.

"Pfft. A Galilean is no scholar," Abel scoffed. "Jesus is well past twenty and still working for his father, not even studying the law in Jerusalem."

Martha set two cakes in front of her father, her temper rising. Yes, Jesus and his parents were Galileans, but they deserved more respect from Abel and Simon. His mother was Mama's cousin and had always been welcomed in Bethany. And Jesus was like a brother to her and Mary and Lazarus. They'd all been disappointed when Jesus hadn't come to Mary's wedding feast.

Abba stroked his beard, its silver streaks glinting in the sun. "There have been many—far too many—who have claimed to be the Messiah. They've ended up dead, and many righteous men have died with them."

Simon eyed the cakes as Martha came closer. "But surely the Anointed One will come. Someday."

Abba frowned. "If we keep the law, the Lord will surely send the Deliverer, but we must be vigilant against false prophets. We must doubt, until his power is proven to us."

Simon tilted his head toward his host. "As always, you are blessed with wisdom, Sirach." He turned to Abel and whispered, "As if the Messiah could come from a poor hovel in Nazareth."

Martha bristled, her temper sizzling like water on hot coals. Simon and Abel wouldn't know the Messiah if he sat down at the table with them and announced the coming of the Kingdom. No one was good enough to be their Messiah.

Abba motioned for Martha to serve the rest of the honey cakes, as if he hadn't heard their disrespectful talk. "Let us enjoy the feast and the last rays of the sun. You know every woman in Bethany wishes they could make cakes as light as the clouds, like my Martha."

Martha plopped a cake in front of Simon before banging the wooden tray beside Abel. Abba raised his brows in surprise, a question in his eyes. She pressed her lips together and looked away, ashamed at her display of temper.

He who honors his father atones for sins. Was it a sin to think badly of her father's friends? If it was, she'd atone tomorrow.

Tomorrow, when Mary moved into her new home with her new husband.

Tomorrow, when Isa left, and she wouldn't see him until Tabernacles.

Abba returned his attention to his guests, but Simon watched her closely. Lately, it seemed he was always watching her.

She crossed her arms and looked at the ground. When would they stop their talk long enough to eat and let her clear the empty dishes before them? It wasn't as though she didn't have other things to do.

Simon licked the last of the honey from his fingers and stretched his arms over his head with a deep sigh. His rounded stomach strained his fine linen tunic. "Your daughter is the best cook in Bethany, Sirach." His words may have been to her father, but his fishlike eyes were on Martha. "Tell me again why she isn't married before her younger sister?"

Martha knew what was coming next. She'd heard it enough from the women in the last year. And with good reason. She was almost seventeen years old, long past time to talk of marriage.

Abba fished a lamb bone from his plate and nibbled the remaining meat from it. "No man in Bethany is worthy of my Martha," he said, his lips shiny with the cumin sauce that every woman in Bethany tried and failed to duplicate.

"But you will let her marry?" Simon smiled.

Martha stilled her hands, waiting for her father's reply.

Abba chewed thoughtfully. "Most women let their hearts rule their heads, but not my Martha. She knows that the way to the Lord is through obedience and purity, just like her mother, blessed be her memory."

"Blessed be her memory forever," Simon repeated. "An obedient daughter is indeed rare and deserves a righteous husband."

Martha's stomach turned. A righteous husband.

Abba nodded. "She is a daughter I won't easily part with. How could I give away such a treasure except to the most righteous man I can find? A man who can give her everything that I have given her."

A treasure. Martha's chest constricted, and despair clogged her throat. Across the meadow, Isa's gaze was turned on her. The lilt of the kinnor joined with his deep voice, his song for her alone. She blinked back tears. Isa could never be the husband her father wanted for her, because he wasn't righteous. He was a pagan. And he could give her nothing, because he had nothing.

Still, her heart cried out for Isa even as her head told her that the boy she'd loved since she was a child would never be worthy of Abba's treasure.

Chapter Two

*When I was my father's child, frail, yet the darling of my
mother, He taught me, and said to me: "Let your heart hold
fast to my words: keep my commands, that you may live!"*
—Proverbs 4:3–4

MARTHA TURNED HER back on the men and began to stack
her father's costly stoneware bowls on the tray. She had only herself to blame. Perhaps if she hadn't been a perfect daughter—if
she hadn't tried so hard to fulfill Mama's dying wish—perhaps
then Abba wouldn't be determined to choose the perfect husband
for her.

Mama was gone, but her last words to Martha echoed in her
mind each day. *Take care of them, my daughter.* And she did. She
cooked Abba's favorite dishes, worked in the gardens, was a
mother to Lazarus, and kept Abba's household running smoothly.
Everything Mama would have wanted.

Martha balanced yet another bowl on top of the stack. Of
course Abba loved her—all the women said they'd never seen
such a devoted father. And he would find a man worthy of his
treasure.

She hoisted the tray, bowls shifting and teetering. Wasn't a
righteous husband what any good Jewish woman wished for? A
respectable husband who owned land and had plenty of servants?
Her own household to run and—if the Most High was kind and
willed it—children to love and care for? That was what a sensible

woman—a woman who didn't let her heart rule her head—wished for. She'd always known she couldn't marry Isa, since they'd first spoken of it years ago. It was hopeless.

She rounded the table and caught sight of her brother. He'd snuck beside the men, sitting as close to them as he dared, listening in on their talk of messiahs and the law and whatever else men spoke of. She peered over the dirty dishes. "Lazarus, go find your friends."

"But I would rather—"

She raised her brows at him. "Go play. You'll have plenty of time to talk with the men when you're older." Her tone brooked no argument. He was only ten years old. Young enough to still be running with the village boys, sneaking food and climbing trees.

"I saved you some honey cakes." She held out the tray. "Share them with Simcha." The shepherd boy who was Lazarus's best friend loved her honey cakes.

Lazarus took the cakes, stretching up to kiss her proffered cheek. "Thanks, Marmar," he said before running off, shouting for Simcha.

Martha lugged her burden down the grassy incline, her sadness lightened as it often did with her little brother's affection. She'd had to grow up fast when Mama died, but Lazarus deserved plenty of time to be a child and she'd make sure he had it.

She arrived at her father's walled courtyard, her arms aching. The poorer residents of Bethany lived in houses of clay and mud in the village, but among the rolling green hills and verdant pastures surrounding Bethany were the houses of the Pharisees—men rich enough to afford land and devout enough to live close to the Temple. Most of them, like her father, made plenty of silver supplying the people of Jerusalem with grain for bread and animals for sacrifice.

Sirach of Bethany lived in a timber-and-brick home with an imposing arched entry guarded by a door of oak and iron. She pushed through it to the spacious courtyard. Smoke and the sharp scent of cumin drifted from three smoldering cooking fires.

Baskets half-filled with onions, cucumbers, and figs littered the ground, along with dirty dishes and a mountain of empty wine amphorae. Servants crouching near the fire jumped to attention when they saw her.

She let out a long breath. Was she the only one who could see what needed to be done? Abba had agreed to pay the extra servants a ridiculous wage. He could afford it, but it was up to her to make sure they earned it. She set her tray down with a clatter. "Clear the dishes and get water for washing. And you"—she motioned to two guilty-looking servants—"bring the rest of the bread to the women and children, please."

Safta, her grandmother on her father's side, sat in the corner, her chin doubled into her chest and her eyes half-closed against the smoke. She liked to call herself the oldest woman in Bethany, and she was probably right. She was as thin and frail as a reed, with a frizz of silver hair perched on the top of her head like a bird's nest. Deep grooves outlined a toothless mouth that could speak words as sharp as arrows.

Safta opened an eye. "Are they gone yet?"

"Some of them," Martha answered. "Tomorrow the rest will leave."

Safta blew air out her nose. "I suppose we'll be holding your feast next, if my son decides which of his friends is worthy to be your husband."

"Safta," Martha whispered, looking at the servants. She didn't need more gossip in the village.

Safta cackled, her laugh as dry as parchment. "We all know what kind of man your abba wants you to marry, even the servants."

Martha tore a round of soft bread into bite-sized pieces and shoved them in an earthen cup. *Yes, a righteous one.* She poured warm goat's milk over the bread and put the cup in her grandmother's hands. That should keep Safta's mouth busy. Now, with the servants working and Abba and his friends sated, she could talk to Isa.

If she was careful.

Martha scooped the last of the roasted lamb into two rounds of bread and added a generous spoonful of seared onions, garlic, and chickpeas. She pinched off a sprig of fresh rosemary, rubbed it between her palms to release the scent, and sprinkled the needlelike leaves over the lamb. Three honey cakes were left, two for Isa—he was too thin—and one for Zerubabbel, the flute player. She broke open a pomegranate and scattered a handful of juicy seeds over the cakes. Isa would eat like a king tonight if she had anything to do with it.

As she balanced the rounds of bread in each hand and turned to the door, her heart dropped. Jael, Simon's mother and their closest neighbor, entered her courtyard like the queen of Sheba entering a palace.

Not her. And not now. Martha glanced at the sky. The sun was setting, casting a pink light over the stone walls. In a few minutes it would be dark.

Jael sauntered toward Martha, a smile pinned to her mouth like a faded flower, and her hair, blackened with expensive dye, swept up into braids so tight they pulled her eyebrows into questioning arches over her critical eyes.

"And just who are you bringing such a fine meal to, hmm?" The older woman's voice scraped on her nerves like a rusty knife.

A response sprung to Martha's lips—*to my sister's marriage tent, in case she and her husband get hungry during their long night of making grandchildren for my abba.* She'd love to see how high Jael's eyebrows would stretch. "Just to the musicians," she said instead.

"That half Jew and the pagan abomination he drags around the countryside with him?" Jael puckered her lips in a disapproving circle. "A good woman does not cast pearls before swine, my dear."

Heat rose in Martha's face. *Isa isn't swine.* "And a worthy woman reaches out her hands to the poor and extends her arms to the needy." She raised her chin, daring—wishing—Jael to respond.

But Jael only narrowed her eyes and harrumphed like a constipated camel.

Martha edged toward the door. Of course Jael would tell Simon of her rudeness, and Simon would surely tell Abba. Abba would be disappointed with her, but by then Isa would be gone with a full belly. He might not eat well again for weeks.

Almost at the door, Jael's mumble reached her. "You'll learn better manners if you are to live in my household and be respected in Bethany."

Martha jerked, and the food teetered in her hands. *Her household? Does she mean what I think she means?* Marriage to Simon? And Martha didn't want to be respected by the women Jael called friends. They kept their homes pure but gossiped with spiteful words about anyone who wasn't the wife of a Pharisee.

Martha pushed through the door without a word, her stomach curdling like sour milk. If Jael meant what she said, Abba must be considering an offer from Simon. How long before a betrothal? How long until even the tiniest hope for her and Isa would be snuffed out like a flame in the wind?

With feet as heavy as stones, Martha carried the laden bowls toward the meadow where Isa and his guardian, Zerubbabel, were finishing a haunting melody. Isa's eyes were closed, his fingers sure on the strings of his kinnor. The last rays of the sun gave his olive skin a burnished glow. His hair was as black as soot, straight as a donkey's mane, and almost as shaggy. Dark, untamed brows curved over slate-gray eyes, and his chin showed the beginnings of a beard.

Each day of Mary's wedding feast had been both sweetness and suffering as she'd dashed between the cooking fires and the wedding guests, knowing his gaze was on her. Knowing they could never be together, not like Mary and Josiah.

They'd met when Martha was just six years old. Isa was taller and a few years older, but back then his voice was still high and clear—the most beautiful voice in Judea, his guardian had bragged.

She'd found him sneaking food from the storage room. He'd run away, but that night after dusk Martha had gone to the orchard with bread and olives. She'd watched him eat, but he hadn't said a word. The next year, not long after Mama died, they came again to play for Purim. He didn't speak when he found her crying in the orchard that night, but sat beside her, as if he understood her sorrow could not be soothed by words.

The next year at Tabernacles, they met again in the orchard. "Question or command?" were the first words he said to her, his voice a hesitant squeak.

She stared at him, more in shock that he spoke than in wonder at his words.

"It's a game. Choose one."

If it got him talking, she was willing to play. "Question."

He fidgeted with a fallen twig, peeling the bark from the wood. "What's it like to have a real father?"

She stared at him. What kind of question was that?

"If you don't answer, you have to do my command." His gray eyes were serious. "That's the rule."

She chewed on her fingernail. What did he mean? Abba was Abba. "He takes care of us," she said slowly, "but he misses Mama."

Isa nodded solemnly. "Does he beat you?"

"Of course not." What a question! Abba would never do that.

"Does he . . . love you?"

"He's our Abba. Why wouldn't he?" She looked sideways at the strange boy who didn't seem to understand family. "Now it's my turn. Question or command?"

After that, they played the game each time he and Zerubabbel visited Bethany. For feasts, for weddings, whenever the rich Pharisees needed the best musicians silver could buy.

Martha always chose questions; Isa chose commands. He asked her about her sister, her brother, living in Bethany. She made him climb trees, hang upside down from branches, and carry her on his back across the stream, their laughter drifting through the dark orchard like petals carried on the wind. She didn't know that he wasn't a Jew. Not until later, and by then it was too late.

As the years passed and her responsibilities weighed heavier on her shoulders, she needed his calm presence like parched land needed rain. And as they grew older, their unlikely friendship went from a spark to a flame, as though they weren't a pagan musician and the daughter of a rich Pharisee. This year, when he strode into town for Mary's wedding, she'd felt its heat like never before.

Martha watched the men and women gather around Isa as he played the last song of the evening, their faces rapt, their bodies swaying to the melody. Isa was taller and broader than he'd been last year, and handsome in the way that made the rabbis nervous. The village girls elbowed each other to dance closest to him and bickered about whom he rested his gaze on. Eliana was the worst. She was bold, too bold—her father should keep a better eye on her. The first night, Eliana had brought an extra cloak to Isa's tent in the meadow. Martha sniffed. *She probably wanted to help him keep warm under it.*

Abba had called Martha beautiful, but Eliana with her almond-shaped eyes and generous mouth was surely the most beautiful girl in the village. Did Isa think Eliana pretty? Martha blew at a strand of hair tickling her face. *What does Isa see when he looks at me?*

Her clothing was finely woven and dyed. The tunic she wore today, deep green with pink embroidery, was made from the best linen Abba could buy. Her hair was thick and fell in plentiful curls almost to her waist. Unless she was working—and there was always much work to be done—then it was pulled in a thick braid under her head covering. She was taller than Mary and not as plump, but she had curves in the right places and her face was said to be pretty. But was she beautiful, as Abba said? As beautiful as Eliana?

It didn't matter. Isa loved her. She knew that like she knew when the bread was perfectly baked, like she knew when her cumin sauce was just right.

The song ended. Guests began packing their cups and knives, getting ready to return to the village. Others laid their cloaks on the grass to sleep their last night in Bethany before journeying home in the morning.

Tomorrow, the meadow would be empty again. No more Isa, no more Mary. Just Martha and Lazarus and Abba. She'd have enough work to keep her busy from sunup to sundown, and plenty of time to worry that she'd be wed to Simon by this time next year.

Zerubbabel laid down his flute and took his food without a word of thanks. She shivered when his hands brushed hers. He was tall, taller than any man she'd ever seen, and his sharp eyes and beaky nose reminded Martha of a hawk looking for its next meal.

She'd heard enough from Isa to fear him. Isa's guardian might act like a Jew in Jerusalem and Bethany, but he was as pagan as the Greeks they sang for in the cities across the Jordan. In the Decapolis, Zerubbabel told fortunes and sold amulets while Isa sang and played his music. If Abba knew that, he'd never let them return to Bethany.

Some of the women talked about what a good man Zerubbabel was, how he'd taken in a boy—a pagan boy abandoned by his own parents—and raised him like a son.

Raised him like a son. Yes, if raising him like a son meant beating him. If it meant not feeding him enough to keep a mouse alive. Martha wished she'd laced the flute player's stew with something that would make his stomach ache. Isa didn't talk about Zerubbabel anymore, not like when they were children, but he didn't have to. She saw the bruises, the way he cowered when his master was angry. She knew how Zerubabbel treated him, and it wasn't like a son.

Isa laid his kinnor carefully on the grass. Without the strings under his fingers and the curved wood between him and the rest of the world, he stood awkwardly. A few of the village men gathered around. "He has the voice of King David," they said to Zerubabbel.

Isa shuffled and looked at his feet as his guardian accepted all the praise. When would he realize he deserved more than Zerubabbel's abuse?

The men wandered off, and Martha approached. Isa, with relief written on his face, took the food from her hand and bent his head toward the other side of the meadow, out of earshot of his guardian and partially hidden by a screen of junipers.

Martha followed him, glancing sideways to see if anyone watched. She whispered to his back. "It's almost dark. Abba will miss me."

He slipped behind the junipers. "Meet me tonight. In the orchard." His words were quick and quiet. His long, calloused fingers curved around her hand.

Her body warmed, as though she stood too close to the cooking fire. Meet alone, in the orchard, at night? When they were young, they'd met at night. They'd talked, looked at the heavens full of stars, and played their favorite game. But since Martha had become a woman, they had found each other only in daylight. If Abba knew that Martha spoke to Isa—even in the day—he would lock her in the courtyard and never let Zerubabbel or Isa near Bethany again. But if he found her in the orchard at night, with a pagan boy . . . she didn't want to think about it.

He turned his serious gray eyes on her. "Please, Martha."

Across the meadow, Zerubabbel stood and wiped his hands on his tunic. "Boy," he barked. "Get our things packed. We leave at first light."

Isa tensed, and his grip on her hand tightened.

"Boy!"

Isa jumped as if he'd been hit by a flying spark. "I'll wait for you," he mouthed as he backed away, his dinner forgotten in his hand.

Martha knew he would. He would wait all night under the apricot trees for her, shivering in his thin cloak. Hoping. Heat crept up her neck at the thought of being alone with him in the night. She couldn't take the chance. But could she bear to let him leave without saying good-bye?

She gazed back over the meadow at the village women, busy with their gossip, at Mary's empty place. At Simon and Abel arguing with the other Pharisees. Tonight might be their last chance to be together before Abba betrothed her to Simon and then . . . it would be too late.

Chapter Three

Get wisdom, get understanding! Do not forget
or turn aside from the words I utter.
—Proverbs 4:5

MARTHA TURNED RESTLESSLY, rustling her straw-stuffed pallet. Abba's deep voice and the murmurs of his friends drifted through the window that opened on the courtyard. It was late, at least halfway through the night. If they didn't go to sleep soon she'd never be able to get to the orchard to see Isa.

The bed she'd shared with Mary felt too big; the space where Mary had warmed her back stretched empty and cold. For six nights, Martha had slept alone—when she slept at all. Lazarus was a good brother and she loved him, but a boy couldn't be the friend that Mary was. That Mary had been.

Since Mama died, Martha had shared everything with her sister. They'd grumbled about their father, cared for their baby brother and ancient grandmother. They were different—two sisters couldn't be more different—but they belonged together. Since the wedding night, when Mary had left her family to join Josiah's, Martha had been alone. Bereft. Like a pot without a spoon. Like a mortar without a pestle.

Martha turned over again, the bedclothes twining around her legs. So many nights they had burrowed into the warm bed, whispering secrets. They spoke of marriage, what every little girl dreamed of. What would it be like? Who would their husbands be? Now Mary knew the answers to their childhood questions, and Martha was happy for her. But Martha's future seemed to stretch before her like a starless night, bleak and hopeless. A future without Mary, and without Isa.

She closed her eyes and pictured the apricot orchard where Isa waited. The boughs were heavy with blossoms, and their heady fragrance scented the night air. He would be standing— no, sitting—with his back against the oldest tree, the one they'd climbed as children.

When she was married, she wouldn't be able to see him again. It wouldn't be right. How could she say good-bye to him forever? She loved him as much as Mary loved Josiah. As much as Abba had loved Mama. And Isa loved her. Not because she could cook and take care of the house. Not because she was obedient to the law and devout in her prayers.

He loved her . . . because she was Martha.

Martha kicked the coverings to the other side of the bed. She had to see him tonight. By the time he came back for Tabernacles, she'd surely be betrothed.

They had to do something, just as Mary had said. If she could convince Isa to talk to Abba. To ask for her . . . surely there was a chance Abba would listen to him.

Slipping off her pallet, she wrapped a fine-spun mantle around her shoulders and padded through the open door, the tile floor cold on her bare feet. She peered around the door frame into the black night.

Abba and his friends sat around a low-burning fire in the center of the courtyard. The only way out of the courtyard was on the other side. Perhaps they'd drunk enough wine that they wouldn't notice her. She slipped out the door, staying in the shadows of the wall.

Simon's slurred voice carried through the dark. "A wife such as Martha is worth more than rubies and emeralds. She is a pearl without price."

Abba's voice returned, quoting the sages as he often did. "Haste in buying land; hesitate in taking a wife."

"You want land?" Simon's voice rose. "Anything, my fields, the olive grove—whatever you want is yours."

Martha clenched her fists. She wasn't a donkey to be bought and sold.

"We will talk of it tomorrow, when you are sober." Abba's voice was serious.

She froze in the shadows. So it was true. Abba was considering Simon. Simon was almost as wealthy as Abba, and at a much younger age. And Isa had nothing but his kinnor to his name.

She wrapped her mantle closer around her shoulders and edged around the courtyard until she reached the door. The latch slid smoothly under her careful hands. She slipped through the opening and closed it behind her without a sound.

Dew soaked her tunic as she ran through the knee-high grass, wishing she could keep running. Away from Abba, away from Bethany. She lifted her tunic high to wade through the icy stream that tumbled down the mountain and toward the Jordan. The rainy season had just ended, and the deep rush of water pulled at her feet like cold hands. She clawed her way up the steep embankment and entered the orchard.

The blossoming trees stood like white-garbed maidens, their branches reaching pale arms to the sky. Fallen flowers blanketed the ground like a layer of sweet-smelling snow that soothed her mind and calmed her spirit. Yes, perhaps there was hope for her and Isa.

A murky shadow moved at the base of the largest tree. A tall, lanky form just as she'd imagined him. "Isa." She let out her breath in a rush.

He stood, his hands reaching out to enfold hers. His chest rose and fell as though he'd been running. She brought her gaze to his face, a face she loved more than any other. His long lashes shadowed his eyes, and his lips slanted in the smile he saved only for her. How could she ever be another man's wife?

"What about Zerubbabel?" The thought of the hawk-faced soothsayer finding them in the orchard was enough to send a shiver down her back.

Isa shook his head. "He won't cross the river."

They were alone. At least for tonight. Shyness suddenly made her look away from him.

She slid her hand over the rough bark of the apricot tree. They had climbed this tree together, eaten apricots in the light of the moon, and played games until the dawn crept into the eastern sky. Each time they'd seen each other, it had become harder to say good-bye. Isa didn't need to speak; she knew that he was reliving the same memories.

"Isa." She swallowed hard. "He's going to—I think Abba is going to settle on a betrothal for me."

Isa straightened, and his jaw firmed. After a long minute, he spoke softly. "If I were your father . . . if I had a daughter like you"—his gray eyes met hers and he brushed a hand down her cheek—"I'd want the best for her."

Tears clogged her throat. Didn't he know he was the best for her? "If you go to him . . . ask him?" At *least* try.

Isa ducked his head, avoiding her pleading gaze. "You know what he'll say. And Zerubbabel—"

"But you could try." *Please.*

He looked at his feet, his throat working. His voice was gentle, but she heard every word like a blow to her heart. "He'd never let us come back. You're not even supposed to speak to me." He brought her hand to his mouth and pressed his lips on her fingers. "I can't bear the thought of you married to someone else. But to never see you again . . ." He closed his eyes and laid his cheek on her palm.

The touch of his lips on her fingers set her heart pounding. She wasn't like other women, Abba had said. She didn't let her heart rule her head. She followed the law, took care of her family, worked from sunrise to sunset—just as Mama had asked. She was the perfect daughter. And because of that, she would never have Isa.

As she saw her lonely future stretch before her, despair welled in her chest and the stars blurred.

Isa leaned in, as if drawn by an invisible force. "Don't cry, Martha. Please."

She heard the pain in his voice, and her heart twisted. At least she would have Abba and Lazarus, a home and people who loved her. What would Isa have? Tears for his loneliness joined those for her own.

He slipped his arms around her and pulled her close. His head lowered. Would he kiss her? Would she let him? His breath brushed her cheek as softly as a flower petal. Didn't she deserve one kiss before he left her? Couldn't they have at least that? She leaned closer and lifted her chin. His lips brushed hers, soft and warm . . . and she couldn't breathe.

Her arms went around his neck like they had always belonged there.

He kissed the corner of her mouth, her cheek, her closed eyes, then back to her lips for a kiss unlike the first tentative touch, but like a starving man at a feast.

Her thoughts muddled as though she'd drunk too much wine. *Unthinkable.* Saying good-bye was unthinkable. She curved into his embrace. A thought whispered in one corner of her intoxicated mind. *This is wrong.*

As though he'd heard her thought, Isa pulled away. "Martha," he whispered against her cheek. He closed his eyes as though to summon strength. "You must go back."

His warning clamored in her mind, but it was dull and distant. *This is what Mary has with Josiah.* This was what Martha wanted. Just a moment longer. Then she would go back to Abba and Lazarus and her life of obedience. Then she would go back to her lonely bed.

She leaned closer to Isa, soaking in his warmth. The tree branches arched over them like a wedding tent; the trees swathed them in their rich perfume. Insects sang a gentle night song, and doves cooed in the branches like lovers whispering their secrets.

She brought her lips to his again and closed her eyes. She felt the moment his strength ebbed and slipped away. He pulled her down with him, onto the bed of velvety blossoms. And for the first time in her life, Martha let her heart rule over her head.

Chapter Four

My son, forget not my teaching, keep in mind my commands; For
many days, and years of life, and peace, will they bring you.
—*Proverbs 3:1–2*

*L*AZARUS WOKE WITH a gasp, the sharp claws of the nightmare
pinning him to his sleeping mat, his heart hammering. The night
closed around him, the darkness a living beast reaching out to
drag him away.

He lay frozen, a wordless prayer his only defense. Finally, his
heart slowed its staccato rhythm. The stars still shone in the
onyx sky, just as they had when he'd fallen asleep on the flat roof
of his father's house. The moon still hung in a golden arc, and his
cousins still snored beside him.

It was just a dream. He knew that. But the threatening
shadow had seemed so real. It always did.

He pushed himself to his feet, stumbled around his sleeping
cousins, and climbed down the ladder. Martha would understand.
She'd let him curl up beside her until the dawn chased away the
memory of the beast. He was too old to be scared by bad dreams,
but Martha wouldn't tell anyone.

He crept into the house, past the open area where Abba
slept on his pallet and Safta snored in the corner, and into the
tiny room in the back of the house. But Martha's bed was empty,
the bed coverings a tangled heap.

The hazy terror of his dream receded as he stood beside Martha's empty bed and contemplated a greater mystery. Where would Martha go in the dark? Abba would be angry if he found out. And if Abba was angry, Martha would work harder—even harder than usual—to make him happy. And she'd make him work, too, instead of listening to the teachers in the synagogue.

He'd have to find her before Abba did.

He returned to the courtyard, where Abba's friends slept near the smoldering fire, their cloaks tucked under their chins against the spring chill. He'd listened to their talk late into the night, at least until Martha sent him to bed. In a few years, when he wouldn't have to obey Martha, he'd stay up all night with the men talking of the law and scriptures. Abba promised he'd study at the Temple with the doctors of the law and become a great scholar. But for now, he ran errands and worked in the garden and did what Martha told him.

He threaded his way around the guests and out the gate, hugging his bare arms to ward away the chill of the night air. In the east, he could see the first lightening of the horizon. Dawn would be here soon, and Abba would expect Martha to be baking their bread.

Poor Marmar. She'd been mad all week. She'd banged the cooking pots and snapped orders. He knew why. It was because she wasn't married and Mary was. Although why Mary wanted to wed Josiah, he couldn't understand. Josiah was never called on to read from the scrolls at the synagogue, and he stumbled through the prayers. No one asked Josiah's opinions on the law, not like they did Abba and Simon. But Lazarus liked Josiah. He was always kind, and he laughed a great deal. He made Mary happy, Abba had said when he agreed to the marriage, and he was a righteous man. If that was enough for Abba, then it was enough for Lazarus.

Lazarus crept across the flat meadow between the gardens and the vineyard, the air damp on his face. Guests clustered in groups around low-burning fires. A few were already waking, rubbing their eyes and pulling their cloaks around them. But Martha wasn't here, with the relatives from Galilee. Maybe she was in the gardens south of the house. He hurried toward the southern fields, where the darkness lingered. His heartbeat quickened. *Even though I walk in the darkest valley, I fear no evil, for you are with me.* Martha had better have a good reason for leaving.

No, Martha didn't want to marry someone like Josiah, but she should have married before Mary. Everyone in the village said it. Just like they said that Mary was the useless sister, the one Abba was ashamed of. That made him angry.

Abba loved Mary. He might wish she followed the law as carefully as Martha, but he wasn't ashamed of her. And Mary was a good sister. She took him to the Temple in Jerusalem. She let him listen to the rabbis who taught in the courtyards. And she hardly ever remembered to check if he'd done his chores.

Martha was more like a mother—the mother he'd never known. She made sure the garden was watered, that the vegetables grew, and that they had good food to eat. And in some ways, she treated him like a grown-up. She asked him which goats were ready to slaughter and to choose the best kids for the Temple sacrifices. She depended on him and didn't treat him like a child all the time, because he wasn't a child. He was almost ten.

Still, he knew why Abba didn't accept any of the men who asked to marry Martha. Abba was afraid to lose Martha. If she were married, she'd leave them and live with her husband. He and Abba would be alone.

If he could find her, maybe he could tell her that. Maybe then she wouldn't be so angry. He reached the gardens and scanned the rows of beans that were just beginning to poke out of the ground. Not even a footprint. He moved farther down, to the long rows of lettuces and herbs, the spring onions, and the hills of cucumber plants. She wasn't here.

The first burst of light broke over the horizon, turning the blossoming trees in the orchard to gold. The orchard. It was her favorite place. Didn't she always go there when she was sad? He should have known.

He sprinted through the rows and reached the stream that cut a narrow gorge between the garden and the orchard. He pushed through the scrub and half slid down the steep bank to the rushing water. During the dry season, the stream was hardly more than a trickle, meandering toward the Jordan. But now the water was deep, sliding over the rocks like a black snake. A shiver slipped up his back at the remembered fear of his dream. He clenched his teeth and hiked up his tunic.

The icy water was deeper than it looked. The current pulled hard at his feet, water swirling above his knees. He slipped on the water-smoothed rocks and went down on one knee. Water surged to his waist. He clambered up, his tunic soaked. The icy wind took his breath away as he climbed to the top of the opposite bank.

She better be in the orchard. He didn't want to cross that river again by himself.

The soft light of dawn slanted over the blossoming trees, illuminating a canopy of pink-and-white petals. He stopped at the first tree and listened. He could call out for her, but what if a wild animal or a bandit heard him? He tiptoed into the deep shadows under the branches.

He jerked to a stop. Was that a voice? Just a low murmur, but yes, a man's voice. And then the soft tone he'd known all his life: Marmar. Relief swept through him. But who would she talk to here in the dark? Father was asleep; he'd seen him in his bed. She wouldn't speak to a man alone, and surely not here in the orchard. Alarm replaced relief.

He picked up a rock the size of his fist. If she was in trouble, he'd help her. He may be small, but he could fight. He'd seen the village boys hitting each other enough. He crept through the trees, his heart skipping. The murmurs grew louder, but Martha didn't sound like a woman in trouble. And the man's voice was familiar.

Lazarus peeked around a trunk to a place where branches hung low enough to form a secluded alcove. His breath caught in his throat. She was with the musician—Isa, the one who sang for the wedding, the one they called the pagan. But what were they doing?

They leaned against the trunk of the old tree. Isa's arms were around Martha, and her head lay pillowed on his chest. Martha's hair was loose over her shoulders, her mantle crumpled beside her on the grass.

Isa dipped his head to kiss Martha . . . on her mouth.

He can't do that. Lazarus jerked back, dropping the rock as he fell on his backside. Abba said one brush against a pagan's cloak was reason to immerse in the mikvah. What happened if you kissed one?

"What was that?" Martha's voice was an alarmed whisper.

This wasn't right. Lazarus squeezed his hands into fists. That Isa deserved a beating, but something kept him from moving forward to stop them. He drew back into the shadow of the tree. Martha would be angry if she saw him. She'd make him promise not to tell Abba. But Abba needed to know.

Isa answered after a moment's silence. "Nothing." Lazarus was close enough to hear him take a deep breath. "Martha, what will we do now?"

"We'll marry, Isa."

Lazarus edged closer, careful not to make a sound. What did Martha mean? A Jewish woman couldn't marry a *pagan*. Everyone knew that.

Isa sounded worried. "Your father would kill me before he'd let me marry you."

"No. He'll have to. It's the law."

Alarm jolted through Lazarus. Martha's voice, always so sure, quivered with doubt. What made her sound like she was going to cry?

"I don't want you shamed, Martha. And your family, they would hate me."

He was right. Abba would never give his blessing. Not to a pagan.

"Then what? What should we do?"

Isa took a deep breath. "Zerubbabel wants to go to the Decapolis next. We always get plenty of work there. I'll get my share of the silver this time. Then I'll come back."

"And then?"

"I've heard in Jerusalem, of non-Jews learning the law, of becoming one of you."

"You'd do that for me?" Martha whispered.

"I'd do anything for you, Martha."

Lazarus almost snorted. Isa, a proselyte? He'd heard his father's friends complaining about how some rabbis in Jerusalem let non-Jews learn the law. After they were circumcised, they welcomed them in the synagogues like members of the Chosen People. They even sacrificed in the Temple. But Abba would never allow it.

Martha's voice was uncertain. "And if he still says no?"

Isa answered quickly, "We'll go away. To Caesarea or Damascus." He held Martha's face between his hands. "You can't marry anyone else. Not now . . ." His voice trailed off.

Lazarus couldn't believe his ears. Martha leave Bethany? She couldn't.

Martha buried her head in Isa's chest and murmured something Lazarus couldn't hear.

Isa's voice was rough. "It won't be long. I promise. Then we'll have a family. We'll raise our children like I always wished I had been. With a mother and father." Isa pulled her closer. "I promise you, Martha. I'll make you the happiest woman in all of Judea."

Lazarus leaned back on his heels. She didn't sound happy now; she sounded like she was crying. And it was Isa's fault, he knew that much. A flurry of blossoms moved by the wind brushed over his nose like a pigeon feather. He tried to stop what was coming, but it was too late. "Ah-ah-choo!"

Martha cried out, branches rustled, and a strong hand grabbed him by the neck of his tunic and pulled him around the tree.

"Lazarus!" Martha's whisper was low and fierce even as tears shone on her face. "What are you doing here?"

He knew that tone of voice. He was in trouble. "I was just . . ." He looked to Isa, and his fear turned to anger. "What are you doing with my sister?"

Isa didn't answer, but Lazarus could tell Isa was afraid. He was afraid of Abba, and he was running away. And he was making Martha sad.

Anger as he'd never known swelled in his chest. Lazarus launched himself at Isa, swinging wildly. His fist connected with a bony rib, and Isa grunted. Before Lazarus could get in another swing, Isa caught his arms and held them. His grip didn't hurt; it only stoked the fury burning inside Lazarus. If he were just bigger . . . older. He'd be able to fight for his sister.

But there was one thing he could do. "I'm telling Abba." Abba always knew what was best.

Martha bent close to him, her face a breath away from his. "You can't tell anyone. Not Abba. And not Mary or Safta." Her breath was rapid and shallow, her face pale in the moonlight. There was something he'd never seen on Martha's face: fear.

A kindred fear rose in his chest, pushing out the heat of anger. What would happen if he told? A shout from across the stream made them all jump and turn to the east, where the sunrise painted the sky with magenta and gold.

Isa tensed. "Zerubbabel. He's looking for me."

Martha took Lazarus from Isa's grasp, her fingers like iron claws on his shoulders. "Don't make a sound." She turned to Isa. "Go now. I'll take him home and make sure he doesn't say anything."

Isa glanced down at Lazarus, then pulled Martha close and kissed her for a long time. Lazarus turned his face away. How could they even breathe? Finally, they pulled away from each other, and Isa ran his hand down Martha's cheek.

Martha looked like she might cry again. "Question or command?" she whispered.

Isa stared at her for a long moment. "Command."

She smoothed a finger over his dark brow. "Come back to me."

He leaned his forehead on hers. "I promise," he whispered, before disappearing into the shadows of the trees.

Martha knelt in front of Lazarus. Tears stood out in her eyes, and her voice was soft and broken. "Lazarus. Swear to me that you won't tell Abba, or anyone. Swear an oath to me right now."

Lazarus looked at his big sister. If he told, Abba could hunt down Isa. Isn't that what he deserved? And then what would happen to Martha? But to swear an oath by the Lord not to tell? That was serious.

"Please, Lazarus," she whispered. "If you love me, swear to me that you will never speak of this to anyone, ever."

Of course he loved Martha; she was his sister. She would do anything for him. He'd swear, then he'd pray that Isa came back soon to make things right with Martha and Abba. "I swear it, Martha. On the name of the Most High, I won't tell anyone, ever." He threw his arms around her neck. "I'll take your secret to my grave."

Seven Years Later

Chapter Five

When one finds a worthy wife, her value is far beyond pearls.
—*Proverbs 31:10*

MARTHA SCOOPED YOGURT from the goat-hide bag into a bowl and drizzled it with deep red pomegranate syrup, then added a round of bread, warm and fragrant.

She glanced at the weak winter sun, already well above the horizon, and frowned. There was much to do today. The cooking pots and utensils must be purified and the prayers sung. Then she and the rest of the household would immerse in the mikvah. Every letter of the law would be followed in preparation for the Sabbath. Abba would surely approve.

Of course, Abba had been dead for almost a year, but his voice still whispered in her mind. His sorrowful eyes watched over her every task.

He who honors his father atones for sins.

A boy shuffled across the courtyard, his arms full of sticks. He was tall for just over six years. His limbs were as angled and bony as a lamb's, and his face had lost the roundness of babyhood. His eyes, the gray of a stormy sky, were outlined with such thick, black lashes they looked to be rimmed with kohl.

He dumped the sticks beside a petite, dark-haired woman stirring the coals of the second cooking fire. "Mama, I'm done with my chores." She nodded without looking up, and he skipped in the other direction toward Martha, his eyes on the bowl in her hand.

Martha smiled and ran a hand over his ebony curls. "Not until you've immersed your hands and prayed, Zakai."

As Zakai hurried to the tall clay jar that held water for purifying their hands, the woman beside the fire made a tiny noise, hardly more than a chirp, but Martha knew what it meant. "He's not too young to follow the law, Penina."

Penina looked over her shoulder and rolled her eyes. Although she was mute—she hadn't spoken a word since she'd come to their family as a slave six years before—Penina made herself abundantly clear.

"She's right, Nina." Lazarus shouldered his way through the courtyard door, his tunic stripped to his waist and a bundle of kindling in his arms. At seventeen, Lazarus was taller than Martha by a head, but still as skinny as a boy. His hair was curly, just like both his sisters', but the dark gold of polished oak instead of their deep brown. Over the past year, his shoulders had broadened, and his suntanned skin stretched tight over bony ribs and a flat belly.

"Zakai will be a man soon." Lazarus winked at the boy. "And when he is, he won't have Martha around to remind him of the law."

Penina said nothing, of course, but the deep dimple on her cheek flashed. She made a sign with her small, expressive hands that sent Lazarus's brows shooting up. He put down the kindling and stood, pushing out his chest. "I am a man, Nina. And the head of this household, which you seem to forget." He looked down his nose at her, but a smile lurked on his mouth as he flexed an arm to show his muscle.

Penina blew out a breath, clearly unimpressed.

Martha shook her head, but a smile threatened. "Stop it, you two. You're both too old for bickering."

Penina might resist following the many precepts of the Pharisees, but she had never been able to resist tormenting Lazarus. She was just a year or two older than he, but seemed younger because of her small frame and petite face. Her high cheekbones and slanted eyes hinted at a heritage far from the hills and valleys of Judea, but her skin, the color of dark honey, was only a shade darker than most Israelites'.

Martha was glad Lazarus had taken on the responsibilities of the man of the family after Abba died, but the household decisions were still her domain. And they would be until Lazarus found a wife. If he ever did.

She rested her eyes on Penina. Perhaps someday, Penina would love the God of Israel as much as she loved to tease Lazarus. And then, perhaps Lazarus would let himself think of Penina as more than another sister.

Martha watched Zakai as he immersed his hands and mumbled the prayer. He came back to her with a smile, and she kissed his soft cheek, resisting the urge to smooth his eyebrows into a tidier line before she handed him his food. She wished she had time today to pull him into her lap for a few minutes, but she had much to do.

Martha filled another dish with yogurt and pomegranate syrup, two rounds of bread, and two handfuls of roasted almonds. That should put some meat on Lazarus's bones. Safta snored in the corner. She would need breakfast, too. And perhaps today she would let Martha brush her hair. It looked like the birds had been nesting in it.

But first, something—other than Penina's taunts—was bothering Lazarus. Her baby brother had never been able to fool her. She handed him his food, sat down on the packed dirt beside him, and waited. She didn't have to wait long.

"Do you know what tomorrow is?" Lazarus asked, ignoring the food in his hands.

"Yes." How could she not know? Tomorrow would be one year since Abba died.

"*Avelut* is done, Martha." His face was serious.

"So it is." The twelve months of mourning for Abba was finished, but she would never stop atoning for her sin against him.

"Abba asked me . . ." Lazarus stopped suddenly and took a bite of bread.

Martha watched her brother fidget with his food. Why was he so uneasy?

Lazarus swallowed. "Abba made me promise to find you a husband. Now that the mourning period is over, I can abide—"

"A husband?" Martha lurched to her feet. How could he even think it?

Lazarus set his bowl aside and pushed himself to standing. "I'm the head of the family now, Martha. It's my duty."

"No." Her brother might be taller than she, but she could still use the voice that had made him jump as a boy. "That is not going to happen."

Penina stopped grinding grain and sat back on her heels. Her eyes flicked between Martha and Lazarus. This time, she wasn't smiling.

"He spoke of it, when he was dying." But Lazarus didn't look her in the eye.

Martha shook her head. This was ridiculous. "Abba said a lot of things when he was dying." Most important, that she must keep her secret. But how could she keep her secret if Lazarus wanted her married?

"This is one that he meant." Lazarus's mouth was firm. "You need a husband. I might not always be here to take care of you."

Anxiety knotted under Martha's heart. "What do you mean?" But she knew what foolishness Lazarus meant. How could Lazarus do this to her, to Penina and Zakai?

"The Messiah has come, Martha. I must be ready to follow him."

"That doesn't change—"

"Martha." Lazarus's eyes widened as if he were seeing the coming of the Kingdom already. "It changes everything."

She blew out a breath of frustration. Their cousin Jesus had visited their home often in the years since he'd started teaching among the people. She was always glad to welcome him into Bethany and feed him and his followers. She loved him as much as Lazarus did. But Jesus of Nazareth, the Messiah?

Yes, there'd been talk—and in the past year Jesus' name had been on everyone's lips. But there was always talk of messiahs. That's what Abba said. Besides, Lazarus was too young to be a disciple, no matter what he thought.

Penina came to Martha's side, slipping her warm hand into Martha's cold one. Martha gripped it as if it were keeping her from falling from a cliff. Penina might be mute, but she understood. *Messiah or not, I can't marry.*

Lazarus knew enough about women and men, enough about the marriage laws. He couldn't ask this of her. At the very least, she'd be humiliated in the eyes of her husband. At worst . . . she refused to think of it.

Lazarus set his hands on her shoulders, his eyes gentle as if she were a frightened animal. "Don't worry, Martha. I've been praying about this. The Lord will provide a husband who—"

The gate squealed open, and Jael swept into the courtyard. Martha's back stiffened. How did that woman always know the worst time to come visit? They couldn't speak of this in front of her, of all people. Martha glared at Lazarus and shrugged out of his grip.

Lazarus eyed Jael and lowered his voice. "Martha, Abba wanted you to marry. It's for the best." He nodded to Jael and ducked out the door, leaving his food untouched.

For whose best? Not hers. She wouldn't be getting married, no matter what Lazarus had promised Abba. She smoothed a hand over her eyes and hair and fixed a smile on her trembling lips.

Jael embraced her as if she hadn't seen her for weeks, instead of just yesterday. "Peace be to you and your house, Martha. And upon all that you have."

"And peace be to you," she answered.

Jael's hair was still as black as a he-goat although she was well past her fifth decade, but her tight braids couldn't smooth the deep furrows on her brow. She cast a critical eye on Zakai, scooping up the last of his breakfast. "Has the household of Sirach become wealthy again, that you can feed the children of your slaves so well?"

Martha didn't have to look at Penina to know she was bristling. She pulled Jael toward the other side of the courtyard and offered her a seat under the fig tree beside her dozing grandmother. *Safta, I beg you, try to hold your tongue today.* "Jael, you know that I gave Penina her freedom almost a year ago. She's not a slave, and neither is her son. They are family." As if she hadn't told Jael a dozen times.

Jael sniffed. "Family?" She sat down heavily on the bench and brought out a tuft of wool and her spindle and distaff. "As my son always says, once a slave, always a slave."

Safta opened her eyes and wet her withered lips with her tongue. "Your son, the leper, says that, eh?"

Jael reared back. "My son is no longer a leper."

"Just as Penina is no longer a slave." Safta put her lips together and blew, making a rude sound that told Jael exactly what she thought.

Martha tapped her temple and shook her head. "Safta," she whispered to Jael. They owed too much to Simon to let Safta insult his mother.

"My mind is as good as it ever was, little girl, and so is my hearing," Safta said sharply.

Jael's eyes narrowed. "At least I still have a child"—she gave Safta a pointed look—"in Bethany."

Safta stared at her for a moment, then settled lower and closed her eyes as if she was going back to sleep. Today's battle was over, and Jael had won.

No one in Bethany spoke of Safta's daughter. At least if they had any kindness in them. When Martha was just a child, Safta's only daughter had forsaken her family to marry a poor man from the lower town in Jerusalem. They'd heard rumors that her husband gambled, that they had stopped worshipping at the Temple—even talk that she herself had sunk into drunkenness. It had broken Safta's heart to lose her only daughter . . . to never know her grandchildren.

Martha turned away, wishing she could tell Jael what she thought of her cruelty to an old woman. Instead, she gathered the rest of the bread into a basket. "Zakai, take this to Mary." She set it in his arms with a warning look. "And come back with news. Don't run off onto the mountain." Perhaps by then Jael would be gone.

Zakai sidled toward the door, a suspicious twitch under his tunic.

"Zakai?"

He stopped and gave her an innocent face.

"What is it?"

He hung his head, tramped back to her, and set down the basket. He dug into the neck of his tunic and pulled out a long green-and-black lizard. "I just wanted to show it to the girls."

Martha heard Jael's sharp breath across the courtyard and tensed. Zakai was just being a little boy. Why did the meddling woman have to act like he'd broken the first commandment?

"Zakai." Martha crouched down to see his face. "You know the lizards are unclean."

He kicked at a stone with his toe. "I know. He was just so pretty."

Martha wished she could lean in and kiss his disappointed face. But not in front of Jael. Instead, she gave him a nudge and a smile. "Let him go outside the walls. And don't forget to immerse your hands again."

Zakai bounded out the door. Martha returned to Jael, passing the corner of the courtyard that held Zakai's collection of cages and discarded baskets. One cage held a desert hare Zakai had rescued last winter, another an assortment of birds that twittered and flapped. A lamb, born too early and with a deformed leg, munched a pile of grass in the corner. Zakai couldn't resist taking care of every animal he found.

Jael looked down her nose at the animal menagerie. "You are far too lenient with your *former* slaves, Martha. I can't believe what you allow." She pursed her lips. "And especially considering your"—she lowered her voice—"reduced circumstances."

Martha bit back a retort and picked up her distaff. Didn't Jael have anything else to do today? Harass her servants, mend Simon's fine garments, or even look over the land that used to be Abba's and now belonged to her son?

She should be used to Jael's comments about the decline of Abba's household. Even before the illness that took his life, there was talk that Abba had lost his senses. He let his fields lie fallow and took no interest in his herds or orchards. Martha knew her father hadn't lost his wits; he'd lost his will to live. Her sin had eaten away at him, until finally, he gave up his spirit.

Jael continued, her own work forgotten in her hands. "Of course, you have no children of your own to consider. Not like Mary, hmm? Perhaps your sister will have a son this time. It is a shame your father, blessed be his memory forever, didn't live to see a grandson."

Martha's fingers fumbled on the distaff, and her throat closed. She waited until she could give an appropriate response without a hitch in her voice. "Let us pray that Mary's child is a boy, to bless my father's memory as your son blesses his father's memory and all those who came before."

Jael nodded, satisfied at the compliment. "You, my dear, are a blessing on your father's memory. The holiest, most devout woman in Bethany, everyone says it."

Martha settled into her work. Jael's feelings were soothed, but hers were in turmoil. *The holiest woman in Bethany.* The people of Bethany may think her holy, but they only saw what they wanted to see. What she let them see. A perfect woman, her value far beyond pearls. A blessing to her father's memory.

But would a holy woman have so many worries? Would she worry about how to keep her household fed and clothed, or if her garden would produce enough for the winter? Would a holy woman wait seven years for a pagan who had abandoned her? Martha quickened her fingers at turning the wool into fine thread. *Don't think of Isa. Don't remember that night in the orchard.*

No. She wasn't as holy as they believed. And now, with Lazarus and his ridiculous idea of marriage, she had even more to worry about.

Chapter Six

Her husband, entrusting his heart to her, has an unfailing prize.
—Proverbs 31:11

MARTHA CUT ACROSS the terraced meadow that sloped from the upper reaches of the Mount of Olives to the wide arches of the Bethany gate. She passed by the two city judges who sat on benches outside the gate, waiting to resolve disagreements between bickering shepherds or disputes between merchants. Both were dozing, their backs resting against the wall, their gray-bearded chins propped on their chests.

She kept her head down. Perhaps this morning, the day after a peaceful Sabbath, she'd make it to the well without having to speak to anyone—without having to listen to gossip about who was betrothed, who was pregnant, or who had breached one of the many laws of the Pharisees.

She hadn't taken ten steps into the city when she saw Elishiva. The old woman struggled to climb down from her rooftop, a basket of clothes under her arm. Martha let herself into Elishiva's tiny courtyard, set down her jar, and hurried to the base of the ladder. "Elishiva, please, let me help you."

Elishiva looked down from the highest rung. She was a tiny woman, made even smaller by a hunched back that bent her almost double and made every movement look painful. Furrows creased her forehead, and channels cut down her mottled cheeks like dry riverbeds. "Martha, child, you are too kind." She lowered the basket to Martha's waiting hands.

Elishiva tottered as she descended each rung. Safta's closest friend had been blessed with three sons. One had gone to Damascus and rarely sent word to his mother; another had died before he reached twenty. Elishiva's youngest son still lived in his mother's house. He worked for Simon, and most of the village thought him an idiot. His speech was so slow he could hardly be understood, and his mind was that of a child. Still, he worked as hard as any man to bring his meager pay home to his mother.

Martha let out a breath of relief when both Elishiva's feet were firmly on the ground.

"Thank you, sweet girl." Elishiva caught her breath and smiled up at Martha. "You are looking as beautiful as your mother, Martha."

Martha carried the basket to the shade of a scrawny fig tree in the courtyard. "Thank you, Elishiva. Next time, send for me. I'll have Zakai spread your laundry to dry." She'd hate to have Elishiva fall; she looked as frail as a twig.

"You are busy enough, what with your brother to take care of and your sister so close to giving birth." She put her gnarled hand on Martha's arm. "Tell Mary I pray for her."

"As do we all," a strident voice added.

Martha's stomach rolled.

Devorah, the wife of Abel, stood in the courtyard entrance, her ample body blocking Martha's only way out. There would be no avoiding gossip today. "Your sister won't be gathering flowers or giving away bread to the beggars at the city wall, not with three little mouths to feed." Devorah smoothed her hair. "Mary would do well to watch over her own before worrying about others."

And you could do the same. Martha clamped her teeth together. Abel was a city judge; it wouldn't do to anger his wife.

"Mary is a good girl." Elishiva lifted her chin at Devorah. "She's always so kind to my boy."

"And we all know what a blessing your boy is." Devorah's words were like arrows.

Elishiva's face fell, and her shoulders hunched even lower.

Martha picked up her water jar. She could at least spare Elishiva any more of Devorah's insults. "Are you on your way to the well, Devorah? Let us go together. You can tell me how your daughters are faring with their cooking."

Devorah glowed as if she'd been asked to visit Herod's palace. "Of course, my dear, although no one can compete with your skill."

Martha bent her lips in a smile.

"Lazarus is indeed blessed to have you for a sister," Devorah gushed, and without a word of good-bye to Elishiva, flounced back into the street.

Martha touched Elishiva's bent back. "I mean it, next time send for me. You shouldn't be up on the roof."

Elishiva nodded, but her eyes blinked back tears of hurt from Devorah's words.

Martha listened halfheartedly to Devorah talk about her perfect children as they walked through the village, wishing she could tell the rude matron just what she thought of her. But what would be the use of angering Devorah? She'd tell her husband, and that wouldn't help any of them.

They reached the well, a wide opening ringed by a low wall of rock. The city walls might unite Bethany, but at the well there was an unspoken division. The wives of the Pharisees, those who followed the law with precision and made their vessels pure, gathered on one side. The village women kept to themselves on the other.

Silva, on the Pharisee side of the well, was pouring water into her jar. She smiled and stood to embrace Martha as if she'd journeyed from Damascus instead of just outside the walls. "Martha. Did you have a blessed Sabbath?"

Martha breathed shallowly. Silva's husband, Tobias, had made an offer for Martha before she had turned thirteen, but

Abba hadn't thought him worthy of her. Now Tobias owned half the olive groves in Bethany, and his wife wore linen and smelled strongly of rose oil. Very strongly.

Without waiting for her answer, Silva went on. "And good wishes to your sister. May she be blessed with a son."

"Thank you, Silva." Martha's eyes watered. Silva meant well, most of the time, but she was easily swayed by the opinions of Devorah and Jael. "I will tell her of your goodwill."

Silva lowered her voice. "I do hope that she will manage with a new baby." Her brows lowered in a show of concern. "She can barely keep those two girls fed and clothed." She glanced at Devorah as if they'd spoken often of the subject. "But, of course, she has you. She is blessed to have such a sister, all the women say it."

"We often wonder what she'd do without you, my dear," Devorah added with an abrasive laugh.

Martha's hand itched to wipe the smirk off Devorah's face. Instead, she threw the gourd down the well and pulled it up from the cool depths. Didn't these women have anything better to do than gossip about Mary? And Mary . . . how angry she'd be if she knew how they talked of her. Her sister made no secret of what she thought of these proud women married to rich Pharisees, of their strict adherence to the law and the lack of love in their hearts.

Mary was a good mother and a good wife. Yes, she sometimes had no bread to feed her family, but no matter how little they had, Mary didn't worry. Trust in the Lord, she would say with a smile. And somehow, the Lord—or more often, Martha herself—provided the bread. But Martha didn't dare defend her sister.

Instead, she feigned surprise at the position of the sun. "Look how late it is. Blessings on you and your family, Silva, Devorah."

They called out their good-byes as Martha fled, her jar half-full of water, but her belly brimming with bitterness. They didn't know her, these women who called her the holy one, the good sister. These women who received her into their midst with honor she didn't deserve.

Yes, she followed the laws and kept her home pure. She immersed her vessels and kept the Sabbath holy. But she stood by in silence as proud peahens like Devorah and Jael pecked at Elishiva and Mary.

Martha couldn't afford to ruffle feathers in Bethany.

She'd spent years building a wall to protect the ones she loved. Each brick—the purity of her food, their tithes to the priests, the daily immersions—made it stronger. Without her fortifications the women of Bethany might guess the truth about her. That she wasn't the good and holy sister. That she had once followed her heart instead of the law. And that she hid a secret that could shake Bethany like an earthquake.

Chapter Seven

She obtains wool and flax and makes cloth with skillful hands.
—Proverbs 31:13

MARTHA SUPPRESSED A yawn and fed more wool from her distaff to the whirling spindle as Jael droned on.

What would it take to get this woman to go home?

If only she could nap through the mid-morning litany, as Safta was doing. She'd sent Penina to water the garden as soon as Jael arrived for her daily visit. Penina had given her a relieved look and the sign for thank you. Even carting water from the stream was better than listening to Jael crowing about her son.

Martha had heard it all before. Hadn't every woman in Bethany? Simon's fields, his business in Jerusalem, his visits to the Temple, and how he would soon be declared a doctor of the law. Jael loved to tell of her son's blessings. Yet everyone still called him Simon the Leper and probably always would.

He'd contracted the grim disease around the time Mary's first child had been born and Simon was sent away in shame. Less than a year later, he returned to Bethany, declared clean by the Temple priests. It wasn't unusual; many lepers came back to their families after their skin had cleared. Some physicians even believed that the white, flaky skin that had afflicted Simon wasn't the same putrid disease that killed other lepers. No one knew for sure, but it didn't matter to the people of Bethany. They never forgot that Simon had once been defiled. Perhaps that's why Jael had to sing her son's praises so loudly.

Martha started from her stupor at the slam of the courtyard gate and Zakai's urgent call. "Marmar!"

She dropped her spindle in the dirt as Zakai ran to her and pulled her to her feet. "It's Mary. Come quick."

A twist of apprehension spiraled through her. "Is it the baby? Already?"

He nodded, his eyes wide.

"Where is Penina?" They'd need her. Mary's births were always so difficult.

Zakai dragged her toward the gate. "She's already there."

Jael darted to her side. "I'll come to help you, Martha. You'll need someone other than that slave."

Martha closed her eyes for a moment. Penina was the best midwife in Bethany. And Jael in the birthing room? Mary would hate it, Penina would never allow it, and Martha would surely lose whatever patience she had left.

Safta pushed herself up with a groan. "Go home, Jael. We'll take care of her ourselves. And *that slave* is better with birthing than you ever will be."

Jael's mouth shriveled like a rotten fig.

Thank the Almighty for Safta, even if she was rude. "I'm sorry, Jael." Martha took the woman's arm and showed her out of the courtyard. "We'll send word as soon as the baby's born." She smiled. "You'll be the first to know." And the first to share the news at the well, which would soothe Jael's feelings more than anything else.

Jael accepted her compromise with a glare at Safta before she strutted out of the courtyard.

Martha turned on her grandmother with a reproving look.

Safta ignored her and hobbled toward the door. "Let's go see to your sister. This isn't gonna be easy."

Martha followed Zakai as quickly as Safta's shuffling steps allowed. They reached her sister's tiny home on the other side of the village. Mary's courtyard was hardly big enough for the three of them. An overgrown riot of flowers choked out the rosemary and garlic in the corner garden. The mint patch had overtaken the vegetables, and the cooking fire was black and cold.

The door was open, and the one-room house was crowded. Mary sat on a bench, her breathing quick, her knuckles white as she clutched her husband's hand. Josiah watched his wife with worried eyes. His hair and beard were wild, as if he'd been pulling at them. Penina crouched close to Mary.

Mary's younger daughter, Sarah, ran to Martha and wrapped her arms around Martha's legs. At two years old, Sarah was usually as chatty as a magpie and twice as naughty. Today, she buried her face in Martha's tunic with a sob. Martha crouched down and untangled the little girl. "Shh, Sarah. Don't worry. We'll get your new brother or sister here soon." She folded the little girl in her arms.

"Adina." Martha held her hand out to Mary's other girl, a waif of five years who stood in the corner with her thumb in her mouth. "Don't worry, sweet one." Adina burrowed into her embrace without a word. Adina rarely spoke, but did the work of a girl twice her age. She could be counted on to take care of her sister.

Martha pushed her fingers through Adina's tangled hair. Mary never had been good with scissors, and her daughters badly needed their curls trimmed. Baths and clean clothes wouldn't hurt them either.

Josiah's mother, Chana, stood behind her son and wrung her hands. She was a thin, nervous woman with a high forehead. Her long face was crisscrossed with lines and as dry as parchment. "Thank the Almighty you're here, Martha. You are so much better at caring for Mary than I am."

Penina snorted. Martha gave her a warning look. Josiah's mother was good at one thing: talking. She knew every tidbit of gossip in the village and spread it like a sower scattering seed. But Mary didn't need gossip right now. She needed space to breathe.

Penina looked up at Martha. With deft hands and a firm expression, she silently said what Martha already knew. *Everyone out.* When it came to birthing a baby, her mute friend made her wishes clear.

"I know," Martha answered. Martha urged Josiah and the children out the door and turned to Chana. "Please, Chana, take the girls to my house and give them something to eat. We'll let you know as soon as the baby is born."

Josiah clutched at Martha's hand, his grip mirroring the worry in his face. "Send word to me as soon as you can."

Martha nodded. Her sympathy rose at the pain in Josiah's eyes. Mary's girls hadn't come easily. When she'd become pregnant a third time, Josiah had been joyful at the prospect of a son. But as she grew large with his child—and then even larger—he spent more time in prayer and even less at work. She patted her brother-in-law's hand and gave him a push. "Pray, Josiah. Pray for your wife and baby."

Mary groaned in pain as her husband ducked out the door.

With the room cleared of everyone but Mary, Penina, and Safta, Martha took a deep breath. There was much to do. *Keep busy. Don't think.*

Penina brought a stool and settled close to Mary.

Mary reached out a shaking hand. "I want Martha," she whimpered, sounding like the little girl she had been when they had lost their mother.

Penina gave up her place to Martha, her face showing a worry that made Martha's stomach clench. Safta crouched in the corner, her eyes closed, her lips moving in prayer.

When the pain waned, Martha helped Mary to her sleeping pallet on the floor. She rubbed Mary's back while Penina rummaged through the disarray of the house. Penina returned, handing Martha a scrap of linen and a bowl of cool water scented with lavender. Penina set her hand on Mary's distended belly, then made the sign for night.

Martha stroked her sister's face with the damp cloth. If Penina was right—and she always was about birthing—it would be a long, hard day for Mary. "Sleep, my sister, for a little while," Martha murmured.

Mary's eyes fluttered closed, and her body relaxed.

Penina nodded in satisfaction, then made the sign for food. She took up watch on Mary as Martha checked Mary's grain and oil jars, both almost empty. Martha might be low on wheat and spices in her home, but Mary was hardly getting by on what Josiah earned working for Simon. And she had two children and a mother-in-law to care for.

Martha scraped the last kernels of barley from the jar. Why hadn't she come earlier, to help with the girls and prepare for the baby instead of sending Zakai with their leftovers? She knew why. There was more than a meadow and the walls of Bethany separating her and her sister. There was Josiah. Mary had a husband to turn to now, a husband she loved. She didn't need Martha.

She found a jar half-filled with lentils. Guilt twisted through her. If she were honest, she couldn't blame Josiah. Mary often asked Martha to go on walks with the children or to share a meal at her home, but Martha found excuses. She was busy—cooking, caring for the garden, getting the vegetables ready for market— always busy.

The real reason she stayed away was more than she could admit to her sister. She couldn't bear to see Mary's beautiful children, or watch her sister's face glow with joy when Josiah came home from his work. Even after seven years, it hurt too much.

Still, a good sister would have taken care of Mary during the last weeks of her pregnancy. A good sister would have stood up for Mary when they talked about her at the well.

Mary should see to her own family before helping strangers.

Josiah should put his foot down.

Martha slammed the top onto the lentil jar. They should all mind their own business. She went outside to the cooking fire and tumbled a handful of kindling into the ashes. Mint tea would soothe Mary, and a thick lentil soup would give them all strength for the long labor ahead. She gathered the lentils, a few dried-up onions, and the rest of the garlic, and got to work.

There was much to do.

AS THE SUN sank in the west, Martha walked with her sister inside the walls of the little house. The pains were closer now, and harder, but Penina's face was grim. As they'd waited through the long afternoon, Martha had purified her sister's cooking vessels and prepared the soup and bread. She'd cleaned the house, stitched the girls' ragged tunics, and swept out the courtyard. There was nothing left to do but wait.

Safta had fallen asleep on the bench in the corner. How could she sleep through Mary's groans?

Zakai poked his head into the house and looked for Martha in the dim light. "Marmar. Lazarus wants you."

Martha stuck her head out the door to find Lazarus leaning against the wall. His chest and long legs were bare, and a pruning hook hung from his hand.

"How is she?" His eyes were worried. "Tell the truth."

Martha let out her breath. "She's weakening."

Lazarus's shoulders slumped.

"She must have the baby soon, or I don't think she'll have the strength . . ." She laid a hand on Lazarus's arm. "Don't tell Josiah. Not yet."

Lazarus's eyes slid to Zakai; the boy's face was worried, too. "Come, Zakai. We'll go to Josiah and pray with him."

As darkness embraced the little house, broken only by a pair of glowing lamps, Mary's pains increased. Her labored breathing turned into moans of pain. Penina motioned to Martha. It was time. Together, they helped her to the birthing stool. Mary, her grip as weak as a baby lamb, held on to Martha. Safta awoke and scooted beside Mary, murmuring into her ear. "You can do this, my girl. You are stronger than you know."

Penina grunted. It was the only sound she could make, but Martha knew what she meant. "Push," Martha whispered. *Please, oh God of Israel, please.* "Push, sister. Your child needs to come into the world."

Oh Lord, save her. Please, Lord, do not punish her, too, for my sins.

Chapter Eight

MARTHA SUPPORTED MARY'S back and shoulders.

Mary pushed. Her face stretched into a grimace as a cry of agony tore from her. She stopped and sucked in a breath.

Penina, her hand on Mary's belly, nodded to Martha.

"Again, my sweet," Martha crooned.

Mary didn't respond; her head lolled forward.

Safta clutched her. "Don't give up, granddaughter. I won't allow it."

Martha lifted her sister's chin. Mary's eyes were closed, her mouth slack. "Mary!" She shook her. Mary must finish—for her own life and the baby's. Martha used her most commanding voice, the one she'd used when Mary was a child. "Push, Mary. Once more, and then you can rest."

"Once more," Safta repeated the command.

Mary's eyelids flickered open.

Please, little sister. This time, a note of pleading crept into Martha's voice. "Once more and you will have your child in your arms."

Mary took a shuddering breath, and her lips firmed. One more push, a cry from her, and she crumpled. Martha folded her sister in her arms.

A warbling cry sounded from below the birthing stool. Penina held the baby, squirming, blue, and very alive. She passed the bundle to Safta's reaching hands.

"A boy, Mary," Safta cackled. "Thanks be to the Almighty."

Joy and relief weakened Martha's legs. "Did you hear, Mary?" Her voice wavered. "Mary, you have a son."

Mary's eyes fluttered open, and the ghost of a smile twitched her lips. Safta pushed the child into Martha's arms and helped Penina lower Mary to her pallet. Penina motioned for Martha to give her room to work.

While Penina cared for Mary, Martha poured salt on the squalling baby boy's wet limbs, gently rubbing it into his soft skin to harden it against disease. Relief and gratitude swelled in her heart. A boy who would carry on Josiah's line, learn the law and faith of his people.

She reached for the linen wrappings and wound them around the infant's arms and legs, murmuring the prayers of thanksgiving and joy. Thanksgiving for another child for Mary. Joy for Josiah, who had a son.

The baby began to snuffle and cry. She took him to her shoulder and patted him, swaying as she sang a tuneless song. She laid her cheek against his tiny head and closed her eyes, reveling in the softness and warmth of a new life.

Josiah burst into the room and stumbled to Mary's side. He dropped to his knees beside his wife. "How is she?"

"Tired, but she'll be fine, Josiah," Martha answered, hoping Josiah couldn't see the line of Penina's mouth, the furrow in her brow that told of another difficult birth.

Josiah stroked his wife's face, and only when she'd opened her eyes and murmured to him did he turn to see the baby.

Martha settled the child in his father's arms. "The Lord has blessed you. You have a son." Martha's throat tightened as Josiah's face transformed from worry to joy. *This boy has a father who will love him.* Mary and her family were blessed indeed.

BY THE TIME dawn stretched fingers of ruby and gold into the eastern sky, Mary was asleep with her new son snuggled to her breast.

Josiah and the two girls nestled close by, and Chana stood watch over them.

Martha pulled on her cloak with leaden arms.

Chana hovered as Martha and Penina crossed the courtyard. "Thanks be to the God of Sarah, the God of Rebecca, and the God of Leah, and the God of Rachel. Martha, you are a blessing to your sister." Chana pulled open the courtyard gate and ushered them through. "Go home now, and take your rest. Safta and I will take good care of them."

Martha glanced sideways in time to catch Penina's brows flicker. It wasn't the first time a village woman had forgotten to thank her after a birth. "Send Adina if you need us." Martha would bet her favorite knife Chana was waiting to run to the well to share the news of her grandson.

Martha stepped into the biting wind, Penina at her side. Penina's face was drawn in fatigue, her bare arms crossed against her chest. Martha slipped off her cloak and wrapped it around them both. If Penina would obey her, she'd order her to sleep for the rest of the day. But when had Penina ever obeyed her? Very little when she was a slave and even less after she was freed.

They threaded their way past houses yet untouched by the sun's first rays and out of the city, nodding at the sleepy gate-keeper.

Martha plodded on, her heart heavy. As the night had turned into dawn, her joy had seeped away. Each moment witnessing the happiness she could never have rubbed her heart as raw as a fresh wound.

When they reached the walls of her father's house, Martha stopped. Inside the impressive gate, there was work to be done. Always more work, always more to worry about. And never a husband who loved her like Josiah loved Mary, never a family. Good Jewish men married virgins. Not women who had shamed their fathers and themselves.

The weight of her sorrow, the loneliness of her life stretching out before her, threatened to crush the breath from her body. A shudder shook her shoulders, and she slumped against the wall.

A warm hand slipped into hers. She may be mute, but Penina could read Martha like the Pharisees read the scrolls of the Torah. The tears that Martha had held back for hours spilled over. Penina wrapped her arms around Martha's shaking shoulders and drew her close.

When her tears were spent, Penina wrapped the cloak around Martha, turned her toward the orchard, and gave her a push. Yes, she needed to be alone there. Penina knew that, too, after all these years. Just for a few moments before she could face the rest of the day . . . and the rest of her life.

Martha shuffled toward the orchard on stiff legs. A dull pain pounded in her temple. She plunged down the bank and splashed through the stream, which was hardly more than a trickle. Up the far bank, and she was under the apricot trees.

No pink blossoms littered the grass under her feet. No hint of the springtime buds or soft green leaves. The branches above were black and gnarled, reaching up to the brightening sky as if begging the heavens for rain. She pulled a dead leaf from an empty branch.

Here, right here, was the only place she let herself think of Isa. The only place she whispered his name or remembered his kiss. The only place she asked the question that had haunted her for more than seven years.

Isa, why didn't you come back to me?

She stroked the dry leaf over her lips. After seven years, how could thoughts of Isa still hurt like a knife in her heart? How could she still look to the east and hope to see him coming back to her? She'd been a fool.

A fool waiting for someone who would never return.

A fool with a secret that made marriage an impossible dream, no matter what Lazarus thought.

For seven years she'd waited. Isa was either dead or he'd deserted her. Either way, it was time to give him up. Time to stop tormenting herself with a ridiculous shred of hope that refused to be crushed. Time to forget about Isa. He wasn't coming back.

Martha crushed the brittle leaf and let the crumbled pieces scatter in the wind.

Isa was either dead or he deserved to be.

Chapter Nine

━━━

Have mercy on me, God, in your goodness; in your
abundant compassion blot out my offense.
—Psalm 51:3

*H*UNGER. THIRST. DESPAIR.

His tortured mind understood nothing more. He writhed on a cold stone bed. The cave was dark but for a murky beam of light seeping through the entrance. Dense, still air choked him with the smell of decay and rot. The voices that had been with him for all eternity shrieked in laughter. Or did they wail in despair?

The cries—the pain of a thousand lifetimes, the torture of an untold number of souls—suffused him. It swept away all thought, all memories of a life before this torment.

Hunger clawed at him. He stumbled from the cave, shielding his eyes from the sun struggling to shine through a bank of gray clouds. His feet found the rocky path to the shore. Food. He needed food. At the water's edge he might find a fish.

The wails increased, became frantic. *Stay away from the water.*

But this time, his hunger won.

Light glinted off the waves like sharp knives. The scent of water ignited a rage of thirst in his dry throat. New cries assailed his ears, echoing off the rocks that lined the shore. A despairing lament, like a monster's heart was breaking. His throat rasped in pain. The voice was his.

He stumbled along the rocky edge of the water. Nothing. Not even a dried-up fish carcass. Nothing but the relentless lapping of the waves. The voices cried out as he approached the wet stretch of shore. They threw him back, away from the water.

Thirst burned through his body.

Despair clouded his vision.

Laughter pounded in his head.

His hand closed around a stone, sharp and flinty. He scraped the rough edge over his naked chest. A line of blood showed bright against his dirty skin. The pain sharpened his vision, cleared his mind. The cacophony subsided for a sweet moment. He rushed to the water, threw himself on the pebbled edge, and drank like an animal.

As the water quenched his thirst, one thought formed like a lamp lit in the night. Someone was waiting for him . . . someone needed him. But who? And where? As the pain faded to a dull ache, the wails swelled to a crescendo of agony.

There is no one. You are alone.

His brief hold on his thoughts loosened and fractured. There were too many of them. The howls surged to a fever pitch, and he knew nothing more.

Nothing but hunger, thirst, and despair.

Chapter Ten

My son, if you receive my words and treasure my commands,
Turning your ear to wisdom, inclining your heart to understanding . . .
—Proverbs 2:1–2

LAZARUS LAID HIS white prayer shawl over his head and shoulders and smoothed the fringes into place. A pair of crows flapped and paced on the ledge above the mouth of the tomb, crying out as if in warning. *Stay out. Stay out.*

Earlier in the day, he'd asked some of the village men to help him push the thick stone slab from the mouth of the tomb. Now the men were gone, and he was alone. It was his duty, and his alone, to lay his father's bones to rest.

The day was cool, and a dry wind blew from the eastern deserts, carrying the smell of the village, the smoke of cooking fires, and the sweet tang of the olive trees on the hillside. The mountainside was peaceful. Why then did the mouth of the tomb seem to gape at him like a hungry animal? Lazarus closed his eyes and breathed deeply of the fresh air before ducking through the opening into the dim stillness, his heart thumping in his chest.

The ceiling was just tall enough for him to stand upright. His eyes adjusted to the gloom, and his heartbeat slowed. In front of him, a funerary bench was carved into the smooth rock wall, long and narrow, large enough for the outstretched body covered in a shroud. No restless spirits prowled the room. No smell of death lingered in the chamber, just the dry scent of old bones and a lingering aroma of myrrh and nard.

Nothing to fear.

Along each of the three sides, a deeply carved niche held a square ossuary. One held the bones of his mother, and the second his grandparents except for old Safta. The third would receive his own bones at the appointed time. His appointed time. . . . A breath of cold air on his neck sent a shiver down his spine.

Just one year ago, Lazarus had watched his father take his last breath, had watched as Sirach's spirit left his body and went to a place none could follow. Martha and Mary had wept and keened at his passing. Lazarus had held Abba's hand as it cooled and became rigid. With his grief, the weight of responsibility settled like a yoke of stone on his shoulders.

He had just passed his seventeenth year, and he'd become the man of the family.

Sirach had been a good father. He had taken care of his family even as his body sickened and his wealth declined. Even as he had kept his son in Bethany to work the land instead of study the law with the teachers at the Temple. And now, Sirach's voice from the grave reminded Lazarus to do what was best for his family.

Sirach's last words to him had been a command. That command weighed heavy on Lazarus as he murmured the kaddish and approached his father's body. *Magnified and sanctified be His great name in the world which He created according to His will . . .*

The wrappings were deflated, like an empty water skin. His father's flesh had gone to dust, just like Adam, Abraham, and Moses. Sirach, like most of the Pharisees, believed that he would wake on the last day. He, with the rest of the pious sons of Abraham, would go to the paradise of the righteous, while the sinful would be forever confronted with their own disgrace. Lazarus, too, believed the dead would rise on the last day and that he would see Abba in paradise.

As Lazarus unwound the stained coverings and stared at the

skeletal remains of his father, Sirach's last words echoed in his ears as though they had been spoken within the empty chamber. *Your sister . . .* Sirach had clutched his hand, and he'd known it was Martha his father spoke of. *Promise me . . . do what is best for her.*

And Lazarus had promised. Now the year of mourning was over, and he must keep his promise and see her securely married. That must have been what his father had meant. It had to be.

But how could he find a husband for Martha? Abba had turned away every would-be suitor for his sister until all of Bethany knew that he would never give her up. They said it was because she was a treasure, and she was. Martha was beautiful, devout, and the best cook in Bethany. But those weren't the reasons Abba hadn't given her in marriage. No. It was because good Jewish men didn't marry women who weren't virgins. If she married, her husband would discover her secret on their wedding night. And then Martha could be stoned or, at the very least, banished from Bethany.

Lazarus cursed the name of the man who had defiled his sister. The pagan, Isa. *May he be thrown into the fiery reaches of Gehenna.* If not for him, Martha would be free to marry, to have a family. And Lazarus would be free as well.

He pulled out the ossuary that housed the bones of the mother he had never known. Stone scraped against stone as he slid the cover back. His mother's skull stared up at him. The perfect woman. Martha was just like her mother; everyone in the village said it. Had Mama been perfect, as his father believed? Or was it just easier to remember the dead without their frailties and sins? He would never know, unless he met her after the last day.

He gathered his father's bones and laid them next to his mother's. Finally, they were together again. *Blessed, praised, glorified, exalted, extolled, honored, adored, and lauded be the name of the Holy One, Blessed be He. May He who makes peace in the heavens, make peace for us and for all Israel.* He set his father's sightless skull on top. *Amen.*

He pushed the stone box back into its niche in the wall and sat down on the bench. His chest ached as though he were underwater. It had started at Tabernacles—a shortness of breath, a pain under his ribs. By the time winter winds swept over the farm, he could hardly work a full hour without sitting down to rest.

He reached under his tunic to feel the hard lump that had swelled under his arm weeks ago. It didn't hurt, but it had grown. Another—just behind his jaw under his ear—was covered by his hair and beard. He'd have to make sure Martha didn't notice when she cut his hair. She would worry . . . and Martha worried too much already.

He pushed himself up, leaving the dim coolness of the tomb for bright sunlight and a cold wind. He'd feel better when the spring sun warmed the air. He must. Because when Abba had made his dying request of Lazarus, there was something his father hadn't known. Something that changed everything.

The Messiah had come.

After centuries of waiting, he was here, and his name was Jesus.

What would Abba have thought, now that there was talk of Jesus—their own cousin—working miracles? Would he believe that Jesus was the Messiah, or would he side with the rest of the Pharisees and call him a fraud? According to Abba, it was the purity of the people of God—the purity that set them apart from the other nations—that would bring about the coming of the Kingdom. But Jesus didn't even follow some of the laws that Abba had held so dear.

Lazarus gazed out over the gardens and fields stretching down to the Jordan. He couldn't ask Abba now what he thought of Jesus. He must decide for himself. And he had. Jesus was the Messiah, and he must follow him. The only thing holding him in Bethany was Martha.

He started down the winding path to Bethany, his heart swelling in his chest. Jesus was coming tonight—he'd sent a message to expect him and his disciples. Soon, Lazarus, too, would follow the Messiah, be part of the new Eden. As soon as he found a husband for Martha, a husband who would be forgiving, merciful—a husband who would give her a second chance.

Chapter Eleven

Like merchant ships, she secures her provisions from afar.
—Proverbs 31:14

MARTHA GAVE THE young goat another turn on the spit. The meat was beginning to brown and crisp, and her cumin sauce bubbled nearby. Two more cooking fires crackled and smoked in the courtyard. Over one, lentils flavored with garlic and onions simmered; on the other, a pot of water heated.

Jesus was coming for dinner, and everything would be perfect.

The goat had been butchered and bled according to the law, the wine touched only by Jewish hands. The first fruits of all the foodstuffs in her larder, from the grain to the eggs, from the mint to the rue, had been given to the priests as an offering. Even her vessels and bowls were made right in Judea, not in Rome, as was the fashion among some of the wealthier families of Bethany. Families not as strict as Abba's.

The purity of Martha's home was second to none in the village, except perhaps Jael's. Just as Abba would have wanted. A twinge of guilt reminded her that the Pharisees grumbled against Jesus' unorthodox teachings, and Abba may have disapproved of him as well. Still, Abba would never deny a hungry man a meal. And Jesus would come hungry. He always did.

Penina bent to sniff the cumin sauce and nodded.

"This will be done just in time," Martha said. The goat

wasn't as young as she'd like—there had been few kids this year—but the spicy sauce would mask the stronger flavor. "We'll eat our fill, Penina. There won't be meat again until after the garden comes in." Thanks to the Roman taxes and the Temple tithe, she had nothing left in her purse but a few brass coins.

Martha glanced at the sky, stretching from the Mount of Olives to the valley of the Jordan River. Not a cloud to be seen. She couldn't remember a drought like this in all her life in Bethany.

They'd need to water the garden again soon if the Almighty didn't bless them with rain. She'd see to it, even if she had to carry the water on her own back. The artichokes and asparagus would be ready in two weeks, and the rich Greeks and Romans who shopped in Jerusalem's upper market would pay a ridiculous price for them. Thank the Lord for their expensive tastes.

The rest of the spring vegetables—cucumbers, chickpeas, and herbs—would bring in enough to reduce their debt to Simon. By Passover, just six weeks away, they would be doing better. And after the apricots ripened in late summer, they would be out of danger, perhaps even able to afford some spices and eat meat again.

Martha checked the lentils. If the Lord smiled on them with a good harvest, they would prosper this year. Well, perhaps not prosper, but they would get by.

Lazarus trooped into the courtyard, Zakai at his heels. "Martha. I spoke to Josiah. They will come for the feast. Mary asked if you needed help." They both dumped armloads of dried sheep's dung near the fires. "Shall I tell her to come early?"

Safta, who had been dozing in the corner, opened an eye. "Mary? Early?"

Martha frowned, but her grandmother was right. Mary had good intentions—she always did—but she was always late. And her help usually involved burning the bread, chasing the children, and wandering off instead of watching the meat. But that wasn't why she hadn't called on Mary to help.

"No. You know she's still impure from Natanel's birth." Abba would never have allowed her to serve his guests so soon after childbirth. Martha blew on a bite of lentils and tasted, then added a pinch of salt. She and Penina could manage, and everything would be perfect.

Martha glanced up and caught a rare smile and the flash of a dimple on Penina's cheek as she cleaned a basket of leeks. Penina nodded toward Lazarus and winked at Martha. Martha suppressed a laugh. Her brother was staggering under an armful of colorful rugs piled higher than his head, whistling a tune through his teeth. He dropped the pile and started arranging the rugs under the fig tree.

Lazarus sometimes forgot that he was the man of the house now and no longer required to help with the women's work. Martha and Penina didn't remind him.

He finished with the rugs and flopped down on a bench under the fig tree, his breathing labored. "His time is coming, Martha," he panted. "I tell you, it won't be long now before everyone knows he is the Messiah."

Martha sprinkled a handful of crushed rosemary over the bubbling lentils. Despite the heat of the cooking fires, a shiver of worry went through her. That kind of talk could be dangerous.

She'd heard of Jesus' miracles, that he healed the sick, cured lepers. There had even been a rumor that he'd given sight to a man born blind. But she'd never actually seen anyone who had been cured. No one agreed: some said he was the Messiah, others a prophet, some even called him a fraud. And now—most worrisome of all—the Sanhedrin called for his arrest. How could Lazarus be so sure that Jesus was the Anointed One?

Martha pulled her knife from her belt and sliced the green top off a radish. Many had claimed the baptizer was the Messiah, and everyone knew what had happened to him. Dead. Killed by Herod and his traitorous wife.

Abba had warned of false messiahs. What had he always said? *We must doubt, until his power is proven to us.* She'd known

Jesus all her life. If anyone was a prophet or a healer, it would be him. But he hadn't proven that he was the Promised One.

Prophet or not, he was in danger. Her worry grew, and she frowned at Lazarus. "Is he safe here? So close to Jerusalem?" There were plenty of Pharisees in Bethany who would be glad to curry favor with the Sanhedrin.

Lazarus waved away her concern. "Don't worry. Jesus knows what he is about."

Martha wasn't so sure. Jesus had never been careful about what he said or who he said it to. She'd have to make sure his visit to Bethany was known only to the family.

Lazarus moved to crouch in front of Penina. "Have you thought about what I said, Nina?"

Penina frowned at the leeks.

Martha sliced another radish into the bowl. Her brother would not give up. Penina wouldn't change her mind. Martha loved her friend, but Penina was as stubborn as a blind donkey.

"Nina." Lazarus put his hands on her shoulders. "He's cured the blind, healed the lame, even brought a boy back from death. He could give you your voice."

She made a sign with her hands, along with a roll of her eyes that made her meaning clear.

Lazarus's back stiffened, and his voice hardened. "He's not a magician; he's the Messiah."

Penina shrugged and turned away. Lazarus stomped back to the ladder.

Martha couldn't blame her. Of course she wished Penina could speak. She could tell them of her life before Damascus, of what happened to her family. Yes, Penina would have to learn to guard her tongue around the women of Bethany—what disrespectful thoughts would her bold friend voice if she could?—but she didn't blame Penina for not putting her trust in a man she hardly knew.

Zakai snuck a slice of radish from the bowl. Martha gave him another one, and he crunched it, his cheek bulging. She pulled him into her arms and rested her cheek on the top of his warm head.

What if Penina asked Jesus to cure her, and he said no? What if he couldn't? Or worse, what if he could? Lazarus always thought the best of everyone, even the smug wives of the Pharisees. But they already mistrusted Penina for her foreign face and mute voice. What would happen if they thought she was part of a ruse by a man who called himself the Messiah? They would tell their husbands, and their husbands would turn against Penina. And against Zakai.

She kissed Zakai's head as he squirmed away, then went back to her radishes. Besides, the Messiah would come in glory, with power to conquer the Romans and restore their land. Everyone knew that. Not like a friend with a hungry belly, clothes that needed mending, and news from his mother.

Penina touched her arm. She pointed to the rooftop, where Lazarus had gone, and then made a sign for sickness.

Martha frowned. "I didn't notice." Lazarus hadn't been sick a day in his life, even when he was a baby. But he hadn't been eating well. And he was too skinny. "I'll ask him after Jesus comes."

Lazarus came down the ladder with another bundle of mats. He did look pale. And just how many mats did he think they needed for a few men and Jesus' mother? "How many are coming with Jesus?"

"He says at least twenty."

Martha fumbled with her knife. "Twenty people? With Jesus?"

"That's what the messenger said. His twelve disciples, some women, others who follow him."

"And you're just telling me now?" Martha jumped up. "That means . . ." She calculated quickly. "With Josiah and Mary and the children—we need food for twenty-eight or even thirty."

She'd cooked feasts for that many—even more when Abba was alive—but never with so little in her storeroom. And how would they keep Jesus' visit a secret from the Pharisees of Bethany if he was bringing such a crowd?

"Penina, add another scoop of lentils to that pot. And more rosemary."

Penina hurried to the storeroom, while Lazarus and Zakai stood in the middle of the courtyard, their arms hanging idle at their sides. What were they waiting for? A voice from the heavens? "Don't just stand there. Get some more water for the jars inside." Lazarus and Zakai jumped and made for the courtyard gate as if they were being chased by Beelzebub himself.

Martha frowned at the goat. The meat would stretch if they only served it to the men. The rest could eat lentils and bread, and she should have just enough wheat.

She knelt at the grinding kern. Thirty people. Why hadn't Lazarus told her sooner? With all his talk about a Messiah . . . she could use some help with the here and now. She lifted the wheat jar but found it far too light in her hand. She looked inside. Just a few handfuls covered the bottom, hardly enough for two rounds of bread. "Safta!"

The old woman opened her drooping eyes.

"Where is the wheat?"

Safta rubbed her whiskery chin. "You gave some to Mary yesterday."

"I know, but there was plenty left." *At least enough for tonight.*

Safta closed her eyes again. "You might ask the boy."

Zakai? "But what would he know of the wheat?"

Safta jerked her head toward the animals in the corner.

Martha's heart sank. He wouldn't have. He couldn't have. She rushed to the corner of the courtyard where his collection of animals scratched and twittered. Kernels of wheat lay scattered among the birdcages.

"He gave my best wheat to his birds?"

"And to the rest of them, I'd guess." Safta settled back on her stool as if she hadn't a care in the world.

Martha checked a cage made of a bushel basket and some

bent willow switches, where Zakai's rabbit stared at her with alarmed eyes beside a heaping pile of the golden wheat. The lamb stood on his three good legs, a kernel dangling from his velvety chin.

Martha stomped to the house. Zakai was in deep trouble. She'd have a few things to say to him when he returned, but right now she had an empty storeroom, no bread, and very little time.

Dinner for Jesus was turning into a perfect disaster.

Chapter Twelve

She rises while it is still night, and distributes food to her household.
—Proverbs 31:15

MARTHA FLEW THROUGH the house as if a whirlwind were on her heels. *Lord of all, give me patience. And wheat.*

She passed by her own room, with baskets holding carded wool, spools of yarn, and clothes in need of mending, then spared a quick glance into the formal dining room, where Abba had entertained so often. Tonight, it would seat Jesus, his disciples, and Lazarus. And they would be hungry.

No bread was unthinkable. Abba would be so disappointed in her.

She darted into the storage room at the back of the house. *Please, there must be something.* The shelves were sparsely stocked with her dwindling supplies of oil, olives, and dried fruit. Goat skins full of curdling milk hung from hooks in the wall. There was plenty of yogurt and cheese, but Abba always said, *Better to starve than serve meat and milk on the same table.* No. Grain was what they needed. Even barley would do.

Lazarus entered through the back door, a dripping water jar in his arms. But instead of bringing it to the dining room, where it would be available for their guests to immerse their hands, he set the jar down and stood in the doorway of the storage room. "Martha." His voice was low and hopeful. "Have you thought about what I asked you?"

"Not now, Lazarus." Had her brother decided to nag all the women of his household today? The last thing she needed to think about was finding a husband. She pulled the corks from the nearest jars. Empty, all of them. She pointed to a jar on the top shelf. "Reach that for me."

Lazarus was as used to taking orders as she was to giving them. He snagged it from the shelf and handed it to her. "Tomorrow then," he relented, "but we will talk about it."

Couldn't Lazarus see she was busy? And why the hurry? She needed to consider his ridiculous idea for a few weeks. Or a few years. She pointed to the last jar. "That one." *Please, there must be something.*

He pulled it down.

She peeked inside, and her heart sank. Nothing but chaff. "What are we going to do?"

Lazarus put his hands on her shoulders and gave her a quick kiss on the cheek, his wispy beard tickling her. "Don't worry so much, Martha. The Lord will provide."

The Lord will provide? It was easy for him to say; feeding their guests wasn't his responsibility. When and what, exactly, would the Lord provide? And how was she supposed to stop worrying?

Lazarus hoisted the water jar and clumped toward the dining room. "He made the Temple lamps burn for eight days, Martha. He'll provide food for our guests."

Martha pressed her lips together. She didn't have time to wait around and see if her trusting brother was right. She'd have to provide, and soon.

She veered into her own room and shed her everyday mantle. The cedar trunk beside her bed had once been full of fine linen in her favorite colors of dark green and soft blue. Now, just one length of linen, dyed pink with pomegranate rinds, remained, and it was far from new. Under it lay the only other item of value left in her father's house. An alabaster jar half-filled with the nard they'd used for Abba's burial. She could sell it in Jerusalem for enough silver to buy oil and wheat for months. She ran a hand over the smooth jar. Only if she had no other choice. If something happened to Safta, they would need it.

For now, she had one option left. She'd go to the market and ask for credit. She draped the pink linen over her hair and around her shoulders. If she was going to beg, at least she'd do it with dignity.

She reached the village as the sun began its descent toward the western horizon. If she could get enough wheat, she'd have bread made when Jesus and his people arrived. Just in time.

At the synagogue, a cluster of men sat on the steps. So Lazarus wanted to find her a husband? She looked sideways at the men as she passed by. *Well, brother, these are my choices.*

They were arguing, of course. Did they have nothing else to do with their days?

"He is a disgrace," Yonah griped. Old Yonah had lived in Bethany as long as Martha could remember. The beautiful Eliana, who had caught the eye of half the village men in her youth, was his much-younger wife and the proud mother of two sons.

"He is the Messiah," argued Simcha, a shepherd who lived on the eastern side of town. He was a good friend of Lazarus's, years younger than Martha, and had a little brother and an old mother to care for. Definitely not marriage material.

"What about Nazareth? He couldn't even work his cures there, they say, in his own town," Yonah said.

Simcha shrugged. "They had no faith in him, that's what I heard. So he couldn't cure them."

Martha dawdled for a moment at the corner. No faith meant no cure from Jesus? If that was true, then Lazarus could stop badgering Penina to ask Jesus for her voice. She had little faith in God, and certainly none in a man.

The debate continued. Was Jesus the Messiah or a fraud? A prophet or a charlatan? As the men voiced their opinions of her cousin, Martha considered each one. Married. Too young. Too poor. She turned her back on the arguing men. Lazarus would just have to admit it. There was no one in Bethany for her to marry.

The marketplace near the northern wall of Bethany was busier than usual. As she strode past stalls and brightly colored awnings, the spice merchant called out to her. "Good day to you. I have saffron from the eastern caravans." She shook her head. Today she couldn't linger at her favorite stall.

The olive seller blocked her path. "The olives stuffed with pistachios that you love." She shook her head. Perhaps after the harvest she'd be able to buy some of the delicacies that they offered.

She reached the awning where mounds of wheat, barley, and spelt shone in the sun. Old Micah measured grain onto a scale. He'd been old when he'd worked for Abba, when Sirach had owned the wheat fields surrounding Bethany. Now he was even older and Simon's steward. His face was as furrowed as the fields he oversaw, his eyes shadowed by brows as thick as hedges.

He put down his scoop and rushed to her side. Like every other merchant in Bethany, he knew she expected the best quality and she bargained well. And she always paid with Jewish coins, never Greek or Roman. He didn't know that today she had no coins at all.

He dipped a hand in a mound of wheat and let it run through his fingers like liquid gold. "The finest wheat in Judea."

Yes, and the most expensive. She nodded to a bin of lesser quality. "I'll take two ephah of the other." Her mouth was dry as chaff. "And I'll have to pay you next week, Micah."

Micah's heavy brows lowered. "Next week? But you know that Simon doesn't allow—"

A curt voice cut him off. "Simon doesn't allow what?"

She turned, her stomach dropping at the familiar tone. Simon stood behind her. His two burly guards, companions he was rarely without, stood at his side, their eyes shifting over the crowds. Did Simon think he was going to be attacked in his own city? Or were his guards there to announce he had something to protect?

His wide eyes and full lips still reminded Martha of a fish, but now silver flecked his well-trimmed beard and gold flashed on his fingers. His hair had thinned over the years, and his fine linen tunic hung on a lean—almost bony—frame. Heavy blue tassels fluttered at the corners of his coat, marking him a pious Pharisee, just like Abba.

Micah stuttered, "You don't . . . you said, no credit for these miserable—"

"Silence, Micah." Simon glared, then offered Martha a small smile and a bow. "Give Martha, daughter of Sirach, may his name be blessed for generations to come, two—no, three—ephah of the best wheat. As my gift to your family."

Martha opened her mouth to decline. She didn't want a gift, especially not from Simon. They already owed him more than they could pay in a year of Sabbaths. But what else could she do? Humiliate the richest man in Bethany? She dipped her head. "My thanks to you, Simon. May the Lord bless you in your generosity."

His gaze dropped to his feet. "I know why you are making a feast tonight."

Her heart faltered. He knew about Jesus? Simon was as close to the leaders in Jerusalem as a flea on a donkey's ear. If he knew Jesus was in Bethany, they would know within hours.

Simon nodded gravely. "Your year of mourning for your father, may his memory be blessed forever, is complete."

Avelut. Of course. During the year after a parent's death, the law discouraged feasting. But now they could celebrate with food and music. In fact, the sages encouraged bringing an end to the mourning period with a feast. But Simon didn't know they would be feasting with a man Abba probably would have disdained.

Simon took her silence as an affirmation. "Well do I remember the many delicious dishes you prepared when your father had me as his guest. Before . . ." He cleared his throat and looked away.

Before he was a leper. Martha glimpsed a flash of pain on Simon's face. Abba had treated Simon like a son for years, but when the leprosy struck, Abba had turned away. The priests had declared him clean, but Abba—like many in Bethany—never welcomed him in his home again. Even as Simon's wealth increased, the people of Bethany had never forgotten his shame.

She watched Micah scoop grain into her basket as the silence between them lengthened. Simon clasped and unclasped his hands. "You honor the memory of your father by your devotion to the law and your dedication to purity."

Purity. Martha looked down at her feet, worry twisting through her.

Simon rubbed a hand over his neck. "Perhaps you can bring a message to your brother for me." It sounded more like an order than a request. "Please have him visit my home at his convenience. Now that avelut is over, we have much to discuss."

Martha glanced at Micah, who was obviously listening. What business could Simon have with Lazarus? And why only after their mourning?

"I will give him your invitation." She clasped the filled basket to her side. "I thank you for the wheat. May your household ever be blessed."

Instead of the traditional response, Simon looked at her with his large, round eyes as though trying to tell her something. "I hope those blessings begin soon. For both of us."

What did that mean? Martha zigzagged through the marketplace. Simon had never been easy to understand. *Just be thankful he doesn't know about Jesus.* Lazarus had been right, the Lord—or at least Simon—had provided.

Anxiety pinched at the back of her neck. But what would it cost her?

Chapter Thirteen

MARTHA GAVE THE cumin sauce one last stir. She would have liked to go with Lazarus to meet Jesus at the outskirts of Bethany, but someone had to keep the food hot and the children clean.

She surveyed her courtyard with satisfaction. The vessels had been immersed, and jars of water stood ready to wash the guests' feet and purify their hands. The meat was perfectly roasted, the bread freshly baked. A breeze lifted the smoke from the courtyard as the last rays of the sun filtered through the clouds. It would be cool tonight but not cold. Perfect for gathering around the fire and visiting with Jesus and his mother.

Adina and Sarah perched on the bench next to Mary, who was nursing Natanel. Martha had brushed and braided their hair and washed their faces. They jumped up as the courtyard door opened, then slumped in disappointment when Zakai came through with an armload of dried dung for the fires. He avoided Martha's eyes, and her heart twinged. His punishment for the wheat disaster had been to stay with her instead of going with the others to meet Jesus on the road. Now she wished she hadn't been so hard on him. He was just a little boy, after all.

Zakai stopped before her, blinking hard at her feet. "I'm sorry, Marmar."

Martha let out a long breath and pulled him into her arms. "I know, my sweet." She kissed his cheek. "Now wash up."

His face brightened. "When will he be here?"

"Soon." She steered him to the water jar. "And don't forget your face."

He splashed some water on his face and rubbed. "Lazarus says he's the Messiah. Is he, Marmar?"

Martha snagged a clean tunic drying on a rosemary bush and pulled it over his head. What could she tell him that wouldn't be disrespectful to her brother or Jesus? That Lazarus thought the best of everyone? She combed through his hair with her fingers. Or that Jesus was wise and good, perhaps a prophet like Elijah? Her problem was solved as the door creaked open once more.

Jesus entered the courtyard with what seemed like a joyful army. Lazarus walked next to Jesus, one arm draped over his shoulder. John, the youngest disciple, not much older than Lazarus, smiled on Jesus' other side. A troop of dusty men, women, and children followed with Mary, the mother of Jesus, at their center.

Zakai, Adina, and Sarah gave a collective shout and ran for Jesus at a full sprint. Jesus saw them coming and crouched down, holding out his arms. They barreled into him, but he held steady, his smile growing wide as they all spoke to him at once.

Jesus embraced each child, whispering in their ears something that made them laugh. His hair, brown and curling over his neck, needed a trim, and so did his beard. He wasn't a big man, and he'd lost weight since Martha had seen him last. She'd need to make sure he got plenty of food tonight.

Jesus stood and turned to Martha. She looked at his hands, strong and calloused, as they closed around hers. For a moment, she felt exposed. Would he know she didn't believe he was the Messiah, as Lazarus did? Would he be angry at her—or worse, disappointed?

She forced herself to look up, into his deep brown eyes. He gazed back at her with friendship and love, just as he had since they were children.

"Welcome, my cousin. We are honored to have you here."

And she meant it. Whatever others said of him, he was family and their beloved friend.

Jesus squeezed her hands. "I hope you haven't been working too hard, Martha." His voice was teasing, and she flushed. He knew her well.

Mary approached with her tiny son in her arms and a proud smile on her face. Her arms jingled with her ever-present bangles. She wore her pink tunic, a green head covering, and a belt of mustard yellow. Martha smiled. Leave it to Mary to be the most colorful woman in Bethany. More colorful than most women thought seemly.

Jesus turned to her and held out his arms. Carefully, she set her new son in the crook of his elbow. He pulled Natanel close and kissed his wrinkled forehead. Natanel squirmed as though Jesus' rough beard tickled him, and his mouth stretched into a smile.

Martha laughed. Even infants loved Jesus.

"Natanel. God gives." Jesus nodded his approval to Josiah. "A good name, my friend." He gave Natanel back to his mother as Penina approached with a bowl of water.

Penina bathed his feet quickly, then hurried away before Jesus could even thank her. Martha caught Lazarus's quick frown. What did he expect? Penina hadn't grown up with Jesus like they had, and she surely didn't believe he was the Messiah.

Within minutes, Jesus and the men reclined on couches in the dining area. It was a large room, one that Abba had been overly proud of. Jesus sat at the head of a low U-shaped table surrounded by raised benches. Lazarus stretched out at Jesus' right side and John at his left. Martha recognized Peter, Andrew, and the ones they called the sons of Zebedee—James and his brother John. Some of the others she had seen before but didn't know their names.

Mary, the mother of Jesus, touched Martha's elbow. "Can I help you with the meal, Martha?" Mary was a small woman—her head only reached Martha's shoulder—and as dainty as a girl.

Her deep brown hair was streaked with gray, and her face showed the lines of age and the pallor of fatigue.

Martha embraced her. "No, Mary. You are all tired from your journey." She shooed Mary and the rest of Jesus' people—a woman from Magdala, and one named Joanna, along with a few servants—into the courtyard. "Go rest beside the fire. I'll bring food after the men are served." When the men were satisfied, she'd have time to catch up with Jesus' mother without hurry, without worry.

Martha rescued the last few rounds of bread from the baking oven just before they burned. She'd sent her sister to watch the bread, but, of course, Mary had disappeared. Penina appeared at her side. "Thank the Most High for you, Penina," Martha whispered. There was much to do, and Penina could always be counted on. "I'll serve the wine; you bring the bread and the olives."

Martha entered the dining room quietly and poured wine for Jesus, then Lazarus. A well-dressed man with a short, trimmed beard was blessing the bread. He sounded like a scholar, perhaps even a Pharisee. And the way his sharp eyes took in the ritual water jars and surveyed the table reminded her of Abba. Was he looking for any type of impurity, any transgression of the law? Her heart fluttered, even as she knew there was nothing amiss on her table.

"Judas," John called to the sharp-eyed man after the blessing. "Are you finding all to your liking, this house that follows the customs of the strictest Pharisees?"

Judas's eyes narrowed. "And why shouldn't we follow the laws that our wisest rabbis favor? Is it not written that we are a people set apart? Can't we be glad to be in a house that values purity tonight instead of a tax collector's den or dinner with a prostitute?"

John shot back, "And hasn't our teacher told us 'judge not, lest you be judged'?"

Martha backed away. Yes, Abba would agree with the one named Judas. Surely even Lazarus, as much as he loved Jesus, wouldn't eat with a prostitute. She dashed to the courtyard to get more wine.

When she returned, Peter was talking. "You are fortunate, indeed, to have such a good cook for a sister."

Lazarus smiled at Martha, and she ducked her head. "My sister is almost as good at cooking as she is at worrying." He leaned toward Jesus. "You know how she is, Jesus. How can I ease her mind?"

That's not fair. Lazarus knew he could say anything he wanted, and she couldn't answer back in front of the men. Embarrassment and irritation sent a flush to her cheeks.

Jesus gave her a teasing smile. He knew what Lazarus was doing, but spoke directly to her. "Don't be angry at him, Martha. And don't worry so much about what you'll make to serve us."

Martha's cheeks burned, and she looked away. Jesus was so improper. What would he do next? Ask her to sit down beside him and share their food?

Martha poured more wine in Lazarus's cup and glared at him. Her brother would have plenty to worry about when she got a chance to talk to him alone, without these men here to protect him. How could Lazarus put her in this position, then sit there looking at her with that ridiculous smirk on his face?

Jesus laughed at her look as if he knew her thoughts. He swept a hand toward the open window. "Look at the birds. They gather nothing, but your heavenly Father feeds them. Aren't you more important than the birds, Martha?"

Judas spoke up, his face more serious. "But is that fair? We must care for our families. We must worry about feeding and clothing our children."

Martha let out a held breath. Judas had voiced her own thoughts. If she didn't worry about what to eat, who would? The grain didn't appear in the jar each morning. The bread didn't bake itself.

Jesus answered Judas with equal seriousness. "You are right that we must care for our families, but worrying cannot add a single moment to your life."

Martha stalked from the room to get the meat. It was easy for *him* to say to stop worrying. If he knew all she had to worry about, perhaps he would understand.

When she returned with the meat, Jesus continued as if she hadn't left the room. "Look at the flowers, Martha." He motioned to the window, where the first flowers showed white on the hillside. "They do not spin. But not even Solomon was as beautifully clothed."

Lazarus nodded. "They are as beautiful as my sister, and worry much less."

She set the platter in front of Lazarus with a clatter. How like a man to think that being beautiful was her only worry. No, she worried for the safety of her family, and about the crops in the garden. About her brother's talk of betrothal. And most of all, about the secret she hid from everyone in Bethany. Jesus might eat with prostitutes, but would he sit at her table if he knew what she'd done?

Jesus leaned toward her. "I tell you, Martha. Don't worry about tomorrow, but trust in your heavenly Father. Tomorrow will take care of itself."

Martha clenched her jaw and turned her back on the men. Hopefully, no one in Bethany would hear about Jesus' impropriety. Even his mother, out in the courtyard with the other women, would be shocked.

As she left the dining room, a jingle of bracelets greeted her. Mary came toward her, her bright robes flowing behind her like a desert sunset. In her hands she held a familiar alabaster jar.

What was Mary doing now? Martha blocked her way into the dining room.

Mary smiled as though she had a wonderful secret. She pulled the stopper from the jar and held it under Martha's nose. "Look what I found."

"Where did you get that?" The costly nard had been tucked safely away in her room.

"From your storage chest." Mary veered around her. "I am going to anoint Jesus."

Tension tightened Martha's chest. What was Mary thinking? Of course she was not going to anoint Jesus. And not with that expensive oil.

Martha moved to keep her from the doorway. "Mary, you're still impure." And she would be for four more days. The one named Judas would surely take offense; he'd just seen her with a newborn baby. Besides, she couldn't anoint a man that wasn't her husband; it just wasn't done.

Mary's face fell. "But it's Jesus. He won't mind. He's not like other men."

Martha's temper rose. That was surely the truth. "*I* mind." And so would Abba. There was enough impropriety going on in her household tonight.

Mary looked at Martha like she'd grown goat horns. "This isn't your house. It's Lazarus's. And he would want me to honor his guest."

"Honor his guest?" Martha's voice rose. And humiliate her family when everyone in Bethany heard of it? "Lazarus might be the head of the family, but Abba left me in charge of the household. And you are *not* using this on Jesus." She took the jar of precious oil from Mary's hands and pulled her out into the courtyard. *Don't I have enough to worry about?* Josiah would probably tell his mother about Jesus, and by tomorrow, everyone in Bethany would know he'd been here. And of his poor manners. She pushed Mary to sit on the bench beside Safta. "Grandmother, tell her she's being ridiculous."

Safta didn't even open her eyes. "You seem to be doing a fine job with that, as usual."

Can't Safta offer some help for once? "Mary, I have more important things to do than watch over you. Stay here with the women, and I'll get you some food."

Mary looked at her, her eyes sad. "Martha, there is nothing more important than honoring the Messiah."

Martha's mouth dropped open. "You believe it, too?" How could she?

Mary didn't flinch, and her eyes were gentle. "How can you not believe it, Martha? He's cured the sick, given sight to the blind. What else do you need to see?"

Martha clamped her mouth shut. She hadn't seen any evidence of a Messiah tonight, just her cousin embarrassing her in front of the rest of the men.

She looked to Safta. "Grandmother? Tell her. Jesus can't be the Messiah! He's . . . he's Jesus. Mary and Joseph's son. We've known him all our lives."

But Safta's face showed nothing, not a hint of help. "The wise man is honored, even if his family is despised."

What? Now Safta was quoting proverbs to her? Martha blew a breath from her nose. Had everyone in her family turned against her?

"For once, Martha, listen to what your heart tells you," Mary whispered.

"It isn't that simple, Mary," Martha bit out. Mary didn't have her responsibilities, her reputation to uphold. It was more complicated than just sitting down at Jesus' feet. There were people to consider. People she loved.

"It is." Mary's voice was gentle. She reached out to Martha. "Just choose to believe in him."

Martha choked out a bitter laugh as her temper snapped. *Choose?* As if it were that easy. "Some of us don't get to choose," she spit out. *Not our messiahs, and not our husbands.*

Chapter Fourteen

MARTHA BRUSHED PAST Mary and Safta. She had to get away from the pity in Mary's eyes and the challenge she didn't understand in Safta's. She had worked so hard to make this dinner perfect. What else did they want from her?

The anxiety, building within her for the whole terrible day, rose like a flood.

Listen to your heart, Mary said. Martha couldn't listen to her heart. She didn't trust it anymore. She stalked through the courtyard, threading her way through the women, avoiding their concerned looks. Scooping up a handful of dried dung and sticks, she threw it on the smoldering cooking fire. *Just choose to believe in him,* Mary said.

Choose?

She poured water into a cooking pot and set it over the fire. A stack of dirty pots and spoons waited to be washed. She scooped a handful of sand from a crock and began to scour a pot crusted with burnt cumin sauce. If she could just scrub away the memories of the night she'd chosen—*chosen,* just like Mary said—to follow her heart. That night had changed her life forever.

That dawn after Mary's wedding feast, she'd said good-bye to Isa, sure that he would return soon. He'd said he would; he'd promised. And then they would marry—with or without Abba's blessing.

But Isa didn't come back to her.

Weeks went by as she watched the road stretching into the east, standing for hours in the heat of the day. Hoping the shadow on the road would turn into the boy she loved. Hoping . . . but always disappointed as the sun set in the west.

When weeks turned into months, she became afraid. Afraid for herself and the secret she carried. She hid the truth from Abba. But when the harvest came and her belly swelled, she had to tell him.

As she poured steaming water over the dirty pot, memories seared her heart anew. She'd found Abba alone in the olive grove, contemplating the fruit hanging on the branches. He smiled at her and kissed her cheek, thanking her for the cold water she'd brought in the heat of the day. He'd always been an affectionate father. Not in public, of course, as the law forbade it. But in their home he showed his love for his children—even his daughters—in his warm embraces and gentle touch. But today, Martha couldn't return his kiss.

Her heart hammered and her voice quivered as she told him simply that she was expecting a child. He didn't shout. He didn't hit her. She knew he wouldn't. He simply sank to his knees and put his head in his hands. When he finally looked up, he seemed to have aged ten years.

"Who is the father?" he choked out. But she didn't tell him. She couldn't. If he knew her child was the offspring of a pagan . . . it would kill him. If—when—Isa returned for her, then together they would beg Abba to allow Isa to become a proselyte. Surely Abba would do that, for his grandchild.

"Does anyone else know?" he'd asked.

She'd told no one. Not even Mary.

He rubbed his hands over his face. "Keep it secret," he'd said, then turned and walked away, his back bent as if carrying the weight of her sin on his shoulders.

For three days, he didn't speak—he didn't eat or sleep. On the morning of the fourth day he came to her with a loaded donkey and told her they were leaving Bethany. She was to help a needy kinswoman in Galilee for the winter. She had time only to kiss Lazarus good-bye and send a message to Mary.

Three days of silent walking brought them to a simple hut in the Galilean wilderness. The woman that met her at the door was familiar—distant kin who had come a time or two to Bethany. Abba had left her there, his face wet with tears as he walked away.

Her kinswoman was not unkind. They worked together, prayed together, made food for her grizzled husband when he returned with the sheep. Martha woke each morning with worry gnawing at her. What would become of the baby growing inside her? Would she be forced to leave the child here, in Galilee? Or would Abba leave them both here forever?

When her time came, the birth was fast and hard. She thought her body would rip apart, that the pain would twist her into a knot. But when it was over, she held Isa's child in her arms.

A son.

A son with no father to accept him. Instead, the old shepherd performed the circumcision and gave him his name.

Zakai.

Martha plunged the cooking spoons into the dirty water, blinking away the tears that sprang to her eyes. Zakai, a child of Israel because the lineage of Abraham was passed through the mother, but also the child of the pagan who had deserted her.

Perhaps Abba should have just left them both in Galilee. But when Zakai was a few weeks old, Abba had returned, and not alone. Penina was with him. She was so young, barely more than a child—a brokenhearted child with no voice and swollen, leaking breasts.

Abba had taken Zakai from Martha and held him a moment, then settled him in Penina's arms. "This is your son," he'd said, his voice rough with grief. "Now, let us return to Bethany."

Just the memory brought an ache to Martha's chest that she

could hardly stand. Her boy, her beautiful boy, who looked like Isa, was taken from her. Penina's arms would hold him, Penina's breasts nurse him. Martha bit down hard on her lip and laid the clean utensils out on a mat to dry.

The trip back to Bethany had been silent. A slave girl carrying an infant, and Martha numb with agony. Tears made hot streaks down her face, and her body shook with silent sobs, but Abba was firm. "I'm doing this for you, Martha, to save you and this family from shame. It is for the best."

From that day forward, they didn't speak of Zakai's birth. Abba never again asked about the father, and Martha told no one. But each day, she watched the road for Isa to return. Each day she was disappointed.

Martha stared at her reflection in the dirty water. Since that night in the orchard, she was tainted, unclean. Abba could have had her stoned, could have denounced her in front of all the village, could have left her and Zakai in Galilee. But he didn't. Instead, he lied for her. And her sin ate away at him. His fields lay fallow; his flocks did not increase. Finally, his health failed. As Abba had sickened and died, she'd known that his sickness, their decline in wealth—everything—was her fault.

Martha closed her eyes, hot tears wetting her face. She'd chosen—*chosen*—to trust her heart, and look what had happened. She'd been deserted. Forsaken. Betrayed. She wouldn't make the same mistake twice. She wouldn't disgrace Abba again.

The children loved Jesus. Lazarus and Mary loved him. *I love him.*

But this time, she couldn't trust her heart. Her cousin was a good man, a good friend, and perhaps even a prophet. But he was not the Messiah.

Chapter Fifteen

Yes, if you call to intelligence, and to understanding raise your voice; If
you seek her like silver, and like hidden treasures search her out . . .
—Proverbs 2:3–4

LAZARUS CLAMPED A hand over the pain under his ribs and
increased his pace. The dawn was late in coming. The sun had
risen over the eastern hills, but its light was blocked by a bank of
thick clouds.

He'd risen early, his pulse pounding in anticipation. He
would immerse and pray, then talk to Jesus. Soon, he would become a disciple, just like John and Peter. Soon, he would be a
part of the world to come.

He descended into the declivity that housed the village mikvah, then pulled up with a start. Two tunics lay on the rock next
to the gaping dark mouth, a boy's and a woman's. Before he could
turn away, a pale form emerged from the mikvah, naked and dripping.

Zakai let out a yell and ran toward him, drops of water flying
from his wet hair.

Lazarus bent to the boy and smiled. "Immersing before your
lessons at the synagogue, Zakai?" His voice broke on the last
word, and he cleared his throat. Martha had surely insisted. Penina went along with the purity laws, but only to please Martha.

Zakai pulled his tunic over his head. "I don't want to go to
my lessons. Have you seen my caterpillar? And the sparrow I

caught yesterday? Can I work with you in the orchard instead?" His words tumbled like pebbles in a mountain stream as he pushed his arms through his sleeves. He looked over his shoulder. "Please, Mama?"

Lazarus didn't follow Zakai's gaze but kept his eyes on the chattering boy until he was sure that Penina had donned her tunic. His neck warmed, and heat crept up his face. Living with two women meant he sometimes glimpsed them leaving the river after bathing or the mikvah after immersing. It wasn't a sin to catch sight of a naked body. It was only a sin if you looked upon a woman with lust in your heart. He swallowed to ease his dry throat. Penina was just like a sister to him. There was no reason for him to feel guilty.

A rumble echoed far in the east, and Zakai clutched Lazarus's hand.

"Don't worry, it's just a storm. And we need the rain it brings. Go to the synagogue, Zakai, before you get wet all over again. You can help me in the orchard this afternoon." After he spoke to Jesus.

"I'll see you in the orchard," Zakai shouted as he bounded down the path.

Lazarus swallowed again, as Penina squeezed water from her long hair. With drops glistening on her polished skin, she looked like a young girl, but her damp tunic clung to a body that was most definitely a woman's.

He'd been little more than a boy when she had come to them. Penina had been a few years older, yet already with an infant at her breast. He had taken his father's word, as everyone had, that Zakai was Penina's child. That Sirach had been moved by pity for the young Hebrew girl sold into slavery with no voice, no family, and a baby.

He watched Penina slip her tiny feet into her sandals next to the ones Zakai had forgotten—already his feet were bigger than hers.

When had he known that Zakai wasn't Penina's child? Perhaps as Zakai had grown and he'd seen his light gray eyes, so unlike Penina's deep brown. Perhaps it had been when he'd seen Martha run her hand over Zakai's face with the look only a mother gave, or exclaim in delight as he learned to walk. Whenever it was, he had grown into the knowledge that Zakai was Martha's son. And as his understanding had grown, so had his anger at what that pagan had done to his sister.

And each day, he wished he'd been old enough—big enough—to teach that cowardly dog a lesson.

But it was too late. And to speak of it would only hurt Martha. So he didn't speak of it, just as they didn't speak of Penina's past or the baby she lost before she was sold to Abba.

When they were young, he'd ferreted out a little information about Nina's life before Bethany. She'd lived in the east, a part of the scattered groups of Jews across the Jordan. She'd been married young, but not long after, her town was raided by nomads, her husband and parents killed. She was taken prisoner and sold as a slave in Damascus.

That was all she would tell—in her way—but he could piece together more. She'd had a child, and the child had surely died. But whether she was mute from birth or from the violence she'd witnessed, he didn't know and most likely never would. But he knew she had lost all faith in their God. That she had turned away from him as she believed he'd turned away from her.

Most of the time, Lazarus understood the signs she made with her hands, and Zakai could translate easily. But Martha and Penina seemed to communicate with little effort through a combination of facial expressions and intuition. When he was young, he'd been sure Penina and Martha could hear each other's thoughts.

Penina looked sideways at him, and he tensed. What would she have to say now? She always teased him—about being younger than her, about his love of the law or the way he did his chores. He gave back as much as he got, and their constant sparring made Martha pull her hair out. But this time, Penina pointed to him and made a sign for sickness. Her delicate face and slanted eyes showed worry.

He stepped back, surprised. "No. I'm fine. Now go, before the lightning starts." He'd have to be careful; Penina was quick to detect any secrets. And if she knew, she'd tell Martha. Martha couldn't know, not if he wanted to follow Jesus. He looked at the sun. He'd need to hurry. Jesus and his people would leave soon for the Temple.

But Penina didn't start down the path. She stood in front of him, waiting.

"What is it?"

Penina shrugged, but something was on her mind.

"Nina. Tell me."

She curled one arm like a pot and stirred it with the other hand, like a woman cooking. Her brows pulled down in either anger or worry.

"Are you worried about Martha?"

She nodded.

Martha had hardly said a word after the meal last night but had worked until the courtyard was spotless. Surely she wasn't still angry about his teasing at dinner. "What is it?"

Penina stepped closer. She took his hand in hers. Her skin was cool from the mikvah, and she smelled like rainwater and lavender. Penina formed his hand into the sign he knew for man. She formed hers into one for woman and brought their two hands together. Then she shook her head violently.

Martha doesn't want to marry. Sometimes Penina could communicate better than anyone he knew. "But she must. I promised Abba." He'd promised Abba he would do what was best for Martha. But wasn't that the same thing?

Penina's mouth pinched, and she shook her head again.

Understanding rushed over him. "Don't worry," he said quickly. "Whoever Martha marries, you'll go with her. And not as a servant, as part of the family." Martha would never leave Penina. And not having Zakai with her was unthinkable.

Penina blew out a frustrated breath. She made the sign for woman again and took his hand, entwining her fingers with his. With her other hand, she pointed to herself.

Heat burned up his neck and into his face as he realized her meaning. "You mean . . . you want to be married?"

She nodded and stepped closer. Penina's smile—rarer than a freshwater pearl—transformed her face.

A pain—unlike any pain he'd known before and in the vicinity of his heart—twisted through him. He backed away a step. Of course Penina would want to marry again. She was no longer a slave, not since Abba died. And she was young enough to have many children. He imagined Penina in another man's home, as another man's wife, and the pain sharpened.

He dropped her cool hand. She belonged to his family; it was his duty to find her a husband. "Of course, Nina." He cleared his throat. "I'm sorry I didn't think of it. I'll find a good husband for you."

Penina's mouth dropped open, and her eyes flashed in anger. She shook her head and stomped a foot on the path.

Now what? She was acting like he just said he'd give her to a slave trader.

Again, she made the symbol for man and woman with each hand and brought them together. Then she poked him in the chest.

"I know, Nina. I understand." Did she think he was stupid? "I'll find you a husband if that's what you want."

Her mouth flattened into an angry line. She pushed past him, making a small sound in her throat, and stomped up the path.

Lazarus watched her go. What was that about? She said she wanted to marry; then she got angry when he agreed to find her a husband. What had he done wrong? The older he got, the less he understood women, and especially her.

It wouldn't be hard to find a husband for Penina, even if she wasn't as devoted to the law as Martha. Men would get in line to marry a girl as lovely as she. But the thought of seeing her married to a village man, bearing his child . . . the pain in his heart doubled.

Martha wouldn't want to lose Penina to another family. And what would they do about Zakai? Everyone in Bethany might believe he was Nina's son, but Zakai loved Martha just as much as Nina. Yes, it was Martha and Zakai he worried for. Not himself, thinking of Penina in a village man's bed.

He pulled his tunic over his head and threw it on the rock before he descended into the darkness of the mikvah. He calmed his mind, letting the water embrace his aching body. He'd immerse and pray, asking the Almighty for wisdom. He would surely need it with these women.

And then he would go talk to Jesus.

LAZARUS STOPPED FOR a moment's rest outside the courtyard gate. The walk from the mikvah had never seemed so far. He took a deep breath and pushed through. The courtyard was deserted, except for Peter sitting in front of the fire, mopping up the last of Martha's cumin sauce with a hunk of bread.

"Where is the teacher?" Lazarus tried to keep his voice from sounding breathless.

"They left," Peter said around the food in his mouth. "Jesus asked me to tell you good-bye."

He'd missed him? "How long ago?" Lazarus turned back to the door. "I must speak with him." Who knew when he'd come back to Bethany?

Peter's bushy brows were pulled so low they met above his prominent nose. "They're gone, my boy. Halfway to the Jordan by now. I'm to take a message to Jerusalem, then catch up to them in Capernaum."

Lazarus's heart sank. All the way to Galilee? He eyed Jesus' closest disciple. Perhaps Peter could help him. He sat down across from him, and the words spilled from his mouth. "I want to join you—to be his disciple. Please, Peter, what must I do to follow him?" He felt like a little boy, asking his father if he could sit with the men in the synagogue.

Peter stopped chewing. "Join us? You sure about that? It's not a very safe occupation these days."

Lazarus leaned in. "He is the Messiah. The Messiah, Peter! After thousands of years of praying and fasting and sacrifice. How could I not be a part of the coming of the Kingdom?"

Peter rubbed his beard and looked at the ground.

"What is it? Don't you believe in him?" How could Peter, of all the disciples, doubt Jesus?

"No, no, boy. You've got it wrong." Peter shook his head. "I believe he is the Messiah, but . . ."

"But what?"

"But this." Peter's face pulled down in a grimace. "I don't understand him. Not but a few days ago, he said to us that he would suffer and die."

Lazarus blinked. Die? How could that be? He opened his mouth, but Peter held up his hand.

"Then he said, 'If anyone wishes to come after me, he must deny himself and take up his cross.'"

"His cross? But—"

Peter went on like he had memorized the words. "'And whoever loses his life for my sake will save it.'" He frowned as if trying to work out a puzzle.

Lazarus stared into the fire. It was like hearing Greek or Latin. He heard the words but didn't understand them. "What did he mean?" he finally asked.

Peter let out a long breath. "I'm not sure. But I think we'll all find out, and soon. The Pharisees want Jesus' head on a platter, like the baptizer. And I think . . ." He looked intently at Lazarus, his eyes filled with sorrow. "I think we'll all end up the same way."

Lazarus felt a chill of fear. Not for himself, but for Jesus. "You aren't going to desert him, are you?"

"No." Peter's answer was quick and sure. "No, I'll never leave him. But you might think about it some before you ask to follow him. You have sisters who need you, a farm to run. Who'll take care of all that while you're gone?"

The thunder rumbled again, this time louder.

"I'm working on that. They will be cared for." His stomach twisted. *Even Penina.* "Do you think . . . do you think Jesus will let me follow him?"

Peter picked up a traveling bag and stood. "Ask him when he returns to Bethany. But remember, his ways are not always clear." He pointed to the sky. "Looks like a storm's coming. It will hit here soon. Good-bye, my boy."

With a sinking heart, Lazarus watched Peter leave the courtyard. When would Jesus return to Bethany? It could be months before they saw him again. And Lazarus didn't have time to waste. Thunder growled, this time closer. He looked to the east. Ominous clouds massed over the horizon. Peter was right. A storm was coming, but would it bring the consolation of rain, or pass over and leave them disappointed?

Chapter Sixteen

*Wash away all my guilt; from my sin cleanse me. For
I know my offense; my sin is always before me.*
—Psalm 51:4-5

*H*IS THROAT BURNED like he'd swallowed a live coal.

He dragged his body out of the darkness. The thin light of a crescent moon struggled against the dark fists of clouds pummeling the sky. The storm had raged for days, keeping him in his tomb as the voices in his head howled amid the wind and thunder.

He stumbled down the rocky path to the shore and fell to the ground, the sharp rocks biting into his hands and knees as he crawled toward the water and collapsed where the white-tipped waves crashed against the shore.

The voices tore at his mind in a frenzy, but thirst won over their fear of the water. Coughing and choking, he gulped mouthfuls, tasting fish and slime, then rolled onto his side, the voices wailing and urging him away from the water. He crawled a few paces before he collapsed, spent in mind and body.

Rain pounded him, soaking him to the bone. The bitter wind tore at his rags, driving sand into his eyes and lips. His belly—empty for how long? Days? A week?—cramped and threatened to disgorge the briny water. They laughed, reveling in his misery.

After what seemed like eternity, the rain lightened and the

wind ebbed. The moon gained a corner on the punishing clouds. Its pale glow illuminated a bulky form gliding over the water, coming closer. For a moment, the clamor within his tormented mind ceased, as though its very breath were stolen. Then terror—a terror such as he had never known—shattered his thoughts.

With a roar he rose to his feet. Utter hatred and primeval fear burned through his veins. Pain ripped through his raw throat as he screamed, but his own voice was drowned by the ones that clawed inside his skull.

Through a haze of red, he saw it charging closer. A boat. And it carried a man. *Not him*, they screamed. He tried to run, but his legs were rooted in the shore. The screams reached a fevered pitch, and his vision darkened. They threw his body down once. Then again. The jagged stones tore into skin. His bones snapped, and his skull cracked.

His one human thought, a wordless wish for death. Anything to stop the torture.

The man, the one who terrified them, was on the shore now, close enough to touch him. They petrified into a twisted coil of hatred in the corner of his mind.

"Unclean spirit, come out of the man!" The voice cut through him like a knife.

Silence. Blessed silence, like a sudden intake of breath. Then a deep, rasping voice tore at his throat. "What have you to do with us?" He tried to close his lips, but he could no more prevent them from speaking than he could rise from the ground. "Jesus, son of the Most High God," the voice said. "I adjure you by God, do not torment us!"

They wailed, their voices rising and twisting like a desert sandstorm.

He crawled closer to the man, willing him to speak again. To silence them again. *Please. Just for a moment.*

"What is your name?" the man—the one they feared—asked.

He tried to remember. Surely he had one. Another voice,

low and sibilant, like a hissing snake, slipped from his lips. "Legion. There are many of us. Do not make us leave here. This is our land, not the land of the Jews."

Shrieks swelled to a feverish pitch. His mouth opened, and a guttural voice begged, "Send us into the swine."

The swine? Am I the swine?

Again, the man standing before him spoke. "Legion, come out of this man."

Pain ripped through his chest. He looked down, sure he'd see his heart torn from his body. His torso convulsed, beating him against the rocks. His legs thrashed wildly, and his back arched high, as if to snap his spine. The voices spiraled like a whirlwind. Howling, moaning, fading . . . and then they were gone.

He collapsed on the rocky ground and silence—peaceful, all-encompassing silence—suffused him.

HE CAME AWAKE, but didn't open his eyes. He didn't twitch a muscle.

Silence. Could it be real?

His throat burned, every bone and sinew throbbed with pain, and his body felt as hollow as a broken bird's egg. No wails. No shrieks. No scrape of claws in his skull. He was empty.

They were gone. All of them. They had called the man Jesus. He had called them Legion.

But who am I?

He opened his eyes. A fire crackled on the beach just a stone's throw from where he lay. Men sat around it, talking in low voices. A smell—a marvelous, wonderful smell—made his mouth water and his stomach twist. He pushed to his knees and crawled toward them.

The men startled, and one got to his feet as if to fight.

He stopped. Would they drive him away? There was the one who had freed him—the one named Jesus—next to the fire. Would he help him? *Please. I'm so hungry.*

Jesus held up a hand to the others, then pulled a fish from the spit and brought it to him. The scent made him weak and dizzy, as though he might again descend into blackness; then the meat was in his hands. He ripped open the fish, burning his fingers, and shoved chunks of flesh and charred skin in his mouth, gulping instead of chewing. Needlelike bones stuck in his throat, but he kept eating until nothing remained in his hands but ashes.

He raised his eyes. Jesus stood beside him, watching him. The other men stared at him with open mouths. He licked the flavor from his lips. He wanted to speak, to talk to this man, but no words came to his dulled mind. The demons had called him son of the Most High God. What did that mean?

They were Jews, he could see that. And he was not one of them, he knew that as well. But he wanted to be. He never wanted to leave the presence of this man in front of him.

One of the Jews backed away. "Master, we'll prepare the boat." He waded into the water, toward a fishing boat anchored in the shallows.

They were leaving him? No. He couldn't be alone again. *They* might come back. One word came to him. "Please." He clutched at Jesus' tunic. His voice was new to his ears. It was deep and husky with disuse, but it was his, not theirs. "Please let me come with you."

A young man with a wispy curl of beard stepped toward him, cautiously, as if he were a wild animal, and held out his hand. He reached for it. His own hand was huge—connected to a muscular forearm and an even thicker upper arm. He pulled, leveraging himself from the ground as the young man staggered against his weight.

He straightened his aching legs, rising taller than both of the men before him. He looked down on a body barely covered with a tattered cloth. Muscles bulged like coiled ropes over his dirt-covered legs and filthy arms. His bare chest was wide and marked with lines of scars, hundreds of them. No wonder these men were afraid of him.

He peeled his tongue from the top of his mouth. "Please." He bowed to the man who had saved him from the torture. "Let me stay with you." *Don't leave me alone again.*

A hand, gentle and yet strong, covered his head. Like anointing oil, warmth flowed over his aching body. The hollow, windswept place that had been filled with terror was refilled—saturated—with a calm, with a peace as he'd never known.

"Go," Jesus said, his voice holding all the authority that he'd used with the demons. "Go home to your family. Announce to them all that the Lord in his pity has done for you."

He sank to the ground and closed his eyes, reveling in the peace that filled him, that radiated inside him like the sun.

WHEN HE OPENED his eyes, the sun had won out over the storm. It shone down on the water and turned the sea to pink and gold. The boat was a tiny spot in the distance, the calls of the men as they adjusted the sails as distant as the cries of the seabirds in the brightening sky.

Jesus was gone.

And something else was missing . . . the fear that he'd lived with, that had been his constant companion for as long as he could remember. The fear was gone.

He breathed deeply of the fresh air, scoured by the storm and swept clean by the wind. *Go home to your family,* Jesus had said. *Announce to them all that the Lord in his pity has done for you.* But where was home? And who was his family? How long had he been in this place of misery?

He had only one word, one clue to lead him where he needed to go. The word that had whispered in his mind as Jesus had touched him. His name.

Isa.

Chapter Seventeen

Then will you understand the fear of the Lord;
the knowledge of God you will find.
—Proverbs 2:5

LAZARUS PICKED HIS way through the dried reeds that crackled
and snapped under his sandals. The stream that cut between the
garden and the orchard was hardly more than a trickle, a meager
offering to the Jordan half a day's journey east. There were faster
paths to Simon's house, but the sound of the trickling water and
the breeze rustling in the treetops soothed his worried mind.

Lazarus had put off his visit—his summons—to Simon for almost a week. Whatever Simon wanted to speak to him about, he
prayed it wasn't money; his purse was as drained as the parched
land. The storm that had blown in after Jesus' visit had produced
no rain—just howling wind and rumbling thunder—and he'd
spent the last four days carting water to the garden.

This morning Lazarus could taste another dry day on the
wind as the rising sun cast a dim glow through clouds the color of
dust. The days were warming, but even beside the cooking fire he
felt chilled, as if his bones were made of cold marble.

His breath was short, but he increased his pace, crossing the
market garden that stretched between his home and Simon's
walled courtyard. Simon was a doctor of the law, a Pharisee, and
a learned man—what Lazarus had hoped to be, before his father

had died. Before he'd learned that Abba had been deep in debt and that most of their land—the wheat fields, the olive groves, even this garden—had been sold to Simon.

In his kindness, Simon had offered them the use of the garden plot to grow their crops for the marketplace, brushing aside any talk of rent. But now that the one-year mourning period was over, Lazarus feared Simon's kindness had also reached its limit. If rent was what Simon had called on him to discuss, it would be a short visit indeed.

Lazarus surveyed the vegetables he and Zakai had planted months ago. The artichokes were growing fat, and asparagus fronds pushed through the sunbaked soil. Both would bring a good price at the upper market in Jerusalem. By Passover, he'd have enough to pay Simon some of what they owed. Perhaps then Martha would stop worrying.

His hand strayed to his side, below his ribs, where a dull ache had been growing for days. If Martha even suspected he was ill, she wouldn't let him follow Jesus—she wouldn't even let him out of his bed.

I'm a man now, the head of the household. I don't need her permission. But he wished for her blessing just the same.

Mary would support him, even against Martha. She believed that Jesus was the Messiah; surely she would see what Lazarus needed to do. But he couldn't set Mary and Martha against each other. They would need each other when he was gone.

And Penina . . . she was still barely speaking to him. After her puzzling behavior at the mikvah, he'd tried to make peace with her. He'd teased her, complimented her, even carried water from the well. Finally, she'd given him her special smile when he brought her an armload of the lavender she loved.

Both his mind and his gaze had lingered on Penina in the past days, a strange emptiness filling his chest when he thought of her married to a village man. Finally, he'd concluded that no man in Bethany would do for Nina. No one he knew would put up with her teasing, and surely none of them deserved her smile. He'd have to find some other way to make sure she was protected when he was gone.

He reached Simon's courtyard and stopped outside the ornately carved entrance. He took a deep breath. *The Lord is my strength and my shield.*

Simon's steward, Micah, opened the iron-girded doors as if he'd been waiting since dawn. Lazarus tried not to stare as Micah led him through the courtyard dense with fountains and flowering trees. Simon's house sprawled on one side, shaded with palm trees and big enough for three families. Servants—surely more than one man and his mother needed—rushed by with urns of water and bundles of parchment.

Simon stepped out of a double-arched doorway at the front of the house. He wore a white linen tunic that fell to his ankles and a belt of soft red leather studded with silver. He placed his hands on Lazarus's shoulders and leaned forward, setting his lips on Lazarus's cheek. "Peace be to you and all in your household." His thinning hair, still damp from his morning immersion, smelled of expensive myrrh.

"And may the God of Abraham, Isaac, and Jacob bless you," Lazarus responded. He'd always thought Simon a tall man, but as he accepted the kiss of peace, he realized he had grown taller than his neighbor in the year since Abba died. Lazarus straightened with a little more confidence.

Simon motioned for Lazarus to sit on a stone bench and snapped his fingers. A young woman with black hair and the dark skin of Egypt knelt before him. A young man who looked like her brother brought a bowl of water with rose petals floating on top.

"I thank you for coming to see me today, Lazarus. I wouldn't wish you to neglect your family or your work in favor of me."

Lazarus felt his shoulders tense. Did Simon think he wasn't working hard enough?

Simon signaled the girl to untie Lazarus's sandals and wash

his feet with the scented water. When Lazarus's feet were bathed, Simon led him into the house. His two guards stood just inside. Simon ignored them but touched the elaborate mezuzah on the door frame and closed his eyes. "Hear, O Israel, the Lord is our God, the Lord is One."

Lazarus did the same, then followed Simon into a spacious chamber with a high ceiling and many doorways leading from it. A servant knelt nearby, scrubbing the tile floor, and another scurried past with a stack of folded linen. The walls were hung with woolen tapestries, embroidered with the words of the Torah. Each of the doorways—he counted eight—were adorned with ornate mezuzahs.

Lazarus followed Simon through one doorway, both of them again touching the mezuzah and repeating the prayer. Simon was a devout man indeed.

The room they entered held a tall table, a stack of wax tablets, and neatly arranged rolls of parchment. Simon motioned to a carved chair with a woolen cushion. "Please, Lazarus, sit."

Lazarus sank down gladly. Simon settled on a simple wooden chair with a hard-looking seat while the Egyptian boy appeared at his elbow with a tray of plump figs and roasted pistachios. Simon passed Lazarus a cup of wine, and he drank. It was a good vintage, fruity and rich, and soothed his tight throat.

Simon silently watched the slave leave the room, then turned to Lazarus with a small smile. "Lazarus, I've known you since you were a boy."

He nodded and took another gulp of wine, feeling like a child called in by his teacher. It should be Sirach sitting across from Simon. It should be Sirach telling Simon they had no silver. *Lord, be my help.*

"You are a grown man now. A man who honors your father's memory. I'm sure you know why I've asked you to come to me." Simon straightened the rolls of parchment on his desk and didn't meet Lazarus's eyes, as if what he was about to say was difficult.

Lazarus braced himself. He knew what was coming.

Simon finally looked up at him. "Martha has spent her best years caring for you and for her sister, Mary." His mouth curled down at Mary's name. "And then for her father as he declined. Surely you can see that now it is time for her to have a family of her own."

Lazarus swallowed quickly and almost choked. Martha? He wanted to talk about Martha, not the rent? And what would Simon have to say about his sister? He bit back his questions. *A man of understanding keeps silent.*

Simon rubbed the side of his neck. "There was a time when your father and I talked of my marriage to Martha, but that was before . . ." His jaw tensed, as though in remembered pain.

Before he was a leper. Lazarus had been twelve, studying under the rabbis in the synagogue, when Simon left Bethany. They said Simon was being punished. He was gone for at least a year, and then he came back. But he was different. Everyone in the village said it. He was more serious, and even more devout. He didn't marry, but spent his days studying the law and praying at the Temple. As he prayed, his crops flourished and his flocks produced in abundance.

Simon laid his hands flat on the table and leaned forward. "Martha is a pearl without price, Lazarus. She is devout and pure, a woman of unequaled virtue. I ask to marry her."

Simon wanted to marry Martha? Lazarus had prayed for this, prayed for a righteous husband for Martha. But Simon? What would the most devout man in Bethany do when he found out his sister was not as pure as he believed?

Lazarus reached for a fig and put the whole thing in his mouth, chewing slowly. The betrothal contract was clear; it stated that the woman being betrothed was a virgin. Lying went against the commandments—and lying about a woman's virtue must be even more grievous—yet he'd sworn never to expose Martha's secret.

Simon went on. "If you . . . if she . . . would agree to marry me"—his throat jerked—"the people of this town would no longer call me Simon the Leper. My name would be restored, and my children would be honored." He bowed his head. "I would be most grateful if you would consider a betrothal to your sister."

Lazarus stared at the man in front of him. It was as though a lamp had been lit, illuminating his path through the night. The people of Bethany had never forgotten Simon's shame, no matter that the priests had declared him clean. Even Abba had turned away from his impurity. Would not Simon be the one man who would understand and forgive Martha's past?

And Lazarus would be free to leave Bethany. To follow the Messiah. His heart swelled in his chest. *Praise the Almighty, who has done great things for me.*

Simon went on, detailing his riches: his wheat fields, his vineyards, his olive trees, and his standing with the Sanhedrin. But Lazarus hardly listened.

Simon, the most respected scholar in Bethany. A doctor of the law. And wealthy beyond even Abba at the height of his riches. Someone Martha deserved so much more than that despicable pagan who had abandoned her.

Simon's voice was more confident now. "And of course, if you do agree to a betrothal, I would forgive the debt that you owe me. Family is family. Your garden will be returned to you and yours—as a betrothal gift, you could say."

Lazarus wouldn't need the garden when he left Bethany, but he did need something else. "She has a servant, Penina. A former slave, but . . ." He tripped over his words, his face heating as he heard his own stumbling voice. "She's like family. And she has a son."

"I've heard this woman is a pagan." Simon's brows lowered.

Lazarus frowned. "Of course not." Even though she had turned away from God, Penina was born a Hebrew, and Zakai was circumcised and studied at the synagogue.

Simon looked relieved. "Well, then. I have many servants." He motioned to the house. "But two more would indeed be welcome. And, of course, your grandmother also." Simon's mouth turned up in a forced smile. "May the Almighty bless her with long life." He rose from his chair, signaling the end of their business.

Lazarus stood, his mind reeling. Could it be that all his problems would be solved so easily?

He just had to convince Martha.

He followed Simon out of the house, praying again at each doorway. Yes, Simon was a demanding man, and living with him wouldn't be easy. But Martha was very much the same. And Martha was practical. She didn't want a handsome husband with sweet words and no honor. Not anymore. *Charm is deceptive and beauty fleeting. Fear of the Lord is to be praised.*

Lazarus submitted to another kiss of peace. "I will consider your offer." His eyes watered from the myrrh slicked over Simon's hair. Martha despised myrrh, but if that was the only complaint she had about a husband, she would be a lucky woman indeed.

As he left the ornate villa behind, his hopes lifted despite the pain in his side. A man as devout as Simon would be forgiving. He would give Martha another chance. She could be betrothed in a week, perhaps less. Then, with his vow fulfilled, he would be free to follow Jesus. And when Jesus came into his glory, all would know he was the Anointed One of the Most High God. Even Penina.

He breathed deeply of the morning air. *Give thanks to the Lord, for he is good.* The Almighty had answered his prayers. And the answer was Simon.

Chapter Eighteen

Against you alone have I sinned; I have done such evil in your sight
that you are just in your sentence, blameless when you condemn.
—Psalm 51:6

HAT WAS THAT horrible stench?

A dead animal? A rotting carcass somewhere on the shores of this pristine lake?

Isa raised his hand to cover his nose, and the smell intensified. He pushed himself to his feet, retching and gagging. It was him. He was covered in filth. Blood crusted over fresh cuts on his chest. And what was he wearing? A scrap of linen that was no color he knew.

His hands—with nails grown out like claws—touched his face. A tangled beard reached to his chest. His hair, matted like an animal's, fell in greasy clumps past his shoulders.

Go to your family. Announce to them all that the Lord in his pity has done for you.

The Lord in his pity . . . yes, he was pitiful. No wonder Jesus didn't want him. He was filthier than the pigs that had run into the water. He stumbled to the lake, splashing through the shallows and plunging into the deep. His arms, of their own accord, spread wide, and his feet kicked.

I know how to swim. He dove down, under the lapping waves, until he heard nothing but silence. Blessed silence. No laughing voices. No torturous pounding at his temples. He held his breath as long as he could and came up gasping. The sun sparkled off the waves, blinding him with its brilliance. His chest swelled with gratitude. *Thank you. For the silence.*

Closer to shore, his feet sank into the silty lake bottom. He watched the filth dissolve in the swirling water. Shivering and as clean as he could get, he waded out. At the edge of the shore, he turned back to the sea, staring in the direction that Jesus had gone. The waves lapped at his ankles; the wind raised bumps on his wet skin.

Who was this Jesus, son of the Most High God? And why had he come to him?

Doubt buffeted him from every side. Jesus had found him—filthy and cowering, a shell of a human. He'd driven out the demons and commanded him to go home. But how could he? He was no prophet. Other than a name, he knew nothing. He had but one memory. Yes, even as the demons had racked his mind with torment and his body with agony, he had known this: someone was waiting for him. But who? And where?

A muffled shout and scrape of rock sounded behind him. "There he is. That's the one." He jerked around to see a boy, his face marked by red spots, pointing to him from the scrubby trees past the shoreline. A cluster of men emerged from the trees behind the boy. Perhaps they were his family, or knew of them.

As the men came closer, his hope turned to fear. There were five of them, and except for the spotty-faced boy, they were old and gray. Two held pruning hooks like spears; three more grasped wooden clubs. He eased away, but the water was at his back.

The men stopped ten paces from him, their faces wary. One pushed his way to the front. His clothing was shabby and patched and his face scarred with pockmarks. From the stoop of his back, he looked to be a hundred years old. "Let me talk to him, you bunch of cowards," he barked in Greek. He advanced a step, his club raised in bony hands. "Who are you?"

Isa's mouth opened. He understood the man, but no reply came to him. Instead a familiar memory pricked at the corner of his mind. The raised stick, the angry voice . . . His heart sped up.

The ancient man's face furrowed. "Tell us." He shook his club.

"I—I don't know." He could speak Greek. He let out a breath.

The man came a step closer. "Where did you come from?"

He shook his head. *I'd hoped you would tell me.*

"So that's how you're going to be." The man narrowed his eyes. "Tell me then, where are my blasted pigs?"

The pigs? Isa remembered pigs, and how he'd wanted to eat them.

The boy spoke up. "There were men here. Jews. They came in a boat. And this one was screaming. Then he fell down, and the pigs—" He gulped and looked at the older man.

"What, boy?"

"They ran into the water." His voice dropped to a whisper. "It wasn't my fault. It was him." The boy pointed to Isa.

Isa tried to remember. "There were demons. They screamed, and Jesus came . . . then they were gone, and the pigs were gone."

The man waved his club like a knife, cutting the story short. "You mean to say that some Jew came and ran my pigs into the Galilee?"

Isa nodded.

The man turned red, and spittle collected in the corner of his mouth. "Why didn't you stop him?"

Stop him? Hadn't the old man heard what he said about the demons?

"Those pigs were mine. And they were worth a month's wages. And I'll take that out of your hide if it's the only way I'll get it." The old men came at him, their weapons raised.

Isa backed into the water. His mouth went dry. This, he knew. He could almost feel the coming blows. Before they reached him, a new man pushed past the others.

He had to be the ugliest man Isa had ever seen. His face was mottled with red, his nose the size and shape of an onion, and his eyes tiny slits under heavy folds of skin. "Let's not be too hasty, Cyrus." His voice sounded like the scrape of a sandal on gravel.

The pig owner turned on the ugly newcomer. "He watched my pigs drown, Nikius. He deserves a beating."

Isa cringed, his heart hammering.

The ugly man stepped in front of him with a quizzical frown. "Are you the one who's been living in these tombs for years, wailing and carrying on?"

Isa's mouth dropped open. Years?

One man raised his club. "Let's make sure he doesn't start in again."

Nikius's bristly brows came together. "Now, now. Take it easy." He eyed Isa from the top of his head to his bare feet. "Are you still mad?"

Isa shook his head. He'd just told them that Jesus had taken away the demons, hadn't he? He was no more mad than they were. Perhaps less.

"Why'rya cowering like an old woman, boy? You could kill us all with one arm tied behind your back." He squinted at Isa. "You're strong, I'll give you that. You look like a half-starved gladiator."

Strong? He looked down at his body. He must be.

Nikius ran a hand over his grizzled face and gazed at Isa, then at the one named Cyrus, as though figuring in his head.

Cyrus snorted. "You're not going to take him in, Nikius? He'll kill you in your sleep."

Nikius muttered, "Yes, by the gods. He's gotta be strong." He peered up at Isa with cloudy eyes. "He might be just what I need."

Cyrus shook his head. "You're crazy. And what about my pigs?"

Nikius grunted. "I'll pay fer your scrawny pigs, Cyrus."

"How much?"

"A week's wages."

"That's robbery!"

"See anyone with a better offer? And I'll get the work out of this boy. Now, get out of here and let him be."

Isa watched the one named Cyrus and ugly Nikius haggle over the pigs. What was going on? After a short shouting match that Cyrus seemed to lose, Nikius grunted at Isa, "Come on, boy. We're going home."

Home? Isa stood uncertainly, looking from the men out to the water where Jesus had disappeared. But he had to find his family. Jesus had commanded it.

Nikius raised a brow. "Unless you have something better to do?"

The old man was right. He had nothing else to do. He didn't even know what direction to go.

Nikius jerked his thumb over his shoulder. "Come on. I have a place for you. Work. Food and some clothes. A week is all I'm askin' to pay me back for savin' your life. Then you can go." He smiled like he had a secret. "If you want to."

Isa looked sideways at him. Food and clothes. He needed that, but something seemed wrong.

Nikius answered his unspoken question. "Don't worry, boy. I'm just an old man who needs some help. That's all." His attempt at a smile with his few blackened teeth failed to reassure Isa. But what else could he do? Set out half-naked and hope he came upon his family? And he was hungry again.

The rest of the men turned and began filing down the path toward the south, away from the lake. Isa fell into step behind Cyrus, stooped and shuffling.

As they climbed up the path, Cyrus looked over his shoulder at Nikius, then raised his brows at Isa. "A week," he snorted. "After a week with Nikius and his . . ." He stopped short.

Alarm trickled through Isa's chest and coiled in his belly. "What?"

Cyrus's mouth twisted in the guise of a smile. "Well, boy, I'd bet my last drachma that you'll never leave Gerasene."

Chapter Nineteen

True, I was born guilty, a sinner, even as my mother conceived me.
—Psalm 51:7

ISA FOLLOWED THE line of old men up the steep bank that rose from the rocky shore. The sun, high in the sky now, warmed a dry and colorless landscape. Where were they? And where were they going?

His bruised body throbbed with every step as a litany of questions pummeled his tired mind. Who was he and where was his family? How long had he been a prisoner of the demons? Could it have been years, as Nikius said? How many years?

His stomach growled, and a cold wind tore at his thin tunic.

What he needed now was food, clothing, and a place to sleep. And Nikius was the only one offering anything more than a beating.

The path dipped into a narrow ravine, and a familiar dread tugged at his mind. Stone cliffs rose up on both sides, throwing murky shadows into the basinlike clearing. A chill shivered down Isa's back and prickled his arms. Gaping mouths ringed the base of the cliffs, some natural caves, others hewn into the rock with inscriptions and symbols.

They were tombs. And he knew them well.

A pair of vultures rose out of the crevice, their screeches fading as they flapped heavily up above the cliffs. The men passed by the tombs without a glance, but Isa came to a halt. A wall of rocks—as tall as a man could reach—rose up on either side of the mouth of one cave. Beside it lay a rotten carcass and a scattering of gnawed bones. The smell of filth and rot was like a punch in the gut.

He choked and covered his nose. "Is this . . . ? Did I live here?"

Nikius grimaced. "You did." He frowned. "For the first few years, we tried to catch you. We tied you up, even put you in chains one time. But you always broke free."

The first few years? "How long . . . ?"

Nikius scratched his chin. "Let me see now, maybe six—no, it would be seven years."

Seven years?

"As I was saying, after the first few, we just let you be. You never came into the village."

Nikius pointed with his stick to the rocks ringing the tomb. "You carried these rocks from the shore, made this whole wall."

His stomach twisted. This was his home. He'd been nothing more than an animal, eating what he could find, sleeping in filth. For seven years. Why had Jesus come to him? He was as vile as the carrion rotting next to him on the ground.

"Come on." Nikius nudged him toward the path up the ridge.

At the top, the chill wind whipped over the height, driving away the smell of death.

Winter-brown hills rolled to the west. To the east, where the boy and the rest of the men were heading, was a barren wasteland of dry, whispering grasses and scrubby pines.

"So," Nikius wheezed, "who are you?"

His name was Isa, but what else did he know? He was no Jew. So why had the son of the Jewish God come to *him*? Gratitude welled in him as he breathed the morning air, as he heard the crunch of feet on loose stones. Jesus—the son of the God of the Jews—had given him a new life. But what was he to do with it?

Nikius continued talking as if Isa had answered his first question. "Who are your people?"

Isa shook his head. He wished he knew. He looked to the south, where a river snaked in a narrow swathe of green. Bits of memory and half-formed images surfaced like flotsam coming to the top of the water. Jerusalem was there; he could picture the Temple, hear the prayers and the call of the trumpets. But Jerusalem was a long way from the Sea of Galilee.

"You don't know much, boy."

Isa grimaced. *That's the truth.* They walked in silence. Perhaps when he'd eaten and slept he'd remember who he had been and where he'd come from. And who was waiting for him to come home.

A ramshackle town rose up against the hard gray sky. A few leaning shops lined a narrow street. Old women clustered at a well, their toothless mouths dropped open as he walked by with the line of men. Gray-haired merchants came to their doorways, eyed him warily, then retreated behind their doors. Except for the spotty-faced swineherd, he didn't see a soul under forty years.

As they passed through the town, Cyrus veered away. "I'll expect payment for those pigs today," he grunted to Nikius. "In case you don't wake up in the morning." He cast one last, disgruntled look at Isa before pushing through the doorway of a seedy inn.

As Isa followed Nikius to the edge of the village, they came upon a field strewn with rocks and boulders. Nikius stopped. "This is it, boy. This is what I need you to do."

Isa's mouth dropped open. Clear this field? Some of the boulders were half the size of a man. How did the old man expect him to clear it in a week?

His face must have shown his thoughts. Nikius slapped him on the back, harder than Isa expected for a man his age. "You're strong enough, boy. Now follow me."

Nikius crossed the field to a courtyard wall the color of dried dung. Isa followed. Half-dead bushes and weeds sprouted along the wall. A pile of broken clay pots lay beside a mound of decaying vegetables and what looked like the carcass of a wild dog.

Nikius passed the pile of refuse like he couldn't see it—or smell it.

Isa followed him through a crookedly hung door into what should have been a courtyard but was more like a maze. Piles of pottery and baskets lay in heaps. In the center, an oxcart with one wheel lay tipped under a load of iron spikes. Rusty mattocks and hoes lay like a heap of dead soldiers beside a smoldering fire.

Isa eyed the debris. What kind of man collected useless refuse?

Nikius bellowed toward the door of the one-room house. "Alexa, get yourself out here, woman." His beady eyes stayed on Isa, and a smile lurked under his bulbous nose.

A woman ducked out of the doorway, shading her eyes from the bright light.

Isa's mouth dropped open, and the chill of the wind changed to a warm flush on his skin.

The woman—young, but no girl—glowed like a precious ruby stuck in a tarnished setting. Her hair was like a raven's wing, black and glossy, and her eyes shone like polished onyx. Isa's gaze was drawn to her skin, tawny and smooth, from a high brow to smooth cheeks, down her long graceful neck. He stopped himself from looking even lower and brought his eyes back to her face. Pomegranate lips parted as she stared at him.

Nikius watched him, a slow smile spreading over his misshapen face. "My daughter. She's a beauty, isn't she?"

Alexa tossed her head, and her tunic slipped off one shoulder, exposing even more smooth skin.

Isa swallowed hard. How could such a beautiful woman have sprung from this man's loins?

She looked at him with wide eyes rimmed in kohl. "Just what did you drag home this time, Pater?" She purred like a jungle cat.

"He's the one from the tombs."

One arched brow rose. "The mad one?"

"Aye. And you're to give him some food. And something to wear."

Her languid gaze went from Isa's matted hair to his dity feet. "What if he tries to kill me?" She didn't look at all frightened by the prospect.

Isa's face burned. *Kill her? Is that what they think of me?* He opened his mouth but couldn't find a word to say to a woman this beautiful.

Nikius pulled a rickety ladder out of a pile and leaned it against the house. "I have a feeling in my gut that this boy wouldn't hurt a flea on a camel's hind end."

Alexa stepped closer to Isa. "I hope you're right." She smelled of juniper berries and something else . . . something earthy and sweet.

Nikius jutted his chin toward the flat roof. "You sleep up there." He stomped through the maze of refuse and pushed open the courtyard door. "Stay out of the village, boy. They'd just as soon kill ya as look at ya there." He threw a glance at Alexa. "Get him some food, before he falls over."

"You're leaving me alone with him?" Alexa's eyes swept over his scarred chest.

He was leaving him alone with her? Isa took a step backward, stumbling over a rusty mattock and quickly righting himself.

Nikius laughed, furrowing his face even more. "Don't worry, son. She don't bite." He slammed the courtyard door behind him.

Isa swallowed hard. He was alone—and practically naked—with a beautiful woman who looked at him as if he were a meal and she hadn't eaten in days.

If she didn't bite, why did he feel like he'd just been thrown into the lion's den?

Chapter Twenty

She picks out a field to purchase; out of her
earnings she plants a vineyard.
—Proverbs 31:16

MARTHA POUNDED THE barley on the stone grinder, wishing she could pound some sense into her brother's head. Betrothal to Simon? Was he turning into a raving madman?

Lazarus stood silently, watching her with a hopeful face. Penina sat beneath the fig tree, mashing chickpeas and roasted garlic into a paste, her mouth pulled down, her eyes darting from Lazarus to Martha.

Martha poured more barley on the grinding stone and bent over it, turning away from Lazarus. She'd woken with anticipation this morning, not the usual twist of anxiety and weight of worry. It was the preparation day for Purim, her favorite day of the year. Tonight, they would take Zakai to the synagogue to hear the story of Esther, how her faith had saved her nation from the evil plans of Haman. After, they would give gifts of food to their friends and alms to the poor.

As she'd immersed in the mikvah earlier in the day, Martha had smiled at the remembrance of last Purim. They had still been in mourning for Abba, but the law allowed them to put their sorrow aside for the feast. They had all eaten together, even Lazarus and Josiah, laughing and acting out the drama of Esther going before her husband, the powerful king of Persia.

Little Adina had played the part of Esther, trembling with fear as she went before the king, asking for his protection of her people. Zakai, as usual, had begged to be Mordecai, the wise counselor, and Lazarus gave in to the children's demands to play the part of the king. No one wanted to be the evil Haman, but Josiah had good-naturedly agreed. Penina laughed along with their antics, and Safta's old face had creased into something resembling a smile.

Martha pounded the barley into fine meal. They wouldn't feast on roasted lamb and honey cakes this year. She had little in her storeroom, far less than when Abba had been alive. But everyone she loved would be together. She and Mary wouldn't talk about Jesus—at least not if she could help it. It would be a chance to put aside her worries for one night.

And now Lazarus stood here, with his preposterous idea.

Martha poured the flour into the mixing bowl. Why must Lazarus even talk of a betrothal? As if he didn't know how impossible it was. "Did you agree to it?"

Lazarus frowned. "I wouldn't do that, Martha. Not without your consent. But, Marmar." He crouched down beside her. "I think this is the answer to our prayers."

Martha raised her eyes to her brother's face. How could he think that?

Safta sidled closer, one of Zakai's birds cooing in her wrinkled hand. "Betrothal to Simon the Leper?" She made a sound like a low whistle. "Jumping from the pot into the fire, are you?"

Martha sank down on her heels and let her hands idle. Even Safta knew this was a bad idea, and she couldn't remember what day it was. Didn't Lazarus understand why she couldn't marry?

Lazarus sighed and glanced at Safta. "Come to the orchard with me, Martha." His gentle hands pulled her up, and he led her out of the courtyard door. He put his arm around her shoulders as they walked. Now they could talk freely, away from Safta's sharp ears. And she knew what Lazarus wanted to talk about.

Lazarus stopped when they reached the trickling stream. The morning clouds had cleared, and the sapphire sky stretched to each horizon. The breeze whispered in the trees, and frogs croaked in the reeds. Across the river, the apricot trees showed the first misting of green on their spreading branches. But the beauty of the morning and the music of water over stones failed to soothe the anxiety quivering in Martha's chest.

Lazarus turned her toward him. "Martha, I promised to look after you. Promised Abba."

She looked at her feet. "I know. But—"

He pushed her chin up with one finger. "Listen, Martha. Simon is a good man. He will be a good husband to you, forgive our debt to him, take in Penina and even Safta. Only a brave man would take on our grandmother." He tried to coax a smile with a small one of his own.

The love she saw in his face was sincere but so was the determination. Her baby brother was the head of the family, and he knew as well as she that they were close to destitute.

Abba had lost everything after she came home with Zakai. He'd never blamed her, but she knew it was her fault. Shouldn't she pay the price?

"But what about . . . ?" She couldn't bring herself to give words to the shame they never spoke of. She motioned to the orchard.

Lazarus pressed his lips together. "I swore an oath that I would tell no one of that night, Martha. Lying is a sin, and we've been lying about Zakai for years." He let out a breath. "I will not bear false witness on your marriage contract."

Martha dropped her chin and leaned against Lazarus. The ketubah that he must witness was clear: *Here, in the city of Bethany, Simon the son of Elezar says to this virgin, Martha, daughter of Sirach . . .*

This virgin, Martha.

The law was equally clear on what happened if the bride was found not to be a virgin on her wedding night: *If the evidence of the woman's virginity is not found, they shall bring her to the gate of her father's house, and there her townsmen shall stone her to death.* And then what would happen to Penina, to Zakai?

Lazarus knew her thoughts; he knew the law as well as any man in Bethany. "Tell him, Martha. Now, before the betrothal. The Almighty showed mercy on him, forgave his sins and cured him from his affliction. Simon will show you the same mercy."

Martha raised her eyes to her brother, who was always willing to see the best in everyone. She couldn't afford to be so trusting. "Give me more time. At least until after the harvest."

Lazarus scowled and ran his hand through his hair as if he wanted to pull it out. "Tell me you're not still waiting for him."

Martha stepped back and shook her head. "Of course not. It's been seven years." It would be foolish to still wait for a boy who was gone.

"Seven years, Martha." He shook his head. "If he ever shows his face in Bethany . . ." His fists clenched at his sides.

"He won't." Martha wrapped her arms around her chest. Isa would never come back. He must be dead; it was the only reason he would have deserted her. And she'd spent seven years mourning him. But could she marry Simon . . . tell him of her shame? Was Lazarus right about his mercy?

"You must tell him soon. We can't wait." Lazarus looked away.

Martha put her hands on her hips. She'd always known when her baby brother was keeping something from her. "Why?"

He answered too quickly. "Because the year of mourning is over. I promised Abba. I told you all that." He looked away, toward Jerusalem.

But it wasn't everything. Her heart sank. Was he really going to leave them?

"Tell me the truth, Lazarus."

But Lazarus didn't answer her. His gaze had sharpened toward the south, and his brows pulled down.

She looked to where goats and sheep grazed in the southern pastureland, and a shadow darkened the horizon. "Is there a storm coming?" Thank the Lord, they needed the rain desperately.

Lazarus shaded his eyes.

Martha looked again. Something wasn't right about the soot-colored cloud hovering past the grazing animals. Rain coming from the south? From Egypt? And it was moving far too fast. Her heart stuttered, then surged in panic.

Lazarus turned to her, his alarmed face confirming her fear.

She grabbed him by the shoulders. "Go. Get Josiah and Mary. Everyone. Anyone you can find." She whirled toward the house. She needed baskets, jars, anything. Why wasn't Lazarus moving? "Go!" she yelled over her shoulder. Martha whispered a desperate prayer as she ran. *Please, please, let them pass by. Not the garden. It's all we have.*

Penina and Safta jumped as Martha burst into the courtyard. "Baskets," she panted, running to the stash in the corner. "Hurry. Locusts."

By the time Martha, Penina, and Zakai had gathered all the baskets they could and ran back to the garden, the black cloud had doubled in size and was heading straight toward Bethany. Martha shoved a basket at Penina. "Hurry!" She began to strip fingerling cucumbers from the vines. "Get the artichokes."

Mary and the girls ran across the meadow, the baby strapped to Mary's back. "Girls, get the beans," Mary directed her daughters. She bent to help Martha with the cucumbers.

Lazarus and Josiah came running with more baskets.

A low buzz vibrated through the air. Martha willed her fingers to move faster. If they saved the vegetables, they could bring them to market tomorrow. It wouldn't be as much as they had hoped, but . . .

Martha glanced over her shoulder. The sun had dimmed, and the blue sky was fast disappearing behind a dusk-colored cloud. The drone of countless wings beating the air swelled to a roar.

She hadn't finished one row, and there were at least a dozen more.

The swarm descended. Each insect, as long as her finger, glistened with iridescent wings. They settled on her hair and crawled on her face, their threadlike legs scratching over her skin, crawling over her legs and up her tunic.

Sarah screamed. Adina brushed frantically at her sister's hair.

Locusts covered every green plant—the cucumbers, the artichokes. They bent the asparagus like trees before a storm. The whir of wings subsided, replaced with the grind of thousands upon thousands of jaws—biting, chewing. The garden, their livelihood, their only chance . . . buried under a living carpet of destruction.

Lazarus pulled her arm and pointed to the half-filled baskets at their feet, locusts covering them like a blanket. "Save what you can."

She gathered the baskets, scooping and brushing the insects away, stacked as many as she could carry, and ran for the house.

They burst into the courtyard. A few locusts crawled in the dirt and landed on the fig trees and shrubs along the courtyard walls. Zakai swatted at them, and Penina crushed them under her sandaled feet.

Martha and Mary dumped what they had saved—asparagus, beans, a handful of artichokes—into empty jars and covered them with cloths. Lazarus and Josiah entered with their baskets, brushing insects from their clothes and hair, stomping them into the ground as they fell.

Lazarus bent over. His face was pale and pinched; his breath came in gasps. "This is it. All we could save." He put his head in his hands. "What will we do now?"

Martha sank down beside the meager remains of their garden, not even a tenth of what they would have harvested. She covered her face with her hands. All the days spent planting, watering, and weeding . . . wasted. What would they do now, with so little to sell at the market? She blinked hard to stop the tears. Weeping would not bring back the harvest, and tears would not feed her family. *Why, Lord? Why have you cursed us?* But she knew why.

She was still being punished for her sin.

Chapter Twenty-One

She is girt about with strength, and sturdy are her arms.
—Proverbs 31:17

*M*ARTHA PULLED ANOTHER jarful of water from the cistern and carried it back to the courtyard, her worries pressing heavier than the jar on her shoulder.

She'd gone to the synagogue last night with Zakai, and again this morning as the feast day of Purim dawned. She'd listened to the story of Esther, responding with "Cursed be Haman" and "Blessed be Mordecai." But gratitude did not fill her heart.

She'd brought gifts of almonds and dates to Elishiva, and bread and olives for Simcha's mother and little brother. Giving gifts of food and charity had always been one of her favorite parts of Purim, but how soon would her own family feel the pinch of hunger? Would the Lord provide, as Lazarus always claimed?

At least she still had the jar of nard; thank the Most High she'd stopped Mary from using it. She'd take it to Jerusalem after Purim and trade it for oil and wheat. That, at least, would see them through until well after Passover.

Martha set the water jar in the shadow of the courtyard wall, close to where Safta huddled, her eyes closed and her mouth open, snoring like a camel. Penina sat at the loom, her hands flying across the weighted threads. The Purim feast would be meager at best. Barley was all she had for bread, but if she flavored it with rosemary and thyme it would do. She would roast what they had of the garden vegetables, seasoning them with garlic and plenty of chopped herbs. A few dried fish and olives would go to Lazarus and Josiah, along with the last of their wine.

Martha leaned against the wall's sun-warmed bricks, suddenly so weary. She needed to speak to Lazarus about their plight, but he'd dragged himself to his sleeping mat last night—without eating and without a word. He hadn't risen even now, with the sun well above the horizon. Her burden of worry magnified. Was Lazarus too young to take on the responsibilities of the head of the family?

She pushed herself away from the wall with a heavy breath. *Keep busy.* There was much to do before the feast. She trudged to the fire to start the immersion of the vessels. At least they would all be together for the feast day.

A sniffle and a muffled sob caught her ear. Zakai sat in the corner, his rabbit in his lap and his face wet with tears.

"What is it?" She crouched down beside him.

He stared at the willow basket where he'd kept a fuzzy caterpillar for days, feeding him handfuls of vetch that grew in the meadow. "My caterpillar is dead."

Martha ran a hand down his sweet face. This, at least, she could fix. "He's not dead, my sweet. Look." She pointed to a lump on one of the willow switches. "He made a cocoon. He's getting ready to be a butterfly."

Zakai's brows bent down. He examined the gray mass carefully. "A butterfly?" He frowned and looked at her suspiciously.

"Trust me. A beautiful butterfly will come out. Just wait and see. Now hurry and help me; we have much to do before the celebration tonight." His face brightened into a smile that warmed her heart and lifted her worries. If only all her problems were this easy to solve.

Zakai rubbed the tears from his face. "Are Mary and Josiah still coming to the feast tonight?"

Martha pulled her knife from her belt and started peeling

the papery skin from an onion. "Yes." Mary wouldn't miss Purim.

"And the baby, right?"

Martha smiled. Little Natanel would be a good distraction from her worries. "Of course. He can't be without his mama."

"And his abba, right?" Zakai brought her a basket for the onion skins.

Martha felt a prick of sadness. *A baby needs his mama, and a boy of six needs his abba.* "Yes, and his abba."

Zakai's unruly brows came together. "Question or command, Marmar?" It was a game they played often, but this time his voice was serious.

Martha cut the onion into quarters. "Question." She could tell he had one.

Zakai's looked sideways at Safta, then whispered to Martha, "Did you know my abba?"

Her eyes stung as the acrid scent of the onions reached them and his words cut into her heart. If only she could answer with the truth. If she could just say it out loud for all to hear and end these years of secrets. *Yes, I knew him, and I loved him. He was sweet and shy and handsome. And he loved me.* And he would have loved Zakai, too. She blinked hard and threw the onion pieces in the pot.

"I just wish I knew something about him." Zakai's mouth trembled.

She wiped her knife on a cloth and tucked it back into the sheath at her waist. He wasn't asking for a lot. Just to know something of the man who was his abba. Wasn't that the least she could do? He'd never meet him, not now.

She laid her hands on his shoulders and looked him in the eyes, her own still stinging. "I knew him."

Penina's head jerked up, her slanted eyes questioning, and she fumbled with her spool of thread. Safta snorted in her sleep. Martha watched her settle back down, her chin drooping to her chest.

Zakai's brows arched. "But, you said—"

"I know. But you're old enough now to keep a secret, aren't you?"

Zakai nodded. "But how did you—"

"I just did." She closed her eyes and brought the picture of Isa to her mind. The Isa that she'd known since he was just a boy like Zakai. "Your father was a good man. A kind man." Or he would have been, if he'd grown to be a man.

She pulled Zakai closer, loving the touch of his soft skin, his boyish smell. "He had a voice like King David and could play the kinnor more beautifully than anyone in Judea."

Penina came to them. She laid one hand on Zakai's messy hair.

"Is it true, Mama?" Zakai looked up at Penina, his eyes bright.

She nodded and laid her other arm around Martha's shoulders, making a three-sided fortress. Martha pulled them closer. They were her family, and she would take care of them both. She just didn't know how. *Holy One, Shepherd of Israel, answer me. How can I take care of them?*

The courtyard door swung opened, and Simon entered. Penina stepped away, pulling Zakai with her. Martha wiped the tears from her eyes and adjusted her head covering. Why was he here?

For once, Simon was without his lumbering guards. His face was grave as he greeted them. "Peace be on your house, Martha."

"And on all of yours."

Simon clasped his hands in front of his thin frame. "I inspected your garden this morning and come to offer my assistance."

Another loan? Or a different kind of assistance? "I—I thank you, Simon," she stammered. "You are most kind."

Safta snorted from her perch in the corner. "Kindness has little to do with it."

"Hush, Safta," Martha whispered, her face heating.

Simon stood before her in silence.

Was he wondering if she had agreed to the betrothal? She snuck a look at his face. His gaunt cheeks were tinged with pink. Could he be as embarrassed as she? Her flush seeped from her cheeks down her neck. What was she supposed to say to him next?

And where is Lazarus?

Chapter Twenty-Two

*L*AZARUS ROLLED OVER, every bone in his body aching. The sun was well over the horizon. How had he slept so long? Then he remembered. The locusts, the garden. It was all gone. He pulled his cloak over his face. With no crop to bring to Jerusalem and no coin for more seed, they were ruined. And the apricots wouldn't be ready for months.

Surely now Martha would see that there was only one choice.

He pushed himself up from the mat, but a sharp pain in his middle doubled him over. He breathed shallowly until it passed, then pulled up his tunic, exposing his flat belly. There, where the ache had been for the past week, was a swollen lump. He probed it with one finger. Pain shot through him like a knife under his ribs.

A sick worry knotted in his stomach. What kind of affliction was this? The growths under his arms, the shortness of breath, and now this? Something was very wrong.

Lord, be my strength and my shield.

Surely the Lord wanted him to follow the Messiah? This could be a test, to make sure he was worthy to be a disciple of the Holy One. Perhaps all of it was a test—this illness, the locusts, even his disquieting feelings about Penina. He would stand firm in his trust and go ahead with his plans. He must. And whatever this affliction was, he would keep it to himself.

• • •

MARTHA WHISPERED TO Zakai, "Go, get Lazarus from the upper room." Of all the days to be sleeping so late and leaving her to talk to Simon. Didn't he know she needed him?

Martha stared at Simon's sandals—fine sandals with thick wooden soles and soft leather straps. The tassels of his coat almost brushed his feet. She couldn't think of one thing to say to the man in her courtyard who wanted to be her husband.

Zakai finally returned. "Lazarus is coming." He looked sideways at Simon. "Can I go tell Adina about my caterpillar?"

Martha nodded. "Go, but be back by midday."

As Zakai dashed across the courtyard, Lazarus climbed down the ladder from the roof. Relief flared within Martha, quickly replaced by concern. Lazarus's face was pinched and pale. She stepped toward him, but Lazarus waved her away.

"Simon. Forgive me. Martha, water, please."

Martha hurried to the water jar; she'd ask him later what was wrong. She poured water in two purified cups.

Penina went back to the loom but gave Martha a raised eyebrow. She was wondering about Simon's visit as well.

Simon repeated his earlier condolences to Lazarus as Martha brought them water and bread. Simon took a seat on the bench under the fig tree while Lazarus settled heavily onto a stool. Martha eyed her brother. His hand shook as he lowered his cup. Was she imagining it, or was his chest rising and falling as though he couldn't catch his breath? She retreated to the corner of the courtyard next to Penina, shadowed by the fig tree but close enough to hear every word.

Lazarus took another long drink. "I thank you for your concern, Simon. How did your crops fare?"

Simon looked at his cup, his answer slow in coming. "The Almighty has blessed me. One of my fields was in the way of the insects, but the others have been spared."

Martha's heart sank. Simon's land—his crops and vineyards—were spared when theirs were not?

"You are indeed blessed," Lazarus said.

"Will you replant?" Simon asked.

Martha stifled a snort. Simon, of all people, knew they had no way to pay for seed.

Simon leaned forward. "Do not worry about the cost. I can give you seed."

Lazarus raised his gaze to the older man. "But I can't repay you. And I already owe you a great deal." The silence weighed on the courtyard like a heavy blanket.

Martha's face began to heat. Were they going to speak of the betrothal again? *Please, no.*

"Have you considered, ah, what we discussed in my home?" Simon's voice was low, but he glanced in her direction.

"I have, but Martha . . ." Lazarus let her name hang in the silence.

Martha felt her ire rise. *I'm right here.* Must they speak of her as if she were deaf and dumb? She caught Penina's sideways glance.

Simon put a hand on Lazarus's shoulder. "You are the head of your family now and must do what you think is best for your sister."

Without her consent? Would Lazarus do that?

Simon continued as if she wasn't there. "With my help, you will soon be as prosperous as your father and be able to marry and have a family of your own. Our children will grow up together." Simon's gaze went to Martha, his eyes wide and unblinking.

Martha wished she could disappear like spilled water into the dry ground. Speaking of their children already? Couldn't they take this one step at a time?

Lazarus stared into his wine cup, his mouth turned down in a grimace.

"Do you not wish for a family of your own someday?" Simon asked Lazarus, his tone puzzled.

Martha frowned. Lazarus looked like he'd been caught sneaking away to the synagogue instead of doing his chores.

Simon took a breath and straightened, as though he'd just solved a riddle. "Ah. I see."

Martha looked harder at her brother. What did Simon see that she couldn't?

"You wish to follow your cousin, to be one of his disciples."

Lazarus glanced first at Simon, then at Martha, the answer written on his face. Penina fumbled with her shuttle. Martha took in a sharp breath and reached for Penina's hand. Was Simon right? Lazarus still wanted to leave them? Now, when they needed him more than ever?

"You'll get yourself killed," Simon said, his voice grave.

Martha's heart stuttered. Penina's hand was cold and limp in hers. Simon was right. Being Jesus' friend was dangerous; being his disciple might be deadly.

"He's the Messiah," Lazarus said.

"He's a fraud," Simon answered, smiling as if to soften his words. He raised his hands, palms out. "But you are young and have every right to be foolish."

Lazarus's jaw firmed in the stubborn look Martha knew well.

"Still . . ." Simon's smile disappeared. "You cannot take care of your household and follow your heart."

Simon was at least talking sense.

Before Lazarus could answer, the door to the courtyard flew open, and Zakai darted in, heading straight for the men. "Lazarus! Jesus is coming."

Lazarus jumped to his feet.

Martha locked eyes with Penina, alarm jolting through her. *Not in front of Simon.* Penina darted out of the corner, reaching Zakai just as he came to stand in front of Lazarus.

Simon's brows rose up to his receding hairline. "Stop," he ordered Penina. "Speak, boy."

Zakai froze at Simon's forceful tone, his eyes widening.

Lazarus crouched down beside him. "Tell me, Zakai. What did you hear?"

Zakai didn't hesitate. "He's coming here, today, for Purim." He wiggled as if he had ants crawling up his tunic.

Lazarus glanced at Simon. "He's back from Galilee already?" he asked Zakai. "Who told you?"

Zakai bounced closer to Lazarus. "Josiah. He just came from the Temple. He saw him there, and Jesus said to expect them. Can I go to meet him on the road? Please, Marmar?"

Martha gave him a look that shushed him for a moment. Everyone knew the priests were looking for Jesus. Simon would get word to the Sanhedrin faster than a swallow's flight.

Lazarus stood quickly. Whatever ailed him earlier seemed forgotten as he turned to Martha. "Martha, can we feed them?"

Martha stared at her brother. Jesus was about to be arrested by the Sanhedrin, and Lazarus was worried about whether they had enough food to feed him and his followers?

"Can we?" he asked again.

Martha pursed her lips and surveyed her cooking area. Purim would be meager for them alone; she couldn't possibly feed the disciples. And the wine. Not enough for twelve grown men and Jesus to have even one cup. And this was Purim, where wine was to flow freely and all drink their fill. It was the perfect excuse to keep Jesus out of Bethany. She shook her head. "Zakai, tell Josiah to find Jesus, to tell him not to—"

"I will host them," Simon interrupted. His thick lips bent into a smile in the silence that followed. "Please, Lazarus. Allow me to host the Purim feast for you and your friends."

Lazarus blinked. "For Jesus and his followers?"

Martha tried to keep her face smooth. Hadn't he just said that Jesus was a fraud? Why would Simon, a Pharisee, invite Jesus to his home? And would he tell the Sanhedrin?

Simon nodded, his eyes on Martha. "If your sister deems my humble home worthy and agrees to cook and serve us."

Martha took a step back, pulling Zakai with her. Simon was asking her to cook in his home? For Jesus? She fumbled for a reply. "But what about Jael? Won't your mother wish to cook for your guests?"

Simon looked pleased. "My mother left this morning to visit her people in Jerusalem. She will return after the feast. She will thank you for serving me in her absence."

Thank her? Jael would rather let vermin in her wheat than let another woman cook in her courtyard. Simon knew that as well as anyone. "Josiah"—she needed an excuse, anything to stop this madness—"and Mary and the children. We always—"

"Invite them as well. I have plenty for all."

Martha watched Lazarus, but he seemed at a loss for words. Josiah at Simon's table? Mary and the children in his courtyard? Jesus, with his blasphemous ideas, in Simon's company?

Simon rubbed his hands together. "It is decided." He pushed himself up from the bench. "Lazarus, I will listen to this kinsman of yours. I will question him." He smiled, as if he already knew the answers to his questions. "Perhaps your faith in him will be justified. Or perhaps I will prove my point about this so-called Messiah."

He snapped his fingers at Zakai. "You. Go to Josiah and invite him to my house."

Zakai looked to Martha, and she nodded, giving him a push to the door.

Simon smoothed his tunic and adjusted his cloak. "And, Lazarus, don't worry. For now, no one in Jerusalem needs to know that your kinsman is here. It will be our secret." Simon turned and leveled his gaze at Martha, his voice full of meaning. "I will begin the preparations. It is time for our two families to become better acquainted."

When the courtyard door had closed behind him, Martha covered her mouth with her hand. Was it relief or fear welling up in her chest? Jesus would be safe for now, but she had even more to worry about.

She would be cooking in Jael's home for Simon, the strictest Pharisee in Bethany, and Jesus, who spoke blasphemy. Not to mention Josiah, a man Simon thought a fool, and the disciples, who bickered like old women. And on Purim, the one night when the law encouraged the men to drink wine until they didn't know the difference between "Blessed be Mordecai" and "Cursed be Haman."

It was a recipe for disaster.

Lazarus pushed himself up from the stool, his face thoughtful. "Martha, I see now how the Lord is comforting us. He is rewarding us for our faithfulness."

Martha stared at her brother. Comforting them? It seemed more like the Lord was mocking them. How could Lazarus think this was a good thing? Jesus—not to mention poor Josiah—was stepping right into the lion's den. And she was cooking in the home of the one woman in Bethany whom she couldn't afford to anger.

Lazarus put a hand on her shoulder. "Martha. Don't you see?" His color was back, his grip strong, his face sure. "The Almighty has found you a husband. One who is generous and even willing to listen to Jesus."

"So that you can leave us." She couldn't keep the hurt from her voice. Now she knew why he wanted her married off.

"So that I can follow the Messiah, Martha. *The Messiah.*" He took a deep breath and leaned forward, nodding as if he'd come to a decision. "Martha, I am going to agree to the betrothal to Simon."

Panic rose in her chest, and her legs weakened. Was he ordering her to marry? "What? But, Lazarus—"

"It is for the best. Everyone's best, Martha." For a moment he looked just like Abba.

His best. He couldn't wait to get out of Bethany. She gripped his arm and lowered her voice, although only Penina and a sleeping Safta were within earshot. "But what about Zakai, Lazarus?"

His voice dropped as well. "You will tell Simon."

Martha's heart sped up. "Me?" How could she do that? How could she risk it? "He could have us driven out of Bethany. He could—"

"He won't." Lazarus's hands on her shoulders gentled. "He's a good man, didn't you just see that? He's going to listen to Jesus; not many Pharisees would do that. And he won't report him to the Sanhedrin. Martha, Simon is the answer to our prayers."

Martha swallowed her fear. She needed time. Time to think, to decide. "Give me a week to think about it, Lazarus."

Lazarus looked troubled for a moment, and his hand cupped his side. "No. You must tell him tomorrow."

Martha jerked back. *Why so soon?* Her legs grew weak. "No. I need more time."

"We don't have it." He grimaced as if in pain. "Show him tonight what a good wife you will be. Then tomorrow you will see. He will show you his mercy and forgiveness."

She tried to breathe, tried to think. Tomorrow? Everyone in Bethany believed the lie she lived—the wall of protection she'd built for Zakai, her reputation as a perfect woman. Simon believed it most of all. Would Simon really forgive her, as Lazarus said, or would he release a flood of retribution?

Her brother's face had the stubborn look that she knew well from Abba. Lazarus was the head of the family, and she was bound to obey him, just as she had been to obey Abba. Tonight, she must prove to Simon what a good wife she would be. Tomorrow, she would be like Esther, depending on Simon's mercy even if he—like King Xerxes—could have her slain with one word.

Trust in the Lord, Lazarus's silent gaze said to her. Instead, she wanted to run away, like Jonah when he heard the Lord's call. Was Simon her King Xerxes, or was he the belly of a fish?

Chapter Twenty-Three

Still, you insist on sincerity of heart; in my inmost being teach me wisdom
—*Psalm 51:8*

*I*SA'S ARMS BULGED, and his back strained at the half-buried rock. The parched earth gave way, and the boulder, three times the size of his head, broke free from its berth. Before he could heft it to his shoulder, a flash of yellow-green startled him, and a scorpion the size of his little finger scuttled from the recess under the rock.

A deathstalker. Its sting was excruciating, and often deadly. He crushed it under his sandal and peered beneath the rock, hoping there weren't more.

He wiped the sweat from his face. With this last boulder moved, the field would be cleared. Then what? He knew nothing more about who he was or where he belonged than he had when he'd come here seven days ago. Jesus' words haunted him. Why would he tell him to go to his family, without telling him where or who? And why had he crossed the Galilee to free a worthless pagan from a legion of demons?

The sun burned high in the hard blue sky, and dust dried his throat. He hefted the stone to the edge of the field and eyed the falling-down house. His stomach cried for food. Alexa would be waiting for him with his midday meal, but he'd be safer among the scorpions than being alone with her. Still, where else could he go?

Isa crossed the field to the house. He made his way through the courtyard, past a pile of broken wheels and a jumble of iron chains covered in rust. Did he have a home and family, or was he just another piece of refuse salvaged by Nikius, unwanted and unclaimed?

Alexa stood over the fire, stirring another pot of what he knew would be tasteless lentils. Not that he would complain—any food was better than nothing—but Alexa's cooking skills were limited to lentils flavored with dirty water, and dirty water flavored with lentils.

Alexa's other skills, though, were impressive. She could make him break out in a cold sweat with just one look of her kohl-rimmed eyes. Then his chill would be replaced by heat as she served him his meal, brushing her body against his so often that it couldn't be an accident. He was strong—he'd learned that as he lifted boulders the size of a man—but his strength was nothing compared to what she could do with one glance.

He felt her watching him now as he bent over a shallow barrel of rainwater. Reflected back at him was the face of a wild man. His hair hung over his shoulders and halfway down his back in thick hanks. A tangled beard clung to his neck. Even his brows were wild and unruly over eyes bruised with the shadows of sleepless nights—nights spent wondering who he was and trying not to think of the woman asleep just steps away from his rooftop bed. He scooped up water and was glad for the shock of cold on his face.

If only Alexa would avoid him like everyone else in Gerasene. The few times he'd gone into the village, women had run for their homes and the men had shouted threats. They knew who he was—what he was—and they were afraid. When he saw his reflection, he could hardly blame them.

He didn't look at Alexa as he lowered himself onto a bench, but his body warmed from more than the feeble fire crackling and snapping before him.

Alexa sauntered toward him with a bowl of water and bent

to untie his sandals. "Doesn't a good woman wash her brother's feet when he comes home?" she murmured in a low purr.

He didn't feel like her brother, and she didn't act like a sister. "Where's Nikius?" he asked, his voice breaking.

"Gone. Who knows how long?"

Isa gripped the edge of the bench, the wood biting into the palms of his hands as Alexa smoothed water over his feet, then caressed them dry with the hem of her tunic.

He let out his breath as she finished and tried to stand.

She pushed him down again. "Nothing to say, my quiet Hercules?"

What could he say when he could barely think? He shook his head.

She leaned closer. "Let me cut your hair."

His hand went to his shaggy head. She'd asked before to take scissors to the long mane of hair, and he'd refused. The less she touched him, the better. "No."

She lifted her hand and ran a finger over one of his brows, smoothing it into place.

The touch of her fingertip on his brow sparked through him like lightning. Not from her caress but the shadowy memory it brought forth. A remembered joy, sweet and intimate. A face, dear to him.

Then it was gone. Only Alexa's face was before him, her red lips drawn into a half smile, her brows arched in question. Who had he seen in that jolt of memory? If he could only get away from Alexa, perhaps he could remember.

But she had lowered herself into his lap, pinning him to the bench. She smoothed her palms over his temples and through his hair. The shadow of memory disappeared, replaced by the warmth of her body, the weight of her on his lap.

Alexa leaned against him, lifting her face to his.

His stomach turned at her cloying scent of sandalwood and smoke. His muscles tensed. How could he get away from her? He didn't want to hurt her. Her face came close to his, and her hand slipped up his chest. His heartbeat quickened, and his thoughts scattered as she leaned closer.

At the creak of the courtyard door and the crash of broken pottery he jerked back. Nikius stood in the doorway, a broken wine amphora at his feet, his brows raised in surprise.

Shame flooded through Isa as he realized what Nikius saw. Alexa straddling his legs, her tunic hiked above her knees, her hand curled around his neck. Isa opened his mouth, but no words loosed his tongue. What could he say? This was how he repaid the old man's kindness? He deserved the beating Nikius had saved him from.

But Nikius approached the fire without even a scowl, leaving the broken amphora in the dirt. "Get us some food, girl," he ordered, settling on the stool next to Isa.

Alexa rose slowly, her eyes on her father but no shame on her face. When she'd brought them each a bowl of lentils, Nikius cleared his throat and jerked his head at her. "Leave us."

Alexa smirked and sauntered into the house.

They ate in silence. When they'd both scraped the bottom of their bowls with the last hunks of dry bread, Nikius stood. Isa looked into the fire, readying himself for a blow, a beating, some punishment. But Nikius disappeared into the chaos of the courtyard, returning a moment later with two chipped cups. "Take this."

Isa accepted the cup filled to the brim with dark wine.

Nikius sat and took a long drink. "So. She finally got you, like a spider in her web." He smacked his lips. "That's my girl." His face twisted into a grimace.

Isa froze, the cup halfway to his lips. Nikius knew how his daughter had tormented him for a week?

Nikius looked into his wine, as if it held his own memories. "Her mother was much the same. Couldn't resist her. Then she ran off with a perfume peddler when Alexa was but a baby." He shook his head. "Don't much know what to do with a daughter."

Isa took a deep drink. The wine was heavy and cloying, sweetened with honey and scented with rose. It did not quench his thirst but overwhelmed his senses and made him wish for a drink of cold water.

Nikius's brows came together like two gray caterpillars as he gazed at Isa. "You don't say a lot, but you're a hard worker. And I could use another man around here."

Isa took another sip of his wine. Was Nikius asking him to stay? The thought both warmed and frightened him.

Nikius drained his cup and smacked his lips. "I don't hold much for marriage. Didn't work for me." He wiped his hand across his mouth. "But if I find my daughter in your bed one of these mornings, consider yourself her husband, and I'll be glad to consider you my son."

Isa's heart jolted, but not at the thought of Alexa slipping into his bed during the cold night. Nikius was offering him a home. He could stay here and make a life, have a family. He wouldn't be alone. All he needed to do was give in to Alexa's temptation.

Or he could leave here—alone, not knowing where to go. Was someone really waiting for him, or had that been another torture sent by the demons? Had the flash of memory at Alexa's touch been real or a trick of his lonely heart?

When dusk finally darkened the sky, Isa climbed the ladder to the roof of the house. He felt Alexa watching him, her gaze like a silken cloth brushing over his body. He fell on his sleeping mat, dragging his borrowed cloak over his shoulders to ward off the chill of the night. Sleep pulled at his worried mind. Tomorrow he'd decide what to do.

Moments—or perhaps hours—later warmth roused him, but his tired eyes stayed sealed. The air was cold on his face, so why did he feel like the sun heated his body? A form—warm and soft—pressed against him, hollows and curves fitting to his own. The scent of sandalwood tickled his nose.

A languorous heat curled through him. Hands slipped around his neck, and fingers threaded into his hair. His sluggish mind struggled to understand even as his pulse quickened.

He pulled his eyes open. Stars burned in the sky above, and moonlight reflected off Alexa's onyx eyes. Her face was close to his, her lips parted. The cloak slipped, revealing smooth skin above her loosened tunic.

Her lips pressed hungrily on his mouth. The taste of honeyed wine, the scent of her hair, the softness of her lips and body, overwhelmed his senses. But something clamored at the edge of his dulled mind.

This is wrong.

He jerked away. The woman in his arms . . . she shouldn't taste of wine, but of apricots. And her touch was sure and bold when it should be innocent and uncertain. The face before him—sly and knowing—was not the face he held dear. His heart constricted at a memory that was so sharp, so clear, he knew it had to be true.

He rolled away, struggled to stand, and staggered to the edge of the roof. He gulped deep breaths of night air as memories unfolded before him. Memories of a laughing girl with skin like polished bronze. A girl who smelled of cinnamon and fresh bread. The girl who was his only friend, his only family.

The woman he loved . . . and her name was Martha.

Chapter Twenty-Four

She enjoys the success of her dealings; at night her lamp is undimmed.
—*Proverbs 31:18*

AS THE SUN reached its zenith, Martha stood before the imposing door to Simon's courtyard, her pulse racing and her hands damp. Penina stood close behind her, and Martha thanked the Most High for her presence.

Simon himself opened the door. He clasped and unclasped his hands in front of his body as he greeted her. "Peace be with you, and peace to your house." He'd changed his clothes in the short time since he left her home. He wore a dull brown linen tunic and a wide belt of leather adorned with silver. Martha caught the strong whiff of myrrh from his freshly anointed hair and combed beard. Why did it have to be myrrh, the smell that would forever remind her of Abba's death?

Martha answered, "And may the Lord, Our Righteousness, bless you."

"I hope you will find my home to your liking and that all your needs are met. Please"—a silver signet ring flashed on his finger as he motioned her inside—"all that I have is yours."

Martha's face heated at his words. With his eyes locked on hers, he seemed to mean more than he said. She cleared her throat. "You honor me with your trust."

"Follow me, Martha," Simon commanded. He didn't acknowledge Penina any more than he acknowledged the ebony-skinned slave that hastened out of his path. He led them into the house. Micah, the old steward, and the two guards lounged in the shade beside the house. A wisp of a woman, one of Simon's servants who Martha knew from the marketplace, slipped along the wall. Martha nodded to her and received a thin smile in return. Were they wondering why she was here or glad Jael wouldn't be the one giving orders today?

Martha followed Simon into a wide hall. His home was bigger than she'd imagined and filled with beautiful and costly items. Jewel-toned carpets cushioned the stone floors, and chests of cedar strapped with iron sat against the walls.

They passed a room with a tall table strewn with parchments and wax tablets. Through the next doorway, she glimpsed a large bed, its thick mattress stuffed with straw and covered with heavy wool blankets. Simon glanced back and caught her eye.

She looked at her feet, her face burning. What was he thinking? That she was imagining their wedding night? She glimpsed a dining table and couches through the next doorway. A bronze brazier stood in one corner, and oil lamps were set on the walls, ready to be lit when the sun went down. There was room enough for at least twenty guests. Simon had not exaggerated his wealth to her brother.

Simon stopped in front of the next doorway. "I hope that you will find all you need. My servants are ready to do your bidding, and if you need anything—anything at all—you have only to ask, and it will be obtained." He flourished his hand toward the room.

Martha stepped into Simon's storeroom, and her mouth fell open. It was twice the size of hers and stocked from floor to ceiling with food, spices, and cooking utensils. It was paradise.

Grain jars lined one whole wall, symbols carved on them for wheat, spelt, and millet. Ropes of fat garlic and papery-skinned onions filled another wall, along with baskets of dried figs, apricots, and pressed cakes of dates. Dried herbs—myrtle, mint, and feathery dill—hung from the ceiling. Bowls of mustard seeds, every color from pale yellow to deep brown, lined another shelf.

A neat line of small jars caught her eye, each with the name of an exotic spice scratched into the clay—saffron and cinnamon, anise, coriander and cumin, as well as some she didn't recognize. She chose one, pulled out the carved wooden stopper, and sniffed. Its pungent aroma tickled her nose, and when she cracked a hard, black kernel between her teeth it seared her tongue, hotter than cumin seeds. She glanced at Simon.

A smile curled his heavy lips. "Pepper, from the eastern caravans."

Pepper. It was so costly, people said that even Herod locked his pepper up with his gold. She put it carefully back on the shelf and wiped a hand across her damp brow, glancing back at Penina.

Her friend's eyes stretched wide, and she raised her brows at Martha. If she married Simon, this would be her domain, Penina's look said. Hers and Jael's.

Martha fixed an expression of respect on her face. "I look forward to serving you. If you will allow me, I will begin preparations."

Simon nodded and brought her back to the courtyard. A short man with a patch over one eye tended a lamb roasting on a spit. The thin woman bent over a hand mill, already grinding the wheat. Two slaves, a girl and boy who must be related, stood by waiting for instructions. What to do first?

Simon still stood beside her, twisting his hands. "Please, let me know if you need anything else."

How many times must he say that, and when would he leave her to her work? "I have all I need, Simon."

He leveled his wide eyes on her. "I look forward to this evening. With you in my home, I know I can expect nothing less than perfection for my guests." With that, he turned abruptly and disappeared into the house.

HOURS LATER, THE feast was almost ready, and Martha felt as frayed as a ten-year-old cloak.

She sent the brother and sister from Egypt to ready the dining room. As they'd worked, she'd coaxed their story from them. Poor children, they'd been under Jael's thumb for just a year but already were counting the days until their seven years were done.

Laman, the old man with the patch, kept his one eye on the lamb and sang to them in a surprisingly good voice. The thin woman had eventually spoken a few words when she realized that Martha wasn't like her mistress. She'd even smiled when Martha had given her a few tidbits of lamb to share with Laman.

Simon had come out of the house several times, his arms crossed in front of his chest, watching her work. She swiped a hand over her brow. If only she could get away—go home, or to the orchard, anywhere but under Simon's gaze—for just an hour before Jesus came for the feast. But she still had too much to do.

Penina poured a jar of heated wine over a deep bowl of dried figs, apricots, and plums. Martha spooned on dark honey and stirred, breathing in the sweet, heady scent. This would be a fitting end to her perfect meal.

Penina sniffed. She hadn't said a word—in her way—since Simon had guessed Lazarus's intention to follow Jesus. But her face was drawn, and now her eyes were bright with unshed tears. Martha covered Penina's hands with her own. She glanced around the courtyard, but no one was close enough to hear her. "Tell him." Maybe if he knew how Penina felt, he'd stay.

Penina shook her head, and her mouth firmed.

Couldn't her brother see what he was leaving behind? A woman who loved him. And for what? Jesus was family, yes, but he also might get Lazarus killed. "Then let me tell him."

Penina grabbed her by the shoulders. She stared with fierce eyes at Martha and shook her head. She made the sign for Jesus and then put her hand over her heart.

Martha understood. "He loves Jesus, I know." *We all do. But that doesn't mean he needs to follow him into danger.*

Penina pointed to herself and shook her head.

Martha felt tears prick her eyes for her friend. "He does love you." He just couldn't see it yet. Penina blinked and turned away. She wouldn't make him choose between her and his Messiah. They both knew whom he'd choose, and it would break Penina's heart.

Martha stirred the fruits, the scent of wine and honey closing her throat. She couldn't do it either. She couldn't deny her brother his greatest wish—to follow the man he believed was the Messiah. It was her fault Lazarus worked from sunrise to dusk on a failing farm instead of studying with the doctors of the law as he had always wanted. Only she could give Lazarus his freedom.

Martha blinked back tears. She must marry Simon.

She turned back to the courtyard and her tasks. There could be no mistakes tonight; everything must be perfect. She would show Simon what a good wife she would be. Tomorrow, when the first light colored the sky, she'd tell Simon about Zakai. She'd just have to hope and pray Simon would be as forgiving as Lazarus believed. And then pray that Jesus wouldn't lead Lazarus to his death.

Chapter Twenty-Five

She reaches out her hands to the poor, and extends her arms to the needy.
—Proverbs 31:20

*M*ARTHA WATCHED PENINA ladle the lamb—so tender it fell from the bone—onto a platter. She stacked hot rounds of bread on another, anxiety twisting through her empty stomach. It was a feast fit for King Herod. A Purim celebration that even Abba would approve of—rich food, fine wine, everything.

Simon would be pleased. He must be pleased. *Please, Lord, let him see what a good wife I will be.*

She hastened to the house. Jesus had arrived with his disciples, but there had been no joyous greeting, no embraces as when he dined at her home. Simon had greeted Jesus correctly, but his mouth turned down in a disapproving frown as he surveyed the band of poorly dressed Galileans.

She peeked into the dining room. Simon reclined on the center couch, Jesus on his left side and Lazarus on his right. Even from here, she could see Lazarus looked pale. Was he as worried as she was about tonight? He should be.

On Lazarus's other side sat two men from Bethany. The husband of Devorah, Abel—a rotund man with hands covered in flashing rings—was a city judge and a Pharisee. Tobias, the olive grower and also a Pharisee, watched Jesus with critical eyes. Farther down the table the disciples reclined with their wine cups, already abiding by the dictate to drink well. When Matthew, the tax collector Jesus kept in his company, laughed loudly at something Peter said, Abel's face looked like he had eaten a bad olive.

She prayed Jesus and his followers would not offend Simon's friends. Not only for her sake but for Jesus'. Simon might not bring the Temple guards to Bethany, but she wasn't so sure about Abel or Tobias. She bustled back to the courtyard. If she could keep them all eating, they wouldn't be able to question Jesus or be angered by his unorthodox teachings.

A shout sounded from outside the courtyard. What now? She went to the door, where Simon's guards held a tired-looking man by both his arms. Beyond him, a woman sat on a skinny donkey. Their clothes were threadbare and foreign, northerners perhaps, coming to Jerusalem on pilgrimage. "What is this?"

One of the guards scowled at her. "Beggars."

Micah jerked a thumb at the guard. "Get rid of them."

Martha turned on him. "Surely not." They couldn't refuse a traveler welcome.

Micah's hard expression didn't alter.

"At least give them some food." She motioned to the Egyptian girl. "Get some bread. And meat."

The girl looked at her with wide eyes, then at Micah.

"No, you don't." Micah shook his head. "The master won't like it."

Martha blew out a breath. "That's ridiculous. It's Purim."

Micah raised his chin in defiance, and a hint of fear showed in his eyes. "No."

What was he afraid of? Whatever it was, she wasn't about to turn away hungry pilgrims on Purim. "Go ahead and ask him."

Micah pivoted and marched into the house. She followed. Simon would clear this up. If she was going to be mistress of this house, the servants must respect her.

In the dining room, Simon straightened as they approached him, his eyes narrowing. Micah bent and whispered to him. Simon's gaze went to Martha. "Foreigners?" Simon asked.

Micah nodded.

"We've already given to the poor, the ones who deserve it." Simon scowled and waved his hand.

Surely he didn't mean it. Abba would never deny food to hungry travelers. "But, Simon—"

The shocked look on Simon's face stopped her. She couldn't speak to him, not here in front of the men. She pressed her lips together and caught Lazarus's eye. The disciples shifted uncomfortably. Jesus watched Simon, his face unreadable.

Simon lifted his wine cup. "He who touches pitch blackens his hands." Abel and Tobias murmured in agreement. Simon nodded to Martha. "Bring the food for my guests."

She followed Micah out of the house and watched helplessly as he shut the door against the tired couple.

Martha turned back to her work. This was Simon's home; he could deny food to a wanderer if he chose. But if he could deny food when he had so much, was he really as upright and merciful as Lazarus thought?

She brought in the bread. Penina carried a wide bowl of the roasted lamb, anointed with cumin sauce and sprinkled with sesame seeds. After Simon said the blessing over the bread, Penina set the meat in the center of the table. The men tore the bread in hunks, dipping and scooping meat into their mouths. Simon closed his eyes as he chewed, then looked at Martha and nodded, but his approval failed to ease her worried mind.

She brought in the next dish, setting it close to Jesus. She'd made it especially for him. A trio of vegetables—onions, artichoke hearts, and fennel—roasted in the best olive oil and sprinkled with briny olives. When he tasted a bite and smiled at her, her heart lightened for a moment.

Simon announced loudly that he had gone to the Temple earlier in the day. There, he had seen a tax collector. "He could do nothing but beat his breast and say, 'Lord, have mercy on me, a sinner.'" Simon shook his head sadly. "I thanked the Lord that I was not like that man," he said, looking pointedly at Matthew, sitting at the foot of the table. Matthew's cheeks reddened, and

Martha felt a surge of sympathy for the disciple everyone knew had been a tax collector before he began to follow Jesus.

One by one, she presented the rest of the dishes. Spiced peahen eggs on a bed of fresh greens and chopped herbs. Dates stuffed with ground almonds and honey. Asparagus drizzled with aged vinegar and sprinkled with Simon's precious pepper.

Jesus ate only small portions of the food she set before him and drank sparingly of the wine. He talked in a low voice to Lazarus and complimented Simon, as was appropriate. Abel and Tobias said nothing, their mouths full and their chins dripping.

Simon boasted to his captive audience, signaling to Martha when a wine cup needed refilling or a guest needed another portion. Before the last dish was served, everyone at the table knew he fasted twice a week, gave ten percent to the Temple, and owned all the wheat fields around Bethany.

Martha returned to the courtyard. It was time for the last dish. Then she could eat with the women and children. Thank the Most High, the dinner had been perfect. Simon would find no fault with her tonight.

Penina held a shallow platter as Martha poured out the warm compote of dried fruit steeped in the honeyed wine. Martha sprinkled handfuls of toasted pistachios over the fruits that glistened like jewels, then hefted the heavy platter. This would be the crowning glory of her perfect meal. It would take long into the night to clean all the pots and leave the courtyard spotless, but Simon would see that she did not shirk the duties of a good wife. And tomorrow, he would overlook her sins. She would be able to keep Penina and Zakai and Safta safe, and Lazarus could go with Jesus.

As she carried the platter carefully toward the house, the jangle of bracelets and a flash of color made her jerk to a stop. The fruits slid sideways, but she righted the platter just in time. Mary swept across the courtyard in her pink tunic and yellow belt, her every movement accompanied by the jingle of brass bangles. Late again.

The girls were dressed in their best tunics, their hair combed and faces washed. Josiah followed behind his wife, his head swiveling to take in the large courtyard and even larger house.

"Is he here?" Mary asked, heading toward the house. "I will greet him, then help you serve."

Martha stepped in front of the door and jerked her head to Micah. "Take Josiah in." There was room for him at the foot of the table.

Martha let Josiah and Micah pass by but blocked Mary with the platter. "You can see Jesus later, after dinner." Mary couldn't embarrass her this time. "I'll finish the serving."

Mary's hand shifted behind her, but Martha caught sight of the jar of nard and irritation rose in her. "Mary. Not this again," Martha snapped. She couldn't have Mary traipsing in to anoint Jesus. It would ruin everything she'd worked for. "Go sit with the children and the other women." She looked for help, but only her grandmother was there, sitting on a bench next to the wall. "Safta, tell her."

But Safta raised her brows. "This is your fight, my girl. But don't make the mistake of thinking it's with your sister."

She let out a breath. Couldn't Safta take her side just once? Or even say something that made sense?

"Jesus will welcome me," Mary said with conviction. "You know he will."

"Mary, please," Martha pleaded. *Please don't embarrass me. Not tonight, not with Simon.* And they needed that nard if they were to eat this spring. But with her hands full, she couldn't stop her sister from brushing past her and entering the dining room like Esther going before the king, but without the fear and trembling.

Martha followed to find Mary settled at the end of Jesus' couch, a loving smile on her face. The scent of nard filled the room as she smoothed the oil over Jesus' feet. Every man's eye was fixed on Mary in shocked silence.

Abel recovered first. "What? Josiah, will you allow your wife to join us at the table?"

Josiah took a bite of bread, chewing thoughtfully and watching Jesus. Judas sputtered about the cost of the precious oil.

Martha sent Lazarus a pleading look. *Please, send her away.*

Mary bent her head and kissed Jesus' feet.

Simon coughed as though he had choked on a mouthful of food. "Lazarus, tell your sister to leave us and join the women in the courtyard."

Lazarus looked to Jesus. "What do you say, teacher?"

"Leave Mary alone," Jesus said finally. "What she has done for me is good."

Simon's face turned red, and a muscle twitched in his jaw. "This is no place for a woman."

Jesus inclined his head to Simon. "You did not give me the kiss of peace when I entered your home, but she has not stopped kissing my feet since she came to me."

Simon turned to Lazarus. "This is an outrage. Surely this proves my point about this . . . *messiah* of yours?"

Jesus went on as if Simon hadn't spoken. "You did not anoint my head with oil, Simon, but she has anointed my feet and prepared me for my burial."

The disciples looked at each other warily.

Martha's hands clenched the tray of fruit as anxiety clamped her chest in a vise. Why did Mary have to be so disgraceful? Lazarus would never go against Jesus, and Simon would lose face in front of his friends. Then what would happen tomorrow when she confessed her own disgrace? She had to do something.

Martha set the tray down next to Jesus. "Lord." Could Jesus hear the plea in her voice? "Do you not care that my sister has left me by myself to do the serving?"

Mary gasped and looked up at her, hurt in her eyes.

I'm sorry, Mary. Martha didn't want to humiliate her sister, and a rebuke from Jesus would wound her, but she had no choice. Jesus would help her; surely he understood. "Please, cousin. Tell her to help me."

Jesus looked at Martha for a long moment. His gaze slipped

to Lazarus, waiting for his response, and then to Simon, whose lips were pulled down in a scowl.

Jesus laid a hand on her arm. "Martha, Martha." His voice was soft, but the words hit her like blows from a hammer. "You are anxious and worried about many things." He nodded to Mary. "But there is need of only one thing. Mary has chosen the better part, and it will not be taken from her."

Chapter Twenty-Six

She fears not the snow for her household; all
her charges are doubly clothed.
—Proverbs 31:21

MARTHA FELT AS though a jar of cold water had been thrown in her face.

Mary had chosen the better part? The silence in the room pressed down on her. Jesus' eyes were filled with sadness and sympathy, as though he knew how much pain his words had caused.

Martha pulled away from Jesus, the burn of humiliation replacing her icy shock. She turned and ran from the room, desperate to get away from Jesus, Mary—all of them.

She rushed through the house blinking back tears, barely seeing the servants scattering before her. In the courtyard, she brushed past Penina, who made a small sound and turned as though to follow her, but Martha shook her head and pushed through the heavy door.

She ran—past the garden, across the stream—and kicked through the carpet of brittle leaves to the center of the orchard. There, next to the ancient tree, she sank down, leaned her face on the rough bark, and let her tears flow.

You are worried about many things. Yes, Jesus was right about that. She had many things to worry about. Her betrothal to Simon. Penina and Zakai. Even about Jesus' own safety and what would happen to Lazarus as his disciple.

Who would worry about all these things if not her?

Jesus didn't know all she had weighing on her. The anxiety that woke her early every morning, the heavy weight of her responsibilities. He didn't know her secret and how, above all else, she must please Simon tonight. Yes, she was worried about many things.

Martha leaned against the thick trunk, as rough and solid as it had been the night she and Isa had lain beside it. That night had been warm, the fragrant breeze drifting over their bodies like a soft blanket. Tonight, the wind punished her, whipping her hair against her face and clawing at her tunic.

Mary has chosen the better part? Mary, who rarely had bread baked? Who said "the Lord will provide" and then thanked the Lord when it was Martha who brought food for her family and clothes for her children? Mary, ridiculed by all the women of Bethany? How could Mary have chosen the better part when Martha tried so hard to do everything right?

She wiped her eyes with the back of her hand. Jesus hadn't wanted to humiliate her; she knew that from the love in his face. But he had. In front of everyone. *There is need of only one thing,* he'd said. What? What was the one thing?

She picked up a fallen twig and began to strip off its curling bark, sniffling. Abba would say the law was the one thing. But Mary didn't follow the laws, not like she should, and neither did Jesus. Mary didn't worry about what the women of Bethany—or the men, she'd proven tonight—thought of her. Just as Jesus didn't seem to care when he angered the powerful Pharisees.

Mary cared only for showing her love for Jesus, for welcoming him and believing that he was the Chosen One. *How does she know?* How could she know without a doubt that Jesus was the Messiah?

It was simple, she'd said last time. But it wasn't simple. Not for Martha.

Martha threw down the stick, now stripped of its outer bark and as smooth and naked as a newborn baby. Her devotion to the law, her hard work and the respect that it bought her in Bethany, those things she knew. Those things protected her and Zakai and Penina. As much as she loved Jesus—she couldn't believe he was the Messiah. Not like Mary and Lazarus did.

If that's the better part Jesus speaks of, I can't choose it.

Chapter Twenty-Seven

*For the Lord gives wisdom, from his mouth
come knowledge and understanding.*
—Proverbs 2:6

LAZARUS RAN UP the path toward the Mount of Olives, his breath wheezing hard and fast in his chest. The moon was barely a sliver and the sky almost without stars. A cold wind whipped his cloak and rustled the leaves in the shadows of the olive grove. Jesus and the disciples couldn't be much farther. He could catch them before they crested the mountain and started down to Jerusalem.

He didn't blame Jesus for leaving so soon. Simon had treated the Galileans more like unwelcome relatives than honored guests. After Martha left, Simon had gone from impolite to rude, quizzing Jesus on his knowledge of the law, scowling deeper with each answer Jesus gave.

After dinner, Jesus and his disciples excused themselves to go pray, but Simon had pulled Lazarus aside. "Your friend," he'd said, "is dangerous. I won't be able to protect him if he continues with this outrageous talk."

Lazarus stumbled to a stop and bent double, the pain in his side intensifying. *It is a test, and I won't let it stop me.*

Simon had been rude, but he would see that he was wrong. Soon, Jesus would dispel all doubt. Even Simon would believe, as would Martha and Penina.

Poor Martha. He'd seen the pain on her face at Jesus' rebuke and felt her humiliation. But Mary had been the only one giving Jesus the honor he was due. Surely Martha could see that. He pushed his feet up the path. He'd find Martha, talk to her, after he spoke to Jesus.

Around a bend in the path, he sighted an indistinct shape and called out with the last of his breath. A few more steps brought him to Peter at the rear of the group. The rest of the disciples and Jesus stopped farther ahead on the path.

"Why are you leaving?" he gasped out.

Peter answered, "He wants to pray in the garden, on the other side of the mountain."

"So late?" Only brigands and thieves traveled in the night. "Why not wait until morning? You can stay with me tonight."

Peter shrugged. "We go with him. We'll sleep there." He pulled his cloak tighter around him, looking as though sleeping in the cold night air wasn't his idea. "Perhaps it's not safe in Bethany."

Lazarus felt a tingle of alarm. Peter might be right about that. He wouldn't be surprised if Simon or one of his Pharisee friends had sent messengers to the Sanhedrin as soon as they'd left the table. He looked past Peter, up the rocky path to where Jesus stood. "Jesus, can I speak to you?" He didn't need the other disciples listening. What would they think of him? Would they want him as one of their number?

Jesus nodded for Peter and the rest to go on and came down the hill to stand in front of Lazarus.

Lazarus's mouth went dry. He'd known this man since he was a child. He'd worked with him, eaten with him, laughed with him. Why was he so nervous to ask a simple question? He looked at Jesus, his worn cloak so familiar, his dark hair and beard the same as any other Jewish man's.

But he was different. This man, this son of Mary and Joseph, was the Messiah. The one they'd hoped for, prayed for, waited for. He knew Jesus was the Anointed One like he knew that the stars still shone beyond the lowering clouds, like he knew the moon would return to a full circle in a few days' time. And he needed to follow this man more than he needed to draw his next breath.

"Jesus, please." He raised his eyes to his friend's face. "I believe you are the One who has come. The Messiah. Let me follow you and be one of your disciples."

Jesus didn't answer for a long moment. Finally, he spoke, his voice gentle. "Lazarus, my friend. Where I am going, you cannot follow."

Lazarus reached out and grasped Jesus' arm. "Lord, please. I can. I can go anywhere you go." He sounded like a child, but he didn't care.

Jesus shook his head, his voice firm. "You cannot come after me."

Lazarus dropped his hand as if he'd been burned. "I beg you, Lord." He heard the desperation in his own voice. He was willing to give up anything—his home, his sisters, Penina. "Let me be part of the coming of the Kingdom."

Jesus wrapped his arms around Lazarus and pulled him to his chest. Lazarus felt Jesus take a deep breath. He closed his eyes. This was where he needed to be. With this man, his friend and his Messiah. Surely Jesus knew that.

Jesus pressed a kiss to his cheek, the kiss of peace. When he pulled back, Lazarus felt bereft, more alone than when Abba had died. Jesus looked into his eyes, speaking clearly and slowly, as though he needed Lazarus to understand not only his words but the meaning behind them. "You have faith in my Father; have faith in me also, my friend." His eyes were bright with tears. "The hour is coming when the dead will hear the voice of the son of God."

Lazarus tried to understand, but Jesus' words made no sense. "But, Jesus . . ." What did he mean by that? When would the hour come?

Jesus gazed at him. "Lazarus, do you love me?"

Lazarus straightened. This he understood. This was the important question. "Yes, Lord, you know that I love you."

"If you love me, do as I ask. Go back to your home and your sisters. You will understand when the time comes."

Lazarus's heart sank, and a burden settled on his shoulders like a yoke of lead. *When the time for what comes?* But Jesus had spoken, and he nodded, unable to speak.

Jesus embraced Lazarus again—fiercely, tightly—as though willing him a strength that Lazarus would need. And then Jesus was gone, through the black trees and into the night.

The gloom closed around Lazarus, and the cold wind bit through his cloak. Jesus didn't want him. He accepted Judas, a man no one trusted, and Peter, an uneducated fisherman. Even Matthew, a tax collector. *But not me.*

The dead will hear the voice of the son of God. What did that mean? His breath caught, and the pain in his side matched the pain in his heart. *If you love me, do as I ask.* He did love Jesus— more than he loved his sisters, more than Zakai or Penina—and Jesus had told him to stay in Bethany. He sank down on a rock and put his head in his hands. Whatever Jesus meant, Lazarus knew one thing. He would not be a part of the coming of the Kingdom.

Yes, Lord, I love you. Even as his heart was breaking.

Chapter Twenty-Eight

Cleanse me with hyssop, that I may be pure;
wash me, make me whiter than snow.
—Psalm 51:9

LIKE DIVING INTO the cold waters of Galilee, the memories flooded through Isa. Her name was Martha, and she lived in Bethany.

Joy surged within his chest even as something else—something akin to panic—pricked at the edges of his mind. There was more, and it was something he didn't want to remember. Something terrible.

Alexa sat up, her tunic gaping low. He had to get away from her. He clambered down the ladder, jumped the last rungs, and pushed through the courtyard door. Then he started to run.

He tried not to think, tried not to let the memories flow through his mind like a river breaking through a dam, choking off his breath, immersing him under a tide of shame and regret.

What have I done? The question drummed through his head as his feet pounded on the dirt. He sprinted through the town and out into the dark wasteland. Only one place could shut out the memories that threatened to drown him.

He reached the tombs and ducked into the mouth of the cave where he'd spent so many anguished nights. He fell to his knees inside, laying his head on the stone bench. But the smell of death and the darkness pressing down on him did not shut out his memories. They attacked him, piercing him like a thousand arrows.

Martha. A smiling girl, the only good thing in his life. Her laughter as they climbed the trees in the orchard, the taste of warm apricots in his mouth . . . How his heart broke for her when she lost her mother . . . Walking into Bethany with a rush of joy when he saw her again. Then the memory that made his heart writhe in regret. Those same trees, this time in full bloom. A carpet of blossoms and Martha, older and even more beautiful, giving herself to him.

Not like Alexa, with brazen hands and a greedy mouth. Not to trap him. But out of love and desperation. She'd asked him—begged him—to go to her father. But he'd been too afraid.

I'll make you the happiest woman in all of Judea. He heard his own voice, saw the trust in her eyes. But he hadn't. Martha had given him—a pagan, despised by everyone in Bethany—her most precious gift. He'd taken what she'd given him and left her. He squeezed his eyes shut . . . Left her seven years ago.

The cool air of the cave wrapped around Isa like a shroud. What had happened after he left Martha in Bethany?

He remembered leaving the orchard at first light with the memory of Martha's love and a joy in his chest that even Zerubbabel's stick couldn't beat out of him. He'd told himself he'd return in glory—with silver enough to satisfy Sirach—and they would marry amid the music of the kinnor and feasting. He put his hand over his face. *I was such a child. Such a fool.*

After that, his memories blurred. Isa knocked his head against the cold stone.

Why hadn't he returned to Bethany for Martha? His head thrummed with a dull ache. And where was Zerubbabel?

He crawled to the farthest recess of the tomb. Even the torment of demons couldn't be worse than facing what he'd done. He groaned and rolled into a miserable ball.

For seven years, a corner of his tortured mind had tried to turn him back to Martha, told him that she was waiting for him.

Surely by now, Sirach had made her marry. But after he had taken her purity, how would she find a husband who would accept her?

The ache in his head turned to throbbing, then pounding. A chill eddied through the cave, a whisper that fed his despair. He couldn't go back to her now. He couldn't face her. If she had married another, she wouldn't want him. And if she wasn't married . . . she wouldn't want the man who had deserted her. A man polluted by demons.

He closed his eyes. He'd be better off here, in this place of darkness.

But the words that Jesus had said to him whispered even in that hidden corner. *Go to your family. Announce to them all that the Lord in his pity has done for you.*

A weak shaft of the morning sun pierced the gloom of the cave.

Martha was his home. She was his family. *Go home*.

He pushed himself up and crawled toward the mouth of the cave. His body felt heavy, like it was filled with sand. He reached the doorway as the sun rose in the east. He breathed deeply of the breeze that brought the scent of water. Jesus, son of the Most High God—the God of the Jews—had come to save him. Jesus had commanded the demons, and they had obeyed. And he had given Isa a command as well.

He stepped out into the lightening day. He would go to her, even as his heart quaked at what he would find in Bethany. He could be there in three days. Not long, compared to seven years, but it seemed like a lifetime.

He longed to see her face. He dreaded seeing her face.

He hoped he wasn't too late.

Chapter Twenty-Nine

She makes her own coverlets; fine linen and purple are her clothing.
—Proverbs 31:22

MARTHA SMOOTHED HER damp hands down her best tunic and arranged her pink linen head covering for the tenth time. Her stomach curdled like spoiled milk, and her mouth tasted of vinegar. No sense putting it off any longer. It was time to go to Simon.

As she'd tossed on her bed during the long, sleepless night, she'd heard Lazarus stumble in close to dawn. He'd probably spent the night praying with Jesus and making plans to follow him as soon as her betrothal was in place. No sense waking him before she went; she knew what she had to do.

Martha nodded to Penina. "Let's go." At least she'd have Penina to strengthen her.

How she wished to have Mary's blessing, Mary's support as she faced Simon. But she knew Mary would be against a marriage to Simon. Mary would never understand, especially after last night. And how could she? Mary didn't know what Martha had done to Abba . . . And she didn't know about Zakai.

Martha brought Zakai's face to her mind. She loved Zakai more than she ever thought she could love. He would have a father and security if Simon was as forgiving as Lazarus believed. And if Lazarus was wrong—she took Penina's hand in hers—she wouldn't think of what might happen.

Martha shook her head at Penina's unvoiced dispute. "Lazarus is right. Simon is the answer to our prayers." If she said it enough, perhaps she, too, would believe it.

They walked the path along the ravaged garden, the wilted brown stalks trampled down in the dirt. Farther on, the thin light of morning lit Simon's flourishing plots of wheat and barley, untouched by the curse of the locusts.

Prosperity rewards the righteous, the Pharisees said. Clearly, the Lord had blessed Simon, who followed the law. Just look at his fields, at his home and wealth. How much clearer did the Lord of All need to be?

Penina made a small noise.

Martha stopped and faced her. The sun shone down on Penina's smooth cheeks and red-rimmed eyes. "You want him to be free to follow his heart, Penina, just like I do. And this is the only way he will be."

Penina lowered her eyes, but Martha had seen her pain. Yes, Penina wanted Lazarus to be free, but when he followed his heart, he would break hers.

"Simon will take in you and Zakai, and Safta, too." He'd even offer protection for Jesus if Lazarus was right. And protection for Jesus meant protection for Lazarus. She'd be a fool to reject what he was offering. She'd been a fool once already. Now the Almighty was giving her a second chance.

Again Penina shook her head and added a stamp of her foot.

Martha took a deep breath. "Lazarus says not to worry." She looked around, but they were alone. Still, she lowered her voice. "He says this is for the best . . . everyone's best."

Penina's look said she didn't believe it. Her hands went to her heart.

Martha snorted. "Love?" But her heart softened toward her friend. Penina was only trying to help. "I chose love once. And look what happened." She needed more than that now. "Simon is a good man. He will be merciful, just as the Lord showed him mercy." But would a man who turned away the hungry on Purim show mercy on her? Especially after Mary had made such a spectacle of herself last night?

Martha continued down the path, but as they reached the door of Simon's courtyard, her feet slowed and her hand tightened in Penina's. The thin servant woman opened the door, her brows arching high as she saw Martha. Simon's ever-present guards lounged against the wall of the house but straightened when they saw her and rested their hands on the daggers in their belts.

Martha glanced sideways at Penina. What did the guards think they were here to do, steal the spices from Simon's storeroom? Martha steadied her breathing. This would be her household soon. The servants and the dim-witted guards needed to respect her. "I would speak to your master." Her voice came out sure and strong.

The woman nodded and hurried away. Martha glanced at Penina, who was scowling again. She nudged her. "Penina, try to look . . ." She blew out a breath.

Penina rolled her eyes and held up her hands as if she didn't know what Martha meant. Penina had never acted like a slave, or even a servant. She probably wouldn't start now.

Martha stepped in front of her friend. "Just stay behind me."

Simon appeared behind the scurrying servant. His brows lifted, and his fishlike eyes widened. "You honor me with your presence, Martha." He clasped his hands over his loose tunic.

How thin Simon was. Martha prayed his habit of fasting twice a week had made him more merciful. She took a deep breath. "Peace be within the walls of your home and upon you and your servants."

He inclined his head, a question still in his eyes. "And may the Lord bless you and yours."

Martha waited. She hadn't come to speak to him in the presence of the nosy servant or his guards. She glanced toward the double doors of his home.

He started, finally understanding. "Please, Martha. Follow

me." Simon turned and walked swiftly through the wide arches. Martha followed without a word. At least he wouldn't bring up her disgrace last night in front of Jesus. A man of importance left the gossip to the women, and they were surely gossiping at the well this morning.

After saying the prayer beside the mezuzahs, Simon led her to his workroom and settled behind a teak desk. He nodded her to a chair with ornately carved arms and curving legs. She perched on the edge. Penina took a post just inside the doorway, her arms folded over her chest, to make sure that no one would lurk close enough to overhear them.

Martha ran her tongue over her dry mouth. It was surely unusual for a woman to visit a man, but at least he was giving her a chance to speak. *Lord of all, give me the words I need to say.* She stilled her hands in her lap, took a gulp of air, and looked up at Simon.

He watched her, his hands toying with a wax tablet.

She'd rehearsed the words in her mind, but still they sounded forced in the quiet room. "Lazarus has spoken to me about your offer of marriage. My father would be pleased."

Simon's face was unreadable. "Your father was a good and holy man. May his memory be forever honored and his name be spoken on the lips of his grandchildren."

A proper response. But the next part was going to be harder. Much harder. "Simon—" No words came to her, and the silence lengthened.

"Martha." Simon leaned forward. "Do you know why I want to marry you?"

Martha blinked. Because he liked her cooking? Because he needed a wife?

His jaw twitched. "Everyone in Bethany calls me Simon the Leper." He looked down at the stylus in his hand. "Except you."

Martha relaxed her grip on the arms of the chair. Lazarus had been right. Simon knew what it was to have a shameful past. He knew how a village never forgets. He would understand. "Simon, I must tell you something. Before the betrothal. And then you can decide if you still want me."

Simon's mouth pulled down in a grimace. "Martha. I already know."

Chapter Thirty

Her husband is prominent at the city gates as
he sits with the elders of the land.
—Proverbs 31:23

ALARM SURGED THROUGH Martha. How could he know?

Simon rubbed his neck. "You are marrying me because you are in debt and your brother wants to follow Jesus. *Jesus*." He rolled his eyes. "A poor Galilean whom Lazarus thinks is the Messiah. Once you, your servants, and your grandmother are taken care of, he can get himself nailed to a—"

Martha pulled in a sharp breath.

"Forgive me," Simon said quickly. "Believe me, I'll do all I can to make sure he is safe." He leaned forward. "Martha, I will be a good husband. And you will be the perfect wife for me."

The perfect wife. Martha's mouth was as dry as an abandoned well. If that's what he wanted, he would be disappointed. She gripped the arms of her chair hard. "Simon. There is something—something else—you must know about me. And then"—she dared a look at him—"if you still want me, we will be married."

Simon sat back in his chair and folded his hands over his lap. "I do, Martha. I will." He smiled at her as if she were a silly child. "But please, say what you need to say."

Martha took a deep breath. "My father . . ." No. She was to blame. Not Abba. "I have kept a secret for many years. A secret that I must tell you now, before we are betrothed."

Simon's brows came together, and he opened his mouth as if to speak. Martha stumbled on; she couldn't stop now. "Do you remember when my father took me to care for a kinswoman in Galilee? I was gone for half a year."

"Yes."

She rushed on. "When I returned, it was with Penina and her infant son, Zakai."

"Yes." His brow furrowed deeper.

Martha ran her tongue over her lips. *Just say it.* She looked down at her hands. "Simon. Zakai is not Penina's son."

"Not her son?" He glanced at Penina, then at her. "I don't understand."

She stared at her hands, unable to look at his face. The nicks from her cooking knives and scars from long-ago burns held her eyes as though they were the words of scripture. "My father made Penina swear to tell no one. But you must know . . ." She clenched her hands on the chair. "You *will* know if we marry. Zakai is my son."

Martha slowly raised her eyes from her lap to his hands, lying flat on the polished wood. To his shoulders. To his face. Simon's mouth worked as if he were choking on an olive pit.

Now that she'd started, she couldn't stop more words leaking from her mouth. "I have not married . . . my father did not let me marry . . . because I am not a virgin."

She should have felt better, confessing to Simon. Should have felt the weight of the lie lessen on her shoulders. Instead, she felt the burden grow. Penina's breath sounded loud in the doorway; the talk of the servants and the bray of a donkey in the courtyard drifted through the room.

Simon found his voice. "Zakai—the boy—is your son?" He frowned, as though learning a difficult lesson. "Sirach took you away to have the baby. He bought you a slave woman and said the child was hers."

Martha didn't speak.

Simon pushed himself away from the table and stood. "Such

a pious man, your father." His lips curled, and his voice was as bitter as willow bark. He paced to the window.

Martha peeked at Penina. She was standing like a statue in the doorway, tense, her hands tight as if ready to protect Martha with her fists if needed.

Simon snorted. "A pious man." He turned to face them. "So pious that after I came back from the leper colony, after I"—he jammed his finger into his chest and his voice rose—"paid for my sin, he turned his back on me. I live with my shame every day in this unforgiving village. But not Sirach's daughter."

Martha's heart sped up. She hadn't realized how much Abba's rejection had hurt Simon. Now, would she pay for Abba's sins as well as her own?

Simon stared out the window as though he'd forgotten Martha's presence. He ran a hand over his neck, again and again until Martha thought he might rub the skin off.

"What a good man, taking in a slave and her infant," he muttered in a voice barely above a whisper. "A holy man. A man who told me his daughter—his sinful, defiled daughter—was too good for me."

Martha's stomach knotted.

Simon spun around, facing her again. "I asked him again, a year after I'd been declared clean, for you. He said no." His face twisted. "And all the while, you were the impure one. You. Not me."

Martha tried to breathe as fear rose in her chest. Simon had assumed Abba had rejected him because he had been a leper. Instead, Abba had been protecting her. Because Abba had known what Lazarus did not . . . Simon was not a merciful man.

Simon crossed the room to tower over her. "I won't bother to ask who the father was. If you didn't tell Sirach, you won't tell me."

She looked up at him, surprised.

"I knew your father, Martha." He answered her unspoken question with a flick of his hand. "He followed the law. He would have found the man and made him marry you. Or seen him punished." Simon took a deep breath and blew it out through his nose. "Does Lazarus know?"

She nodded.

"And he expects me to take them in?" He motioned to Penina. "Your slave and your own bastard son. As well as your ill-natured grandmother?"

Martha looked him in the face and straightened her back. Now was not the time to cower. "She's not a slave. And Zakai knows nothing of this. I would expect you to treat them all with respect and"—she swallowed—"teach Zakai a trade."

Simon jerked again to the window, where he looked out at his courtyard. He rubbed his hands over his eyes and through his hair. Martha snuck a glance at Penina. Her friend's face was pale.

Simon turned back, crossing his arms over his chest. "I could have you driven from Bethany. All of you."

Martha didn't answer. They both knew it was the truth.

"But I won't."

She let out a breath she didn't know she was holding.

Simon sat again at his desk, as if preparing to do business with a seed merchant or buy a yoke of oxen. "In three days, Lazarus will sign the ketubah, and our betrothal will be announced."

Martha leaned forward. He was accepting her? So easily?

He picked up the stylus and made a note on the wax tablet. "Send Lazarus to me on the morning of the day after the Sabbath. Early." His mouth twisted. "We will announce our happy news at the village gate that afternoon."

Three days. Three days until she was legally bound to Simon.

He set down the stylus and stood, walking around the desk and coming to stand before her. He rested his hands on the carved arms of her chair and leaned forward, his face just a breath from hers.

"Hear me, Martha. For this is the only time I will say this to you. You will never—*never*—dishonor me." His voice was soft, but in it was the threat she understood. To her, her son, and everyone she loved. "In my home you will follow my laws. You will be hardworking, modest, and obedient to my every word. By the God of Abraham, the God of Isaac, and the God of Jacob, you will not speak to *anyone* of whom I do not approve." Simon did not move, but watched as understanding flooded through her.

Martha caught her breath. "Jesus?" she whispered. She'd never get to speak to him again?

Simon nodded. "Jesus, his followers, including your brother if he is among them. Even your disgraceful sister if she doesn't behave. You dishonored your father, but you will not make that mistake with me."

Martha couldn't breathe. Couldn't think. How could he ask this of her? Turn her back on Jesus? On Lazarus and Mary? "What if . . . ? What if I can't agree to this?"

Simon stared at her, his eyes flat and cold. "What is the punishment for having a child with no father?"

Stoning, if the judges commanded it. If they were merciful, banishment for both her and Zakai, and probably Penina.

Simon leaned even closer. "And the punishment for blasphemy?"

Death. A flush of anger rose in her. "You can't order the death of a man." Could he?

Simon's mouth hardened. "If I see Jesus here again, I'll have no choice but to report him to the Sanhedrin. They will take it up with the Romans."

She swallowed. "And Lazarus?"

"If you do exactly as I say, I can protect him. But without me speaking for him, the Sanhedrin will arrest all Jesus' followers, your gullible brother included."

Panic swelled in her. There was no going back. She'd thought telling Simon her secret might free her from her burden; instead she was bound even more tightly. And now, it wasn't only Penina and Zakai who depended on her. Lazarus and Jesus—perhaps even Mary—would be in danger if she failed.

Still, Simon wasn't done with her. His next words, cold and precise, chilled her blood. "Martha, remember this. I am no longer a boy, running after the approval of your father. I am a man. And you will be the perfect wife in every way."

He leaned close enough for her to smell the sweat of his clothes and the clinging fragrance of myrrh in his hair. "In three days, we will be betrothed." His breath brushed over her face. "And if I ever find out who the father of your child is, I'll make sure he is punished exactly as the law commands."

Chapter Thirty-One

Let me hear sounds of joy and gladness; let
the bones you have crushed rejoice.
—Psalm 51:10

ISA FORCED HIS weary body up the hill. He'd pushed himself hard for two days, but it wasn't much farther to the Jordan crossing. And then just a half day's journey to Bethany. He could be there by midday tomorrow, perhaps even earlier.

Nikius hadn't been surprised when Isa had said good-bye. "Not sure whether to thank or curse you, boy." Nikius had shoved a water skin and a bag of food into Isa's hands. "You worked hard." He jerked his head to where Alexa leaned sullenly against the door frame of the house. "But living with her now won't be easy."

Isa ducked his head as he saw the disappointment in the old man's eyes. Nikius had wanted a son. And Alexa . . . he'd seen her hurt when he'd come back from the tomb. If he was doing what he had to do—what Jesus had commanded—why did he feel like he was running away again?

"May the gods go with you, boy." Nikius's words followed him down the road.

Now sweat dampened his tunic and stung his eyes as he crested the hill. The dust-brown land stretched before him, cut through with the green furrow of the Jordan. Wool-colored clouds massed in the east while in the west the sun sank into a golden sky streaked with crimson.

The bread and almonds that Nikius gave him when he left Gerasene two days ago were gone, his stomach as empty as the limp bag slung over his shoulder. His limbs trembled with a hollow weakness. He leaned heavily on the stout branch he'd picked up to use as a walking stick. It didn't matter. Nothing mattered, except that he'd soon be with Martha again.

He could see her, more real than his feet on the dusty road, more vivid than the setting sun. The Purim after her mother died, he'd gone looking for the girl who had brought him food. He'd found her in the orchard, crying in the light of the moon. He knew the sound of loneliness, but he didn't know how to help her except to sit beside her in the crook of the oldest apricot tree.

At the next feast, he'd found her there again, as if she was waiting for him. He didn't know what to say to a girl so pretty, a girl who smelled like fresh-baked bread and cinnamon. But he did know a game. Question or command, he'd asked, desperate to hear her voice.

She chose question, as he'd hoped she would. He asked her about her abba, about Mary and the baby, Lazarus. About life with a family. She answered easily, as if she didn't know how fortunate she was to have these people . . . to belong to a family.

When it was his turn, he chose commands. He didn't want to answer what she was sure to ask—about Zerubbabel, about their life of travel and homelessness . . . about his bruises. But he was happy to do whatever she asked of him. Especially if he could see her smile.

When he couldn't be with her in the orchard, he watched her as he sang his songs and played the kinnor. He saw how hard she worked. How she never strayed far from Mary, how she cared for Lazarus like a mother.

Her family fascinated him. He watched how they laughed and smiled—and the way they touched each other! They embraced when they saw each other, and again as they said goodbye. Martha held Mary's hand as they walked through the meadow and kissed her brother's scraped knees and elbows. He'd even seen stern Sirach scoop up his young son in his arms and swing him onto his shoulder.

What would it be like to feel something other than the back of Zerubbabel's hand each day? What would it be like to know that so many people loved you?

It was the Purim he was seventeen when he knew Martha had claimed his heart and soul. He and Zerubbabel had arrived in Bethany late in the night, and he'd slept in the orchard, waiting for her. She had come to him as dawn filtered through the new green leaves of the apricot trees, no longer a girl but a woman. She'd smiled at him . . . and he was lost. He'd known in an instant he would do anything for Martha—anything she commanded, anything to make her happy.

That dawn in the orchard they spoke of marriage for the first time. Abba would never allow it—not to a pagan. That year, he buried his statues of the pagan gods and threw away his amulet. He listened to the teachers in the Jerusalem Temple and learned about the God of Abraham.

He'd do anything for Martha. Even worship her God if it meant being with her.

Every year he returned to Martha, yearning to see her face, terrified that she'd be betrothed. But that last time, when she begged him to speak to Abba, he had been too afraid. Afraid that Sirach would banish him from Bethany forever.

Isa kicked at a loose stone on the road. Yes, he'd do anything for Martha . . . except face her father. *Coward.*

Running away, that's what he was good at.

The first night out of Gerasene, Isa had found a shepherd's hut. The man had offered him food and a place to sleep . . . until he'd told him about the demons, about Jesus. Then the frail old shepherd had brandished his staff and driven him out into the night.

Today, he'd walked far without food but had hoped for a meal when he came to a village on the slopes of Mount Gilead.

The people there had seemed good and kind. They'd given him water at the well, and one brave matron had offered a midday meal. But when they'd asked him who he was, he'd told his story. The woman's husband had pulled a knife while his wife cowered with the children. Isa had made do with water and a few dried pods from a spindly carob tree.

Is that what Martha would do? Would she be afraid of him or, worse—despise him and call him defiled? Did he dare tell her about the demons and how he'd become an animal under their power? Or would he be giving Sirach one more reason to drive him away?

A wave of dizziness slowed his plodding feet. He remembered this road dimly, as if from a dream. The crossroad to the Jordan was close, just around the bend. There was a spring where he could fill his water skin, maybe even find a few green figs or wild onions to eat, and sleep another night beside the road. But tomorrow, he'd be in Bethany.

He rounded the bend and stopped suddenly.

A camp was pitched at the spring—a tent, a fire, a grazing camel. In front of the tent stood a tall man, two servants huddled close to him. Three other men, one holding a heavy club, advanced on the tall man, their backs to Isa. One snarled in thick Greek, "Give them over. Everything. And the camel."

Isa veered into the shadow of an oak tree. They hadn't seen him. He could turn back or cut through the brush. He didn't want any trouble, not now, so close to Bethany. And this looked like trouble.

He eyed the tall man—a foreigner and clearly wealthy. His tunic was dyed a deep blue, embroidered along the hems and sleeves in gold thread. A finely woven head covering threw shadows over a long face and deep-set eyes.

The foreigner held up his arms in front of his servants—an old man and a half-grown boy—as if to protect them. "Take what you will, *nothoi*, but leave my people alone." His voice was deep and his bearing as stately as a king's.

The thief with the club advanced. He turned his head, and Isa could see his face was scarred, as if he'd lost a fight with a mountain cat. "We'll do what we want with them, and you'll be thankful if we don't leave you bleeding to death on the road."

Isa's mouth went dry. He couldn't let this man fight off three thieves with just a boy and an old man to help him.

He gripped his walking stick and slipped out of the shadows. One of the thieves was close, his back to Isa. Isa stepped quietly behind him and swung with all his strength at the back of his head. The man dropped to the ground. The second one charged. Isa pulled the stick back and jabbed the knobbed base straight at the oncoming man's gut. With a grunt, his attacker doubled over and fell to the ground, clutching his belly.

Isa spun toward the leader, but the tall foreigner had already yanked the club from the man's hands and used it on his head. Isa faced the prostrate attackers, shoulder to shoulder with the tall man.

The thieves scrambled to their feet, scowls on their faces and curses in their mouths. Their eyes widened when they saw Isa. He stepped toward them, his walking stick held high. They looked at each other and stumbled away, crashing through the brush toward the river.

Isa watched the brush until he was sure the men were gone, then turned to the trio staring at him in silence. He could imagine what they saw. A hulking man, wild hair tangled down his back, in a thin scrap of a tunic. A man who had sent three men running. Of course they were afraid.

But the foreigner bowed to him. "I thank you from my heart."

Isa nodded and backed toward the road. Any moment now, they would order him away.

The stately man moved forward slowly, as though approaching a wild animal. "Where are you going, my friend, as the sun is setting?"

My *friend?* Isa pointed across the Jordan.

"It will be dark soon." The man lifted a brow. His eyes were deep brown and looked almost . . . welcoming. "Are you hungry?"

The smoke from the cooking fire brought Isa the smell of meat, and his mouth watered. Would they share their food with him? Perhaps. Unless he told them about the demons.

A smile played on the man's generous mouth. "Look." He held out his empty hands. "You just saved my life and my servants' lives. The least I can do is give you some food and a place to lay your head."

Within moments, Isa was served a stew of creamy red lentils and chunks of goat meat. The unfamiliar spices stung his tongue, but food filled the void in his belly and left him sleepy and satisfied.

As he ate, he listened. The man's name was Melech. He was a Jew from Caesarea, although he looked and sounded like someone from a farther land. Melech signaled to the boy servant for more stew. "We journey to find Jesus, the Nazarene."

Isa looked up from his bowl. "You know of Jesus?"

"So you can speak? Good!" Melech clapped him on the shoulder with a grin. "Yes, I know of him. Who doesn't in all of Judea?" He held out his hands. "I was a leper, almost dead, my flesh rotting from my bones."

Isa's stomach turned as he peered at the man's hands and face. His skin was smooth and unblemished.

"I was driven from my home in Caesarea to Dotham, with the rest of the unclean. And then we heard about him." He shook his head in wonder. "Finally, outside Jerusalem, we found him. He healed us all."

Jesus could do more than drive out demons? "What else has he done?"

Melech's teeth flashed white against skin the color of polished oak. "My boy, there is nothing he cannot do if you have faith. He has healed the sick, the mute, the deaf. He's given sight to the blind. They say he even brought a dead boy back to life, the son of a Roman."

"But isn't he a Jew?"

Melech laughed. "Yes. And that's the part no one understands. It seems he can cure all, Jews and gentiles alike. He asks only one thing."

Isa's heart quickened. "One thing? And what is that?"

"That you believe he is the one sent by God."

Sent by God? The demons had believed in him. The son of the Most High God, they'd called him. A rush of warmth poured through Isa that had nothing to do with the spicy stew.

"Who is he?"

"He's the Messiah, my boy. The one the Jews have been waiting for." Melech smiled.

"The one in the old songs?" He'd sung about the Messiah many times, just as he'd sung of Zeus and Adonis to the pagans.

"The very same. And he goes over the country, healing the sick and speaking of his father, the God of Abraham and Isaac."

Could it be true? The God of the Jews had sent the Anointed One that they sang of at every feast? The demons had known it, and they had obeyed him. Isa's heart burned in his chest.

"Some of the Jews in Jerusalem despise him." Melech's face twisted, and he spat on the dust. "The fools called for his arrest. He left, I found out, with his followers and is teaching in Bethabara, just a day's journey from here." Melech waved to the east. "I will go tomorrow, to give thanks to him. But tonight . . ." Melech slapped his thighs and signaled to the old servant. "Tonight we celebrate. We were strangers, and now we are brothers."

Brothers? Hope sparked within him. If he could be brothers with a Jew from Caesarea, perhaps there was hope for him in Bethany. As long as he didn't speak about the past seven years.

The boy servant appeared, and what he held in his arms made Isa's breath catch in his throat. The firelight danced and flickered on its polished wood. The taut strings gleamed. He rose to his feet, his hands reaching out of their own accord.

"Do you play the kinnor?" Melech asked.

Isa stared at it. His fingers could already feel the strings beneath them. Melech nodded to the boy. "Give it to our new brother. Let us sing together. But first, my friend, you must tell us your story."

Isa took the kinnor in his arms and eyed Melech and the servants. Tell them of the demons? He couldn't.

Melech looked at him closely. "Come now. I told you I was once a leper. It couldn't be worse than that."

But it was. At least lepers could think. Could remember.

His hands slipped over the delicate curves of the kinnor, so familiar, so comforting. He sat down beside the fire and stroked the wood. He plucked a string, then twisted a knob on top. He strummed a chord.

Melech's face was expectant. Waiting. The servants watched him.

His heart sped up, and a cold sweat chilled his back. If he told them, they'd drive him away into the night just like the others. Or threaten him, like the old Greeks. He couldn't chance it. Not when he'd just found a friend.

Melech's eyes were kind, and his face showed understanding. "Whatever it was, my boy, I can tell that you met him and he changed you, like he healed me. I could see it on your face when I said his name."

Isa's shoulders relaxed, and his grip on the kinnor loosened.

The servants crouched down beside the fire. Melech settled himself, his smile flashing in the dim light. "Let us sing. Perhaps you can tell us in song what you can't put into words."

And with that, the melodies came to him, brimming in his mind.

His fingers found their places and strummed a chord that filled the night air. Melech grinned, and the two servants leaned close. Isa's voice swelled from his chest, no longer tentative, but sure and strong.

Sing to the Lord a new song; sing to the Lord, all the earth. Sing to the Lord, bless his name; announce his salvation day after day.

The words of the Jews he'd sung so many times, always with

Martha in his mind's eye. This time, a new feeling stirred in his heart. As the music rang through the night and Melech's deep voice joined his, he saw the face of Jesus.

The man who had power over demons.

The son of the Most High God.

The Messiah who had given him a new life.

Chapter Thirty-Two

Turn away your face from my sins; blot out all my guilt. A clean
heart create for me, God; renew in me a steadfast spirit.
—*Psalm 51:11*

ISA LET THE old servant pour another jar of icy springwater over his head and shoulders, wetting his thin tunic. The sun was already well over the horizon, glinting down on the green grass and sparkling waters of the spring.

The boy pulled the stakes from around the tent and began to roll it. Melech tossed Isa a round of warm bread. "Stay with us, my friend," he said for the tenth time that morning. "Come to Bethabara. We will give Jesus homage together."

Isa tore the bread and stuffed it in his mouth.

They'd stayed awake long into the night. He played song after song on the kinnor while Melech told him of Jesus.

"All that he requires is faith, my brother," Melech said again. "Come with us, and see him."

It would be good to travel with them, to play the kinnor and have companions. And how he longed to see Jesus again. But he shook his head at Melech's hopeful face. "I must go to Bethany." Even if it meant facing Martha's anger and her father's hatred.

Melech sighed. "I was afraid you'd say that." He winked at Isa. "I'm guessing there's a woman."

Isa looked at the ground, and his face heated.

Melech laughed and signaled to the old servant. "At least I

can send you to her looking better than that." The servant brought a clean tunic, creamy white and embroidered with gold thread, and a coat of deep brown wool, finer than anything he'd ever seen. Isa looked at Melech in confusion and fingered the new tunic, the soft wool smelling of lye and cedar.

Melech elbowed him. "Put it on."

Isa pulled it over the thin rag Nikius had given him. Then the coat, thick and heavy.

The old man ran an ivory comb through his tangled hair and beard, then Melech pulled him toward the pool at the base of the spring. Isa stared at the man reflected back in the rippling water. Was that really him? That man with wide shoulders covered in fine clothing? Would Martha even recognize him from the ragged, beaten boy he had been the day he left her? Hope trickled through him. Surely Sirach would give him a chance to explain when he looked less like a poor musician and more like a rich merchant.

Melech smiled like a proud father. "Your hair and beard need cutting, son. But that can wait for your woman to do."

The young servant came to him, shyly holding out the kinnor.

"Take it, my boy," Melech prodded him. "He wants you to have it."

"But I have nothing to give him."

Melech grinned. "He thinks you're a hero, the way you took care of those vermin." Melech pulled a silver drachma from his belt. "And take this. Go back to your home, and your woman, as a prince."

Isa stepped back, shaking his head at the silver. "I can't."

Melech smiled. "You can and you will."

It was too much. Melech didn't even know him—didn't know what he had been—and treated him like a son. "Why are you doing this?"

Melech pressed the coin into Isa's hand. "Let's just say some-one helped me once, and I'm passing it on." His smile faded. "And a girl told me this: *Do not be afraid. He is the Messiah.*" He looked into Isa's eyes, his own full of wonder. "Just a girl I didn't know, and I never saw her again, but she changed my life." Melech threw his arms around him and slapped his back. "Now, go. May we meet again someday."

Isa's throat ached with words he couldn't say.

Melech gripped his shoulders and looked into his eyes. "Whatever Jesus did for you, my friend, know this: he made you a new man."

Isa's chest warmed, as if a spark had been fanned to a flame. He'd turned away from his pagan gods for Martha. But he hadn't believed—not really—in the God of the Jews. Now he had met their Messiah and been healed by him. Could he be a new man? *Do not be afraid*, Melech said. He would try.

After a lifetime spent in fear and what seemed like eternity with the demons, he was free. Free to do what Jesus had asked of him and to return to Martha as he'd promised. And this time, perhaps he would be worthy of her.

After Melech and his servants headed east to Bethabara, Isa faced the ford across the Jordan. Not much farther now.

Mustard bushes with bright yellow blossoms dotted the banks. The cypress trees were green, as were the leaves of the mighty oaks that lined the riverbed, but the marsh grasses were brown and defeated. Dried-up myrtle and broom bush rattled in the wind, and the Jordan was reduced to a sluggish channel.

He checked that the kinnor was secure in his bag and his silver tucked into his belt, then lifted his new tunic and coat and tied them around his waist. Memories surfaced as the cool water swirled over his legs, both sending a shiver up his spine. When they'd left Bethany that last time, Zerubbabel had feared the water here at the ford. He'd clutched Isa like an old woman as the water had risen almost to their waists. What had happened to his guardian after that? Where was Zerubbabel now?

He reached the other side and scrambled up the steep bank, pulling himself up on the dried grass and thorny bushes. Bethany was just two hours' journey from here, uphill all the way, on a path that wound through the rocky hills filled with caves.

He'd see Martha by the time the sun reached its peak. His pulse quickened, and he started out, swinging his walking stick at a fast pace. He'd left her for seven years. He wouldn't waste another moment. He'd walk into Sirach's home dressed like a prince, with silver in his pocket and his kinnor in his hands to sing to her. Surely Martha would forgive him. And Sirach might take a moment to listen to him.

But he wouldn't tell them about the demons. Not right away. He couldn't bear to have Martha fear him or for Sirach to call him defiled. But what could he say to her? How would she react when he walked into Bethany? She would be angry, that he knew. And she'd want to know where he'd been for so many years.

But perhaps—worse than her anger—she was already married to a good man, someone her father had chosen. She could already have a child. His stomach twisted in a knot.

His strong legs hardly felt the steep climb. His breath didn't falter. His thoughts drifted to Martha's childhood laughter as they'd eaten half-ripe apricots. As they'd hidden and found each other under the light of the moon. Then, to the last night in the orchard. She'd been so sad. He'd watched her all seven days of the feast. He'd seen her sadness in her bowed shoulders, in her slow steps. How she'd watched Mary and had blinked away tears. She would miss her sister.

When she had come to him in the garden, he'd had nothing to say to ease her loneliness, and her tears had broken his heart. It had been so natural to pull her into his arms to comfort her. To heal her heartache with a kiss.

But comfort had turned into something more . . . and he hadn't been strong enough to stop what happened next.

His heart sped up as he remembered her lips on his, her soft body as they'd lain on the carpet of blossoms. What they had done was wrong, and it was his fault. He had failed her, but now he would make it up to her.

Isa quickened his steps, his eyes on the horizon, his thoughts on Martha. He didn't hear them approach. Didn't see them until he was surrounded. Three of them. Two from the front, appearing out of the cypress trees like spirits. One coming up behind him, a man with a scarred face he recognized.

The scarred man held a heavy club wrapped in iron bands. "He's the one," he called out to the others. "And this time, he's getting the surprise."

Fear froze Isa's limbs for a moment; then a surge of anger went through him like a brush fire. These men stood between him and Bethany, and he wouldn't let anyone separate him from Martha again.

The scarred one ran at Isa and swung the club.

Isa jumped back, avoiding the blow. He turned to see the other two almost on him. He lashed out with his stick, landing it on the side of one attacker's head. A hit in the throat sent the third man reeling and coughing.

Isa backed away. He heard a shuffle behind him and turned, but too late. The man behind him landed the club in his middle. His breath left him in a great gust. The faces around him blurred, his vision darkening as the road rose up to meet him.

Hands ripped his bag from his shoulder and searched his belt. His kinnor, the silver. He needed that for Martha, for Sirach. He pushed them away and staggered to his feet. He swayed, the trees and road tipping wildly as he tried to suck in air.

The scarred man's ugly face came close, but his guttural curse sounded far away. Isa saw the club arcing toward his head but was helpless to stop it. Pain burst through his temple, and the sun exploded into a thousand stars . . . then, there was nothing but darkness.

Chapter Thirty-Three

He has counsel in store for the upright, he is the shield
of those who walk honestly, guarding the paths of
justice, protecting the way of his pious ones.
—Proverbs 2:7–8

*L*AZARUS STEPPED DOWN the stone stairs into the dark, cold waters of the mikvah.

Blessed are you, Lord our God. Be my strength.

He'd hardly been able to drag himself from his sleeping mat as the sun rose on the day of Martha's betrothal. Since Jesus had sent him away, he'd felt his strength—his very life—draining away like water from a cracked jar.

There was no denying it. The swelling in his side had grown and now was hot to the touch. He'd begun waking up at night drenched in sweat, dreaming he was drowning. Penina already knew there was something wrong. She didn't tease him, and he caught her worried eyes on him more than once. Soon Martha would know as well.

Today he would go to Simon's and sign the ketubah. Simon would announce the betrothal to the village this afternoon, and Lazarus's vow would be fulfilled. He would be free to leave them, and not to follow the Messiah.

He took a breath and immersed, letting the cool water flow over his head. Is this what death would feel like? Would it be cool and peaceful like slipping underwater? Or would it come for him like the terrifying demons of his childhood nightmares, wrapping around him and stealing the breath from his body?

He came up gasping for air. *The hour is coming when the dead will hear the voice of the son of God.* He'd thought that Jesus' words were a riddle—but now he was beginning to understand.

He was dying.

He staggered up the steps and out into the thin light of dawn, pulled on his tunic, and slumped on the stone bench. Slowly, he breathed in and out while the pain in his side ebbed and turned into a dull ache.

I don't want to die.

Lazarus rubbed his hands over his eyes. He wouldn't live long enough to see Jesus come into his glory, when all would believe in him and know that the Messiah had come. He wouldn't see Martha marry and have more children or Zakai grow into a man. And he would never see Penina's smile again. The pain under his ribs turned into an ache in his heart. Who would she tease when he was gone? Who would carry water for her and bring her lavender?

At least, with the ketubah signed, his family would be safely under Simon's protection.

Martha had been pale when she and Penina returned from Simon's home. She'd said little, just told him Simon knew about Zakai—knew she wasn't a virgin—and still would marry her. She hadn't met his eyes, and Lazarus saw what her admission to Simon had cost her in the tightness around her mouth, in the jerky movement of her hands as she set about her tasks.

"Did he ask about . . . his father?" Lazarus whispered, although only Safta was near, sleeping in her corner, Zakai's rabbit curled on her lap.

Martha shook her head.

Lazarus had embraced his sister, pulling her close as relief eased the pain in his chest. "We were right to believe that he would give you a second chance, just as he has received. He is an honorable man." But he'd felt her tremble against him, and she'd said no more about Simon or the upcoming betrothal. He didn't tell her that he would not be following Jesus. He couldn't speak of it, just as he couldn't tell her about the sickness that weakened him more each day.

For two days, the courtyard had been heavy with silence. Martha worked—scouring every pot, immersing every vessel, sweeping the house until not a speck of dirt dared show itself. Even Zakai was subdued. When he wasn't doing his chores, he sat in the corner with his animals or curled up next to Safta.

Anyone would think they were preparing for a burial instead of a betrothal.

Penina worked beside Martha, her usual smile when she served Lazarus replaced with a frown, her dimple absent. How he would miss that smile, the dimple that was his daily bread.

A scrambling of sandals on the pathway brought him to his feet, and the object of his thoughts hurried around the bend in the path. Penina's hair was woven into a braid that shone blue-black, and her rich skin glowed in the morning light. She didn't look surprised to find him.

She came to a stop in front of him and bowed, like a slave to a master.

What was she doing? He reached for her hands and pulled her up. "What do you want, Nina?" He'd give her whatever he could. She didn't have to beg him.

She began to make her signs, slowly and carefully. Lazarus's eyes went from her hands to her expressive face.

Martha, marriage, no.

"You don't want Martha to marry?" Is that what she'd said?

She nodded, relief brightening her face.

Lazarus leaned back. "Why? It's a good marriage, Nina. It's what Martha wants."

Penina shook her head violently. She leaned forward, her expressive hands moving quickly.

Please. No marriage.

Lazarus rubbed his eyes. Penina didn't understand this was

how it had to be. "Penina, I won't be here much longer. Martha needs to be married to someone who can take care of you and Zakai. You know this."

Penina signed furiously, fast and jerky, her dark eyes flashing. He caught some of what she was trying to say, but he must be wrong. *Simon.* And then a sign he didn't understand, but her face told the meaning.

"You don't like Simon?"

She clenched her jaw, her hands closed into fists, and she nodded.

Lazarus relaxed. That's all it was. "Don't worry. I know he's not . . . well, he can be fussy."

Penina raised her brows. *Fussy?* she seemed to say.

Lazarus blew out a breath. "All right. He's arrogant. And difficult. And his mother is worse." He set his hands on her soft shoulders. "But Martha can handle him and Jael. She'll take care of you."

Penina shook her head and looked up at him, her eyes filled with tears.

His heart lurched. His Nina—always so full of vinegar—crying? "Nina. What is it?" He ran his hands down her arms and captured her hands in his, so small and soft. If only he could make her understand. "Please. I know you don't believe in God's goodness; I wish you did. But trust me if you can't trust in him."

She leaned closer. Her eyes pleaded with him; her mouth trembled.

He'd touched her many times like this, as a sister. But this time, his heart beat faster and a warm flush crept up his neck. She was so sad. And so close. He could bend his head and kiss her—comfort her—so easily.

She leaned forward until her warm curves pressed against him. She tipped her face up. Her lips parted, and her eyes met his. The look she gave him was not that of a sister, and the feelings he'd denied for too long were hardly brotherly. *One kiss.* Her body, her face, her eyes said it as clearly as if she'd spoken.

He breathed in her scent of lavender and rainwater. Didn't he deserve as much—one kiss from the woman he loved—before he left this world?

Chapter Thirty-Four

Do not drive me from your presence, nor take from me your holy spirit. Restore my joy in your salvation; sustain in me a willing spirit.
—*Psalm 51:12–13*

*I*SA DRIFTED IN a sea of darkness and pain.

He breathed in the scent of earth and the sweet, metallic tang of blood. Dry grass rustled in a cold wind, and the chant of insects throbbed in his ears. He pried open his eyes and glimpsed the amber sky, the sun rising like a flame on the horizon.

Was he dead? He tried to rise, but pain suffused his head. His hands searched his body. His bag . . . gone. His belt and the silver . . . gone. He shivered in the wind. Even the new tunic and coat had been stripped from him.

He'd lost everything. A wave of despair washed over him like a flood. He closed his eyes and gave in to the pain that coursed through him. With it, unbidden, came the memory of another night of agony.

He and Zerubbabel. On a boat. In a storm.

The wind had come up just after they'd left shore in Capernaum. Zerubbabel was terrified, but Isa, for once, had insisted. It would be an easy ride to the Greek side of the lake, where they could make plenty of silver playing for the pagans. Isa's thoughts were on Martha . . . how he needed the silver. He hadn't seen the storm coming.

*Brutal gusts whipped at the sail. The waves rose, tossing
the boat and its two passengers from side to side. Isa clutched
at their pack with the flute and kinnor inside and pushed it into
the prow. They couldn't lose their livelihood, not now.*

*"Help me!" Zerubabbel cried, grabbing at Isa as the boat
listed to one side, water pouring in and pooling around their
ankles. Isa struggled with the oars, trying to turn the boat into
the waves.*

*Zerubabbel's eyes rolled in terror. "Don't let me fall in."
His long fingers wrapped like shackles around Isa's wrists.*

*Isa pried him loose. "Grab the other oar." If Zerubabbel
could balance the other side of the boat, they could use the
oars to face the waves. Then they wouldn't take on more
water.*

But Zerubabbel clung to him like a terrified child.

*A massive wave broke over the boat, tipping it sideways.
As they tumbled into the water, Isa held his breath. He stroked
upward, breaking the surface to find the boat out of his reach
and Zerubabbel thrashing beside him. The pack—his kinnor!
It was sinking under the waves.*

*"Help us!" the old man screamed, grabbing at Isa, pushing
them both under. Isa struggled against Zerubabbel, coughing
out water. His kinnor—it was gone.*

Isa opened his eyes to the burning sky. His heart hammered,
his breath lodged in his chest. Only the breeze and rustle of grass
assured him that he was, indeed, no longer in the water. But it
wasn't a dream. It was a memory. A memory as clear as if it had
happened yesterday.

He groaned and tried to stop the images that followed.

*Zerubabbel was strong, unnaturally strong. Shrieks like a
thousand tortured souls spewed from his mouth. Isa wrapped
one arm around his guardian's neck and swam with the other.*

He reached the listing boat and pulled himself onto the hull. "Grab the side!" he shouted. But Zerubabbel was consumed by a terror so deep, he was blind and deaf.

Zerubabbel slipped from Isa's grasp, disappearing under the churning water. Isa grabbed his hair and pulled him up, but it was no longer the face of his lifelong guardian that he saw rising from the water. Zerubabbel's eyes rolled back to show just the gleaming white orbs; his mouth stretched open— too wide, as though pulled by invisible hands.

An inhuman voice howled from Zerubabbel's cavernous mouth: "Save us."

Fear coursed through Isa, but he didn't release his hold on Zerubabbel. What was happening? Then a mist, like breath on a cold day, snaked out of Zerubabbel's open mouth. It slipped upward, coiling around Isa's hand. His grip on Zerubabbel faltered, and the man's lifeless body was pulled down, into the dark depths.

But the mist didn't follow Zerubabbel. It slithered up Isa's arm, then higher—over his chest and neck. Tendrils slipped into his nostrils like smoke. Taking hold.

The frigid presence filled his mind, laughing like a pack of jackals. His last thought—the one he clung to like a drowning man—was of Martha. Her face. Her voice. Until even her memory was swallowed by the unrelenting terror.

Isa stirred. The wind was cold, but his body was on fire, melting on a bed of agony. His throat felt like a cauterized wound. He cracked open his eyes. The sun burned above the horizon.

How long had Zerubabbel been infested with demons before that storm on Galilee? And then, when his body was slipping under the waters of Galilee, the demons had found a new host. Him.

He choked and felt hot tears on his face. Zerubabbel was gone, drowned in the waters that he feared so much. His guardian had been unkind and even cruel. But he was the only father

Isa had ever known. Now he was indeed all alone. And he would die alone on this road if he didn't find the strength to get to Bethany.

The shadows of the cypress trees stretched toward him—reaching out as if to pull him into their depths. Fear seized him.

When they reach me, I know I'll die.

He called out to the only God he knew. The God who had sent his son to him. The God of the Messiah, the God of the songs he'd sung since he was a boy. *Please, God of Abraham and Isaac, God of Jacob . . . give me strength.*

He pushed himself up, the sun swinging wildly in the sky as his head swam with pain. To his knees, then to his feet. He found his stick lying in the ditch next to his trampled traveling bag. Inside, his kinnor was broken into a pile of kindling.

He clutched it to his chest and shuffled onto the road. At his back, the sun blazed. In front of him, the shadows stretched over the western hills.

Martha, I'm coming back to you.

One step, then another, and another . . . toward Bethany.

Chapter Thirty-Five

LAZARUS STRAIGHTENED AND stepped back, putting enough space between himself and Penina for his mind to start working again. Yes. He loved her. And not as a sister.

But he couldn't tell her. Not now. To tell her, to show her how he felt with the kiss he wanted, would be cruel. He would be leaving soon, and forever. He'd be no better than the heartless musician who had abandoned Martha.

He cleared his throat and looked at her tiny feet. "You'll see, Penina." He smoothed his tunic. "This is best for all of us."

He caught the glint of tears on her cheeks as she turned away, and Lazarus's heart wrenched. She disappeared around the bend, and his legs buckled. He collapsed onto the bench and closed his eyes.

Please, Lord of All, take this away. But was his plea to be rid of his affliction or his love for Penina? Both were too painful to bear. At least he could make sure his household would be protected when he left them. He staggered to his feet and started down the mountain.

Lord, give me time. Time to make sure they would be cared for. Time to say good-bye.

By the time he reached Simon's home, his chest burned and his tunic was damp with sweat. The courtyard door swung open at his first knock, and Micah led him to Simon's workroom in the cool stone house.

Simon sat at the same table where they had first spoken, with an unrolled parchment, a reed quill, and a jar of ink at his elbow. A scribe stood beside him—not the usual scribe from Bethany, whom Sirach had used for many years. This man was thin and sallow-faced, with sharp teeth and sharper eyes.

Simon stood and embraced him. "Shalom, Lazarus. You honor me and the memory of your father, may his name ever be remembered among his descendants." Simon nodded to the chair opposite his table. "Where is your sister?"

Lazarus sat, trying to keep his breathing even. Martha had asked only one favor of him, that she not be present at the betrothal. He hadn't been able to say no. "She asked me to act on her behalf."

Simon's brows went high. "It is not the usual way."

Lazarus nodded. "But within the law."

"Yes," Simon agreed with a small smile. "And we can allow her some leeway, to save her from embarrassment."

Lazarus gripped the arm of the chair. Simon's tone held a note of disrespect that made the back of his neck prickle. "Who is this?" Lazarus jerked his head to the unfamiliar scribe.

"This scribe shall record the details of the ketubah. He is"— Simon cleared his throat—"aware of our needs and has been well paid to stay silent. No one in the village will know the details of this document."

Lazarus's hands were damp, and he resisted the urge to wipe them on his tunic. Simon was right to bring in an outsider. The Bethany scribes would gossip—they all did—and the details of this ketubah must be kept secret. But the shifty scribe and Simon's disrespect toward Martha grated on him.

Simon poured wine into an etched silver goblet. "Let us begin." He passed the cup to Lazarus and motioned for him to drink. Lazarus took a long gulp. It was strong and sweet and made him wish for cold water. He gave it back, and Simon drank.

With the cup passed, the scribe read from the parchment. "On this, the first day of the week, the nineteenth day of the month of Adar, in the city of Bethany, Simon son of Elezar is betrothed to a woman, Martha, daughter of Sirach, may his light ever shine."

Lazarus tensed. *To a woman.* The ketubah should say *to a virgin.* Just a small word, but it made all the difference. If Simon had used one of the village scribes, Martha's reputation would be ruined before she could walk across the garden.

The room was suddenly hot, the air too heavy to breathe. Was he doing what was best for Martha? Was this what he had promised Abba?

The scribe droned on, "Be thou my wife by the law of Moses and Israel, and I will work for thee, honor and support thee . . ."

Lazarus glanced at Simon. His eyes were on the scroll, his mouth moving along with the scribe's words. Would he honor her? Or would he forever remember that she was not a virgin bride?

". . . thy food, clothing, and necessaries, and live with thee in conjugal relations according to the laws of Israel." The scribe took a breath and shuffled the scroll upward.

A flush of heat swept over Lazarus, along with a wave of dizziness that made the room spin. He clutched the arms of the chair and pulled in a careful breath. This was the part that he needed to hear.

"I, Simon of Bethany, forgive all the debt of Sirach's household, and at the time of the marriage, will take into my home the servant Penina, the boy Zakai, and grandmother of the bride to support and care for them as my own family."

Lazarus felt some tension leave his cramped chest. Simon would take care of them. But the scribe continued, his voice scraping in Lazarus's ears.

"This ketubah shall be forfeited and all rights within it revoked if the bride is found guilty of adultery, or accused of any impropriety, or if she is accused of any transgression to the laws of decency." The scribe paused for a moment and glanced at Lazarus warily. "And she shall be punished under the laws of our rabbis and sages, may their memory be a blessing."

Lazarus straightened. Accused of impropriety? Since when was an accusation reason for divorce? His head ached with the effort to stay upright as the pain in his side sharpened. He swayed in his chair. Was this what Penina had been trying to tell him?

Simon caught his frown. "I can have not a whisper of disgrace on my household, you understand, my friend." He glanced at the scribe. "Of course, Martha is the holiest woman in Bethany. This is just a formality." His eyes were flat and hard.

The scribe finished with, "The betrothal period shall be for one month."

Lazarus's heart pounded. Accusations of impropriety. The scribe's smug expression. And now just a month's betrothal? This felt wrong. Very wrong.

Simon strode to the door, barking a command, then returned with a look of satisfaction on his face. A parade of servants entered, each bearing an armful of gifts. The thin woman he'd seen earlier held out fine linen, dyed in all the colors of a rainbow. A man with a patch on his eye brought a tray filled with small clay pots, each marked with the name of an exotic spice. A third servant, the Egyptian girl, held an array of silver bangles and gold chains, enough to charm a dozen women.

The servants looked at the floor, their faces drawn as if even they knew this marriage was a bad idea. Simon was talking. Something about sending the gifts to Martha this afternoon. About the plans for the announcement.

Lazarus moved his head up and down and swallowed the bile that rose in his throat. On the outside, all was as it should be. The gifts, the contract, the forgiveness of their debt. He just had to sign, and his duty would be done.

Lazarus took a shallow breath. He couldn't do this. Martha deserved a better man than Isa. And she deserved a better man than Simon.

The scribe gave the quill to Simon, who dipped it in the ink jar and signed the bottom of the scroll. Simon held out the quill to Lazarus, his face expectant.

Lazarus pushed himself up from the chair. *Hear me, oh Lord, and be my help.* He waited for the room to settle. It made sense now. Martha's silence, Penina's appeal at the mikvah. They had known what Simon was like, and Lazarus had been too set on his own needs—first following Jesus, then hiding his illness—to listen. "Forgive me, Simon. I can't do this."

Simon's brows rose to the top of his domed forehead. "It is done. Everything is prepared." His voice rose with each word.

Lazarus staggered toward the door. "No. I won't sign this. I will not allow Martha to marry you." He just needed to get to the orchard. To rest under the trees, alone.

He stumbled through the courtyard, ignoring the stares of the servants and Simon's shouts behind him. He would talk to Martha, tell her about his sickness. He'd tell her everything. They would find another way. His breath rasped in his ears as he rushed past the gardens, through the stream, and up the bank, finally reaching the shade of the blossoming apricot trees. He stopped, gasping for breath. Somehow, he'd provide for her and Penina and Zakai. Some way that didn't include marriage to Simon.

Pain stabbed through his chest. He swayed and reached for a tree to steady himself but clutched nothing but air. He hit the ground, his breath left his body, and he knew nothing more.

Chapter Thirty-Six

She is clothed with strength and dignity, and
she laughs at the days to come.
—*Proverbs 31:25*

MARTHA SCRAPED HER feet on the path through the village, kicking up dust that clung to the hem of her tunic. She'd lain awake all night, worry choking her mind. Her eyes were gritty, and her head felt like it was stuffed with wool.

Lazarus had been gone since dawn. He'd left early to immerse, then to go to Simon's. Now the sun was well above the horizon. Her betrothal was no doubt complete and the ketubah signed. In almost every way she was a married woman. Simon could talk to her, touch her, even kiss her if he desired. She shuddered at the thought of his thick lips. And when the betrothal period was over, she would share his home and his bed.

Halfway to the village, she'd met Penina coming back from the mikvah. Penina had fallen into step beside her, as if she knew Martha couldn't face the well on her own. Not today. Jael was back from Jerusalem and surely would be there, catching up on the scandal of Purim. How Mary had embarrassed her family in Jael's own home.

But Jael's horror at what happened while she was gone would pale compared to the news of Martha and Simon's betrothal. Simon would have told her immediately on her return, but had Jael told her friends—the inner circle of Silva and Devorah—

even though it was her son's privilege to make the announcement? Could Martha have one more day before the news swept through Bethany like a brush fire?

At least Simon wouldn't tell Jael about Zakai. His pride wouldn't let him, Martha was sure. But Jael would find plenty of other transgressions to hold against her new daughter-in-law, now and for years to come. As Martha came in sight of the well, her heart sank. At least ten women gathered around the low casement, squawking like a pack of buzzards. As she and Penina approached, Devorah and Jael turned to watch her. Her heart sped up, and her hands dampened.

Jael sauntered close and linked her arm through Martha's. "You've been busy, my dear." She smirked. "It's too bad your sister was so foolish. She ruined a perfect meal, from what my son says."

Martha tried to pull away. She didn't want to hear again about how Mary had shamed the family. They didn't know the real story.

Jael's hand closed over her arm like a claw. She pulled Martha along the low watering trough where shepherds brought their sheep to drink. "I want you to know," she whispered, "Simon tells me everything." She raised her brows in a knowing look.

Martha sealed her lips shut before she could speak words she would regret. *Not everything.* If he had, Jael would hardly be acting like they were best friends going for a stroll.

Jael continued walking around the sheep trough to the other side of the well. "You are a fortunate woman, Martha, that my son wants you as his wife." Her fingers dug into Martha's arm. "There are many women—younger women—who could give him a houseful of sons. But he has chosen you, my dear." Jael's face looked like she was having a tooth pulled.

Martha didn't answer, but she could imagine how Jael had reacted to Simon's news when she returned from Jerusalem. It's a wonder they hadn't heard from across the meadow.

"I'm sure by this time next year you'll have a grandchild for me." Her words sounded more like a threat than a blessing. "And when you are my daughter-in-law, you will learn how to please my son as well as be respectful to me." Jael ran a hand over her oiled braids. "And don't worry"—she nodded to Martha—"I won't say a word about the betrothal until Simon makes the announcement."

Martha turned to the well. Now that Jael had made it clear that life would be miserable under her roof, perhaps she could get her water and go. But as she lowered the gourd into the well, she saw Mary approaching with her water jar. Martha's mouth dried; she hadn't spoken to Mary since the debacle at Simon's. She just didn't know what to say. Especially about Simon. Anxiety tightened at her neck as Jael intercepted Mary and whispered in her ear.

Mary looked from Jael to Martha, her brow furrowed.

Jael covered her mouth with her hand, but a hint of glee was in her voice. "Forgive me, my dear Martha. I just assumed your sister, of all people, would know."

Martha gritted her teeth.

"Is it true?" Mary's voice rose.

"I can't believe she kept a secret from you that even her slave knows," Jael whispered. "Just keep it quiet, especially from that talkative mother-in-law of yours, until Simon makes the announcement."

Mary's eyes were bright as she took Martha's elbow and pulled her away from Jael's listening ears. "How can this be?"

"Mary, I—I meant to tell you. I just—"

"Martha, no." She took Martha's hand in hers and brought it to her heart. "Sister, you can't. You'll never be happy with Simon."

Martha's body was flushed with heat, and her mouth tasted of curdled milk. As always, Mary didn't understand. "Happy?" she choked out. "Not everyone gets happiness, Mary. You know that." Many women married for protection, for security. Happiness may come later, or it may not.

She picked up her half-full jar. If she could just get away.

Away from Jael and her disapproving eyes. Away from her own sister, who didn't understand the here and now. Martha turned away from the well but stopped in the act of hefting the water jar to her shoulder.

A stranger stumbled across the square. A tall man, in a short tunic like the Greeks wore—not much more than a scrap of wool streaked with dirt and what looked like blood. He clutched one hand against the side of his head. Long, dark hair hung over his shoulders, and a tangled beard covered most of his face.

"Help me," the man choked out.

The women drew closer together like sheep under threat of a wolf.

A stone's throw from the well, the injured man careened sideways, then crumpled to the ground with a muffled groan and was still.

Mary rushed to him. "Get me some water," she called over her shoulder.

Devorah moved toward the well.

"No." Jael stopped Devorah with a raised hand. "Look at him. He isn't from here. He's not even a Jew." Jael jerked her head toward the city gate. "Devorah, get your husband. Let the city judges take care of him."

Mary sat up on her knees. "The city judges? They'll throw him outside the gate." She glanced at Martha. "Martha, help me get him to my home. I'll take care of him."

Martha moved toward her sister. Mary was right. If this man was a pagan—or worse, a Samaritan—Abel and the other men would let him die rather than help him.

"Martha," Jael's voice rang out. "Don't you dare touch that man. Simon would not approve."

Martha stood like a statue, one step away from the group of women, two steps from Mary and the injured man. Panic rose in her throat, and her damp hands slipped on the water jar. Mary, silently begging her. Jael, watching her with narrowed eyes as if this was a test.

Her heart pounded. It *was* a test. One that she couldn't fail, not now with Simon's threats still ringing in her ears.

You will never dishonor me.

Martha looked at the man lying on the ground. He was hurt, maybe dying. But Simon's wrath would threaten not only her but Zakai and Penina. Maybe even Mary and Lazarus. She couldn't risk it. She looked away. "Mary, let the men decide what to do with him."

"Martha!" Mary's voice held shock, and her face showed her disbelief. She turned toward Penina. "Penina, you'll help me." It wasn't a question.

Penina stepped forward, but Martha grabbed her arm. Penina pulled, and Martha firmed her grip. "I forbid it."

Penina's brows went up, but she stayed put. Martha had never treated her like a slave, or even a servant. But this time she had to or Simon would hear about it. *Forgive me, Penina.*

Martha turned away, unable to look another moment at the injured man. Her gaze fell on the women who watched Mary with disdain, and shame washed over her. She was one of them now. She had turned into the kind of woman she despised.

Jael sidled up to her. "Don't worry. You can't be held accountable for your sister's actions. Simon will hear that you chose wisely, my dear."

A bubble of hysterical laughter rose in her. Jael couldn't be more wrong. She hadn't chosen wisely; Mary had. Mary had chosen the better part, once again.

Chapter Thirty-Seven

She opens her mouth in wisdom, and on her tongue is kindly counsel.
—Proverbs 31:26

PENINA STAYED THREE steps behind Martha as they carried the water through the village and past the olive groves, just like a slave would.

Martha's mind whirled with regret. She'd had to do it. Surely Penina could see that?

Mary would care for the injured man. She'd get Josiah, and probably Simcha, to carry him to her house. She would treat his wound and give him food and water. *Mary can afford to choose the better part.*

If she was so sure, a small voice asked, why was shame welling in her like an overfilled pot, threatening to choke her? Why did her heart feel like a cold, blackened cinder in her chest?

Martha pushed through the gate and glanced around the courtyard. Lazarus still wasn't home. Where had he gone after Simon's—to the mountain to pray or perhaps to the orchard? He was probably planning how soon he could leave to follow Jesus.

She collapsed in the corner next to Zakai's animal farm, her arms still around the jar, her face pressed on its cool, smooth surface.

Penina slammed her jar down beside Martha.

Martha stayed huddled on the ground. "You know I didn't have a choice," she said without looking at Penina.

Jael would have marched straight to Simon like a tattling child. The betrothal would be ended before the ink dried on the ketubah and with it, their life in Bethany. Martha reached out to Zakai's rabbit. He hopped away and cowered in the corner of his basket, his ears twitching. Even the rabbit hated her.

She didn't want to be like them—like Jael and Devorah—but it had happened. She touched the willow twig where Zakai's caterpillar hid in its cocoon, looking like a lump of hardened pitch. After Zakai's birth, she'd been forced to build a shell—a fortress—to protect her son. Now her cocoon was so hard—so petrified—she would never be able to break out.

I'm not like them. I'm not. She pushed herself up and gathered the leftover rounds of bread into a basket. She found a handful of dried figs and some almonds. The man had been big, but he'd also looked half-starved, all muscle and bone, as if he'd gone years without a good meal.

"Here." She shoved the basket toward Penina. "Take this to him."

But Penina crossed her arms and turned her head away.

Now what? "Don't you want to help him?"

Penina shook her head. She lifted her hand and placed her finger above Martha's heart. Her eyes softened as she made her meaning clear.

Martha stepped back. "No. I can't do it." Mary probably wouldn't even let her in the door. And Simon would find out.

Penina pointed back to the well and then at Martha's heart again, shaking her head. That woman—the one at the well—that wasn't her. Penina knew it, and so did Martha.

Martha's lips trembled, and tears welled in her eyes. Penina took the basket from Martha's hands and set it on the ground, then gathered her in her arms like a mother, murmuring the only sounds she could, like the coos of a dove.

Martha pressed her face to Penina's shoulder. She'd denied help to an injured man. That was never what Abba would have wanted from her. And Mama would have been ashamed to see her today.

Penina stepped back. Her hands said go. *Go to Mary. Help her.*

Martha gulped down a sob. Could she? Mary had chosen the better part. Was it too late for her to choose it as well?

Penina picked up the basket and put it in her hands, then pushed her toward the door. Martha took a deep breath and straightened her shoulders. She gave Penina a trembling smile, but her legs shook like a newborn lamb's as she walked out the door.

She walked across the meadow and through the city gate. The nearer she came to Mary's door, the more her worry grew. What if Simon found out? He'd told her what would happen if she defied him. What if Chana was there? Or Jael saw her?

Was this the better part? Was this what Jesus meant? To do something that made your legs quake and your hands shake? That made your mouth as dry as dust?

The door to Mary's courtyard stood half-open. She slipped inside silently, her hands clutching the handles of the basket. Sarah saw her first. The little girl threw her arms around Martha's legs and buried her face in her tunic. Adina held a fussing baby Natanel.

"What is it?" Had he already died? Was she too late?

"Mama's crying," came Sarah's muffled voice.

Martha stepped into the house. Mary bent over the hulk of a man lying on a pallet in a dim corner, her back to the door. The sunlight slanted through the square-cut windows on each wall. Martha could see the man's long legs, caked with dirt. A roughly woven bag lay beside him, lumpy, as though it held a load of kindling.

"Stay outside, girls," Mary commanded without turning, a hitch of a sob in her voice.

Martha gave the basket to Sarah. "Take this and do as your mother says."

Mary turned to Martha. Her eyes were red and her cheeks shone with tears, but she said nothing. Shame burned through Martha.

"Mary . . ." What could she say? How could she ever explain how she'd become so bound from a long-ago sin that she couldn't break free? "I'm sorry." It was all she could manage.

"I know." Mary, as she always had, held out her arms.

Martha fell into her sister's embrace, but her heart was still raw. She didn't deserve Mary's forgiveness.

Mary knelt beside the unconscious man, but Martha hesitated. She was here now, but what could she do? The man lay on his back, his face hidden in shadow and smeared with blood. His long, soot-colored hair tangled in his matted beard.

Who was he, and how did he get so injured when he looked as though he could take on an army? Jael was right; he wasn't a Jew. Was he a Samaritan? Or perhaps a pagan?

Martha wavered. She could still leave. Maybe Jael wouldn't find out she'd been here. Mary raised her eyes to Martha's. "You were always better at cutting hair."

Martha's heart turned in her chest.

Mary sniffled. "Remember when I cut Lazarus's hair?"

Emotion welled in Martha as she recalled how small Mary had been, not even as old as Zakai, and how proud of herself. "He looked like he'd been in a fight with pruning shears." She smiled at the memory.

Mary held out the scissors.

Martha hesitated, the moment weighing on her like a cloak of lead. Could she take the scissors—make the choice—that Mary offered?

Choose the better part.

Martha went to her knees beside her sister and took the scissors from her hand. The decision was made. The walls of the little house were still standing; the sun hadn't fallen from the sky. At least not yet.

"Be careful," Mary whispered. "Don't reopen the wound."

"I won't." As if she was going to be rough with this man who looked like he might attack them both if he awoke.

They worked together in silence. Gently, Martha pinched hanks of hair and snipped around the crusted wound. The gash started above his ear and wrapped around his head as if he'd been in the jaws of a lion. It was deep and already festering. Mary poured wine on a scrap of cloth and gently wiped the wound.

"I know what they say about me," Mary whispered as they worked. "The women, my own mother-in-law." Mary pressed her lips together as if to stop their trembling. "That I'm not a good wife, that I don't follow the law." She waved at the proof of it in the man laid out on her floor. "That Abba was ashamed of me."

Martha's hands stopped; her heart ached in her chest. *I am the one who didn't follow the law. The one Abba was ashamed of.* Yet she'd let them push that shame on Mary for years. Let them ridicule her sister. "You are a good wife, Mary." She reached out and took her sister's hand. "And Abba loved you, you know that."

Mary looked at her doubtfully.

Martha turned the unconscious man's head and snipped carefully until a pile of dark hair lay on the floor beside her and he looked almost human.

Mary laid her hand on Martha's arm. "What happened to us, Martha? When did we become strangers instead of sisters?"

Martha's throat closed. She knew when. Her words came out in a whispered croak. "You got married . . . you got Josiah . . ."

"And you got Penina." Mary's voice was small and childlike.

What did Mary mean? "But Penina is . . ." Her friend. Her sister. The only one who knew her secret. The only one who understood. Could Mary be as hurt by Martha turning to Penina as Martha was when Mary wed Josiah?

Mary's mouth turned down like it had when she was a baby, trying not to cry. "After she came home with you, you didn't talk to me anymore. It was just her."

Martha blinked back her own tears. *And Zakai.* She should

have told her from the beginning. "You had Josiah and the girls . . ."

"He's my husband, Martha, but I needed my sister. I needed you, especially after Abba died." Twin tears trickled over her cheeks. "I miss Abba . . . and I miss you."

Martha put her arms around Mary and pulled her to her. All these years, Mary thought Penina had replaced her in Martha's heart, just as Martha felt like Josiah had taken Mary from her. Martha pulled back and wiped the tears from Mary's face with the corner of her mantle. "I love Penina. She is like a sister to me."

Mary blinked as though she would cry again.

"But you *are* my sister. I love you and always will. Always. And nothing and no one will ever change that." As she said it, she knew it was true. Even Jael, even Simon. She wouldn't turn her back on Mary ever again. "Please, Mary. Forgive me for being such an idiot."

Mary's face became serious. "We have much to talk about, Martha."

Martha nodded. They did. It was time to tell Mary everything. Relief lightened the weight in her chest. It would be good to share her burden with Mary. They would have no secrets now.

The man beside them moaned and shifted.

Martha leaned over him. "He's waking up." They would talk later, after he was cared for.

Mary rolled to her feet. "He'll need something for the pain. Elishiva will have willow bark. I'll get it." She hesitated. "Will you—can you stay here with him?"

Martha took Mary's hand in hers and kissed it. "I'm not going anywhere."

In a moment, Mary was gone. The stranger jerked and rolled, as if he were fighting off an attacker, then quieted again.

Martha leaned over his shadowed face. At least she could trim his awful beard while he was still asleep. She snipped carefully under his chin and up around his jaw.

How could she not have seen that it wasn't easy for Mary to

choose the better part? It was hard. But she did it anyway instead of hiding. Instead of pretending. *Like I have.* How would her life be different if she'd been more like her brave sister?

She shifted her attention to the man before her. Carefully, she trimmed around his mouth until his beard was short and neat, just as the Pharisees wore theirs. As she angled the scissors around his jaw to cut away the last of the knots, a feeling of recognition crept over Martha. Her heartbeat quickened. Why did that chin look so familiar?

Regret and heartache for Mary disappeared, replaced with confusion, then with fear. Her hands trembled as she smoothed the stranger's hair and leaned back on her heels, letting the light from the window illuminate his face.

Her heart jumped into her throat.

It can't be him.

But she knew that mouth, that smooth forehead, those wild eyebrows. Panic pounded through her chest. She knew the slate gray that hid behind those closed eyes.

She inched back from the body in front of her. *He is dead. He has to be dead.*

That mouth had kissed her and whispered promises. Those arms—no longer those of a boy, but hard and muscular—had held her close. How could he be here? And why now? *Why now, Isa?*

His hands twitched and flexed. His eyes opened.

She couldn't move. Couldn't think. Couldn't even breathe. The moment slowed and stopped until there was nothing, not the sounds of the birds outside the window or the warmth of the sun.

Only his voice, like a knife plunging into her heart. "Martha." Just one word, but it changed everything.

Isa. He wasn't dead. *But if he isn't dead, where has he been for seven years?*

Chapter Thirty-Eight

MARTHA'S HEART BEGAN to beat again. Her breath rose and fell in her breast. The birds sang, and the sun warmed her shoulders. His hand searched and found hers. He lifted it and pressed her fingers to his mouth.

She snatched her hand back, her mind spinning like a whirlwind. Isa. He had come back to her, but too late. Seven years too late. One day too late. Cold shock gave way to the heat of anger. If he wasn't dead, this man who had promised to come back to her, where had he been all this time?

She lurched to her feet, backing away from him. It didn't even matter, not anymore. She was Simon's wife now, or as good as married to him. And if Simon suspected, if he found out . . .

She stared at him. Anyone with eyes would see that Zakai was his son.

Zakai. He couldn't know about Zakai. Not now, not ever. If he knew he had a son . . . *he'd be so happy.*

She covered her mouth with her hand. He couldn't know. He had to leave. Soon, before anyone saw what was right in front of their eyes. It was the only way for her and Zakai. And for him. She'd send him away and make him promise never to return. That's the least he could do after what he'd put her through. But he was in no shape to leave Bethany.

She dropped to her knees beside him. He didn't speak. At

least that part of him hasn't changed. She whispered fiercely, "Don't tell anyone. I mean it, Isa. Not your name. Not that you know me." She heard the pleading in her voice. She shook him by the shoulder, and he flinched. Could he possibly know how important this was? "Please, Isa. Do you understand?"

He blinked, and his head moved in what could have been a nod. His eyes rolled back in his head, and he was gone, his face slack, his limp hand falling to his side.

Mary rushed through the door and dropped to her knees beside Martha, a jar in her hand. She struggled with the wooden stopper. "We'll put it in water and—" Mary caught her breath, the jar forgotten in her hand. "Martha. Isn't that—?" She stared at the man on the floor. "Martha, it's Isa."

Martha's heart sank. She needed Mary's help to keep him hidden. And for that, she'd have to tell her. About Zakai, the orchard. All of it.

Mary nudged her aside and laid her hand on Isa's slack face. "Thank the Almighty. Zakai will finally have his father."

Martha stared at her sister, her mouth dropping open. Mary knew? "How did you . . . How long have you known?"

Mary blew a breath through closed lips, sounding much like Safta. "You didn't think I believed Abba's story, did you?"

Martha blinked. Yes, she had thought that. "Why didn't you tell me?" What a relief it would have been to not hide her secret from Mary.

"I wanted you to tell me." Mary's face showed the years of hurt. Years Martha couldn't get back. "When you left with Abba . . . I wanted to ask. Then you came back with Penina, and you were so different. So sad. I thought something had happened to Isa."

Something *had* happened to him, but she didn't know what it was. "I'm sorry, Mary. I should have . . . I wanted to . . ."

"I know." Mary squeezed her hand. "But now you can marry, and Zakai will have his abba."

"I'm betrothed, Mary. It's too late. *He's* too late."

Mary looked at her like she was speaking Greek. "You can't marry Simon. Not now. Isa is Zakai's father."

"But Lazarus will never—not to a pagan." And Lazarus had never made a secret of how he felt about Isa. "Besides, Simon would have to break the betrothal."

And Simon would make her—and Isa—pay the price.

"The Lord will give us a way, Martha." Mary pulled her close. "You'll see."

How could she believe that? What way and how?

Suddenly, a frantic shout came from the courtyard, and Chana burst through the door. "Girls!" she gasped out. "Come quick!" Her thin face was red, as though she'd run all the way across Bethany.

Martha jumped to her feet. What now? Had Simon already found out about Isa?

Chana panted. "It's Lazarus." She caught another breath. "Come, both of you. Your brother is sick."

MARTHA'S FEET POUNDED alongside Mary's as they ran through Bethany, their tunics tangling around their legs. They lifted them to their knees, not caring about the startled looks as they passed the houses in the village and raced through the village gate.

Martha's chest ached for breath. They'd left Isa in the care of the biggest gossip in Bethany, and all Martha could do was pray. Pray Isa would stay quiet. Pray Simon wouldn't find out who lay injured in Chana's home. And pray Lazarus wasn't seriously ill.

Their sandals clattered into the courtyard and through the house. Lazarus lay on Martha's bed, his eyes closed, his face ashen. Penina sat beside him, worry on her face and Zakai clinging to her tunic. Simon stood in the corner, wringing his hands. A flash of relief crossed his face, and something else—guilt?—when he saw Martha. She didn't have time to think about it.

She went to Penina's side. "What happened?"

Simon spoke up, his voice loud in the small room. "I found him in the orchard. I didn't know what to do."

Martha cut Simon off with a look. "Penina? What's wrong with him?" She bent over Lazarus. Her brother looked old. Ancient. His eyes were sunken, his skin the color of parchment.

Penina's mouth trembled, and tears shone bright in her eyes. She brought Martha's hand to Lazarus's forehead. His skin was hot and dry, as if he'd been standing next to a fire. "Get water; we must cool him."

Simon stepped closer, the fragrance of myrrh making her stomach turn. "He seemed fine when he came to my home." He cleared his throat and stood straighter. "Maybe a little quiet. Now that I think on it, a bit pale. He left quickly."

"And then?" Martha loosened Lazarus's tunic.

"I checked on my workers in the southern field. When I returned, I found him in the orchard."

Penina came with a bowl of water and a cloth. She leaned over Lazarus and pulled down his tunic, uncovering him to his waist.

Martha's heart wrenched at his bony ribs. When had he become so thin? But as Penina straightened, Martha's heart seemed to stop beating altogether. A lump, swollen and the size of her fist, protruded from her brother's side.

Martha gasped, and a sob broke from Mary.

Martha thought back desperately. He hadn't been eating well for weeks. And he'd gone to his bed early and stayed there late into the morning. She'd been so worried about Simon, about Penina and Zakai. Her eyes blurred with tears. How could she not have seen what was happening to Lazarus?

Martha rubbed her eyes. She needed to think. As she took Simon's arm and pulled him toward the doorway, he stiffened at her touch. Why should he when they were betrothed? "Accept our gratitude, Simon. The Most High surely brought you to Lazarus in his moment of need. And now he needs his family."

He swallowed and lowered his voice. "If he doesn't recover..."

She shook her head. "He will." *He has to.*

He rubbed his reddening neck. "Please send word if you need anything. Anything at all, all I have is yours."

There was one thing he could do. "Simon, would you—I mean, if you could—"

He stepped closer. "Anything, Martha."

She leaned back, away from his round-eyed stare. "A physician. The one from the upper town in Jerusalem." He'd treated Abba. He would know what to do. And it would get Simon out of Bethany for a few hours.

"Of course."

She returned to Penina, Mary, and Zakai in the bedroom.

Zakai ran to her, and she wrapped him in her arms. "He'll get better, won't he, Marmar?"

"He will, Zakai. I promise you, he'll get better." She pressed her face to his shaggy hair, shutting her eyes to the scene in front of her. But when she looked up, it was all still there. Lazarus, lying motionless on the bed. Mary and Penina, looking at her with tear-filled eyes. Waiting for her to tell them what to do.

But Martha didn't know what to do.

Chapter Thirty-Nine

She watches the conduct of her household,
and eats not her food in idleness.
—Proverbs 31:27

SIMON BROUGHT THE physician within hours. He was thin, with sad eyes and a nose like a vulture. Lazarus opened his eyes and tried to answer his questions, but his voice was weak.

"How long have you felt the pain?" Months, Lazarus said.

"Weakness?" Every day.

"Have you been able to eat?" Lazarus shook his head before closing his eyes and dropping back into the netherworld—somewhere between a restless sleep and senseless pain.

The physician examined him. The lumps under his arms, his pallid skin. Lazarus groaned and moved restlessly when the man prodded the swelling beneath his ribs.

"There is nothing to do but pray," he said to Martha, his eyes drooping above his beaky nose. "This will help the pain." He gave Martha a small jar. Simon passed the physician a silver coin as he showed him out.

Nothing to do but pray? There had to be some way to help him. In her storeroom, she ransacked her supplies. Rosemary, dill, a pinch of cinnamon. Bottles of unguents she had used for Abba—camphor, mustard, sandalwood. Surely there was something that would cure him? She couldn't stand by helplessly and watch Lazarus die.

Simon stood nearby as she sifted through bottles and jars. "Martha, about the betrothal." He twisted his hands together. His face was guarded, as if he wasn't sure what to say.

Martha pressed her lips together. Now wasn't the time to talk of marriage, not with Lazarus struggling for breath. "Yes, Simon." She tried to keep her voice calm; he had just paid for the poppy extract they would never have been able to afford. "When Lazarus recovers, we will announce the betrothal, just as he wanted."

Simon's brows shot up in surprise, and he seemed to search for words. "Of course," he finally said. "Your brother will recover. And then we will announce the betrothal." He ducked out the door as if wild dogs were chasing him.

Martha swallowed her irritation. Yes, the betrothal should be announced, but didn't she have enough to worry about with Lazarus ill? Finally, she unearthed cumin and dried rue. They were said to cure many illnesses. If she mixed them with a dose of the poppy juice, perhaps he would sleep well. And sleep would restore him, everyone knew that.

In the courtyard, Martha poured boiling water over the powdered rue. How could Lazarus have kept this from her? And for so long? When he was well—when he got better—she'd tell him what she thought of his foolishness. She wiped a hand across her wet eyes. And he *would* get better.

For hours, Zakai had worn a path between Lazarus's side and his animals in the corner, watching Lazarus for signs of life as closely as he watched his cocoon. Waiting for both to emerge from their silence. Now, he came to her. "Can I go to Mary's?"

"I told you no, Zakai," she almost shouted. He couldn't go there, not with Isa.

His mouth trembled, and he blinked hard. Safta glared at her and put her arm around Zakai, pulling him close.

Martha turned back to the fire, wishing she could take back her harsh words. But she couldn't risk Isa seeing him. Mary and Josiah had gone to the Temple to pray, but before she left, Mary had checked on Isa. He hadn't spoken a word, Chana had reported, and only woken to take water and a little food.

Martha swirled the rue in the hot water. She needed to see him, to send him away. And she would, as soon as Lazarus was better. She strained the mixture and added a few drops of poppy juice and a spoonful of honey to make it go down easily.

In the house, she pushed the cup into Penina's hands. "Give him this. I'll stoke the fire." Hot coals in the brazier beside his bed would fight the chill on his skin that had replaced the fever. Martha pushed more wood into the flames, then straightened the coverings on the bed.

Penina hadn't left Lazarus for a moment, but now she took Martha's hands in hers, stopping her frenzy of activity. She pressed Martha down to sit beside Lazarus. *Stay*, she motioned.

Martha tried to rise. "No. I must . . ." There must be something more to do than sit with anxiety eating like a worm in her belly.

Penina signed again. *Stay with him*. Then she settled at the foot of the bed and closed her eyes.

Martha covered her face with her hands. She didn't want to look at Lazarus, didn't want to see his sunken cheeks, the hollows around his eyes, his skin the color of ash. He was dying. She could hear it with his wheezing breath, smell it on his skin. Was this really all they could do? Be with him. Stay with him as he left this world?

He stirred, and his eyes opened, cloudy with pain. "Martha."

"I'm here, Lazarus." She offered him a weak smile.

He grimaced. "The betrothal."

She set her hand over his cool fingers. First Simon, now Lazarus. Why must they talk about that now? "Don't worry. I've spoken to Simon."

Lazarus struggled to speak again, his voice so soft she had to bend close to him to hear. "I'm sorry, Martha." He winced and closed his eyes.

Martha stroked his cheek. Why should he be sorry? He was

doing what he thought was best for her. For all of them. It must be the poppy juice, muddling his thoughts.

He seemed relieved, squeezing her hand and letting out a rattling breath. He closed his eyes and drifted away. Martha laid her head on his chest. Just a moment's rest, that's all she needed.

MARTHA JERKED AS she heard the courtyard gate slam. The light was dim. Had she slept that long? As she sat up, Mary rushed in. "Martha," she said, her voice breathless. "There is something we can do."

"What?" Anything. She'd do anything.

"We must send for Jesus."

Jesus? "Do you think—could he?" Hope flickered in her heart. Could he heal Lazarus?

Mary grasped Martha's hands in hers. "I know he can. We've heard so much. He's cured the blind, made the lame walk. Surely for someone he loves like Lazarus?"

Lazarus stirred. "No," he whispered. He tried to rise. "I forbid it," he gasped, slumping back down on the bed.

Martha looked from Lazarus to Mary. It would be dangerous for Jesus. Everyone knew the authorities were looking for him. And Lazarus didn't even know about Simon's threats. Bringing Jesus to Bethany would be dangerous for them all.

"Martha," Mary went on as if her brother hadn't spoken. "He can save Lazarus. We must send for him."

A tide of doubt flooded her spark of hope. What had the men said when they talked of Jesus? That there was one place he couldn't heal . . . Nazareth. *They had no faith in him.*

Lazarus moaned, as if trying to speak, then faded back into a restless sleep.

Martha pulled Mary from the room and out into the twilight where Josiah hunched over the fire. Penina followed, her brows pulled down.

"I don't know, Mary." Her voice wavered.

"We have to, Martha," Mary whispered.

"But Lazarus said no." He'd forbidden it. And if he knew what Simon had said . . . What if she put them all in danger, and then Jesus couldn't heal Lazarus because of her lack of faith?

"He doesn't know what he's saying," Mary countered.

Mary waited. Penina watched, Martha's own doubt reflected on her face. Josiah stared at the fire. Martha's pulse quickened; the familiar anxiety seeped through her limbs, paralyzing her. Even if Jesus could cure him—if they brought him to Bethany despite the risk—there was still one problem. "Where is he?"

Josiah shrugged. "They say he's hiding. But I could ask in Jerusalem. Someone may know."

They all waited on her decision. Josiah and Mary. Penina. Martha's chest tightened, cutting off her breath. *I don't know what to do.* She needed to be alone. Until this wave of panic passed, she couldn't even think. She turned away and stumbled out the door. Mary's voice calling her name faded as she ran into the gathering dusk, across the meadow, and through the stream. She scrambled into the orchard and threw herself down under the shadows of the apricot trees, burying her face in her hands.

You are anxious and worried about many things, Jesus had said. She was. Worried for him and for Lazarus. Worried for herself and Zakai and Penina. And now there was Isa to worry about as well. Her worry weighed on her like a mountain of stone. She couldn't think. Couldn't decide. How could she know what to do?

There is nothing to do but pray, the physician had said. She closed her eyes and prayed as she had never prayed before. *Please, Lord. Tell me what to do.*

Chapter Forty

I will teach the wicked your ways, that sinners may return
to you. Rescue me from death, God, my saving God,
that my tongue may praise your healing power.
—Psalm 51:15–16

*P*AIN SHOT BEHIND Isa's eyes as he stumbled toward the wall around Bethany. His head pounded, and the streets tilted.

He wasn't waiting a moment longer to see Martha.

When the old woman who had given him water and food left the house, he'd seen his chance. He'd dragged himself from the pallet and crept through the falling dusk. A cold wind brought the scent of cooking fires, but the smell of food didn't tempt his empty stomach.

He recalled bits and pieces since the men had attacked him. Women gathered around a well. Raised voices. Martha's stricken face when he opened his eyes. She hadn't been happy to see him. *Don't tell anyone.* His heart dropped at the memory. But what had he expected? For her to slaughter the fatted calf and prepare him a homecoming feast?

He hadn't said a word—as if he could have gotten a word in. The old woman hardly took time to draw a breath. The little girl—Sarah was her name—she was tiny, but brave enough to creep close to him when she thought he was sleeping. He'd whispered questions to her.

"Martha . . . do you know her?"

She nodded, her eyes big.

"Where does she live?"

She looked over her shoulder, where the grandmother babbled to the baby. "In my grandfather Sirach's house, blessed be his memory."

Blessed be his memory. Sirach was dead and Martha yet unmarried. Hope warred with shame and regret. He knew why she hadn't married, and it was his fault.

He must speak to her.

He passed through the village gate, deserted while the men had their evening meal. Dust spiraled through the dry meadow, filling his eyes with grit. The world shifted as a wave of dizziness passed over him, and the emerging stars lurched over his head.

The pain beating in his head magnified his despair. If Sirach was gone, Lazarus would be the man of the family, and he surely hated Isa. Lazarus had seen them that morning in the orchard, seen Isa make a vow to Martha that he didn't keep. *Lazarus knows what a coward I was.* And if Lazarus knew about the demons, he would despise him even more.

He reached the imposing gate to Sirach's courtyard. Torches blazed on the arched entrance, the wind making the shadows twist against the walls. His thoughts jumped and tangled, as chaotic as the dancing shadows. He couldn't go in there. Not like this. He'd wait for her in the orchard, like he always had. She would come there.

He splashed through the shallow trickle of the stream. Dead leaves blew in the chill wind, fluttering against his wet calves. If she came, what would he tell her? It didn't matter; he just wanted to see her.

He pushed aside the low-hanging branches. There was the tree he sought, the oldest tree, in the center of the garden. Its branches swayed and creaked in the wind. His heart jumped. There, underneath the heavy branches, a form as familiar to him as his own face.

Martha.

Her knees were drawn up and her head bowed. The wind teased at her uncovered hair and plastered her tunic to her legs.

Isa lurched toward her and fell to his knees.

She jerked up, and her breath escaped in a gasp. Her face was pale and covered in tears. He reached out to her, cupping her cheek in his hand. Words swam in his mind but wouldn't form on his tongue. *Please, Martha, don't cry.*

She jerked away and buried her face in her knees. Sobs shook her shoulders and wrenched at his heart.

His head hurt. The orchard was spinning, and he didn't know what to do with the woman in front of him. He ached to gather her shaking body in his arms and hold her close, to comfort her in the only way he knew how. But he couldn't, not this time.

When at last her sobs waned, she raised her head and took a quivering breath. "Lazarus is dying," she said.

Lazarus? He pictured the young boy who had found them here in the orchard. He couldn't be twenty years old yet. What could have happened to him?

She let out her breath. "I don't know what to do . . . and now you're here." She bit down on her trembling lip as another tear slid down her cheek. "Seven years, Isa." Her voice gained an edge of anger. "Why didn't you come back?"

He looked at her tear-stained face, heard the accusation in her voice, but didn't answer. If he told her, she would despise him, and so would her family. He needed time to prove himself to her, to make her trust him again. And then, he promised himself, he would tell her about the demons, about how Jesus had healed him.

Jesus. The idea jolted him upright. Jesus could heal Lazarus.

Hadn't Melech said he'd cured the sick and healed the blind and lame? In fact—understanding passed through him like a bolt of lightning—this was why Jesus sent him here, to Bethany.

Go home to your family. Announce to them all that the Lord in his pity has done for you.

He'd thought only of himself, of finding Martha. But perhaps the real reason Jesus had sent him to Bethany was for Lazarus. God had given him a way to redeem himself in the eyes of Martha, her family, perhaps all of Bethany. If he saved Lazarus, then they would accept him, listen to him. And find him worthy to marry Martha.

MARTHA HUDDLED BESIDE the tree, the wind sending fingers of cold down her back.

Isa. He was here, with her. And as silent as ever.

He had left her. Abandoned her. And now, when her world was falling apart, he'd returned. And there he sat, unwilling to even answer the question that had plagued her every day—every hour—for seven years.

She pulled away from him. She shouldn't even speak to him. She should send him away, make him suffer as she had suffered for seven years. Instead, she wanted him to move closer. She wanted his arms around her, wanted him to hold her until her racing heart stilled, until her worried mind was soothed by his quiet presence.

Isa wrapped his hands around hers, bringing them close to his heart. "Martha. You must send for Jesus."

She jerked away as though he'd burned her. "How . . . what? Did Chana tell you?"

He leaned closer, his voice rising. "Chana? No, Martha. That's why I'm here. Why I came to you. To tell you to send for Jesus."

"Send for Jesus." She repeated his words dumbly. Wasn't that the question she'd come to the orchard to answer? "Do you know Jesus?" Isa hadn't met him in Bethany, she knew that. He'd never spoken to anyone but her.

"Yes. I know him." He swallowed hard and squeezed her fingers.

A shiver chilled her. For a moment, she'd seen a flash of fear, of desolation, in his face. Then it was gone, replaced by a conviction, a fervor, an intensity she'd seen before—when Lazarus spoke of Jesus.

"Jesus can save Lazarus, Martha. Believe me." Moonlight illuminated his face, his eyes pleading with her. "He is the Messiah."

Her heart twisted. *The Messiah.* Just like Lazarus and Mary believed. And now Isa, too? A pagan believed Jesus was the Messiah? *How do you know?* she wanted to shout. How did any of them know? She snatched her hands back and shrank away from him. "Why should I even listen to you? You left me—after you promised to come back—and you haven't even told me why."

A muscle jerked in Isa's jaw, but he didn't speak. He rubbed a hand over his chest as if remembering a hidden pain.

Martha pressed her trembling lips together. He wasn't going to tell her, and she wouldn't ask again. She let out a breath. "Besides, even if he is the Messiah, I can't send for him. I don't even know where he is."

"That's just it." Isa leaned toward her, his eyes burning as with a fever. "I know where he is, Martha. I know where you can find Jesus."

Chapter Forty-One

MARTHA PUSHED HERSELF up from her pallet on the floor, every muscle stiff. Her swollen eyes felt full of sand, her throat coated with wool. The first rays of dawn trickled through the window with the cool breeze. Mary slept next to her, baby Natanel curled in her arms. Safta snored in the corner, and Penina sprawled at the foot of Lazarus's bed. All of them, keeping a desperate vigil at Lazarus's side.

She'd sent Josiah to Bethabara two days ago, at dawn the morning after Isa had found her in the orchard. Isa had wanted to go, but he could hardly stand. She'd ordered him back to Chana's, warning him to stay out of sight.

Two full days of waiting, of praying, of worrying. Had she done the right thing? She prayed that Josiah hadn't told his mother. That Simon wouldn't find out. That her own lack of faith wouldn't fail her brother.

As quiet as a moth, she stepped around Mary and bent over Lazarus, her heart pushing hard on her chest. *Thank the Lord, Healer of the Sick, he breathes.*

Penina jerked awake, a panicked question in her sleepy eyes.

"He's still with us," Martha whispered. "Go back to sleep."

Penina crawled up the bed and curled beside Lazarus's still body. She laid her cheek on his hair and closed her eyes. Martha brushed Penina's tangled hair from her childlike face. Was it

right for Penina to lie beside him when they weren't even betrothed? Abba would be outraged. But Lazarus's breathing seemed
to ease as she curled next to him. Penina's face smoothed from
worry to peace.

Martha couldn't separate them. Not when they had so little
time.

*Lord, Almighty One, Most High. I beg you. If he is your
Anointed, bring Jesus to us in time.*

Safta awoke and held out her hand to Martha. Martha sank
down beside her, burying her face in her grandmother's shoulder.

Safta stroked her wrinkled hand over Martha's face. "You are
stronger than you think, my girl," she whispered.

Martha breathed in Safta's scent of dust and ashes and
blinked back tears. Her grandmother was wrong. Safta didn't
know how weak she really was.

Lazarus began to move restlessly, his face creased in pain.
She pulled away from Safta. Lazarus would need the poppy juice
again. And Penina and Mary needed food. She couldn't remember the last time they'd eaten.

There was much to do.

She crossed the courtyard, hovering for a moment over
Zakai, asleep in his corner beside his animals. His face was
smooth and untroubled, but she knew the toll these days had
taken on him. She'd snapped at him more than once as worry
shortened her temper. She ran her hand softly over his hair. *Forgive me, my son.* Soon, Jesus would be here and the agonizing
wait would be over.

The rising sun marked the third day of waiting. If Josiah
had walked fast, he would have gotten to Bethabara late yesterday. If they had left immediately, Jesus could be here
tomorrow—midday at the earliest, surely by sunset. Lazarus
would hold on. He must. Anxiety squeezed her chest like a vise.
Please, Jesus, hurry.

Martha stirred the blackened remains of the fire, looking for
an ember. Could Jesus really be the Messiah? Lazarus and Mary

believed it. And Isa said he was. He had even known where Jesus could be found. A wisp of smoke curled from the ashes.

But Abba . . . *we must doubt.* Abba would have needed proof to believe.

She found a handful of straw and set it over the ember, blowing until a tiny lick of flame took hold. But if Jesus came, if he healed Lazarus . . . perhaps her doubt would finally be put to rest.

The flame spread, and she added a handful of kindling. *Please, Lord, be my help. Let him heal my brother.* That was all she asked. Nothing for herself, just for Lazarus to live. She'd marry Simon and be the perfect wife.

And she'd send Isa away.

"I'll wait for you here, every night," Isa had said when she'd left him in the orchard two nights ago.

As dusk fell each evening, she'd told herself that she wouldn't see him, that it was wrong for a betrothed woman to meet a man alone, in the dark. It was adultery if anyone discovered them. Still, as the moon rose, she would find herself in the orchard, and she would find Isa waiting.

She didn't tell him about the betrothal.

He didn't tell her where he'd been for seven years.

The first night, he'd brought a battered kinnor, repaired with twine and missing a string. He played softly, hardly louder than the whisper of the wind in the branches. The rustle of the new leaves added their own accompaniment, and the chirp of the night insects joined in the song.

The music seeped into her heart like water into parched soil. Just for those brief moments, her pounding heart eased and the weight of her worries lightened. For just a short time, she was free of worry, free of doubt. Isa's music, more than anything he could say or do, reminded Martha of his love for her. He had loved her not because she was the perfect daughter, or the sister who took care of everything, or the woman who made the meals and sewed the clothing. He loved her just because she was Martha.

The second night, he sang to her. His voice was deeper, richer than seven years ago. He sang to her of the Lord's love, of his people calling out to him in fear and trembling.

I sought the Lord, who answered me,
Delivered me from all my fears.

As he sang, she watched him. He'd changed. He wasn't just bigger and stronger. When they were younger, he had put aside his pagan ways for her. But now his faith in the God of the Jews wasn't for her or even for Abba's approval. She could hear it in his voice and see it in his eyes. It was his own, and it was strong. What had happened to bring him to this? And why now, when it was too late for them?

As a girl, she'd watched his hands move over the strings, his lips as he sang the songs. So many times she'd thought about those hands touching her, those lips kissing her. His touch may have been what she wanted then, but his strength—his faith in the God they both believed in—was what she needed now.

Now, as she fed tinder into the fire, watching it grow, she heard Isa's song echoing in her mind. Would the Lord answer her call and deliver them from all their fears? Isa believed Jesus was the Messiah. Could his faith in Jesus be enough to kindle her own?

How does he know? How can he be so sure?

Zakai rose from his corner and stumbled to her side. She pulled him close, leaning down to kiss the top of his head. How Isa would love to know of his son, but it was impossible. Nothing would protect Isa if Simon found out about him. And this time, no one would save him.

Zakai leaned against her leg. "Is Lazarus going to die, Marmar?"

She sank down on the ground and pulled him into her lap. "No." She forced the words through her raw throat. "Jesus will come; he will heal him. You'll see." If only she could be as sure as she sounded.

The courtyard door creaked. Zakai straightened, her own thought reflected in his face. *Could it be Jesus and Josiah? So soon?*

Instead, Jael stepped into the courtyard with a steaming pot. "Peace and strength to you, my dear." Her words were correct, but her mouth pulled down in a disapproving frown as her critical eyes surveyed the courtyard.

Zakai scrambled out of Martha's embrace. Martha glanced at her own dirty robe, the jumble of dishes beside the fire and soiled tunics in a pile. Her household was in disarray and so was she, but must Jael look at her as if she had been sleeping with a herd of pigs?

Jael handed her the pot as if she were giving a treasure of jewels. "At least you will have some food now."

"Peace be to you, and our thanks," Martha managed to say politely, taking the pot and passing it to Zakai. The lentils smelled wrong and had bits of black floating in them. Zakai wrinkled his nose, and she gave him a warning look. Jael may have burned the lentils, but at least she was here to offer sympathy.

Jael crossed her arms. "Is it true that you've sent for that fool, Jesus?"

Alarm prickled the back of Martha's neck. Simon's mother wasn't here to sympathize but to voice her disapproval. Why had she thought Chana could keep Josiah's journey a secret? If Jael knew, then surely Simon did as well.

"It's a waste of time, and you know it. Jesus." Jael's mouth puckered like a dried fig. "What would Sirach, blessed be his memory, say?"

Martha turned back to the dwindling fire, the mention of her father stinging her conscience. "Jesus is Lazarus's friend. He would want to know."

"Hmph." Jael crossed to the collection of pottery and bowls that Martha had dropped in a heap. "You think he'll heal your brother, but mark my words, he's a fraud." She sorted the pottery by size, stacking them precisely.

Martha rubbed her hand over her tired eyes. He may not be the Messiah, but plenty of people had seen him cure lepers, heal the lame, bring sight to the blind. If Jesus couldn't heal Lazarus, it would be Martha's fault, not his own. But why argue with Jael when she'd soon have to live with her?

Jael examined a wine cup. "Anyway. He'd be a fool to show up in Bethany, him and those rough friends."

Martha advanced on Jael. "Then he is a fool, because he will be here." She snatched the cup from Jael's hands and threw it in the corner, shattering it to pieces.

Jael raised her brows and stepped back. "You should be more careful, my dear. Those are expensive vessels." She brushed her hands over her tunic. "I will pray for your brother, Martha. But remember, he who touches pitch blackens his hands."

Heat crept up Martha's neck and into her face. So Jael thought the Almighty was punishing Lazarus, for what? Being Jesus' friend? She fisted her hands at her sides, angry words choking her. If the Almighty was punishing anyone, it was her. Not Lazarus, who had done nothing but love his family and follow the law all the days of his short life.

Before Martha could utter her thoughts, the courtyard door burst open.

"Josiah!" Zakai ran to the lone man who stumbled into the courtyard, the neck of his tunic dark with sweat as if he'd run all the way from the Jordan.

Jael moved close, her eyes alight with curiosity.

Martha brushed past Jael to scoop a cup of water. She put it in Josiah's hand. "Did you find him?"

He gulped, water spilling from the corners of his mouth and dribbling over his dusty beard. "Yes," he choked out. "In Bethabara."

Martha's heart sped up. Just where Isa said he would be.

Jael grunted like a goat choking on her cud.

"And you told him?" She looked through the open doorway. Would he be coming? Would she see him on the road?

"Can I go? Can I meet him?" Zakai asked quickly.

Josiah drank down more water and wiped his mouth with the back of his hand.

Martha clenched her hands into fists, wishing she could shake the words out of Josiah.

Josiah gave her back the cup and sank onto the bench under the fig tree, hunching his shoulders in exhaustion. "You know how he is." He let out a deep breath. "He told me to go back. Didn't explain why."

"But he's coming?" *Please, say that he's coming.*

"Can I go, Marmar, please? Can I go to the road?" Zakai pulled at her.

"Hush, Zakai!"

Zakai's face fell, and he blinked back tears.

Josiah shrugged and ran a hand over his face. "I told him. I told him to hurry. I got there late in the afternoon, ate and slept, then left early the next morning. I walked all yesterday and through the night."

Mary appeared at the door of the house, blinking in the weak sunlight. She ran to Josiah and threw herself at his feet, burying her face in his lap while he stroked her hair and murmured to her.

"Then he should be here," Martha calculated quickly. "If he left yesterday morning and stopped for the night. By this afternoon, certainly." No later than that. Her stomach twisted. And then they would see if he could heal Lazarus. Or if her lack of faith would fail her brother.

Jael wagged her pointy chin at Martha. "I'll pray for Lazarus, and so will Simon. The Holy One, blessed be he, hears the prayers of the righteous, my dear, not the prayers of sinners." She bent her lips at Josiah and Mary and flounced to the gate.

Martha ushered Jael out the gate, wishing she could slam it on her generous backside. Instead, she stood in the arched entrance, gazing down the road to the Jordan framed before her by oak trees and green fields of wheat. How many times had she stared down it, praying for Isa to appear? Hoping long after all hope was gone that he would come back to her and their son?

Now Isa was here, in Bethany, and she watched the road for another man.

Hurry, Jesus. Hurry.

Jesus wouldn't be too late. Not like Isa. Jesus would come in time.

Chapter Forty-Two

Then you will understand rectitude and justice, honesty, every good path;
For wisdom will enter your heart, knowledge will please your soul.
—Proverbs 2:9–10

LAZARUS OPENED HIS eyes. The golden light of late afternoon filtered through the window with the aroma of garlic and lentils. For a moment, he was a child again, waking from an afternoon rest, ready to run out to the courtyard, asking Martha for a taste of whatever she was cooking.

But the pain in his chest, the weakness in his limbs, drove away the memory. What had happened to him? He'd been in the orchard. Then men, carrying him to the house. Simon, wringing his hands. Zakai's worried face.

Later—had it been days or just moments?—Martha and Mary talking about Jesus. They had sent for him. He tried to sit up, but his head was as heavy as an iron ball. They didn't understand. It was too dangerous. If Jesus came, the Pharisees of Bethany would get in line to report him to the Sanhedrin. Jesus knew that as well as any of them.

Jesus had told him he would understand when the time came, and he did.

The hour is coming when the dead will hear the voice of the son of God. That meant him. The dead.

He had failed at all of it. He had been so sure that Simon was the answer to his prayers, and now he was out of time. He would die, and Martha would be left without a husband, Penina and Zakai with no protection. And he wouldn't be with Jesus to herald the coming of the new Eden.

Sinister shadows—he knew them from his childhood dreams—waited in the corners of the room. Patient. Vigilant. Resolute. Like sentries, they were ready to take him away.

He didn't have long.

Again, he tried to move, but his body was weighted with something warm and soft. He shifted to see Penina asleep beside him, her head pillowed on his shoulder. Her arm encircled him, as if holding him in this world. She wouldn't let the shadows come for him. Not yet. He lifted his hand to touch her silky hair.

Penina stirred and opened her sleep-clouded eyes. Her lids were red and swollen, and a fold in his tunic had pressed a deep crease in her cheek. She was the most beautiful woman he'd ever seen.

He'd been such a fool.

He opened his mouth to speak, but his throat was like an arid desert, his lips dry and cracked.

Penina slipped from the bed. *Don't leave.* But she was back, holding a cup of water to his lips. A few drops trickled down his throat; most ran down his chin and into his beard.

She wiped his beard with her sleeve, touched her fingers to a small jar, and smoothed sweet-smelling balm over his cracked lips.

"Penina," he whispered. If he could, he'd marry her today. Keep her beside him, like this, for the rest of his life—however long that would be. She looked away from his searching eyes and made the signs for Martha and Mary.

He lifted his heavy hand and captured hers, the effort almost too much for him. "No." His voice was not much more than a whisper. "You."

She eyed him warily.

"I've been an idiot, Nina," he croaked.

Her hands curled over his. So small and yet stronger than they looked. Then she nodded.

A laugh tickled his tortured chest. How could she make him smile even now? He pulled in a breath, scented with her, the smell of rainwater and lavender.

Her lips trembled, and she blinked back tears.

"I should have . . ." He waited for more air. ". . . married you." He would still be leaving her, still be dying, but they would have had some time together.

She let out a breath and nodded again, one tear spilling over.

He smoothed the tear away with his thumb. His strength was ebbing. The darkness leaned in. *Not yet.* The Lord had given him Penina to comfort him in his last moments. And Jesus had given him strength, had told him that he would hear his voice and call him out of darkness on the last day. "God is good, Penina."

Penina's mouth turned down, and she shook her head.

He pulled her back onto his chest. "He is. Penina. He is."

She burrowed closer to him, resting her head under his chin, wrapping her arms around him.

He wouldn't give in to the shadows that beckoned. Not yet. This was all he wanted. To watch the last rays of the sun slant through the window and hold Penina in his arms.

If this was dying, then he would die content.

WHEN HE AWOKE, the light pierced his eyes like arrows. The taste of iron filled his mouth, and pain lashed him to the bed.

Penina still sprawled beside him, and now Martha sat on a low stool, her head propped against the wall, her eyes closed. She looked terrible. Her hair was dull and tangled around her face, her tunic stained and wrinkled as though she'd worn it for weeks.

"He's awake!" Zakai's voice roused Martha and Penina like a trumpet blast.

Martha swayed forward. She laid her cool hand on his cheek, set her lips to his forehead. "Stay with me, brother," she whispered. "Jesus will come."

The shadows pulled at him. They were getting stronger. He

fumbled for her hand, and her fingers found his. "Martha . . ." He didn't have much time. The end beckoned like cool water—a deep pool free from pain.

"Jesus . . . he is the Messiah."

She smoothed his brow as if he were again a child with a bad dream. "Yes, Lazarus, he's going to heal you. Just like the lepers and the blind man. He knows you need him." But her voice was thick with the worry that always laid so heavy on her. She didn't believe in Jesus. Not yet.

If he could ease her worry. If he could lift the burden of her secret from her before he left this world . . . if he could only free her.

At least he'd seen the truth about Simon before it was too late. Thank the Almighty he'd stopped the betrothal. Simon would have made Martha's life miserable. Still, what would she do when he was gone? Who would take care of her and Penina? Who would teach Zakai to be a man? Who would put up with Safta?

The shadows pulled. A wave of pain clamped over his chest like an iron band. He was drowning. He wrenched his eyes open to see Mary, her face wet with tears. Martha's, full of worry. Safta's, reflecting his own suffering. "Penina?" He clutched at the air.

"She's here." Mary moved aside. "Right here." Penina slipped her hand in his. Zakai buried his head in Lazarus's side, shaking with sobs.

He pulled in a shallow breath, and a sharp pain followed. Martha held a cup for him, but as he put his lips to it, he smelled the bitterness of the poppy juice and turned his face away.

No more. It was time to go.

He held out his hand to his grandmother. She kissed it, laying her wrinkled cheek on his palm. "Go, my boy. Go where you need to go," she whispered. Her eyes were filled with peace. Safta understood. If only Martha and Penina did.

The room grew dim. "Marmar," he breathed. *I'll take your secret to my grave.* His childhood vow would soon be fulfilled.

"I'm here." Her face appeared close to his. She squeezed his hand, and her voice was tinged with fear.

"Don't be afraid." *Not for me. Not for yourself.*

Mary wept, her keening coming from the depths of her soul. "Lazarus, stay with us. He'll be here soon."

Mary. She didn't understand, but she would. Someday. *Don't despair, Mary.*

He reached out to Penina with the last of his strength, pulling her close. His labored breath seemed to ease as he felt her heart beat against his. He was so tired. So cold.

Martha whispered in his ear, begging him. "Stay with me. My brother, my sweet boy. Please."

His vision darkened. The shadows would wait no longer.

Penina's cheek pressed on his face, her tears on his lips. Zakai called his name, his little-boy voice breaking. Lazarus reached out. One hand found Martha's, the other Mary's. They held tight, but not tightly enough.

He couldn't stay. Not for Martha or Mary, not even for Penina or Zakai. He must give them all up.

Zakai. *Give him a father.*

Mary. *Comfort her.*

Martha. *Free her.*

Penina. The scent of lavender . . . *Give her faith.*

The light was gone now. The sounds of their voices, the touch of their hands . . . gone. There was nothing holding him back.

Lazarus, do you love me? Jesus' words whispered to him.

Yes, Lord, I love you. And he sank into the depths of infinite dark.

Chapter Forty-Three

Her children rise up and praise her; her husband, too, extols her.
—Proverbs 31:28

*D*USK DARKENED THE sky to the color of old ashes.

Martha sat in the corner of the courtyard, her hair loose and uncombed, her tunic gray with the dust of the tombs. Mary lay crumpled in a heap beside her. The third day of mourning was ending, the third day without Lazarus.

The courtyard, the meadow, every home in the village, was filled with mourners. Pharisees who had known Abba, merchants from Jerusalem, friends from Jericho and Emmaus. All to mourn for her brother, who had just begun to live. The mourning of shivah would continue until seven days had passed, and then, thankfully, the visitors would go home.

Martha pushed herself to her feet and walked on legs as stiff and aching as an old woman's. She felt nothing. She was a breath of air, as insubstantial as the mist that moved down from the hills into the valley, scattering at the whisper of wind.

For three days, she'd felt Lazarus's presence. In his clothes still hanging on the rosemary bush outside. His cup by the fire, next to the stool he used. The tools he'd left propped in the corner. She'd felt him, lingering. Perhaps his spirit had been waiting for Jesus as well, wondering why his friend hadn't come. Now she didn't feel him on the breeze or hear his voice whisper on the wind. Her brother was gone.

Lazarus had believed in Jesus. Now Lazarus was dead. Mary had believed in him. Now her heart was as broken as Martha's. Isa had believed in him, and he had been wrong. Now Isa must go, before anyone saw him. She must send him away before someone in the village realized who he was.

She'd sent word with Sarah, warning him to stay away from the mourning, not to come to the burial. And she'd stopped going to the orchard, where she knew he'd waited for her every night. It was too late for them, just as it was too late for Lazarus. Tonight she would send Isa away forever.

But first she would see to her family . . . what was left of it.

She slipped inside the house, to the room where Lazarus had breathed his last. Penina lay in a ball of misery on the bed, her hand clutching the bedclothes as if Lazarus's hand were still in hers, her eyes open but unseeing. She hadn't moved since Lazarus had taken his last breath.

That moment—an eternity ago—when he had left them forever.

As though dead herself, Martha had sat beside Lazarus as his hands had grown cold and his face lost its color. Mary had keened, Zakai had sobbed into the bed, Penina had held on to his body as if she wished to follow him into the afterlife.

Finally, Martha had kissed his face and closed his unseeing eyes.

With Mary, she had washed Lazarus with clean water and anointed him with myrrh and sandalwood. They'd had none of their own, but both Elishiva and Chana had provided from their meager stores. They dressed him in his white tunic and his *tallit*. With her scissors—the ones she'd used to cut his hair since he was a baby—Martha snipped the blue tassels from his tallit, as the law required. Mary wrapped his face in the burial veil while Martha tied his hands and feet with cloth strips and wrapped his body loosely in a linen winding sheet.

Word spread in the village.

Josiah and Chana arrived with the children. Villagers came

by twos and threes—some silent, some singing the plaintive songs of mourning. Elishiva and her quiet son. Devorah and Silva with their husbands. Simcha and his brother, who sat beside Zakai. Simon and Jael. They had been right; Jesus hadn't saved her brother. Jael was probably biting her tongue not to crow about it.

Martha brought each friend and villager to stand before Lazarus's body. They lamented and tore their tunics at the neck. The women put dust in their hair. The men sprinkled ashes on their clothing, praying, "Blessed art Thou, Lord our God, the True Judge." Martha touched his hands and ran her fingers over his face again and again, remembering him as a baby, a toddler, a young man.

Her baby brother. So peaceful. How could he look so peaceful?

As the sun rose high in the sky, they proceeded to the tomb. The low beat of a drum joined with the plaintive call of flutes. Songs of grief rose to the skies like the mournful cries of lost lambs.

Josiah and Simcha carried Lazarus on a cedar plank. Mary and Martha walked beside them, Zakai following behind with Sarah and Adina. A few of the men carried Safta in a litter, her old legs too weak to make the climb. Martha had pleaded and begged, but Penina refused to see Lazarus laid to rest.

At the tomb, three men pushed aside the slab of rock and laid Lazarus on the narrow stone bench inside. Martha and Mary knelt beside his body while the rest of the village gathered outside and mourned.

Mary's keening filled the enclosed space like a flood of despair, but Martha's tears had run dry. She kissed her brother's shrouded face one last time. *Good-bye, my sweet boy.* Since the day Mama had put him in her arms and with her dying breath asked her to take care of him, he had been like her own child. Now he was gone.

Was it her fault? Had her sin poisoned him, as it had destroyed Abba? The thought turned like a knife in her heart.

When the last rays of the sun filtered through the doorway, Josiah entered, lifted Mary to her feet, and led them out. The men rolled the stone over the mouth of the tomb, and they left him, their prayers of lamentation echoing over the hills.

Now Martha stood numb and lifeless in the room where Lazarus had died, and Penina looked as if she was next for the tomb. Safta shuffled into the room with a steaming bowl of soup. "Eat something, my girl."

Martha's stomach roiled at the warm scent of garlic, and she shook her head. How could she eat? How could she eat when she would never again see her brother's smile? "Give it to Penina."

Penina turned her face away.

"Lazarus wants you to keep up your strength, both of you," Safta said.

Something had happened to her grandmother with Lazarus's death. It was as if she didn't understand. She spoke of him as if he were still alive, as though he had only journeyed to Jerusalem for a few days. More than once, Martha had found Safta looking down the road toward the Jordan as if she was still waiting for Jesus to arrive.

Was Safta losing her senses? Didn't she understand it was too late? Perhaps she, too, was not long for this world. Martha rubbed a hand over her eyes, surprised to find them wet with tears again. They couldn't lose Safta, too. How could Zakai lose another person he loved?

Penina signed a word and pointed to herself.

What was Penina talking about? Martha's voice rose. "You can't die. That's not what Lazarus would have wanted." Martha reached to touch her friend, but Penina shrank back and closed her eyes. She made another sign and the one for Zakai.

Alarm rose in Martha and with it, anger at her friend. "Penina. I will not take Zakai." Because Penina could not give up. She must be strong so that Martha could be strong. They were all hurting, and they must face it together. "Please," she begged, "don't leave us. I can't do this without you."

Penina turned her face to the wall and didn't answer.

Was it possible, what Penina wanted? To die of despair?

A sob built in her. How could Penina desert her like this? "Grandmother," she choked out, and leaned on Safta. "What am I to do?"

"Give her time," Safta murmured. Her hand, surprisingly strong, closed over Martha's and tugged her out of the house and through the courtyard. She brought her to the gate and looked down the road into the deepening evening gloom. "He will come. And you must be strong."

Martha's heart ached for her grandmother. The loss of her daughter in Jerusalem, then Sirach, and now Lazarus had broken Safta's aged mind. Martha turned back to the courtyard and led her shuffling grandmother to the warmth of the fire. Mary was there, her mantle pulled over her head. She hadn't spoken to anyone since the burial, not even Josiah. She'd been so sure of Jesus, even to the last moments of Lazarus's life. Now she'd lost both her brother and her Messiah.

Martha put more wood on the fire, her heart sinking as Simon and Jael came through the gate. Could she not have one day of peace?

Jael swept toward her. "The souls of the righteous will find mercy, my dear. We must depend on that in your brother's case." Her voice was a whisper, as was proper in a house of mourning, but her words were as harsh as sand scraping against a wound.

Martha's ire rose to choke her. What did Jael know of mercy? If she had any mercy, she would leave them alone in their grief.

Simon cleared his throat. "I pray that your brother will rise again on the last day, Martha." He rubbed the back of his neck. "But now we must talk of our wedding." He kept his voice low enough so no one in the courtyard could hear, but Safta's head bobbed up.

"Now is not the time for that," Safta said.

Jael raised her brows. "It is the time. She has no father, no brother. She must be married immediately. Who do you think is going to take care of you all?"

Martha straightened and took a long breath. Jael was right. Lazarus would have wanted that. And the betrothal had been his last act. She could do no less than honor his wish—to see her married to Simon quickly.

Simon bowed stiffly. "I made the announcement at the city gate today." His mouth twisted. "It is better for everyone if we marry quickly, is it not?"

Martha understood his unsaid threat. Quickly . . . before she had a chance to dishonor him again. "You are right, of course, Simon." She wouldn't shame him. She would abide by the agreement she—and Lazarus—had made. She would be the perfect wife—never dishonoring him, and never welcoming Jesus into Bethany again.

Chapter Forty-Four

░░

*M*ARTHA MURMURED AGREEMENT as Simon and Jael whispered details of the wedding feast that would take place when the thirty days of mourning were done. Although the law required a year's mourning for a parent and only thirty days for a brother, Martha knew she'd mourn Lazarus for the rest of her life. Finally she breathed a sigh of relief as darkness and a chill wind sent Simon and Jael back to their home.

The rest of the mourners curled in their cloaks around the fire. Martha stared into the flames—trying not to think, trying not to feel—until the moon was high in the sky and everyone was asleep.

Isa must go. Tonight. And she knew what to say to make sure he never came back.

She crept through the bodies strewn about the courtyard, slipped out the gate, and stumbled toward the dark blur of the orchard, feeling as if another death were upon her. Down the embankment and across the trickle of river, and she was in the orchard.

She found him standing in the shadow of their tree, just where she knew he would be. He straightened when he saw her and stepped out to meet her. He looked better—steadier on his feet—than he had the last time they'd met. His slate-gray eyes were filled with pain but this time not his own.

"Martha." In his voice—just saying her name—was the solace she'd needed these past days. All she needed to soothe her grieving soul was right here, just a step away.

But she couldn't receive the comfort he would give. Not this time. *You are stronger than you think*, Safta had said. Now she must be. She couldn't give up, as Penina was doing. She could still protect Isa and Zakai.

"Martha." His voice was choked. "I thought he'd come. . . ."

She crossed her arms and stepped back, swallowing the tears that threatened.

"He is the Messiah." Isa reached out, his voice desperate as if he knew her doubt. "You must believe me, Martha."

"Believe you?" She pulled away as if his touch were a scorpion's sting. She'd wanted so badly to believe in Jesus. Just as she'd wanted to believe that Isa would come back to her. But like Isa, Jesus had abandoned her in her time of need. She closed her eyes to shut out his face, his earnest eyes.

She hardened her heart. It was the only way to get through what she had to do next. But before she sent him away, she must know. She opened her eyes. "Question or command, Isa?" *Please, say question. Please, Isa, answer my question.*

ISA CLENCHED HIS jaw and tried to think of something—anything—to say. He knew the question she had for him. Where had he been? Why hadn't he come back to her? And he couldn't answer it. He couldn't bear to see her pull away from him even more. He had been so sure that Jesus would come. That the Messiah would heal Lazarus and then Lazarus would embrace him as a brother and bless his marriage to Martha.

But Jesus hadn't come, and Lazarus was dead. How could he tell her now and make her despise him?

"Question or command?" she asked again.

He stepped back, crossing his arms over his chest. "I can't . . ." He looked at the ground, his feet—anywhere but at her accusing eyes. "I can't answer your question."

Her words were as sharp as flint and hit him like arrows. "Then your command is to leave, Isa. Leave Bethany, and never come back."

Go away and never come back? She didn't understand. He had to make her understand. "No, Martha. Please. I came back to you."

Her mouth trembled, and her eyes were bright with tears. "It's too late. *You're* too late."

Go home to your family, Jesus had said. Surely he wouldn't have sent Isa to Bethany if he had no one waiting for him. He spoke quickly. "Please, Martha, we'll marry like we planned, I don't have much—"

"I can't marry you, Isa." She took a shaking breath.

If she would only listen to him. He would take care of her; he'd do whatever he must to make her happy. "Martha, I—"

She cut him off with a fierce look. "Isa, I'm betrothed."

He heard her voice but couldn't make himself believe her words. Betrothed? She couldn't be. Why hadn't she told him?

Martha's voice dropped to a whisper. "As soon as the mourning is over, I'll marry."

It couldn't be true. She was his. She'd waited for him. And he'd come so far for her.

She turned aside, as if she couldn't bear to look at him. Her voice cracked. "You ran away, Isa. And you stayed away." She shook her head and swallowed hard. "It's too late."

Understanding pierced his heart. It had always been too late. His dreams of life with Martha and her family had been just that—ridiculous, foolish dreams. She deserved better than him. Sirach had known it. Lazarus had known it even as a boy. And if he was honest with himself, he'd known it all along.

She closed her eyes. "You need to go, Isa. Before Simon finds out about you."

Simon. He'd heard that name from Chana. Simon's fields, Simon's olive groves. Simon, the doctor of the law. The kind of man Sirach had wanted for Martha. The kind of man she deserved. "But what about . . ." He couldn't bring himself to say it. "Does he know about us?"

She met his eyes. "He knows I'm not a virgin."

Her words hit him like a slap in the face. What he and Martha had shared in this orchard was nothing more than a shameful picture in another man's mind. A defilement that lessened her worth in this other man's eyes. And it was his fault.

She turned her face away. "He's a good man, Isa. But if he finds you here . . ."

She didn't have to say it. Simon would want to kill him, and Isa didn't blame him. Isa had taken what wasn't his and run away like a thief, a coward. Martha deserved someone better.

And she'd found him.

He leaned closer, almost close enough to touch her. Everything in him demanded to pull her to him. But it was too late—he was too late. She stared up at him, her lips so close he could kiss them. But they weren't his to kiss, not anymore. They never had been.

He stepped away, and the cold night wind cut between them. "Is this what will make you happy? Is this really what you want, Martha?"

She covered her face with her hands and laughed—a short, joyless laugh. His heart felt like it would tear in two. If she was betrothed to such a good man, why did she look so miserable? But her next words were like a stone rolling over his tomb.

"I want you to run away again, Isa." Her voice dropped to a whisper, and she didn't meet his eyes. "And this time, don't come back."

Chapter Forty-Five

She brings him good, and not evil, all the days of her life.
—*Proverbs 31:12*

MARTHA DRAGGED HER body across the dark meadow, her last words to Isa echoing in her mind like the beat of the funeral drum.

Don't come back.

Don't come back.

She didn't see the sky lightening in the east; she saw the pain dawning in Isa's eyes, the hurt in the face that she loved more than any other. At least now he'd be safe from Simon's wrath.

Is this what will make you happy? Happy? She would never be happy again.

Her breath hitched in her throat. How quickly Isa had believed her. How willingly. She'd thought it would be harder to send him away, but it had been easy. Easy to convince him she'd chosen a better man.

As she pushed through the gate, she found her courtyard in an uproar. Women threw on their cloaks; men shouted orders and filled water skins. What was going on, an exodus?

Penina ran to her, her hands flying, her eyes filled with worry.

"Slow down, Penina." Martha couldn't understand a thing except that something had happened to raise Penina from her stupor of grief.

Chana came, wringing her thin hands before her. "I thought he was with you, I did. Here, with his cousins."

Martha's heart jumped to her throat. "Who?" Not Zakai. *Please, Lord of Mercy.* "Penina, what—when did you see him last?"

Penina signed. *Yesterday.* She'd seen him in the corner with his animals. Not long before dusk.

"And he wasn't with you last night?" She clutched Chana's arm.

"No. You told him he couldn't."

Safta's old face pinched. "I woke up, and he was gone. So were the animals."

Penina pulled at her sleeve. Martha followed her to the corner of the courtyard where a torch sputtered, illuminating empty willow cages and baskets. The birds and the lamb. All gone. Even his rabbit cage was empty. Her stomach twisted into a knot.

"But where would he go?" And why would he take his animals? She hadn't seen him sleeping before she left for the orchard; she'd been so worried about Simon, about Isa. "Where's Mary?"

"She went home last night."

"Safta, did he say anything, anything at all?"

The old woman shook her head. "He didn't say a word all day, but . . . he might've heard you carrying on with Penina."

"Penina?" What did Safta mean?

"About Penina leaving and her not wanting Zakai, and then you said you wouldn't take him. I'm guessing they could hear you all the way to Jerusalem."

"We didn't . . . I didn't mean . . ." Martha stumbled. That's not what she'd said, was it? She looked to Penina, who shook her head, her eyes wide and worried.

Martha rubbed her face and pushed herself to her feet. Zakai had hardly spoken since the burial. And she'd been so caught up in her own grief . . . Could he really have run away? And with so many mourners here, had no one seen a little boy leave with enough animals to fill an ark?

Martha didn't know what to do next. But Safta did.

Safta raised her voice. "Go," she ordered the women, "to the village, ask at every house. He must be somewhere." She squeezed Martha's arm. "Josiah. Check Simcha's."

Martha leaned against her grandmother, taking strength from her thin frame. He wouldn't have gone anywhere else, would he? Not to Jerusalem or toward the Jordan. Not on the roads filled with bandits and wild animals. Panic rose in her.

Not Zakai. She couldn't lose him, too.

Safta turned to the rest of the men—relatives, merchants, a few Pharisees. "Check the river and the path to Jerusalem." She sent them in every direction. "That boy knows every cranny and cave in the valley," she mumbled to herself. "If he doesn't want to be found, he won't be found."

Martha sank to her knees. Lazarus, and then Isa. *Please, Lord, don't take Zakai, too.*

Chapter Forty-Six

Lord, open my lips; my mouth will proclaim your praise. For you do not desire sacrifice; a burnt offering you would not accept. My sacrifice, God, is a broken spirit; God, do not spurn a broken, humbled heart.
—Psalm 51:17–19

*I*SA LEANED AGAINST the trunk of the tree, too weary to move.

A dove cooed in the oak tree; the spring frogs and insects sang along the stream. His world had ended. How could life go on around him?

Run away again. And this time, don't come back.

Her words hurt more than Zerubbabel's stick, more than the demons' torture. Isa's head pounded in the rhythm of the chirping insects. This time, he wouldn't act like a child. He would do what was best for Martha.

She'd left, walking across the carpet of brown leaves, and she hadn't looked back. And why would she? She had a good man waiting for her. A righteous Jew, just as her father had always wanted for her. She would be happy. Surely that was a small comfort?

He watched the sun rise over the eastern hills, his eyes gritty, his heart raw.

He'd been so sure that Jesus had sent him to Bethany for a reason. But it hadn't been to save Lazarus. He had died anyway. And not to marry Martha. Before the summer heat, Martha would marry another man, a better man.

Go home to your family, Jesus had said. He'd gone back to the only family he'd ever known, and been sent away.

Announce to them all that the Lord in his pity has done for you. He'd been too afraid to tell them what Jesus had done.

He'd failed in everything. He wouldn't go back to Chana's. He had his kinnor and the clothes on his back. He'd follow the stream to the Jordan. It didn't matter where he went now. Without Martha, he'd always be alone.

He started downstream, passing the outskirts of Bethany and continuing east to the Jordan. As he pushed past a copse of juniper bushes, a snuffling by the stream stopped him.

Could it be an animal, drinking from the trickle of water? He peeked through the branches. No, it was a boy. Probably seven or eight years. He sat curled in a ball, his head on his knobby knees. Shaggy black hair hid his face, and his skinny back shook with sobs. Next to the boy lay a lumpy traveling bag and a battered water skin. The bag twitched suspiciously.

Isa cleared his throat. The boy jerked his head up, his red-rimmed eyes widening at Isa. Isa held out his empty hands. He didn't want to scare the boy.

"Who are you?" the boy asked, wiping his nose with the back of his hand.

Was he lost? Isa took a step forward. "My name's Isa. And Bethany's that way." He motioned behind him.

The boy put his hand on his bag. "I'm never going back there."

So he was from Bethany. Isa took a few steps closer. The boy seemed familiar. "Who's your father?" He was probably looking for him right now.

"Don't have a father." The boy shrugged. "And my mama doesn't want me. Nobody wants me there." He sniffled again.

He was younger than Isa had thought, probably no more than seven years. And running away. A mother in Bethany was frantic by now. Isa sat down beside him and swung his kinnor from his back. "Who's that in the bag?"

"My rabbit. He's going with me." His mouth trembled. "I let the rest go."

"The rest?" If he kept him talking, perhaps he could find out where he belonged.

"A lamb. And a dove and two sparrows. And a snake Mama didn't know about."

Isa nodded gravely. "It was good to let them go. They wouldn't have got along in that bag." He plucked at a string; the note hung in the air.

"No," the boy agreed, his eyes on the kinnor. "Where are you going?"

"Across the Jordan. No one in Bethany wants me either." He strummed a minor chord. It was the truth.

The boy straightened. "Can you really play that? Can you teach me?"

"Maybe." Isa felt a smile tug at his mouth. He'd been younger when he'd learned. "We'd have to ask your mother."

The boy's mouth trembled. He turned earnest eyes on Isa. "Take me with you. I can make a fire, cart water. I'm a good worker."

Isa looked at the boy, and something warmed his torn heart. This boy would be good company. Isa could teach him to play. He'd treat him better than Zerubbabel had treated him. And he wouldn't be alone. Isa settled his back against the sandy bank and strummed a new chord. "Your mother, did she beat you?"

"No," he scoffed, as if it were unthinkable. Fortunate boy.

"Starve you?" Isa raised one brow. Not with those strong legs and bright eyes.

The boy looked down and didn't answer.

No, this boy was well cared for, maybe even loved. "Perhaps she wanted you to take a bath." He looked like he'd slept in the mud beside the stream.

But the boy didn't smile. "She said she didn't want me."

"She said that? You heard her?" His fingers slipped on the fret to sound a discordant chime.

Zakai nodded, and a tear slipped out of the corner of his eye and slid a clean path down his dirty cheek. "I'm sure. She told Marmar to take me, and Marmar said no." His voice hitched at the last word.

Isa straightened. Marmar? "Martha, the daughter of Sirach?"

The boy nodded. "Mama cries all the time. And Lazarus . . ." He sniffled again. "Marmar told me he wouldn't die. She promised." His voice dropped to a whisper. "I miss him so much."

So this was Penina's child? He'd heard about Martha's former slave. She was a foreigner, and mute. Chana said most of the village women didn't trust her. What did she say? That Sirach had taken Martha to Galilee, and they had come home with a slave girl and an infant. Just as Mary's first child had been born.

The boy pushed his shaggy hair away from eyes the color of river rocks. How could he be so familiar when he'd been born after Isa had left Martha in Bethany? And to a woman he'd never seen?

Something wasn't right. "What's your name?"

"Zakai."

"And where is your father?"

Zakai shrugged. "I don't know. Marmar said . . ." He stopped and clamped his mouth shut as if he'd almost spilled a secret.

Isa leaned closer. "Did she—did Martha know him?"

Zakai's unruly brows came together, and he looked uncertain. "She said once that she did."

"What else did she say about him?"

Zakai eyed the instrument in his hands. "She said that he was kind and good. And that he played the kinnor and had the voice of King David."

Isa's heart stopped. Time slowed as he looked at the boy in front of him. His gray eyes . . . *So much like mine.* His smooth brown skin . . . *So much like Martha's.* Understanding flowed over him like a river, each truth flowing into the next, too quick to grasp at once.

How could he be so stupid?

He had left Martha with child. Sirach had hidden her shame under the guise of a slave's child. Martha waited for him—how she must have wished him back—had borne his child, and never told who the father was. A wave of nausea passed over him. If she'd been found out, the judges could have had her stoned or, at the very least, driven her out of Bethany with her child. Alone and unprotected, a death sentence in itself.

Martha, I'm sorry.

Isa reached out as if to touch Zakai's hair. He had a son. A child that was his and Martha's. A family. *Go home to your family.*

Anger welled within him, but with it, realization and understanding. He had a son, and Martha had kept that from him. But she had been afraid, he could see that now. Afraid of what would happen if the people of Bethany found out who Zakai really was. *He knows I'm not a virgin,* she'd said of her betrothed. But did he know that the father of her child was back in Bethany? No. Martha had been protecting him when he should have been protecting her. And his son.

He stood up, swinging the kinnor behind him on his back. "Come, Zakai."

Zakai slung his bag over his shoulder and looked up at Isa, expectation lighting those familiar eyes. "Are you running away with me?"

Isa looked down on his boy. "No, Zakai. We're going back to Martha."

Zakai's face fell, and worry flashed over it. "I'll be scraping out the pigeon coop for a week."

Isa took Zakai's hand in his. It was small and warm and sent a jolt of something through his chest. Martha had been afraid, and so had he. He'd been afraid to tell Martha about the demons. Afraid of what she would think of him, that her family would hate him. But now he knew . . . he had a son, a family of his own. And he wasn't giving them up.

Melech had told him, *Do not be afraid.* This time, he'd do what Jesus had commanded. He'd tell all of Bethany what the Lord in his pity had done for him.

This time, he wasn't running away.

~~~~~~

Chapter Forty-Seven

*M*ARTHA PACED, HER mind dulled by the sleepless night. As the sun inched above the horizon, the men had come back tired and empty-handed. The women had found no sign of Zakai in Bethany.

Simcha went out again, taking every man to scour the fields and orchards. Penina went to look in the olive groves. Safta prayed in the corner, her eyes closed, her wrinkled lips moving. Martha had sent the rest of the women to Josiah's house to mourn with her sister. She couldn't stand the sight of their pity, their worried whispers.

Zakai, where are you?

What was he thinking? Every part of her wanted to run out of the courtyard, to shout his name through the fields and into the valleys. But someone had to wait here, in case he came home. *Please, Zakai, come home.*

For the tenth time, she stirred the stew of onions and chick-peas. They had plenty of food brought in by the mourners, but she must do something. Anything but think about Zakai bleeding in the wild or taken by bandits.

At the sound of steps and the creak of the courtyard door, her heart jumped. But it wasn't her son shouldering through the door. Simon swept into the courtyard, followed by his two guards. "Peace be to thee and to thy house," he announced.

Her shoulders slumped. *Not now, Simon.* "And to yours."

He crossed his arms in front of his chest. "I am sorry to hear of the boy. I've sent all my servants to look for him."

His servants, but not the two guards who followed at his heels. "Thank you, Simon—"

"And in doing so," he interrupted, his face grim, "they saw your friend Jesus and his people on the Jordan road."

She blinked at him in surprise. Jesus? Why was Jesus here now?

"He sent a message." Simon's mouth pursed. "He waits for you, Martha."

For me? "Why?" The question popped out of her mouth without thought.

Simon raised his brows. "You did send for him, did you not?"

She nodded, not meeting Simon's eyes. "Yes, but . . . for Lazarus . . ."

Simon blew out a breath. After a long moment, he finally spoke. "Martha. You did what I commanded you not to do. But your brother was dying, and you are just a woman, after all." His eyes narrowed. "But I won't suffer your disobedience again."

Martha bit down on her tongue, reminding herself that he was her betrothed. She was bound to obey him just as she would obey a husband.

"Jesus waits for you. To welcome him into Bethany or . . ." He didn't have to finish.

Or send him away. No one would blame her if she did.

He stepped closer, his words low and smooth, as if he were talking about a deal on wheat. "We have an agreement, Martha. As my future wife, it is not seemly for you to welcome such a man and his followers into your home." He put his hand on her shoulder, and his voice brooked no argument. "Go to Jesus and send him away. Before someone sends word to the Sanhedrin."

Simon's touch, damp and warm through the thin fabric of her tunic, made her cringe. This was the price she'd agreed to pay. His silence for her obedience. And it would be best—safer—for Jesus to stay away from Bethany. There was nothing else she could do. She opened her mouth to agree, but a sound as precious as gold—as sweet as honey—reached her ears.

Laughter. Zakai's laughter.

She looked past Simon to the open courtyard gate, and her heart swelled as if it would burst from her chest. Isa ducked through the arched doorway and, riding on his shoulders—with Isa's kinnor in his hands and a smile as wide as the Jordan—was her son.

"Zakai!" She stumbled past Simon, her arms open wide.

Isa swung Zakai down, and Martha dragged him into her arms, burying her face in his neck. *Thank you, thank you.* But whether she was thanking Isa or the Lord, she didn't know. Tears welled, and she couldn't stop them. Her sobs rent through her chest.

Zakai clung to her. "I'm sorry, Marmar."

"Don't you ever do that again." The words choked through her tears. She pulled him tight against her.

Isa crouched beside them and laid one hand on Zakai's shoulder.

Martha's breath stuck in her throat. Isa's face was no longer full of hurt but shining with something else. Pride. Joy. And determination.

He knows.

She couldn't help it. Her gaze flew to Simon. He scrutinized Isa, then narrowed his gaze at Zakai, held between them. Anger flared on his face, and he drew a sharp breath.

Martha's pulse pounded in her ears as fear weakened her limbs.

They both know.

Chapter Forty-Eight

Many are the women of proven worth, but you have excelled them all.
—*Proverbs 31:29*

MARTHA ROSE ON trembling legs, pressing Zakai against her side.

Simon's eyes narrowed. "This is the one who defiled you." It wasn't a question. His guards closed in on Isa.

Martha looked over her shoulder. Isa rose slowly, but he didn't look afraid. *Why doesn't he look afraid?* "Isa. Go. I told you to go."

Isa stood tall, his voice strong. "I'm not going anywhere."

With a patter of sandals and an intake of breath, Penina rushed into the courtyard. She fell before Zakai and took him in her arms, crushing him to her. After a moment, she looked at Martha, then at Simon and his guards. Her brow creased when she saw Isa.

Martha gave Penina a look that said she couldn't explain now. She wasn't sure if she ever could. "Take him," she whispered, nodding her head to Zakai.

Penina watched Martha over her shoulder as she prodded Zakai to the corner of the courtyard. Safta held out her arms to Zakai, and he ran to her.

Simon's chest heaved; red crept up his neck and into his face. "Now I see why you didn't admit who fathered the boy. A pagan." His lips curled in disgust. "How could you defile yourself like that?" He turned his gaze on Isa. "And why did he come back now, so late?"

Martha's hands curled into fists. *Don't answer, Isa. Don't mention Jesus.*

Isa lifted his chin. He took a deep breath and looked not at Simon but at Martha. "Jesus sent me here."

Martha's stomach rolled in fear. Now Simon would have no mercy.

Simon snorted. "A fool—another fool!—who believes in that blasphemer!" He turned on Martha. "They're just the same. Both cowards, both frauds." He shook his head. "And both here too late."

Isa's gaze flashed to Martha. "Jesus is here?"

Simon answered back, "He's waiting on the road. She'll go and send him away if she wants to save him." He threw a scowl toward Zakai. "And herself."

Isa stepped toward Martha, his brow furrowed. "You can't send him away, Martha."

Martha looked at the ground. Isa didn't understand. She had to obey Simon now.

Isa touched her chin, raising her face to his. Simon bristled and pulled in a breath, but Isa ignored him. "Martha, Jesus is the Messiah. He sent me back to you."

Martha let out a shaky breath. How could he still believe that after Jesus let Lazarus die? Where had he found this faith? And where had this courage come from, now that he was too late?

Isa's slate-gray eyes met hers, and there was nothing in them but truth. "Ask me a question, Martha. Anything. I'll answer you this time."

Martha's mouth went dry. A question. She'd asked him where he had been—why he hadn't returned to her—and he'd refused to answer. But now she had only one question, the question she hadn't asked Lazarus before he died, that she couldn't ask Mary. The question she feared no one could answer.

Her throat closed so that she couldn't speak above a whisper. "How do you know? How do you know that Jesus is the Messiah?"

Martha watched Isa's face. All else fell away—Simon staring at her, the guards hovering so close. She must know the answer to this question.

Isa's jaw twitched as if he were in pain; then he let out a heavy breath. "They knew."

A shiver passed over Martha at the tremble in his voice.

"They?" Simon bit out. "Who are they?"

Isa didn't even look at Simon. "Martha, for seven years, they tortured me." His breath became heavy, as if he were drowning in the memory. "They filled me, Martha." He reached up and loosened the neck of his tunic, pulling it low.

She caught her breath. Countless scars crosshatched his chest. Some long and jagged, others as straight as a knife blade. "Who . . . who did this to you?"

He swallowed. "Demons. A legion of them. They were why I couldn't come back to you. And they are how I know Jesus is the Holy One of God."

Simon stumbled back toward the wall, his face stricken.

A cold shiver passed down Martha's back. Demons? He'd been possessed by demons, like the men she'd heard of who wail and beat their heads against the rocks. *My Isa.* How he must have suffered. Martha stepped closer, her hand rising of its own accord toward the proof of his words.

He clenched his jaw. "I'm sorry, Martha." He closed his eyes.

Martha laid her hand over a jagged scar above his heart. Something in her own chest loosened, a shackle that had choked her heart for years. Isa hadn't been dead. He hadn't deserted her. He'd been imprisoned.

Isa let out a deep breath and pressed his hand over hers. "Then Jesus came to me, across the water. And *they* knew him. They called him son of the Most High." His heart pounded under her palm. "He destroyed them. And then he told me to come here and tell you what he had done."

Isa's hand was warm over hers, his face close. "The son of the Most High, Martha," he whispered. "Your Messiah—and mine—has come."

Martha stared at Isa, at the scars, trying to understand. Jesus had freed him from demons and sent him home to her.

Could Isa be right? Could Jesus really be the Messiah?

Isa let out a breath as if a weight had lifted from his shoulders. "I should have told you earlier, but I was afraid." His eyes went to Zakai. "I think we both were."

Simon staggered forward. "Get your hands off her." His face was pale, and he stayed far enough away that Isa couldn't touch him. "He's an abomination." At his signal, the guards charged Isa, each grabbing one of his arms in their thick hands.

A sob caught in Martha's throat. Yes, she had been afraid, so afraid for all of them. And now she had more to fear. Jesus wasn't here to save Isa this time. Only she could do that.

Martha went to her knees before Simon. She grasped the hem of his cloak in supplication. "Please, Simon. For me, let him go."

"For you?" Simon bellowed. "I'm doing this for you. He defiled you—a woman he had no right to touch—and ran away like the coward he is." He threw a disgusted look at Isa. "The Lord blesses the righteous, but his curse is on the head of the wicked. And you were cursed."

Martha turned to Isa. He could get away; he was strong enough to throw off the guards. "Go, Isa. Run."

The guards strengthened their hold, but Isa didn't resist. "I'm not running away again, Martha."

Simon stepped around Martha and advanced on Isa. "You are a coward, a liar, and a pagan. Coming here with your story of demons, with your belief in a false messiah." Spit flew from his mouth and landed on Isa's face.

Isa didn't blink. "I believe in the God of Abraham and Moses. Jesus is his son, the son of the Most High God."

Simon's face turned red. "A blasphemer and a fornicator." He turned and wrapped one hand around Martha's arm, jerking her up and against his side. "As this woman's betrothed, I'd be within my rights to have you punished right here by my own men."

Martha's blood pounded in her ears. He was. The men of Bethany wouldn't object to Simon beating a pagan who had defiled his betrothed. Even if he killed him. Martha looked at Zakai, huddled between Penina and Safta, watching. She couldn't let Isa die in front of the son he'd just found. "Please, Simon. He didn't mean it. He doesn't know what he's talking about."

Simon raised a brow. "He doesn't? I don't believe that for a minute. He's as taken in by this false messiah as your brother was."

A sob caught in Martha's throat. "Please, Simon. He's no one." She didn't look at Isa. She couldn't. "He means nothing to me now. Send him away, and we'll marry, just as you wanted."

Simon stared at her, his jaw clamped firmly. He rubbed his neck. "For you, Martha, I'll give this pathetic excuse of a man a chance to save his skin."

A chance? Martha tensed.

Simon made a sweeping gesture toward the courtyard gate. "You may leave Bethany, forever . . . if"—his gaze hardened—"you admit your lies." Silence fell on the courtyard. Simon raised his brows. "Admit that you lied—that Jesus is a fraud and a liar—and I will let you run away like the cowardly dog you are."

Martha twisted toward Isa. *Do it. Please, Isa.*

Isa straightened, and his jaw tensed. His eyes met Martha's. Her heart dropped as her mind grasped the truth. Isa was no longer the frightened, beaten boy she'd known. He was a man—a strong man who knew what he believed. And he wouldn't run away, not even to save himself.

Isa looked Simon in the eye as he sealed his fate. "They called him the son of the Most High, and I know this: he is the Messiah."

Martha's breath froze in her chest.

Simon let out a snort and flicked a hand at the guards. One jerked Isa close, pulling both his arms behind his back. The other one landed a solid punch in his midsection. Isa doubled over with a groan.

"Isa!" Martha lurched toward him, but Simon's grip was unbreakable.

Isa straightened, gasping. "Don't be afraid, Martha. I'm not." The guard landed a heavy blow to his face, snapping his head back. Blood streamed from his nose.

Martha covered her face with her hands. The guard raised his malletlike fists and landed two quick blows to Isa's ribs. Isa slumped to the ground and groaned.

Zakai shouted and struggled in Penina's arms. Martha sent her a look. *Don't let him go.* Who knows what Simon would do to Isa's son?

The first guard held Isa up; the other landed more blows, battering his face.

Anger built up in Martha like a fire. She strained against the hands that held her, but she couldn't break free. *Fight them, Isa.* He was strong; at least he could try. But he was letting them beat him. Just like he'd let Zerubbabel hit him when he was a boy.

Isa crumpled to the ground. The guards backed away as if their job was done.

Martha choked out a sob. *Isa. Stay down.*

But Isa didn't stay down. He staggered to his feet, swaying drunkenly. Bright red blood flowed from the wound above his ear. "Jesus sent me . . . to my family"—he clutched his side and his expression hardened into resolve—"He is the Messiah."

The guards looked at each other like they couldn't believe what they were seeing.

Simon raised his brows. "Finish it."

They stepped in. One slammed a fist into his face. The other punched him in the gut. He stumbled and went down. Both guards landed brutal kicks to his back, his side, and his chest until finally, Isa lay unmoving in the dirt. The guards backed away.

Martha wrenched away from Simon and threw herself beside Isa. Her blood pounded in her ears, and her mouth tasted of dust. Was he dead? Because he wouldn't run? Wouldn't deny what he believed about Jesus? *Please, God of Mercy, don't let him be dead.*

Simon loomed over her. "Look at him, Martha. I think I've proven my point." His lips curled, and he pointed to the court-yard gate. "You know what you have to do. Send Jesus and his people away. Now. And make sure they don't come back to Bethany."

Martha shuddered and looked at the face of the man Abba would have chosen for her. The man Lazarus had betrothed her to. How could she bear to be his wife after what he'd done to Isa?

He narrowed his eyes at her hesitation, and his mouth hardened. "Martha, do as I say or I will have no choice but to bring you before the judges. And I don't have to remind you . . . you have no man to speak in your defense." Simon signaled for the guards to precede him. "If it comes to that—and I pray for your sake it doesn't—may the Lord have mercy on you. Because the people of Bethany surely will not."

Martha watched Simon walk out the door, so sure of his own righteousness. And Isa, lifeless on the dirt, a pagan who had never learned the law but was willing to die for the Messiah.

Simon's words echoed in her mind. *I think I've proven my point.* Yes, Simon had proven his point. And Isa had proven his.

ᴹARTHA PRESSED A wet cloth to Isa's broken face. He didn't flinch. His eyes didn't flutter. She glanced at Penina. Her friend's face was drawn in worry. She didn't need to tell Penina about Isa now. She knew.

Penina nudged her aside and took the cloth from her hand. *Go,* her hands said. *I'll take care of him.*

Martha stepped back. She wanted only to stay with Isa, to wait and pray for his eyes to open. But Jesus waited on the road, and Simon waited for her decision. Obey him and send Jesus away? Or welcome Jesus and condemn herself to the judges of Bethany?

She looked at Isa's battered face. He hadn't abandoned her; he'd been imprisoned for seven years. And he'd been willing to die for the man who had freed him. But how could she go against all Abba had believed in? How could she put Zakai and everyone she loved in danger and trust in a man who had left Lazarus to die?

He is the Messiah, Isa had said, even as he knew it might cost him his life.

He is the Messiah, Lazarus had said as he died.

She closed her eyes as a tiny spark flared in her. Could she really believe Jesus was the Messiah?

Isa had said that demons had known Jesus. Demons had *obeyed* him. With every breath, the tiny spark of faith grew into what she should have known all along. The Messiah. The Anointed One of God. Her legs weakened, and she covered her hands with her face. The one they waited for had come.

He is here. He is Jesus.

But what was she to do now?

A soft, wrinkled hand slipped into hers. She opened her eyes. Safta tugged at her, shuffling out of the house, leading her into the corner of the courtyard where the empty crates and baskets had once held Zakai's animals. What was Safta up to now?

"Look, my girl." Safta pointed, her voice tinged with triumph.

As Martha's gaze followed Safta's bent finger, she caught her breath.

The dark cocoon, the hardened sarcophagus that had held Zakai's caterpillar, was split open and empty. Beside it, perched on a twig, sat a new and beautiful creature. Martha reached out a hand but didn't touch the vibrant wings that trembled in the breeze—so fragile, so easily destroyed. A hungry bird, a sudden storm, and this new life would be cut short. It pumped its wings, letting the life flow into them, readying them to fly.

Safta squeezed her hand and turned bright eyes on her. "What will you do now, my girl? Will you crawl back inside that safe little cocoon of yours, or will you finally come out and live?"

Martha stared at her grandmother. "What do you mean?" But she knew. Could she do it? Even if choosing Jesus meant a death sentence for her and the ones she loved?

Choose to believe, Mary had said. Lazarus had believed in Jesus, and he had died. Isa had believed, and he lay beaten and broken, perhaps dying. Should she follow her heart or what her head told her was the safer path?

The butterfly fluttered its wings and lifted on the breeze, drifting up and over the courtyard wall. Safta watched it go, then turned to Martha. "What are you waiting for, girl? Make your choice."

Make her choice? Between a caterpillar and a butterfly. Between Simon and Isa. Between death and new life.

Martha forced her feet to leave the courtyard, her mind still in turmoil, her body numb. The path to the Jordan stretched under her feet. Far in the distance, she saw movement. Emerging from the haze on the road, a group of at least ten people. A few more steps, and she could see Peter and Judas, James and John, a few women. And Jesus, watching her. He broke away from the group and walked toward her.

Her heart pounded, and her legs trembled.

Do not be afraid, Lazarus had said.

Do not be afraid, Isa had told her.

The Messiah had come. She had denied him, doubted him. She had hardened her heart to him, had closed her eyes when Lazarus and Mary had seen clearly. How could she face him? Her throat dried, her steps faltered. What would he say to her? What could she say to him?

Worry weighed on her like a mountain. Anxiety stole her very breath. With every step, her burden grew heavier, until she was sure she would be crushed beneath it. Just as she was certain she couldn't take one more step, he was there, in front of her.

Jesus' words whispered to her. *You are worried and anxious about many things. There is need of only one thing, Martha.*

She fell to her knees and bowed her head, unable to voice the words that she longed to say but that her fear and doubt and guilt had silenced. This time, she would choose the better part.

I believe, Lord.

His hands reached down, closing over her cold, trembling fingers. Warmth flowed over her—through her. She heard his voice like a whisper in her ear.

Give me your worries, Martha. Give me your pain.

Yes. She could carry them no more. But he could.

The burden of sin she'd carried for seven years lifted. Every shred of guilt over Abba's death was washed away in the warmth of his touch. Her doubt, her shame for all the times she had denied him, swept away in the flood of his presence. Her breath eased in her chest. He raised her to her feet. Like a lily lifting its face to the sun or a bird soaring into the sky, she was free.

She dared a look at his face. The face of her Messiah. Tears wet his cheeks. Tears of sorrow that she knew were for her pain. Tears of joy for her newfound faith. He loved her—not because she could cook a feast and keep her household clothed, not because she immersed the vessels and kept the law. He had always loved her . . . because she was Martha.

She brought his hand to her cheek, then turned and kissed it, washing it with her tears. She didn't try to hide the pain—the confusion—in her voice. She wouldn't hide anything from him again. "Lord, if you had been here, my brother would not have died." But she also knew that he came for a reason, a reason she didn't understand. "Even now I know that whatever you ask of God, God will give you."

Jesus' voice was broken, as if his heart hurt for her. "Your brother Lazarus will rise."

Yes, she knew that. Lazarus was not gone forever, only sleeping until the end of days. "I know he will rise on the last day." But she missed him so much right now. Her grief welled up again, as sharp as when Lazarus had drawn his last breath.

Jesus pulled her to his chest. He was warm and smelled of dirt and sweat. His voice rumbled in her ears, so familiar, but his words were unfathomable. "I am the resurrection. I am the life. Whoever believes in me, even if he dies, will live." His soft beard brushed her cheek. "And everyone who lives and believes in me will never die."

She closed her eyes. She didn't understand. It was a circle without end. Lazarus was dead, but he would live? When? How?

Jesus leaned back and looked at her, as if he needed more from her. "Do you believe this, Martha?"

She looked into the face of her cousin, her friend. The tears spilled from her eyes, and her throat ached. *There is need of only one thing, Martha.* She would trust him with her life and the lives of all those she loved.

She took a deep breath. "Yes, Lord. I believe." She gulped a breath of air, strength she hadn't known she possessed surging in her veins. "I have come to believe you are the Messiah who is coming into the world, the son of God."

Jesus looked down at her, his eyes as kind as a father's—a brother's—the touch of his hands warm and solid. He smiled through the tears still on his cheeks. "Go then, Martha, and get your sister."

Chapter Fifty

Charm is deceptive and beauty fleeting; the woman
who fears the Lord is to be praised.
—Proverbs 31:30

MARTHA SPRINTED TO Mary's house.

The brilliant blue sky arched over her, and the sun warmed
her shoulders. The scent of lilies floated on the breeze. Sparrows
darted and swooped in the sky, their song lifting her heart. Had
their calls and trills always been so sweet?

*Whoever believes in me, even if he dies, will live. Everyone who
lives and believes in me will never die.* What did it mean?

She passed by Simon's house. He would soon know that she
had defied him, but worry failed to slow her flying feet. She came
to her own imposing gate. Was Isa alive? Would he recover only
to be brought in front of the judges? She passed by. Isa wouldn't
want fear for him to keep her from doing what Jesus had commanded.

Whatever you ask of God, God will give you. She hadn't
known the words that would come out of her mouth. But when
she heard them, she knew them to be true. What would Jesus ask
of the one who was his Father?

She burst into Mary's courtyard, careened into the house,
and found her sister crumpled in the corner, Natanel in her arms.
A few of the mourning women followed Martha from the courtyard and clustered in the doorway.

Martha whispered in Mary's ear. "Mary." She didn't need all the women of the village to follow them. "Come quickly. The teacher is asking for you."

Mary's head jerked up, and her voice was hardly more than a croak. "Did he tell you why he didn't come?"

Martha shook her head and pulled at Mary's shoulders. There was too much to explain. "Come. He is on the road, waiting for us."

Mary curled around the baby and shut her eyes. "I can't go to him."

"You must, Mary. You told me he was the Messiah. You told me to choose to believe in him. Now I have chosen. And you must do the same."

Mary looked at her, her eyes showing a spark of life, of hope.

"Come, my sister. Be strong. The Messiah is at our door and is asking for you." Martha pulled her sister to her feet and put her arm around her waist. She urged her through the house, past the curious women.

"Are you going to weep at the tomb?" Elishiva asked.

"It's Jesus," Martha whispered. But Chana was hovering close enough to hear.

"Jesus? He's here?" Chana's shrill voice carried over the room as she took the baby from Mary's arms.

"Jesus?" Jael shoved her way into the little courtyard. "What are you going to do?"

Martha didn't answer. Jael would see soon enough. She quickened her steps out the door, not looking behind. She heard the low murmurs of the women. They were following, surely to see what she and Mary would say to Jesus.

Silva's whine reached her ears. "He's come so late. Why bother at all?"

Elishiva answered her. "He loved Lazarus. Perhaps he's come to mourn for him."

They neared the spot on the road where Jesus and his disciples still waited.

Jael's piercing voice carried on the breeze. "He opened the eyes of a man born blind yet didn't even save his friend from death."

Martha wished she could shut the mouths of the women behind her, but Jesus had already heard. He let out a short burst of breath, like she so often had when Zakai had failed to listen to her for the hundredth time. Then he held out his hands to Mary.

Mary threw herself at his feet. She bowed her head and kissed the hem of his tunic. "Lord." Her voice was filled with sorrow and a note of reproach. "If you had been here, Lazarus would not have died."

Martha heard her own words from her sister's mouth. Why had he waited?

Jesus pulled Mary to her feet and wrapped his arms around her as she wept. Jael gasped. The women huddled together and whispered.

After a long moment, Jesus pulled away from Mary and looked to Martha. "Where have you laid him?"

Martha held out her hand. "Come and see."

He took her hand, and with Mary clinging to his other side, they started toward the mountain. She took comfort in Jesus' warm hand holding hers. Whatever came next, she would trust him. Simon had demanded that she choose between him and Isa. But this time, she'd chosen the better part . . . she'd chosen Jesus.

As they passed the walls of Bethany, Abel left his post at the gate. Tobias wasn't far behind. Simcha and his brother, on their way to the well to water their sheep, left their flock and joined in.

By the time they reached the serpentine path up the hill, they'd been joined by workers from Simon's fields, Micah, even old Yonah and his wife, the beautiful Eliana. They climbed halfway up the mountain, then down the sharp decline into the valley that held the tombs.

Jesus stopped in front of the massive stone covering the entrance to the tomb. He released his hold on her and stepped forward. Martha closed the gap between her and her sister and grasped Mary's hand.

Jesus lifted his eyes to the sky, a sharp, clear blue with only a few wisps of clouds.

Was he praying? Mourning? Martha's grip on Mary's hand tightened.

Silence fell over the valley. All of Bethany waited to see what Jesus would do now that he had finally come.

ISA PRIED HIS eyes open. Arrows of light pierced his throbbing head, his ribs burned with every breath, and his face felt like an overfilled wineskin. Even in his pain, relief and something else—a feeling he didn't know—filled him. He'd done it. He hadn't run; he hadn't even fought back. He'd fulfilled what Jesus had commanded. It was peace, what he felt. Instead of the shame and disgrace he'd lived with all his life, he felt at peace.

Where was he? He was propped up on a bed. A high square window lit a cozy room, and a delicious aroma drifted in on the breeze. If not for the pain in his head, he'd think he was in the afterlife. An old woman stared at him from the corner. She looked familiar. Martha's old grandmother was still alive after all these years? "Martha," he rasped out of his dry throat.

She leaned forward and croaked, "Thank the Holy One, he's alive."

He tried to rise, but the walls of the room spun around him. A face appeared above him. Not Martha. This must be the woman called Penina. She leaned over him. A cup touched his lips, and he drank. Cool water, sweetened with honey and flavored with mint. It soothed his throat and cleared his muddled thoughts.

He gripped the soft hand that held the cup. "Did she go to him? Did she go to Jesus?" *Please say yes.*

She set down the cup and made a motion with her hand, then looked at him expectantly.

What was she trying to say?

Zakai popped up beside her. "Everyone is going to the tomb with Jesus. The whole village." He turned to Penina. "Can we go, please? Can I go to see?"

Isa's head pounded, and he rubbed his temple. Jesus was going to the tomb? Lazarus's tomb? Jesus. The man—the Messiah—who had saved him. He'd done what Jesus had commanded; now he could go to him without shame. He sat up slowly, waiting for the room to settle.

His tunic had been pulled down and tied at his waist, his scarred chest naked but for a linen wrapping around his ribs. He pulled in a shallow breath, and a sharp pain pierced his chest. He slid his legs over the side of the bed and set his feet on the floor. "Yes," he answered Zakai. "We're going to the tomb."

Penina's mouth turned down.

Zakai frowned. "Mama won't go." His brow furrowed. "And Safta, she can't walk that far."

Isa tested the strength of his legs. They wobbled under his weight, and he sat down again. *I hope I can walk that far.*

Penina shook her head and put a hand on his shoulder to restrain him. She was a tiny thing, this woman Zakai still called Mama. But stubborn, he could see from the set of her mouth and the determination in her eyes.

A door slammed, sending a new dart of pain through his head. With a clatter and a gust of wind, Chana careened around the door and into the room, baby Natanel clutched to her side. Her breathing was hard and fast. "Quick. Where are they? Jesus and Martha and Mary?"

Penina took the baby and settled Chana on a stool to catch her breath.

Safta hobbled from the corner. "Not here. They went to the tomb, we heard."

"The tomb?" Chana's face crumpled. "Oh no. Oh my. There isn't much time." She wrung her hands frantically and looked from one face to another.

"What is it?" Isa demanded. Had something happened to Martha?

"Simon came with his guards. He's furious." Chana choked on her words, as if she were holding back tears. "He said something about Martha—that she would pay for her betrayal—and about bringing Jesus to the Sanhedrin."

Urgency surged in Isa's pain-filled body. Martha—and Jesus—were in danger, and he needed to protect them both.

Safta snorted. "Since when do you worry about Jesus?"

Chana stiffened, her face showing hurt. "I've known Jesus since he was a baby in his mother's arms. I wouldn't see him hurt, and my Josiah wouldn't want it." She turned to Isa. "And Martha . . . Simon was so angry."

Isa clutched his ribs and stood, the room swaying around him. "What did you tell him?"

Chana looked at her hands, guilt written on her brow. "He was coming here next. I thought I could warn Martha, so I told him . . . I told him they went to the synagogue to hear Jesus teach."

Safta grunted. "Good. Then we have some time." She leveled sharp eyes on Isa. "You and Penina, take Zakai and go to the tomb."

Penina glared at the old woman and her hands fluttered, but Safta interrupted. "Do you love Martha, my girl?"

Penina's face lost its stubborn bent, and she nodded.

Safta frowned, her face creasing. "You heard what Simon said to her, what he'd do to her. Martha will need her family before this day is over. And so will Jesus."

Tears brightened Penina's eyes as she pointed to the old woman.

"I can't make it." Safta's face wrinkled more deeply. She turned to Isa. "Well, boy, what are you waiting for?"

Isa breathed slowly, trying to gather his strength. He took a good look at Zakai, Penina, and the twig of an old woman. They were family—Martha's family. Whatever was going to happen at the tomb, she needed them beside her. And he needed to get them there. Even the grandmother, who looked like she might break in a harsh breeze.

He set his feet firmly on the floor and scooped the old woman into his arms. She let out a surprised chirp, but her arms went around his neck. He swallowed a groan as pain ripped through his ribs. She might look like a bird, but she weighed more than one.

Isa adjusted his hold on Safta, then nodded to Zakai. "Bring us to Jesus."

Chapter Fifty-One

*M*ARTHA STOOD IN front of the tomb. Jesus remained silent, his face raised in prayer, his cheeks wet with tears.

Her grief lay heavy on her heart, as heavy as the day Lazarus died. But now, with Jesus beside her, she could bear it with more strength, with a sense of peace that she didn't have before. Martha squeezed Mary's hand. How she wished she could tell Lazarus he was right.

The Messiah, the Holy One of God, had come. And it changed everything.

The people of Bethany trickled into the valley, filling it like spring floodwaters. Jael and Devorah near the front, behind them Elishiva and Silva and the other women. Josiah and Simcha stood close to Jesus and his disciples, while most of the other men crowded back against the wall of the valley, well away from the tomb, to avoid impurity.

A trio of sparrows dipped and soared, their brown feathers dull against the piercing blue of the sky. A dry wind eddied through the rocky valley and whispered in the leaves of the terebinth trees as the murmurs of the crowd grew to a hum of anticipation. One by one, the sparrows landed on the stone in front of the tomb.

Jesus wiped the tears from his face and stepped closer.

The murmurs ceased.

Jesus' voice carried over the crowded valley like a commanding general. "Take away the stone."

Martha frowned. It had been four days. "Lord, there will be a stench." As soon as the words left her mouth, she regretted them. Hadn't she just decided not to question Jesus?

When Jesus turned to her, his eyes were kind and his tone like that of a loving parent. "Did I not tell you that if you believe you will see God's glory?"

Her face flushed with heat. He *had* told her that. And instead of trusting him, she had worried again. Still, it had taken three of Simon's servants to push the stone in place. Who would move it away? Abel and Tobias frowned and stepped back. Josiah and Simcha hesitated.

The crowd parted like the Red Sea, and a voice called out, "Here I am, Lord. I'll do it."

Martha's heart skipped a beat as Isa shouldered through the onlookers. *He's alive.* But he was pale and his mouth was pinched as if every step was torture. In his arms he carried Safta, her thin legs dangling and her arms circling his neck. Zakai ducked past him, running to Martha's side. Behind Isa's wide shoulders came Penina. Martha held out her hands, and Penina ran to her.

Isa set Safta beside them, holding her steady until she had found her feet. Martha caught his gaze. His eyes held questions she couldn't answer. Why were they here? What would happen now? Only Jesus knew. But they were here. Everyone she loved. Whatever happened, they would face it together.

With a scuffle, Simon pushed through the crowd, his burly guards making a path for him. His eyes narrowed on Isa, and his mouth flattened. But he turned to Jesus and barked out, "What is the meaning of this?"

The disciples snapped to attention. They gathered into a knot around Jesus.

Jael piped up. "He's asked to take away the stone."

Simon scowled. "That's ridiculous. After four days?" He motioned to the guards. "Take him. We'll see what the Sanhedrin has to say."

Isa stepped in front of Jesus and leveled his gaze at Simon. "If you want him, you'll have to get past me." His arm cradled his bandaged ribs, but his voice was strong and he looked like a man ready to fight.

Martha pulled Zakai closer, her heart racing. Isa could barely stand upright; he couldn't fight the guards alone.

Josiah stepped up beside Isa. "And me."

"And me." Simcha joined them.

The disciples fanned out beside them, their faces set like stone and their fists clenched.

The guards glanced warily at each other. Simon snorted. "He won't be able to hide behind his friends for long."

Jesus ignored Simon and nodded to Isa. "Take away the stone."

Isa, limping and bent, approached the tomb. Martha's heart twisted at his pain. Surely Isa couldn't move that heavy stone without help, but she held her tongue. She'd questioned Jesus once already; this time she'd trust him.

Isa put his hands on the edge of the stone and set his feet firmly on the rocky ground. The muscles in his arms bunched and strained. His bare feet dug into the dirt as he pushed. The stone didn't budge.

Peter stepped forward, pushing up the sleeves of his tunic, but Jesus laid a hand on Peter's arm, stopping him without a word.

Isa pushed again, a low groan escaping his lips. Then he dropped his hands, his chest heaving with effort and his face shining with sweat.

Everything in Martha strained toward him, but she forced herself to wait. Jesus knew what he was doing.

Suddenly, Zakai darted from her side and scrambled to stand beside Isa.

Isa looked at the boy, who hardly reached up to his waist, and made room for him beside the towering stone.

Martha's legs trembled, and her bones felt like softened wax. Her son and his father. Together in front of all of Bethany. They both took a deep breath and set their jaws. Isa pushed, his back straining, his legs taut. Zakai pushed, his face red with effort.

The stone budged. Then—with a groan from Isa and a shout of victory from Zakai—it rolled, revealing the black mouth of the tomb. The people stepped back as one body. Some covered their faces with their sleeves, others turned away, but no stench of death came from the darkness. Isa took Zakai by the hand and retreated until they stood just an arm's reach from Martha, but he didn't look at her. Like everyone else, he watched Jesus.

Martha squeezed Mary's hand on one side, Penina's on the other. What would Jesus do now?

Jesus stepped forward, approaching the open tomb as if he were approaching the altar at the Temple. He raised his eyes to the blue sky. "Abba, thank you for hearing me. I know you always hear me, but because of the crowd I say this that they will believe you sent me."

Jael gasped. Simon grunted like he'd been kicked by a donkey. Martha looked sideways at Mary, whose eyes were riveted on Jesus. Penina frowned, her brows pulled down.

The wind ceased and the trees stilled, as if all the valley held its breath.

Jesus' voice rang out. "Lazarus, come out!"

Chapter Fifty-Two

Thus you may walk in the way of good men,
and keep to the paths of the just.
—Proverbs 2:20

DARKNESS.

Silence.

No pain, no sadness, no fear. The void was like a blanket—comfortable, heavy.

Then words reached into the eternal emptiness. Something—someone—pulled at him. A tug out of the darkness. "Lazarus, come out!"

Slowly he understood the meaning of the words. The voice called to him, asked him to leave what he knew and go out, into the unknown. It was a choice. He knew that. He could stay here in the dark, where nothing could hurt him. Here, he would never again know suffering.

Or he could follow the voice. The voice promised joy. Life. Light. But also suffering. There would always be suffering outside, in the light.

The hour is coming when the dead will hear the voice of the son of God.

The hour was here. He knew that voice, and it was the voice of the one he loved. Jesus. The voice of the Messiah.

A pinprick of light penetrated the darkness, like a star in the night sky. He concentrated on the tiny speck of light.

The star brightened. It beckoned.

I'm coming. He tried to answer. *I'm coming out.*

Lazarus felt cold stone, smelled the heavy scent of myrrh, and tasted the coolness of the air. His eyes fluttered open, but he saw only muffled whiteness.

The voice echoed in his ears. *Lazarus, come out!*

His body jerked. Life surged through him like a river breaking loose from a dam. Breath filled his lungs, his heart swelled, blood pumped through his veins. A power, like a rushing fire, filled his limbs. Not his own, he knew. This was from Jesus.

Urgency welled within him. He struggled to rise. His arms were bound, his legs entangled. Why couldn't he move? Why couldn't he see? He wrenched an arm free and lifted it to his face, pulling at the linen covering. He blinked. Bright light poured from the arched opening. Outside, an indistinct figure stood, the sun behind him, but he knew who it was.

Jesus.

He pushed himself up. The loose burial cloths still bound his legs, and one hand was still banded to his side. His bare feet touching the cold ground. Air. Earth. Sunlight. Familiar, but also new.

Voices murmured outside, in the light.

He staggered to his feet. Martha, Mary. And Penina. Were they waiting for him? Zakai, was he out in the light? He shuffled across the smooth stone toward the light. His blood pumped; air filled his lungs. He was strong. Stronger than he'd ever been.

Voices drifted into the dark. "He's a fraud." A face came to his mind—gaunt, with large eyes. Simon.

"He's a liar and blasphemer." Who was that?

Lazarus stood in the cool shadows. Now they would know. The Messiah had come. *When I step into the light, they will all believe.* He ducked his head under the arched doorway and stepped outside. He blinked in the bright, hard light.

The murmurs ceased, replaced by utter silence.

Jesus stood before him. Tears shone on his cheeks. Jesus had wept for him, just as he had wept on the mountain when Lazarus had begged to be his follower.

Jesus came to him; he pulled him close. Lazarus understood now. Jesus, his friend—the Messiah—had kept his promise. *You will understand when the time comes. The dead will hear the voice of the son of God.* The power of the Most High ignited him like a flame. He could run over mountains, jump to the heavens, lift the heaviest stone. He had died. And Jesus had brought him back to life. A new life as a new man.

Jesus drew back without speaking and stepped aside.

Behind him, Martha and Mary, their hands linked together, their eyes wide and their mouths agape.

Jesus spoke to them. "Untie him and let him go."

They stared at Lazarus like he was a spirit. No one in the crowd behind them spoke or even moved. Finally, slowly, Martha loosed her hand from Mary's. She took one step toward him. Then another. She reached out with trembling hands and pulled the shroud from his shoulders.

Mary, her face white as the burial cloths, bent down before him and untied the bindings at his ankles, her eyes never leaving his face. The winding cloths fell from his legs like loosed chains. The wind tugged at his tunic as if to cleanse him of the clinging scent of myrrh. Martha and Mary held his burial cloths to their breasts like shields.

Don't be afraid. But the words froze in his throat as they backed away, and his gaze fell on Penina.

Penina.

Her eyes were wide, her mouth trembling. She looked from Jesus to Lazarus and back to Jesus. Then, before he could move— before he could even speak—she stumbled forward and was in his arms, pressed close to his pounding heart.

Nina, I came back to you. The surge of power—the healing that had brought him from death into life—flooded through him in a torrent. He felt the power leave him, and, at the same moment, Penina cried out as if in pain.

He caught her weight as her body went limp in his arms. What had he done? "Nina!" Her eyes opened. Her face tipped toward his, and her lips parted. A voice, as sweet and soft as a dove, came from her lips. "You're alive." Her hand flew to cover her mouth, and her eyes stretched wide. "I can—"

Lazarus crushed her to him. She could speak!

Martha dropped the shroud and flew at him. Mary followed. He gathered his sisters close. They babbled and laughed—Mary, Martha, and Nina—his family. Jesus had brought him back to his family.

Small arms clamped around his legs. He looked down. Zakai grinned up at him. Lazarus leaned down and threw his arms around the boy, lifting him into the tight huddle.

"She can talk!" Zakai shouted. Penina's laugh rang out like the tinkling of bells.

Penina could speak, and she was in his arms. He would never let her go again.

Safta shuffled close, her bright eyes filled with tears. Lazarus made room for her in the cluster of bodies. She clutched his hand, brought it to her face, and pressed her lips against it. "God is good, my boy."

Mary was the first to break away. She ran to Jesus and threw herself at his feet. "The Messiah has come!"

The crowd surged to crowd around Jesus. Touching his cloak, asking him questions. He disappeared behind the throng, and even the disciples were swallowed by the mob.

"He has power over death. Alleluia! Alleluia!"

"Praise to the Lord, blessed be his name!"

Lazarus lifted his head to look out at the crowd. Now they would know. They would all know that Jesus was the Messiah. Simcha, on his knees, raising his eyes to heaven. Simon, standing alone before the tomb, his face slack with shock. John and Peter looking at each other in amazement. And next to Peter—

Lazarus stiffened. There was a face he knew from another lifetime. He set Zakai down and untangled himself from the huddle of his family, staring at the man before him. The man he'd despised since he was a child.

He was older, and bigger. And he looked like he'd been in a fight. But it was him. The pagan who had defiled his sister, then abandoned her. Now Lazarus was strong enough to make him atone for his sin. Old enough to see him punished for what he had done to Martha.

He took two great strides until he was face-to-face with Isa. They were the same in height, but what Isa had gained in muscle, Lazarus made up for in righteous anger.

Isa didn't flinch. And he didn't look afraid. *He should be afraid.*

Lazarus squared his shoulders and leaned close to the vermin who had broken his sister's heart. "What is this man doing back in Bethany, Martha?"

Chapter Fifty-Three

Give her a reward of her labors, and let her
works praise her at the city gates.
—Proverbs 31:31

*M*ARTHA COULDN'T BELIEVE what she was seeing.

Her brother was alive. Alive! Jesus—the Messiah—had raised him from the dead after he had lain in the tomb for four days. Jesus had freed her brother, and now from the look on Lazarus's face, she saw he might use his new life to end Isa's.

The nearest villagers—Elishiva, Simcha, Simon, and Jael—pushed closer. Voices rose in a buzz of excitement.

"Who is it?"

"Does Lazarus know him?"

Jael's voice rang out. "Martha, who is this man?" Her voice turned heads, and villagers left the throng around Jesus to peer at Lazarus and Isa. Silva and Devorah, their husbands, and a few men came closer.

Martha pushed herself between the two men. She looked at her brother, who loved her enough to take her secret to his grave. "You've kept my secret long enough, Lazarus. It's time for us both to be free." It might be a death sentence. It would surely change her life. But she could not lie anymore.

Martha took Isa's hand in hers. Isa, the man she loved, the man Jesus had found and sent back to her. He looked at her, a question in his eyes. She reached for Zakai with her other hand and drew them together.

Mary broke from the crowd around Jesus to stand beside her. Penina edged in on her other side. Even Safta came closer, her wrinkled face unreadable. Martha's heart fluttered, but the peace she'd felt on the road—the peace Jesus had given her—filled her again. She was strong now.

She faced the people she'd known all her life. The men who knew Abba, who had been told they weren't good enough for her. The women who believed her to be the holiest woman in Bethany. She would tell them all. But first, she would tell Zakai.

She crouched down in front of Zakai. His face was full of questions. She kissed his small brown hand. "Zakai, my sweet. You have always called Penina your mother. And she loves you as much as a mother could. But you must know now that you are my son, my child."

A gasp hissed through the crowd, but Martha kept her eyes on Zakai. His brows came down. He looked at Martha. "You're my mama?"

She nodded.

His gaze went to Penina. "Not you?"

Penina bent down beside him and whispered in her new voice, "I love you, Zakai. And I always will, but Martha is your mama and always has been."

Zakai's forehead puckered. "But you won't leave us, will you?"

She shook her head. "Never." She looked up at Lazarus, and he moved closer, his face reflecting her certainty. "This is my family."

Martha looked at Isa before she went on. He nodded, his jaw firm. The time for secrets was over. It was time to bring everything out into the light.

"Zakai." Martha made herself look only at her son. Not at the gathering crowd around them, the people who could sentence her and Isa to death. "This man." She swallowed hard. Isa's hand, strong and calloused, tightened around hers, and she found the strength to finish. "This good man that I have loved all my life—is your father."

Zakai took a step back. He looked at Penina, who nodded. He blinked hard and long at Isa. His voice rang out in disbelief, carrying over the gathered crowd and echoing against the stones. "*You* are my abba?"

ISA LOOKED AT the beautiful boy who was his son and the strong woman who was everything to him and always had been.

Yes, he was poor, beaten, and didn't have a shekel to his name. Lazarus despised him, and these people gathering around him would either stone him or drive him out of town before the end of the day.

But Martha loved him. She'd said it in front of all of Bethany.

He wanted to shout it to the heavens. He was this beautiful boy's abba, and Martha loved him. He looked into his son's face. "Yes, I'm your abba."

Zakai's slate-gray eyes widened. He let out a yell, dropped his mother's hand, and launched himself at Isa, barreling into his legs with a force that almost knocked him to the ground. Small arms clamped around him, and a muffled sob of pure joy came from his son.

Isa crouched down and circled the boy in his arms, laying his head on his shaggy hair. His throat clogged with tears, and gratitude filled his chest until he thought he might burst. *Thank you, son of the Most High God, for bringing me back to Bethany.*

Martha fell to her knees beside Isa. He wrapped his arms around them both, pulling them close. He'd thought Martha was the only good thing that had ever happened to him, but this . . . this was more than he had ever dared to hope for. Something beautiful and new swelled in his chest, threatening to burst from him in a great flood. He was no longer alone. He had a family.

And with the help of the God of Abraham, he would do whatever he must to protect them, for as much time as he had left.

MARTHA STAYED FOR a moment more in the safety of Isa's arms, happiness welling between them. They were together, finally—no more lies, no more secrets. Too soon, the voices of the crowd intruded on their joy.

"Martha's son?" Devorah squawked like a hen disturbed from her roost. "Not the slave's?"

"Her father would be ashamed."

Through the din, Safta's cackling voice reached her. "How does it feel, my girl, to let go of that burden?"

Martha snapped her gaze to her grandmother. "You knew?"

Safta raised her brows. "Of course I knew. My son could never keep a secret from me."

Martha lurched to her feet. "And you?" She looked at Elishiva.

Safta elbowed Elishiva, who looked sheepishly at the ground. "I saw how you loved the boy."

Chana nodded, too. "I knew from the moment I saw the boy. He couldn't be anyone's but yours. I just thought everyone knew. It isn't the kind of thing you talk about, now is it?"

Martha's bemused gaze went to Penina, then Mary. Both looked as surprised as she. Chana had known about Zakai but hadn't said anything? Elishiva and Safta knew what she'd done and still stood beside her? A spark of hope kindled within her. Perhaps others would be as forgiving.

Jael pushed forward. "How can this be? How did they know?"

Devorah sputtered. "Well, I didn't know. I've always thought you were such a holy woman. It's a disgrace."

A bubble of hysteria rose in Martha's chest. What bothered Jael and Devorah more, that Zakai was her son or that they were the last to know? But Jael's next words brought a shot of alarm.

"We can't let this stand, not in Bethany."

Martha lifted her chin. Now she would take her punishment. What she had feared for seven years. She looked over the crowd to where Jesus stood silently. He watched, his face betraying no surprise, and no judgment either. She drew again on the peace he had given her, and the fear in her heart quieted.

"Did you know about this?" Jael squawked to her son. "That she was defiled by this—this . . . foreigner?"

Martha eyed Simon, wondering why he didn't join the outrage. Isn't this what he wanted? Her and Isa before the judgment of Bethany? Taking their punishment as they deserved? Instead, he glanced warily at Lazarus. "Don't, Mother—"

"Don't?" Jael's voice rose to a higher pitch. "You are betrothed to her! This harlot."

Simon looked alarmed. "Mother—"

"Betrothed?" Lazarus took a sharp breath, and his voice held a note of disbelief.

Martha turned to Lazarus. Didn't he remember? "The betrothal you signed just before you—"

"Yes, of course I remember," Lazarus answered quickly, but something in his face was wrong. What did Lazarus know that she did not?

LAZARUS COULD SEE the worry in Simon's eyes. The wretch was right to be worried. The man had lied, believing that the only one who knew the truth was dead.

A man of understanding keeps silent.

Jael, ignoring her son's distress, looked down her nose at Lazarus. "Your father would demand punishment." She turned to Abel. "What punishment is enough for this pagan and this harlot?"

Lazarus's heart beat fast. What would Isa do now? Run away again, or beg for mercy from Abel? Would he leave Martha to face her punishment alone?

Abel blinked at Jael as if he were coming out of a daze, and his eyes flicked warily to Jesus at the edge of the crowd. Finally he spoke, but his voice lacked its usual confidence. "We would be within the law to give him to the Sanhedrin for judgment. And they could have him stoned."

Jael looked satisfied. "And what of her? Her disregard for the purity of our people?"

Abel looked uncertainly at Simon. "The law says that if an unmarried woman is with child and refuses to name the father, the punishment is stoning at the city gate. If the woman is betrothed and is found not to be a virgin, she shall suffer the same."

Jael, mouth pursed, nodded. "And she is betrothed to my son."

Lazarus watched Isa put Martha and Zakai behind him. The pagan didn't look like he was going anywhere.

Abel held up his hand for quiet. "It is a difficult case." He pulled on his beard. "She is betrothed, but her sin was while she was under the hand of her father. Now," he went on, "if he were a Jew, he would be required to marry her, but a pagan . . ."

Lazarus waited. He knew what was coming. In a case such as this, it was always the father's right to decide. And with Sirach gone, that responsibility fell to him alone.

Abel turned to Lazarus, frowning. "You are the head of Sirach's household now. You shall decide both how your sister will be punished and what will happen to the pagan."

Lazarus looked over the villagers, all gathered now watching the spectacle. This was his chance to see his sister's misery these last seven years atoned for. His chance to see Isa pay for his sin. His gaze stopped at Jesus, watching silently. What would the Messiah want from him?

Isa—a pagan—deserved nothing less than death. Abba would have demanded it. The people of Bethany expected it. Before Lazarus had died—before he'd been brought out from the tomb by Jesus—he would have agreed. But what did he think now? Now that he had felt the Messiah's power and seen his mercy? And now that he had been given a new life with Penina?

He stepped in front of Martha and Isa and nodded to Abel. "You judge wisely in this matter, Abel. I will decide what is right and just."

Chapter Fifty-Four

Those who worship vain idols forsake their source of mercy.
But I, with resounding praise, will sacrifice to you; What I
have vowed I will pay: deliverance is from the Lord.
—Jonah 2:9–10

ISA FACED LAZARUS—THE boy who had witnessed his promise to Martha and had also seen him break it. Now Lazarus was a man and held Isa's fate in his hands. Isa deserved whatever punishment Lazarus demanded.

The past few moments had been like a dream. His son and Martha beside him. But like a dream, over too soon. He crouched down in front of Zakai and kissed his forehead, then took one last look at Martha. He didn't want to leave her, not now when he'd just found them both. But he would do what he had to do to keep them safe.

She nodded, her mouth trembling. She knew what he couldn't say. *I love you. Take care of our son.* He faced the people of Bethany. At Martha's side stood the old grandmother, Safta, and Penina. Mary and Josiah on the other. Martha's family that he would never know. *Please, take care of Martha.*

He straightened his shoulders and took a deep breath as he faced Lazarus.

"You told her you'd come back to her." Lazarus's voice was filled with contempt and something else. . . . Was it uncertainty? "Why didn't you?"

Lazarus raised his eyes to Jesus. The man—the Messiah—who had saved him said nothing, but the memory of the peace that Isa had felt at the edge of the Galilee gave him the strength to form the words he had to say. To find the voice he'd never had.

"I lived on the shores of the Galilee for seven years, possessed by a legion of demons."

The crowd drew back. Shocked voices rose around him, but he couldn't stop now. Isa raised his voice. "They held me. I didn't know who I was. I didn't know what I was." He started to tremble, his legs weakening as he remembered. "And then your God, the one God, in his mercy, had pity on me. Jesus came to me."

The drone of voices subsided as faces turned uncertainly toward Jesus.

"They knew him," Isa went on. "The demons. They called him son of the Most High God. He ordered them to leave me and"—he took a shaky breath—"the demons obeyed him." He went on, the words flowing like a remembered song from his mouth. "I knew your God from the songs I sang, and I knew he was a righteous God. But I learned from this man, from this son of the Most High, that he is a merciful God. And he has shown me, a sinful man, his mercy."

Silence fell in the clearing. The only sound was the wind in the trees and the distant calls of the birds in the blue sky.

Isa knelt before the man who would decide his fate but hardly felt the sharp rocks digging into his battered knees. "He sent me back here, to Martha. I've done what he commanded, Lazarus. Now you can send me to your judges; stone me. Do whatever your law commands." His eyes strayed to Zakai, and he clenched his jaw. "I ask only that you have mercy on your sister and Zakai." He bowed his head to the ground. "I beg you. Let this punishment be borne by me alone."

LAZARUS LOOKED AT the man before him. Then at Jesus, watching him along with the disciples. Isa was telling the truth, he could see it in Jesus' face. Jesus had gone to this pagan, delivered him from demons, and sent him back to Martha. Jesus had given Isa a new life just as surely as he had raised Lazarus himself from the grave. Now Jesus waited with the rest of Bethany for Lazarus's decision.

Whispers reached his ears.

"Demons."

"Send him into the desert."

"Stone him."

He would be within the law to send him into the desert, even to call for his death. He saw Zakai, clinging to Martha's hand, and his heart ached. Could he take away his father when he'd just found him? And Martha. She loved this man. And Isa loved them both enough to offer his life for theirs.

Lazarus's gaze went to Simon, standing beside Jael like a statue. Lazarus had been wrong before. Very wrong. He'd almost made an irreversible mistake.

But now he knew what to do.

Lazarus raised his hands. Immediately, the crowd quieted. "When my father died, he asked me to take care of Martha." He looked at his sister, who had raised him like her own son. "And so I thought to betroth her to this man." He nodded to Simon. "A righteous man, a man who knew the law, who was respected. I thought I was doing what was best for my sister, what Abba would have wanted."

Jael pulled herself up like a preening pigeon. Simon remained silent, his gaze on the ground as if he knew what was coming.

"I was wrong. He had everything—respect, wealth—but he had no honor. And I realized it almost too late. Almost." He turned to Simon. "How long did you wait after I was dead before forging my name on the ketubah?" Lazarus asked him, his voice ringing out over the crowd.

Martha gasped. "What—but you went to him, you—"

"You were never betrothed to him." Lazarus scowled.

"What do you mean?" Abel demanded.

"I didn't sign the ketubah. I called off the betrothal."

Jael harrumphed. "This can't be true. What is he saying, Simon?"

Simon took a step back, his face hardening in stubborn pride. "She had no one. She assumed . . . and I thought . . ." He glared at the crowd. "It's what Sirach would have wanted."

"My father wanted what was best for Martha."

Lazarus turned to Isa, still bowed before him.

Martha seemed to hold her breath, her eyes on Lazarus.

Lazarus spoke to Isa, but his soft voice carried over the quiet of the waiting crowd. "You would give your life for Martha and Zakai?"

Isa nodded his head in assent.

"There is no greater courage." Lazarus laid his hand on Isa's bent head. "And you are no longer a pagan?"

Isa spoke. "I believe in the God of Abraham. And in Jesus, his son and the Messiah."

Certainty filled Lazarus. This time he was doing what was best for Martha. "There is no greater faith." Lazarus pulled Isa to his feet. "If she will still have you, you have my blessing. To be a husband to Martha and a father to Zakai. And to be welcomed in our family."

Martha muffled a sob behind her hand. A hum of shock ran through the crowd.

Abel scowled at Isa but nodded. "It is within the law."

Lazarus lifted his gaze to Jesus, who dipped his chin in a subtle nod—like a father whose son had made the right choice. Then Lazarus leaned forward, giving Isa the kiss of peace. "I could not have given my sister to anyone who was not willing to die for her."

MARTHA COULDN'T BELIEVE what she'd just heard. How could this be? She wasn't betrothed to Simon? And now she was given her brother's blessing to marry Isa? She didn't know what to do first. Throw herself at Lazarus . . . go to Isa . . . give thanks to Jesus for bringing both her brother and Isa back to her?

Mary decided for her. Her sister fell into her arms, kissing her cheek. "Praise be to God." Then they were all surrounding her. Mary and Zakai, Penina and Safta. All laughing and crying, pulling her to Isa.

Martha gulped air, her face wet with tears as she stood before the man she loved. A lopsided smile broke over his bruised face. He looked at his feet, as if suddenly shy with her again, like the little boy in the orchard. She stumbled forward. His arms closed around her, warm and strong, but her body still shook with sobs. Why was she crying? How could she cry when she was so happy?

Lazarus lived. Isa was hers forever. The Messiah had come.

Isa didn't speak, but he didn't have to. His heart pounded under her cheek like a joyful song. She lifted her face to his . . . and felt a tug on her tunic. She looked down. Zakai stood beside them with a grin as wide as the sky. Isa scooped him into his arms and pressed him between them.

Zakai wrapped one brown arm around Martha's neck and the other around Isa's, drawing them together. "This is the best day of my whole life."

Isa brought them even closer, cheek against cheek, beard against smooth skin. Slate-gray eyes looking into deep brown.

"Let us go to Jesus." Isa voiced Martha's own thought.

The crowd parted as they approached him. Martha fell to her knees, fresh tears flowing down her cheeks. She kissed the hem of his garment, washing his feet with tears. Isa knelt beside her. Zakai threw his arms around Jesus' legs.

Jesus' warm hands closed around hers, and he pulled her up to stand in front of him. "Martha, your brother lives." Jesus smiled, the corners of his eyes crinkling. "Don't you think it's time to get him something to eat?"

Something to eat? Of course, they all needed food, and she was suddenly hungrier than she'd been in weeks. "Yes, Lord."

She would. She would make a feast like Bethany had never seen. For Jesus and Lazarus. For Isa. Where she would get the food, she didn't know. The Lord would surely provide. And so would some of her friends in Bethany.

Lazarus raised his voice. "Come, everyone, join us for a feast! The Messiah has come!"

A shout went up among the men and women. They surrounded Jesus and the disciples, praising and singing. Martha caught sight of Jael and Simon slinking up the path with Tobias and Devorah close behind. Sorrow dulled her joy for a moment. How could they see what Jesus had done and not believe? Then she was surrounded by a tide of rejoicing villagers, rushing through the valley like a spring flood.

"Alleluia! Alleluia!"

"The Messiah has come. Glory be to God, the Most High."

Jesus and the disciples climbed the path out of the valley. Lazarus and Penina followed, with Mary and Josiah beside them. Simcha scooped up a smiling Safta and carried her through the crowd. The rest of Bethany eddied around Martha and Isa as they stood with Zakai between them.

Martha took Zakai's small hand in one of hers, and Isa took the other. They climbed the steep path together. At the top of the ridge, Martha stopped. The dark valley of the tombs lay behind them like a half-forgotten dream. Before them, in the sunlight, lay Bethany, bright and filled with rejoicing. The birds swooped and sang against the blue sky; the flowers turned their faces to the sun. Her brother, who was dead, was alive again, and the one who was lost had been found.

Jesus—the Messiah, the Holy One of God—had come, and he had given them all a new life.

Epilogue

There are also many other things that Jesus did, but if these
were to be described individually, I do not think the whole
world would contain the books that would be written.
—John 21:25

MARTHA CAUGHT MARY'S eye as her sister poured another cup of wine for Lazarus. Mary smiled and moved around the table, the brass bangles on her wrist tinkling like bells.

Martha hadn't made the meal, and she hadn't immersed the vessels. She hadn't ground the wheat or roasted the lamb on the spit. She didn't join the women as they served warm bread and vegetables cooked in olive oil and garlic. She'd even given her recipe for cumin sauce to Chana, and now the whole of Bethany would know her secret. She dipped her bread in the savory sauce and tasted. Almost as good as hers.

The sun was low on the horizon, casting golden light on the meadow where the wedding guests sat around the table or lay on the grass in the shade of the trees.

Lazarus, at her side, was deep in conversation with the man reclining next to him. "How is it in Jerusalem, Peter?"

Peter talked around the chunk of bread in his mouth. "Dangerous. Since he rose, they look for us." He tore off another mouthful. "Their anger grows. Especially when we speak in the Temple."

John leaned in from beside Peter. "They threaten, but every day our numbers grow. Every day, more believe in him."

The bread was gone again. Had these men not been fed in the month since Jesus had been crucified and then risen from the grave? She pushed herself up. She'd just run to the courtyard to get some more.

Isa's hand on hers was warm and gentle. "Let Mary."

She settled back. He was right. Today was the first day of her wedding feast. Her place was beside her husband. Soon the sun would set, and they would go to the marriage tent in the privacy of the orchard. Her cheeks heated, and Isa's hand tightened on hers. Was he as impatient as she to leave the feast?

Martha surveyed the wedding guests. If Abba were here, what would he think of the men reclining at his table? Galileans, a tax collector, and one of the *am-ha-arez*. A Samaritan and a Roman soldier. Even she was still amazed. But how could anyone have known how the world would change in just a few short weeks?

These men and women—these believers in the Christ— came often to Bethany since the events of Passover less than a month ago: Jesus' betrayal by one of his own, the horror of his death. Martha and Isa, along with all of Bethany, had mourned on that Passover day—shocked and heartbroken at the news from Jerusalem, none of them knowing what to do when they heard that Jesus had been put to death. Until that morning of the third day . . .

They should have known that death could not defeat their Messiah. They should have trusted him after what they'd seen him do here in Bethany. But now they knew, and so did the rest of Judea and all of Galilee, even Samaria.

Jesus had power over death itself. And he had promised to return.

And so they waited, gathering when they could to share bread and news. Some had seen Jesus. Others had not. Peter spoke of how Jesus had appeared to his disciples, alive, in the upper room, and Thomas told of how he'd touched him and all his doubt had fled.

But the question they all asked was the same. What were they to do now?

"You could stay here," Lazarus said. "Most of Bethany believes in Jesus. They won't betray you to the Sanhedrin."

Since Lazarus had been raised, Bethany had changed. Most of Bethany. Not Jael, not Abel or some of the other Pharisees. But they had an unlikely ally—Simon. He didn't yet believe Jesus was the Messiah; he didn't seem to know what he believed. But any Pharisee who reported Lazarus's guests to the Jews in Jerusalem would face his displeasure.

Stephen, the Samaritan who had been with them since the morning they gathered at the empty tomb, spoke up. "We will continue to testify to the truth in Jerusalem, even if the Jews persecute us." His eyes burned with an intensity she'd seen before—in Lazarus and in her new husband. "Even if they kill us."

Lazarus caught Martha's eye. Stephen was outspoken, perhaps too much for his own good. He had no fear, and he was making enemies among the most powerful Jews. Lazarus worried about him.

"Tell me again what you heard, what you felt, when he called you from the tomb." Stephen had heard the story many times, but he always had more questions.

A man with a long nose and teak-colored skin—the Cyrenian, the men called him—grumbled. "And now more lies from the Sanhedrin. They say he wasn't really dead. That it was some kind of a trick."

John and Peter glanced warily toward the end of the table where the Roman stiffened in anger. He was dressed in plain clothes like any Jew would wear, but his red hair and pale face covered in freckles made him stand out like a fox in a sheepfold.

"He was dead, mark my words," the Roman growled in a voice like thunder.

A woman came in with a stack of charred bread. She was small, hardly bigger than a child. "I'm sorry." She approached Martha, looking like she might cry. "I burned them again."

Martha glanced at the inedible bread. "Don't worry, Nissa." Who had let Nissa take over the bread baking? She tried to think of something nice to say, but what compliment could she give these hideous loaves? "The ones on the bottom look"—she searched for a word that wasn't too harsh—"better." The poor girl would never be able to cook. Perhaps Safta could teach her to weave instead.

Nissa and her brother, Cedron, were yet another miracle. Safta had discovered them, her lost grandchildren, among the believers in the Christ. The daughter who had left so many years ago was still sadly missed, but Cedron and Nissa were taken into the fold at Bethany like found lambs. Martha welcomed them into her home, along with the Roman soldier who stuck to Nissa like black on a cooking pot.

A zealot, a Roman soldier, and a girl who seemed to know nothing about taking care of a household—an unlikely trio with little in common but their belief in Jesus. What would Abba think? But their family had increased, and the house brimmed with debate, laughter, and—if she wasn't wrong—love.

The Roman smiled at Nissa. "I'll eat them, little Nissa." He snagged the blackest loaf. His jaws worked over the charred bread like it was made of wood, but his blue eyes watched Nissa and he winked at her.

Nissa's cheeks turned pink, and she ducked her head.

Martha whispered close to Isa's ear, "Why don't they just announce their betrothal already?" They may be Jew and Roman, but they were both believers in the Christ and it was obvious they adored each other. Besides, no one else was going to marry Nissa with the way she cooked.

Isa lifted her hand to his lips. "Give them time."

Zakai's laughter rang out in the meadow where Elishiva and Safta sat with the children. Martha looked at the sun dipping behind the Mount of Olives. There wasn't much more time before she and Isa would be alone. And then they'd have the rest of their lives together and hopefully more children. Her stomach fluttered, and she wished the dinner to be over.

Cedron's voice rose in argument. Again he was bickering with Stephen. "But when will he return?" He turned to the rest of the table. "What are we supposed to do until then?"

Stephen answered smoothly, "He will tell us when we need to know."

The Roman grunted as if he'd heard the Samaritan's cryptic comments a few times too many.

As for her, she knew what to do. *Choose the better part,* he'd said. It was so easy, and yet it was so difficult. But she was getting better at it.

Penina hurried over the meadow toward Martha. "Sister, a beggar. He looks like he's traveled far." Penina's voice still filled Martha with joy. Her brother had married Penina immediately— with no betrothal period—after he was raised. No one in Bethany objected.

Martha looked to Lazarus for confirmation, and he nodded his head. She signaled to Penina to clear a space at the table. "Invite him to eat with us." They'd waited seven years; the wedding tent could wait until this man was fed.

Penina came back in moments with a man who looked like he hadn't had a decent meal in weeks. Or a bath. His clothes hung on him like rags, and his hair was as matted as a wild donkey's.

Lazarus rose from his place at the head of the table and sat the man down on his own dining couch. "Martha, water."

Martha poured water into a wide bowl. She knelt before the old man, scooping the cool water on his dirty feet, then dried them with a scrap of linen.

"Come." Lazarus signaled for more food. "Eat with us. Today we celebrate my sister's marriage."

The man sat and seemed to gain strength as he looked around the table. Mary offered him a round of bread and poured a cup of wine at his right hand. As he took the bread in his hands, a soft breeze swept over the meadow, raising a shiver on Martha's neck.

The man held the bread before him to say the blessing.

Beside her, Isa sat up straighter. Across the table, the Roman put down his wine. Cedron and Stephen stopped their argument. Nissa dropped her burnt bread, and Mary's sharp breath was heard in the stillness. Each person—Jew, Gentile, and Samaritan—fell silent and stared at the man next to Lazarus.

He held the bread before him, broke it, and said the blessing. And then, as if her eyes had been opened, the old man covered in dirt and sores disappeared, and Jesus sat before them.

Jesus, the friend who called Lazarus from the tomb.

The man who died on a cross.

The Messiah, who had risen.

Peter let out a shout. Stephen jumped to his feet. The Roman fell to his knees. Martha's heart burned in her chest as if it had been lit afire.

"Do not be troubled or afraid," Jesus said. "This is what I command you, love one another, as I have loved you." Then, as mist rises from the water and disappears into the air, he was gone from their sight. His last words left a lingering warmth within Martha, like the rays of the setting sun. "And remember, my friends, I am with you always . . . even to the end of the world."

Martha held his words in her heart. Jesus, the Messiah, had died and risen from the dead. He was with them even now and always would be.

And that changed everything.

Author's Note

$\mathcal{T}$HE STORY OF Jesus raising Lazarus from the tomb is one of the best-known narratives in the New Testament and has been referred to in countless sermons, Bible studies, and devotionals. Because we know this story of Martha, Mary, and Lazarus so well, I encountered some unique challenges as I researched and wrote *The Tomb: A Novel of Martha*.

The first two books of The Living Water Series, *The Well* and *The Thief*, focused on characters that met Jesus only briefly. In them, I explored the question: What was it like to meet Jesus? In *The Tomb*, I was able to explore a slightly different question: What was it like to realize that a close friend—a man who came to visit "with a hungry belly, clothes that needed mending, and news from his mother"—was the Messiah?

John's gospel says, "Jesus loved Martha and her sister and Lazarus" (John 11:5). From what we read, Martha and her family had a long, intimate friendship with Jesus. Since nothing written in scripture indicates that Jesus was not related to the family in Bethany, it isn't too hard to imagine Jesus having cousins that lived close to Jerusalem, people who would have known him all his life, whom he'd visited often on his way to the feasts in Jerusalem. How would these intimate friends react as they came to realize Jesus' true nature? And what would happen if a family was divided in their belief?

The scene in which a woman anoints Jesus' feet is another

well-known New Testament story. It appears in different forms in all four of the gospels, but the details, timing, and even the participants differ. Some biblical scholars claim that there was more than one anointing involving two different women. I chose to show the anointing at the house of Simon the Leper, as stated in both Matthew and Mark, and to place the event within the same dinner conversation in Luke where Jesus gently rebukes Martha as "worried about many things." Although the gospel accounts do not indicate that these events occurred together, I condensed them into one event to highlight the differences between Martha's worry and anxiety and Mary's acceptance of "the better part" of giving honor to Jesus above all else.

There are plenty of mentions of demonic possession in the gospels. Three of them recount the cure of the Gerasene demoniac, each with different details. There is plenty of debate about where, when, and even who was freed from the legion of demons. In *The Tomb*, Isa's story of demonic possession roughly follows the accounts in Mark and Luke, but is mainly one of fiction and imaginative guesses. Isa and Jesus' interaction were what I wanted most for my readers to experience, so I chose to use the account in Mark to supply most of the details and returned to Isa's fictional story as the men from the village entered the scene.

In all three books of The Living Water Series, my goal is the same. I will never contradict the Bible, but neither do I want to rewrite it. I strive to reimagine encounters with Jesus in a way that will help my readers see, hear, touch, and even smell the time of Jesus. My fervent prayer is that readers of *The Well*, *The Thief*, and *The Tomb* will turn to the Bible with fresh understanding and experience their own encounter with Jesus, the Incarnation.

Acknowledgments

$\mathscr{I}$T HAS BEEN a privilege and an honor to write The Living Water Series, and I could never have done so without the help of God-given family, friends, colleagues, and readers. The Holy Spirit has always been behind the scenes, directing the process and putting advocates in my path when I most needed them.

The Tomb is dedicated to my sisters and brother. As I worked on the story of Martha, Mary, and Lazarus, I drew upon my own experiences of growing up in a large, loving, and faith-filled family. Heartfelt thanks to Jennifer, Rebecca, Rachel, and Steve from the baby of the family. Your examples and encouragement have shaped my life. Even though we live far apart, I know that I am only a phone call, text, or email away from unconditional love and the kind of friendship that only comes from siblings.

As always, thank you to Bruce, my ever-supportive husband, and to Rachel, Andy, Joey, and Anna, who put up with a messy house, empty cupboards, and no answer to the question "what's for dinner?" while I inhabited my fictional world.

After months of research and writing, an author is too close to her work to look at it objectively, and that is when brilliant critiquers are essential. I'm lucky to have honest yet gentle critiquers, all excellent writers themselves, that I count on to improve my manuscript and make me look good to readers. Thank you, Regina Jennings, LeAnne Hardy, Celia Waldock, Laura Sobiech, and Cheryl Booms for your time and effort. Alex Luloff,

Megan Rondeau, Anne Brown, and Wacek Kucy—you lend your own brand of help that lifts me up.

Thank you to my agent, Chris Park, and editor, Jessica Wong, for your wisdom, faithful advice, and guidance. You are both blessings to my writing and my life. As always, thanks to Bruce Gore for the beautiful covers and the team at Howard Books for their professional expertise.

And most important of all, thank you to my readers. You are the reason I get to do this amazing thing called writing books. Your emails, texts, Facebook posts, and tweets keep me inspired. That moment you took to tell me how my story touched your life and faith was exactly what I needed to keep going. I thank you from the bottom of my heart.

Reading Group Guide

1 Martha and Mary are well known and beloved biblical women. What was your impression of Martha and Mary before reading *The Tomb*? Were either Martha or Mary different from what you expected?

2 Martha has always been characterized as "the worker" and the "the worrier," while her sister, Mary, has been called "the holy one" or "the mystic." Do you relate more to Martha or to Mary? Why?

3 Martha is highly respected in Bethany, even as she despises herself for a long-ago sin and her inability to stand up for her sister, who is ridiculed by the elite women of Bethany. How does her need to keep her perfect reputation hinder her belief in Jesus?

4 Martha struggles with fulfilling the law as her father wished and with showing her love for both her family and Jesus. Are you ever torn between the precepts of your faith and the compassion and love that Jesus asks us to show to others? How do you reconcile these two important aspects of your faith life?

5 Isa is haunted by the parting words Jesus speaks to him, but he is not sure how to act on them and instead starts to settle into Nikius's household. Have you ever struggled similarly? How did you break out of what was easy and comfortable?

6 Martha's relationship with her sister suffers as she keeps herself busy with her many duties, responsibilities, and worries. In what ways do we sometimes allow everyday tasks and worry about the future to take up our lives and shut out what we are afraid to face? How does this ultimately hurt us and the people around us?

7 The author chose to depict Lazarus as a young man, just reaching adulthood and stepping into his own, only to have his life cut short by a deadly illness. We see young people and even children die of cancer and other illnesses today. Have you ever questioned God's goodness when you see the young die in a seemingly needless way?

8 Did you think Lazarus was selfish or selfless as he worked to provide for and settle his family so that he could follow the Messiah, even as he knew it would be dangerous to be a follower of Jesus?

9 Lazarus feels sure that the Messiah has come and that God is calling him to follow, yet Jesus has a different plan for him. Have you ever been sure of God's plan, only to find you were wrong? How do you obey when it doesn't make sense to you?

10 Isa is discouraged and even afraid after his first attempts to share his story result in rejection, and he slowly begins to convince himself it is better to ap-

proach things his own way. When have you tried to follow your calling, only to be rebuffed by others? Did you soldier on, or did you find yourself justifying moving ahead according to your own wisdom?

11 Martha often thinks of things other people have said to her, from her mother to her father to her siblings and Simon. The voices of others eventually build into a cacophony in her mind—much as the legion's voices built in Isa's—and she must choose to either bow to them or truly hear the one voice that matters. Have you ever been buried under the weight of many voices? How did you find clarity and freedom?

12 Mary is certain that Jesus is the Messiah and equally sure that he will come in time to save Lazarus. When he doesn't, she falls into despair. Martha's new faith in Jesus is strong enough to renew Mary's hope. How did the two sisters' different paths to faith work together to bring them both to Jesus?

13 Even after she has resolved to trust Jesus, Martha finds herself questioning him at the tomb with "Lord, there will be a stench." Can you relate to her falling back into her doubts so quickly after professing her belief in him? Share a time when you did the same and what you learned through it.

14 Martha inadvertently buried herself in a tomb of her own making as she sought to protect herself and her family from the consequences of her sin, and in some ways Isa did the same. Have you ever found yourself in a similar situation, so entangled by your own efforts that you cannot get out? In what ways did Jesus free not only Lazarus but Martha and Isa from death? How has Jesus done the same for you?

15 In the epilogue, the followers of Jesus wondered what they should do now that their Messiah had risen from the dead. Martha knows she must continue to "choose the better part." How can we choose the better part daily as we wait for the return of Jesus?

Keep reading for a peek at the start of
The Living Water Series, *The Thief!*

Chapter One

꧁꧁꧁

*M*OUSE DARTED THROUGH the crowded streets of Jerusalem. His name suited him. Small and drab, he fled from one street corner to the next as though stalked by an unseen predator. Dirt and ash streaked his face, and the tatter of wool covering his head was no less filthy. Both his worn tunic and the cloak over it looked like they had been made for a man twice his size.

Not a head turned as he zigzagged around caravans, street vendors, and plodding donkeys. He was invisible—poor, dirty, worthless. Just another half-grown boy in the lower city whose parents couldn't afford to feed him. If a Greek trader or a Jewish woman noticed him at all, that's what they'd see—just what Mouse wanted them to see.

Mouse skirted the Hippodrome, built by Herod the Great to show off his fastest horses, and moved like a trickle of water past slaves carting oil jars and women haggling over the price of grain. He didn't stop to admire the trinkets laid out under bright awnings. He couldn't be late.

There had been no food in his house for days, and the rent was due. Another week and the landlord would throw them into the street.

Thou shalt not steal, the commandment said.

A familiar voice whispered in his mind, dark and compelling. *You don't have a choice.*

He'd seen the mark on the wall this morning, just across from the Pool of Siloam. Scraped on the bricks with a chalky stone, the straight line down and one across had made his heart race and his fingers tingle. It meant Dismas would meet him in the usual place when the trumpets blew. After, Mouse would have enough silver to satisfy the landlord and his empty stomach.

Mouse bounded up the Stepped Street toward the temple. The drone of prayers and the odors of incense and burnt animal flesh drifted on the afternoon breeze. The Day of Atonement had brought throngs of pilgrims to Jerusalem to witness the sacrifices of bulls and goats—atonements for the sins of the Chosen People. Soon these tired, hungry pilgrims would swarm the upper market. Easy targets for talented pickpockets.

Three trumpet blasts rang out across the city. The sacrifices complete already? He wasn't even past the temple. He pushed by a pair of loaded donkeys and broke into a run. A stream of pilgrims poured out of the temple gates like a libation, flooding the street. Mouse plunged into the packed crowd. He'd be late if he couldn't get through this river of pious Jews. And Dismas wouldn't wait.

The high priest, Caiaphas, led the procession with a goat beside him—the scapegoat, on which he had laid the sins of Israel. Pilgrims followed wearing sackcloth, their faces and hair covered in ashes. They sang songs, begging for mercy from their sins, as they processed toward the Jaffa Gate to drive the goat out of the city and into the rocky northern desert.

Guilt pressed upon him as firmly as the bodies crowding on every side. His father came from the seed of Abraham, just like the priests and the pilgrims. And Mouse had fasted today, just like the men in sackcloth and ashes. But his father didn't offer sacrifice anymore, and his fast wasn't by choice. *The scapegoat won't atone for my sins.*

Mouse broke through the crowd and skirted the procession, picking up speed as he reached the bridge that stretched over the

Tyropoeon Valley. He couldn't afford to worry about sins and the law like the rich priests and Levites. The Day of Atonement would end tonight at the first sight of the evening star. Jews were already hurrying to the market for food to break their daylong fast. And that's where he and Dismas would be, ready for them.

A frisson of anticipation tingled up his arms. He slipped through streets flanked by high walls. Beyond them rose fine homes with cool marble halls, quiet gardens, and rich food, but here the air was thick with dust and the odor of animal dung and unwashed bodies.

A labyrinth of streets crisscrossed the upper city leading to the market that sat just south of Herod's magnificent palace. Mouse turned into an alley hardly wider than a crack and slid into the meeting place—an alcove between the buildings, shadowed and scarcely big enough for two people. His breath sounded loud in the close space.

"You're late." A tall shadow parted from the gloom.

The scent of peppermint oil and cloves tickled Mouse's nose even before Dismas stepped into a dim shaft of light. He wore a tunic and robe like the Jews of the city and spoke Aramaic, but his accent betrayed his Greek heritage. Mouse spoke enough Greek to barter with merchants in the marketplace and understood even more, but Dismas didn't know that. There was much Dismas didn't know about Mouse.

Dismas's face was narrow, with deep grooves curving on each side of his mouth. The afternoon sun picked out glints of gray in his dirt-brown hair and short beard. How old he was, Mouse couldn't guess and didn't ask. Old enough to have a wife and a flock of children, maybe even grandchildren. But instead of a family, he had a slew of fallen women, if his stories could be believed.

"Maybe you couldn't find me?" Dismas's grin showed crooked teeth the color of a stag's horn.

Mouse bristled. He hadn't gotten lost in the upper city for months. "I just followed my nose until my eyes watered."

Dismas let out a bark of laughter. "At least I don't smell like a tannery." He flicked a long finger at Mouse's dirty tunic.

Mouse lifted his shoulder and pressed his nose to it, sniffing. He did smell bad. Maybe he'd overdone it a little. He bounced up and down on the balls of his feet, his chest cramped with tension. It was always like this before they started, but once they reached the market, he would be focused and calm.

Dismas rubbed his beard. "Settle down, Mouse. The gods will smile on us today."

The gods? A knot tightened in Mouse's belly. Maybe Dismas's Greek gods smiled on what they were about to do, but the God of Abraham surely did not. "Let's just go."

Dismas raised his brows. "What's the first rule?"

Mouse huffed out a breath. "You get half."

Dismas's deep-set eyes scanned the street. "And the second, boy?"

"Do whatever you say."

The tall man nodded and shifted past him into the street. Mouse counted to ten, as Dismas had taught him, and followed.

The upper market, stretching before Herod's palace in a chaotic maze of stalls and tents, resounded with clamor and babble. Donkeys brayed, their feet clattering on the stone street. Greek and Aramaic voices rose in heated debate over the price of oil and the quality of wheat. Merchants haggled with loud-voiced women over pyramids of brightly colored fruits and vegetables.

Dismas pushed through the crowds, his head visible above the bent backs of patrons looking for their evening meal. He glanced over his shoulder, caught Mouse's eye, and winked.

Mouse's taut anxiety lifted; his mind cleared.

Dismas stepped in front of a portly Greek woman weighed down with a basket of bread and dried fish. Her arms jingled with gold bangles. Mouse bumped her from behind, spilling the basket.

"Watch where you're going!" She bent to gather the bread.

Mouse mumbled an apology and fumbled to help her, dropping more than he gathered.

"Just let me! You're filthy." She brushed him off and hurried away.

Mouse shoved the gold bangle up his sleeve as he caught up with Dismas at a stall selling gleaming jewelry. A well-dressed Jew haggled with the merchant over a jade-and-ivory necklace. The Jew shook his head. "I wouldn't pay more than a drachma for that."

"Robbery!" The merchant swept away the necklace.

Dismas eased up to the men. "You judge well, sir." He nodded to the Jew. "I know a shop down the street with better quality at half the price."

The merchant grabbed Dismas by the neck of his tunic. "Mind your own business."

Dismas pushed back, protesting in Greek. Passersby stopped to watch. The scuffle was short, but long enough for Mouse to do his job and melt back into the crowd. Dismas backed off with a bow and an apology.

A coin here, a brooch or bangle there. Mouse pushed the treasures deep into the pocket of his cloak. He pushed his guilt even deeper.

You don't have a choice.

As the setting sun cast a golden glow across the marketplace, Dismas glided past him. "Last one." He jerked his head toward a Pharisee speaking to a burly shopkeeper. His striped tunic was made of fine wool, and its deep-blue tassels lifted in the evening breeze. A fat purse peeked over the folds of his belt.

Mouse shook his head. The crowds were thinning. *Too dangerous.*

But Dismas was already gone. He approached the man with his head down, knocking into him. "Excuse me, Rabbi!" he said in loud Greek as he righted the man, both hands on his shoulders. As the Pharisee shouted about defilement, Mouse sidled by, snagging the purse and slipping it into his pocket with one smooth movement. He'd done it dozens of times.

A thick hand closed hard around his wrist.

"Little thief!" The words rang out in the marketplace and echoed off the palace walls. The shopkeeper snagged Mouse's other arm in an iron grip.

Mouse wrenched forward, pain shooting through his shoulder. "Dismas!"

But Dismas had disappeared like the last rays of the sun. Mouse struggled, the third rule goading him into panic: If there's trouble, every man for himself.

A ring of angry faces closed in around Mouse. Hooves clattered on stone, and the angry men turned toward the sound. Two Romans on horseback—both centurions—parted the gathering crowd. One of them jumped from his horse. His polished breastplate glinted over a bloodred tunic. A crimson-plumed helmet sat low on his forehead, and curved cheek flaps covered most of his face. "What's going on here?"

Fear weakened Mouse's legs. Dismas had been wrong. No gods smiled on him today.

The crowd loosened. Some of the men faded away; others started explaining.

The Roman pushed the remaining men aside. "It takes two Jews to hold this little thief?" His Aramaic was heavily accented, but good by Roman standards. He pulled off his helmet to reveal a shock of hair the color of fire. Blue eyes narrowed at Mouse. He grabbed Mouse by one arm, like he was holding nothing more than a sparrow, and motioned to the crowd with the other. "Clear out."

Mouse's heart hammered. *I can't let them take me.* He twisted in the centurion's grip. In an instant, both his arms were wrenched behind his back. Pain brought tears to his eyes. He kicked out at the Roman's shins but hit only the hard metal greaves that protected them.

"By Pollux, you're a fighter." The centurion smacked him across the head—a light slap for a soldier, but it made Mouse's ears ring and his eyes water. He blinked hard.

The Pharisee drew himself up. "That worthless boy has my purse."

With one hand, the centurion gripped both Mouse's hands behind his back. He patted the other over Mouse's chest and midsection.

Mouse gasped. Heat surged up his neck and into his face.

The centurion found the deep pocket in Mouse's cloak, and out came the purse. He threw it at the Pharisee. "Take more care with your money, Rabbi." Then he shoved his hand back into the pocket and drew out a gold bangle, a brooch of jade and ivory, a Greek drachma, and two denarii.

He showed them to the other centurion, still seated on his horse. "See that, Cornelius? It was a lucky day for this boy . . . until now." He pocketed the stolen pieces and pulled Mouse sharply toward him. "Now he'll see how Romans deal with thieves."

Mouse's mouth went as dry as dust. Thieves were scourged, that he knew. But he was more than a thief. If he didn't get away—now—they would find out everything. The Romans wouldn't have to scourge him because he'd be stoned by his own people.

Despair and fear rose in his throat, choking him.

As the centurion dragged Mouse toward his horse and his companion, a shadow shifted in a doorway across the street. A heartbeat later, the Roman's horse whinnied and reared. A stone pinged off armor.

"Mouse! Go!" Dismas shouted.

The redheaded soldier reached one hand toward his shying horse, and Mouse saw his only chance. He wrenched, twisted, and ripped his arms from his cloak. He ran, leaving the soldier with nothing but a billowing cloak and a skittish horse.

Mouse sprinted away from the market. He glanced behind. The second soldier whirled his horse toward the shadow with a shout. Dismas ran toward the palace, the mounted Roman pounding after him. The redheaded centurion was gaining ground on Mouse.

Mouse veered into a side street. The centurion's hobnailed

sandals skidded on the smooth paving stones of the square. A shout and a Latin curse echoed down the narrow passageway.

The centurion was fast, but Mouse was faster. He wove through the back alleys. He darted down a side street, then dove into another that looked like a dead end—to someone who didn't know better. A muffled shout sounded behind him. His pursuer was losing ground. After a quick corner, he ducked through the narrow back door of a wineshop, pushed his way through the crowd of drunks, and sprinted out the front door.

Mouse kept running, his heart pounding faster than his bare feet. *Dismas broke the third rule*.

Mouse circled the upper city and slunk back on the north side of the market. Long shadows darkened the streets. The Jaffa Gate and the meeting spot weren't far, but was it safe to go there?

He stopped, holding his breath to hear something other than his own labored gasps. No hobnailed Roman sandals on the street. No pounding horse's hooves or shouts of pursuit. He approached the gate, staying close to the walls.

What if Dismas had been caught? Dismas knew almost nothing about Mouse, other than that he was an excellent thief. He didn't know Mouse's secret—or even his real name—so he couldn't send soldiers after him. Mouse was safe, but Dismas would be scourged. He might die.

A shiver of dread crawled up Mouse's back. He checked the street behind him. Empty. He crept into the cleft between the walls. Empty. He leaned his hot cheek against smooth stone and closed his eyes. Dismas had been caught. *He shouldn't have come back for me*.

At a whisper of wind and a breath of peppermint, Mouse's eyes flew open, and relief poured through his limbs. Dismas had entered the meeting spot like a wisp of smoke.

Mouse released his held breath. "I thought they'd caught you."

Dismas clapped his big hand on Mouse's shoulder, grinning like he'd just won a game of dice, not run through the city for his life. "They'll never catch me. Did you see that Roman dog's face?" Dismas shook with laughter but kept his voice low. "And you! You were fast, Mouse. I'll give you that. You were made to be a thief."

Mouse slumped against the wall. They'd done it. They'd gotten away. Dismas was right; he was good at this. Good enough to escape a Roman centurion.

Dismas reached into his pockets and pulled out an amber necklace, two silver drachmas, a shekel, and a handful of figs.

"Not bad," he said, popping a fig into his mouth. "How'd you do?"

"The centurion took it all." Mouse's shoulders drooped. How would he pay the landlord? Buy food?

Dismas chewed and leaned a shoulder against the wall. "Too bad. That means I don't get my cut."

Mouse studied his dirty feet. That had been the deal they'd made almost a year ago when Dismas had found him picking pockets in the lower city, rarely pinching enough to buy a handful of food. Dismas had offered to teach him to steal more than copper coins. With Dismas's help, Mouse pocketed silver, jewels—plenty, even after Dismas took his cut. But tonight, Mouse hadn't held up his end of the bargain. And Dismas had almost paid the price.

Dismas straightened and popped another fig in his mouth. "Don't worry about it, Mouse. We're partners."

He slapped the rest of the figs into Mouse's right hand, the silver shekel in the other. "Take this. I know your people don't trade in graven images." The shekel was stamped with a sheaf of wheat, the drachma with the face of Athena.

"But—"

"Shut up and take it, Mouse. I won't offer again." Dismas shoved him in the shoulder, but a smile lurked around his mouth.

Mouse closed his fingers around the coin. He chewed on the inside of his lip. "You broke your rule."

Dismas folded his arms over his chest, his smile gone. "Next time, I'll leave you."

Mouse shoved the coin into his pocket and a fig into his mouth.

Dismas elbowed Mouse aside and peered out into the street. He glanced back over his shoulder, his dark eyes serious. "You aren't worth dying for, Mouse. Nobody is." He faded into the shadows of the city.

Next time? Mouse chewed his lip until he tasted blood. Tonight had been close—too close. If he was caught . . . if they found out who he was, what he was . . . he'd have more to fear than a Roman centurion.

No. He was done stealing. Dismas was safe, and Mouse had enough silver to keep the landlord quiet for a month. He would find a job—anything that would bring in the money they needed.

This time, Mouse vowed, he would stop stealing for good.

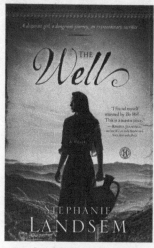
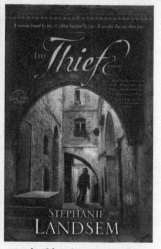